Jennifer Hayward has been a fan of romance since filching her sister's novels to escape her teenage angst. Her career in journalism and PR, including years of working alongside powerful, charismatic CEOs and travelling the world, has provided perfect fodder for the fast-paced, sexy stories she likes to write—always with a touch of humour. A native of Canada's East Coast, Jennifer lives in Toronto, with her Viking husband and young Viking-in-training.

With two university degrees and a variety of false career starts under her belt, **Michelle Conder** decided to satisfy her lifelong desire to write and finally found her dream job. She currently lives in Melbourne, Australia, with one super-indulgent husband, three self-indulgent but exquisite children, a menagerie of over-indulged pets, and the intention of doing some form of exercise daily. She loves to hear from her readers at michelleconder.com.

HIS
MILLION-DOLLAR
MARRIAGE
PROPOSAL

JENNIFER HAYWARD

BOUND TO HER
DESERT CAPTOR

MICHELLE CONDER

MILLS & BOON

First Published in Great Britain 2018
by Mills & Boon, an imprint of HarperCollins*Publishers*
1 London Bridge Street, London, SE1 9GF

His Million-Dollar Marriage Proposal © 2018 by Jennifer Hayward

Bound to Her Desert Captor © 2018 by Michelle Conder

ISBN: 978-0-263-93541-7

MIX
Paper from
responsible sources
FSC® C007454

Printed and bound in Spain
by CPI, Barcelona

HIS MILLION-DOLLAR MARRIAGE PROPOSAL

JENNIFER HAYWARD

For Mary Sullivan and Stefanie London,
my walking partners and brainstormers extraordinaire.
Thank you for being such amazing writers and women!
Our Wed writing craft chats make my week.

CHAPTER ONE

THURSDAY NIGHT DRINKS at Di Fiore's had been a weekly ritual for Lazzero Di Fiore and his brothers ever since Lazzero and his younger brother, Santo, had parlayed a dream of creating the world's hottest athletic wear into a reality at a tiny table near the back as students at Columbia University.

The jagged slash of red fire, the logo they had scratched into the thick mahogany tabletop to represent the high-octane Supersonic brand, now graced the finely tuned bodies of some of the world's highest paid athletes, a visibility which had, in turn, made the brand a household name.

Unfortunately, Lazzero conceded blackly as he wound his way through the crowd in the packed, buzzing, European-style sports bar he and Santo ran in midtown Manhattan, success had also meant their personal lives had become public fodder. A fact of life he normally took in stride. The breech of his inner sanctum, however, had been the final straw.

He absorbed the show of feminine leg on display on what was supposed to be Triple-Play Thursdays—a ritual for Manhattan baseball fans. Inhaled the cloud of expensive perfume in the air, thick enough to take down a lesser man. *This* was all *her* doing. He'd like to strangle her.

"This is turning into a three-ring circus," he muttered, sliding into a chair at the table already occupied by his brothers, Santo and Nico.

"Because the city's most talked-about gossip columnist chose to make us number two on her most-wanted bachelor list?" Santo, elegant in black Hugo Boss, cocked a brow. "If we sue, it'd have to be for finishing behind Barnaby Alexander. He puts his dates to sleep recounting his billions. I find it highly insulting."

"Old money," Nico supplied helpfully. "She had to mix it up a bit."

Lazzero eyed his elder brother, who was probably thanking his lucky stars he'd taken himself off the market with his recent engagement to Chloe, with whom he ran Evolution—one of the world's most successful cosmetic companies. "I'm glad you're finding this amusing," he growled.

Nico shrugged. "You would too if you were in the middle of *my* three-ring circus. Why I ever agreed to a Christmas wedding is beyond me."

Lazzero couldn't muster an ounce of sympathy, because the entire concept of marriage was insanity to him.

"*Show it* to me," he demanded, glaring at Santo.

Santo slid the offending magazine across the table, his attention captured by a glamorous-looking blonde staring unashamedly at him from the bar. Loosening his tie, he sat back in his chair and gave her a thorough once-over. "Not bad at all."

Utterly Santo's type. She looked ready for anything.

Lazzero fixed his smoldering attention on the list of New York's most eligible bachelors as selected by Samara Jones of *Entertainment Buzz.* A follow-up to her earlier piece that had declared the "Summer Lover" the year's hottest trend, the article, cheekily entitled "The Summer Shag" in a nod to Jones's British heritage, featured her top twenty bachelors with which to fulfill that seasonal pursuit.

Lazzero scanned the list, his perusal sliding to a halt at entry number two:

Since they're gorgeous and run the most popular athletic-wear company on the planet—Lazzero and Santo Di Fiore clock in at number two. Young, rich and powerful, they are without a doubt the most delicious double dose of testosterone in Manhattan. Find them at Di Fiore's on Thursday nights, where they still run their weekly strategy sessions from the corner table where it all started.

Lazzero threw the magazine on the table, a look of disgust claiming his face. "You do realize that *this*," he said, waving a hand around them, "is never going to be ours again?"

"Relax," Santo drawled, eyes now locked with the sophisticated blonde who couldn't take her eyes off his equally glamorous profile. "Give it a few weeks and it'll die down."

"Or not."

Santo shifted his attention back to the table. "What's got you so twisted in a knot?" he queried. "It can't be *that*," he said, inclining his head toward the magazine. "You've been off for weeks."

Lazzero blew out a breath and sat back in his chair. "Gianni Casale," he said flatly. "I had a call with him this afternoon. He isn't biting on the licensing deal. He's mired in red ink, knows his brand has lost its luster, knows we're eating his lunch, and still he won't admit he needs this partnership."

Which was a problem given Lazzero had forecast Supersonic would be the number two sportswear company in the world by the end of the following year, a promise his influential backers were banking on. Which meant acquiring Gianni Casale's legendary Fiammata running shoe technology, Volare, was his top priority.

Santo pointed his glass at him. "Let's be honest here. The *real* problem with Casale is that he hates your guts."

Lazzero blinked. "*Hate* is a strong word."

"Not when you used to date his wife. Everyone knows Carolina married Gianni on the rebound from you, his bank balance a salve for her wounded heart. She makes it clear every time you're in a room together. She's still in love with you, Laz, her marriage is on the rocks and Casale is afraid he can't hold her. *That's* our problem."

Guilt gnawed at his insides. He'd told Carolina he would never commit—that he just didn't have it in him. The truth, given his parents' disastrous, toxic wreck of a marriage he'd sworn never to repeat. And she'd been fine with it, until all of a sudden, a couple of months into their relationship, she'd grown far too comfortable with his penthouse key, showing up uninvited to cook him dinner after a trip to Asia—a skill he hadn't even known she'd possessed.

Maybe he'd ignored one too many warning signs, had been so wrapped up in his work and insane travel schedule he hadn't called it off soon enough, but he'd made it a clean break when he had.

"Gianni cannot possibly be making this personal," he grated. "This is a fifty-million-dollar deal. It would be the height of stupidity."

"He wouldn't be the first man to let his pride get in his way," Santo observed drily. He arched a brow. "You want to solve your problem? Come play in La Coppa Estiva next week. Gianni is playing. Bring a beautiful woman with you to convince him you are off the market and use the unfettered access to him to talk him straight."

Lazzero considered his jam-packed schedule. "I don't have time to come to Milan," he dismissed. "While you're off gallivanting around Italy, wooing your celebrities, someone needs to steer the ship."

Santo eyed him. "*Gallivanting?* Do you have any idea

how much work it is to coordinate a charity game at this level? I want to shoot myself by the end of it."

Lazzero held up a hand. "Okay, I take it back. You are brilliant, you know you are."

La Coppa Estiva, a charity soccer game played in football-crazy Milan, was sponsored by a handful of the most popular brands in the world, including both Supersonic and Fiammata. The biggest names in the business played in the game as well as sponsors and their partners, which made for a logistical nightmare of huge egos and impossible demands. It was only because of his skill managing such a circus that Santo had been named chairman for the second year in a row.

Lazzero exhaled. Took a pull of his beer. Santo was right—he should go. La Coppa Estiva was the only event in the foreseeable future he would get any access to Gianni. "I'll make it work," he conceded, "but I have no idea who I'd take."

"Says the man with an address book full of the most beautiful women in New York," Nico countered drily.

Lazzero shrugged. "I'm too damn busy to date."

"How about a *summer shag*?" Santo directed a pointed look at the strategically placed females around the room. "Apparently, they're all the rage. According to Samara Jones, you keep them around until you've finished the last events in the Hamptons, then say arrivederci after Labor Day. It's ideal, *perfect* actually. It might even put you in a better mood."

"Excellent idea," Nico drawled. "I like it a lot. Particularly the part where we recover his good humor."

Lazzero was not amused. Acquiring himself a temporary girlfriend was the last thing he had the bandwidth for right now. But if that's what it took to convince Gianni he was of no threat to him, then that's what he would do.

Making that choice from the flock of ambitious types

presently hunting him and ending up in Samara Jones's column, however, was not an option. What he needed was an utterly discrete, trustworthy woman who would take this on as the business arrangement it would be and wouldn't expect anything more from him when it was done.

Surely that couldn't be too hard to find?

Friday mornings at the Daily Grind on the Upper West Side were a nonstop marathon. Students from nearby Columbia University, attracted by its urban cool vibe, drifted in like sleepy, rumpled sheep, sprawling across the leather sofas with their coffee, while the slick-suited urban warriors who lived in the area dashed in on the way to the office, desperate for a fix before that dreaded early meeting.

Today, however, had tested the limits of even coolheaded barista Chiara Ferrante's even-keeled disposition. It might have been the expensive suit who'd just rolled up to the counter, a set of Porsche keys dangling from his fingertips, a cell phone glued to his ear, and ordered a grande, half-caff soy latte at exactly 120 degrees, *no more, no less*, on the heels of half a dozen such ridiculous orders.

You need this job, Chiara. Now more than ever. Suck it up and just do it.

She took a deep, Zen-inducing breath and cleared the lineup with ruthless efficiency, dispatching the walking Gucci billboard with a 119-degree latte—a minor act of rebellion she couldn't resist. A brief lull ensuing, she turned to take inventory of the coffee bar on the back wall before the next wave hit.

"You okay?" Kat, her fellow barista and roommate asked, as she replenished the stack of take-out cups. "You seem off today."

Chiara gathered up the empty carafes and set them in the sink. "The bank turned down my father's request for a loan. It hasn't been a good morning."

Kat's face fell. "Oh, God. I'm sorry. I know it's been hard for him to make a go of it lately. Are there any other banks he can try?"

"That was the last." Chiara bit her lip. "Maybe Todd can give me some more shifts."

"And turn you into the walking dead? You've been working double shifts for months, Chiara. You're going to fall flat on your face." Kat leaned a hip against the bar. "What you need," she said decisively, "is a rich man. It would solve all your problems. They're constantly propositioning you and yet you never take them up on their offers."

Because the one time she had, he'd shattered her heart into pieces.

"I'm not interested in a rich man," she said flatly. "They come in here in their beautiful suits, drunk on their power, thinking their money gives them license to do anything they like. It's all a big game to them, the way they play with women."

Kat flashed her an amused look. "That's an awfully big generalization don't you think?"

Chiara folded her arms over her chest. "Bonnie, Sivi and Tara went out the other night to Tempesta Di Fuoco, Stefan Bianco's place in Chelsea. They're sitting at the bar when this group of investment bankers starts chatting them up. Bonnie's thrilled when *Phil* asks her out for dinner at Lido. She goes home early because she's opening here in the morning. Sivi and Tara stay." She lifted a brow. "What does *Phil* do? He asks Sivi out to lunch."

"Pig," Kat agreed, making a face. "But you can't paint all men with the same brush."

"Not all men. *Them.* The suit," Chiara declared scathingly, "may change, but the man inside it doesn't."

"I'm afraid I have to disagree," a deep, lightly accented voice intoned, rippling a reactionary path down her spine. "It would be a shame for *Phil* to give us all a bad name."

Chiara froze. Turned around slowly, her hands gripping the marble. Absorbed the tall, dark male leaning indolently against the counter near the silver bell she wished fervently he'd rung. Clad in a silver Tom Ford suit that set off his swarthy skin to perfection, Lazzero Di Fiore was beautiful in a predatory, hawk-like way—oozing an overt sex appeal that short-circuited the synapses in her brain.

The deadpan expression on his striking face indicated he'd heard every last word of her ill-advised speech. "I—" she croaked, utterly unsure of what to say "—you should have rung the bell."

"And missed your fascinatingly candid appraisal of Manhattan's finest?" His sensual mouth twisted. "Not for the world. Although I do wonder if I could have an espresso to fuel my *overinflated ego*? I have a report I need to review for a big hotshot meeting in exactly fifty minutes."

Kat made a sound at the back of her throat. Chiara's cheeks flamed. "Of course," she mumbled. "It's on the house."

On the house. Oh, my God. Chiara unlocked her frozen knees as Lazzero strode off to find a table near the window. Chitchatting with Lazzero when he came in in the mornings was par for the course. Insulting the regulars and losing her job was not.

Amused rather than insulted by the normally composed barista's diatribe, Lazzero ensconced himself at a table near the windows and pulled out his report. Given his cynical attitude of late, it was refreshing to discover not all women in Manhattan were bounty hunters intent on razing his pockets.

It was also, he conceded, fascinating insight into the ultracool Chiara and what lay beneath those impenetrable layers of hers. He'd watched so many men crash and burn in their attempts to scale those defences over the past year he'd been coming here, he could have fashioned a graveyard out of their pitiful efforts. But now, it all made sense. She had been burned and burned badly by a man with power and influence and she wasn't ever going there again.

None of which, he admitted, flipping open the report on the Italian fashion market his team had prepared, was helping him nail his strategy for winning Gianni Casale over at La Coppa Estiva. The fifty-page report he needed to inhale might. As for a woman to take to Milan to satisfy Gianni's territorial nature? He was coming up blank.

He'd gone through his entire contact list last night in an effort to find a woman who would be appropriate for the business arrangement he had in mind, but none of them was right for the job. All of his ex-girlfriends would interpret the invitation in entirely the wrong light. Ask someone new and she would do the same. And since he had no interest of any kind in a relationship—summer shag or otherwise—that was out too.

Chiara broke his train of thought as she arrived with his espresso. Bottom lip caught between her teeth, a frown pleating her brow, she seemed to be searching for something to say. Then, clearly changing her mind, she reached jerkily for one of the cups on her tray. The steaming dark brew sloshed precariously close to the sides, his expensive suit a potential target. Lazzero reached up to take it from her before she dumped it all over him, his fingers brushing against hers as he did.

A sizzling electrical pulse traveled from her fingers through his, unfurling a curl of heat beneath his skin. Their gazes collided. *Held.* He watched her pupils flare in reaction—her beautiful eyes darkening to a deep, lagoon green.

It was nothing new. They'd been dancing around this particular attraction for weeks, *months*. He, because he was a creature of habit, and destroying his morning routine when it all went south hadn't appealed. She, apparently because he was one of the last men on earth she wanted to date.

Teeth sinking deeper into that lush, delectable lower lip, her long, dark lashes came down to veil her expression. "Enjoy your coffee," she murmured, taking a step back and continuing on her way.

Lazzero sat back in his chair, absorbing the pulse of attraction that zigzagged through him. He didn't remember the last time he'd felt it—felt *anything* beyond the adrenaline that came with closing a big deal and even that was losing its effect on him. That it would be the untouchable enigma that was Chiara who inspired it was an irony that didn't escape him.

He watched her deliver an espresso to an old Italian guy a couple of tables away. At least sixty with a shock of white hair and weathered olive skin, the Italian flirted outrageously with her in his native language, making her smile and wiping the pinched, distracted look from her face.

She was more than pretty when she smiled, he acknowledged. The type of woman who needed no makeup at all to look beautiful with her flawless skin and amazing green eyes. Not to mention her very Italian curves presently holding poor Claudio riveted. With the right clothes and the raw edges smoothed out, she might even be stunning.

And she spoke Italian.

She was perfect, it dawned on him. Smart, gorgeous and clearly not interested in him or his money. She did, however, need to help her father. *He* needed a beautiful woman on his arm to take to Italy who would allow him to focus on the job at hand. One who would have no expectations about the relationship when it was over.

For the price of a couple of pieces of expensive jewelry, what he'd undoubtedly have to fork out for any woman he invited to go with him, he could solve both their problems.

He lifted the espresso to his mouth with a satisfied twist

of his lips and took a sip. Nearly spit it out. Chiara looked over at him from where she stood chatting with Claudio. "What's wrong?"

"*Sugar.*" He grimaced and pushed the cup away. "Since when did I ever take sugar?"

"Oh, God." She pressed a hand to her mouth. "It's Claudio that takes sugar." She bustled over to retrieve his cup. "I'm sorry," she murmured. "I'm so distracted today. I'll fix it."

Lazzero waved her into the chair opposite him when she returned. "Sit."

Chiara gave him a wary look. She'd started to apologize a few minutes ago, then stopped because she'd meant every word she'd said and Lazzero Di Fiore was the worst offender of them all when it came to the broken hearts he'd left strewn across Manhattan. Avoiding her attraction to him *was* the right strategy.

She crossed one ankle over the other, her fingers tightening around her tray. "I should get back to work."

"Five minutes," Lazzero countered. "I have something I want to discuss with you."

Something he wanted to discuss with her? A glance at the bar revealed Kat had the couple of customers well in hand. Utterly against her better judgment, she set her tray down and slid into the chair opposite Lazzero.

The silver-gray suit and crisp, tailored white shirt set off his olive skin and toned muscular physique to perfection. He looked so gorgeous every woman in the café was gawking at him. Resolutely, she lifted her gaze to his, refusing to be one of them.

He took a sip of his espresso. Set the cup down, his gaze on her. "Your father is having trouble with the bakery?"

She frowned. "You heard that part too?"

"*Sì.* I had a phone call to make. I thought I'd let the

lineup die down." He cocked his head to the side. "You once said he makes the best cannoli in the Bronx. Why is business so dire?"

"The rent," she said flatly. "The neighborhood is booming. His landlord has gotten greedy. That, along with some unexpected expenses he's had, are killing him."

"What about a small business loan from the government?"

"We've explored that. They don't want to lend money to someone my father's age. It's too much of a risk."

A flash of something she couldn't read moved through his gaze. "In that case," he murmured, "I have a business proposition for you."

A business proposition?

Lazzero sat back in his chair and rested his cup on his thigh. "I am attending La Coppa Estiva in Milan next week." He lifted a brow. "You've heard of it?"

"Of course."

"Gianni Casale, the CEO of Fiammata, an Italian sportswear company I'm working on a deal with, will be there as will my ex, Carolina, who is married to Gianni. Gianni is very territorial when it comes to his wife. It's making it difficult to convince him he should do this deal with me, because the personal is getting mixed up with the business."

"*Are* you involved with his wife?" The question tumbled out of Chiara's mouth before she could stop it.

"No." He flashed her a dark look. "I am not Phil. It was over with Carolina when I ended it. It will, however, smooth things out considerably if I take a companion with me to Italy to convince Gianni I am of no threat to him."

Her tongue cleaved to the roof of her mouth. "You're suggesting I go to Italy with you and play your *girlfriend*?"

"Yes. I would, of course, compensate you accordingly."

"*How?*"

"With the money to help your father."

Her jaw dropped. "Why would you do that? Surely a man like you has dozens of women you could take to Italy."

He shook his head. "I don't want to take any of them. It will give them the wrong idea. What I *need* is someone who will be discreet, charming with my business associates and treat this as the business arrangement it would be. I think it could be an advantageous arrangement for us both."

An advantageous arrangement. A bitter taste filled her mouth. Her ex, Antonio, had proposed a *convenient arrangement.* Except in Antonio's case, she had been good enough to share his bed, but not blue-blooded enough to grace his arm in public.

Her stomach curled. Never would she voluntarily walk into that world again. Suffer that kind of humiliation. Be told she *didn't belong.* Not for all the money in the world.

She shook her head. "I'm not the right choice for this. Clearly I'm not after what I said earlier."

"That makes you the perfect choice," Lazzero countered. "This thing with Samara Jones has made my life a circus. I need someone I can trust who has no ulterior motives. Someone I don't have to worry about babysitting while I'm negotiating a multimillion-dollar deal. I just want to know she's going to keep up her end of the bargain."

"No." She waved a hand at him. "It's ridiculous. We don't even know each other. Not really."

"You've known me for over a year. We talk every day."

"Yes," she agreed, skepticism lacing her tone. "I ask you how business is, or 'What's the weather like out there, Lazzero?' Or, 'How about that presidential debate?' We spend five minutes chitchatting, then I make your espresso. End of conversation."

His sensual mouth twisted in a mocking smile. "So we have dinner together. I'm quite sure we can master the pertinent facts over a bottle of wine."

Her stomach muscles coiled. He was disconcerting

enough in his tailored, three-piece suit. She could only imagine what it would be like if he took the jacket off, loosened his tie and focused all that intensity on the woman involved over a bottle of wine. She knew exactly how that scenario went and it was not a mistake she was repeating.

"It would be impossible," she dismissed. "I have my shifts here. I can't afford to lose them."

"Trade them off."

"No," she said firmly. "I don't belong in that world, Lazzero. I have no *desire* to put myself in that world. I would stick out like a sore thumb. Not to mention the fact that I would never be believable as your current love interest."

"I disagree," he murmured, setting his espresso on the table and leaning forward, arms folded in front of him, eyes on hers. "You are beautiful, smart and adept at putting people at ease. With the right wardrobe and a little added... *gloss*, you would easily be the most stunning woman in the room."

Gloss? A slow curl of heat unraveled inside of her, coiling around an ancient wound that had never healed. "A diamond in the rough so to speak," she suggested, her voice pure frost.

His brow furrowed. "I didn't say that."

"But you meant it."

"You know what I mean, Chiara. I was giving you a compliment. La Coppa Estiva is a different world."

She flicked a wrist at him. "Exactly why I have no interest in this proposal of yours. In these high-stakes games you play. I thought I'd made that clear earlier."

His gaze narrowed. "What I *heard* was you on your soapbox making wild generalizations about men of a certain tax bracket."

"Hardly generalizations," she refuted. "You need someone to take to Italy with you because you've left a trail of refuse behind you, Lazzero. Because Gianni Casale doesn't trust you with his wife. I won't be part of aiding and abetting that kind of behavior."

"A trail of refuse?" His gaze chilled to a cool, hard ebony. "I think you're reading too many tabloids."

"I think not. You're exactly the sort of man I want nothing to do with."

"I'm not asking you to get involved with me," he rebutted coolly. "I'm suggesting you get over this personal bias you have against a man with a bank balance and solve your financial problems while you're at it. I have no doubt we can pull this off if you put your mind to it."

"No." She slid to the edge of the chair. "Ask someone else. I'm sure one of the other baristas would jump at the chance."

"I don't want them," he said evenly, "I want you." He threw an exorbitant figure of money at her that made her eyes widen. "It would go a long way toward helping your father."

Chiara's head buzzed. It would *pay* her father's rent for the rest of the year. Would be enough to get him back on his feet after the unexpected expenses he'd incurred having to replace some machinery at the bakery. But surely what Lazzero was proposing *was* insane? She could never pull this off and even if she could, it would put her smack in the middle of a world she wanted nothing to do with.

She got to her feet before she abandoned her common sense completely. "I need to get back to work."

Lazzero pulled a card out of his wallet, scribbled something on the back and handed it to her. "My cell number if you change your mind."

CHAPTER TWO

CHIARA'S HEAD WAS still spinning as she finished up her shift at the café and walked home on a gorgeous summer evening in Manhattan. She was too distracted, however, to take in the vibrant New York she loved, too worried about her father's financial situation to focus.

If he couldn't pay off the new equipment he'd purchased, he was going to lose the bakery—the only thing that seemed to get him up in the morning since her mother died. She couldn't conceive of that prospect happening. Which left Lazzero's shocking business proposition to consider.

She couldn't possibly do it. Would be crazy to even consider it. But how could she not?

Her head no clearer by the time she'd picked up groceries at the corner store for a quiet night in, she carried them up the three flights of stairs of the old brick walk-up she and Kat shared in Spanish Harlem, and let herself in.

They'd done their best to make the tiny, two-bedroom apartment warm and cozy despite its distinct lack of appeal, covering the dingy walls in a cherry-colored paint, adding dark refinished furniture from the antiques store around the corner, and topping it all off with colorful throws and pillows.

It wasn't much, but it was home.

Kat, who was busy getting ready for a date, joined her in the shoebox of a kitchen as Chiara stowed the groceries away. Possessing a much more robust social life than she, her roommate had plans to see a popular play with a new boyfriend she was crazy about. At the moment, however, lounging against the counter in a tomato-red silk dress and impossibly slender black heels, her roommate was hot on the trail of a juicy story.

"So," she said. "What really happened with Lazzero Di Fiore today? And no blowing me off like you did earlier."

Chiara—who thought Kat should've been a lawyer rather than the doctor she was training to be, she was so relentless in the pursuit of the facts—stowed the carton of milk in the fridge and stood up. "You can't say anything to anyone."

Kat lifted her hands. "Who am I going to tell?"

Chiara filled her in on Lazzero's business proposition. Kat's eyes went as big as saucers. "He's always had the hots for you. Maybe he's making his move."

Chiara cut that idea off at the pass. "It is strictly a business arrangement. He made that clear."

"And you said *no*? Are you crazy?" Her friend waved a red tipped hand at her. "He is offering to solve all your financial problems, Chiara, for a *week in Italy*. La Coppa Estiva is the celebrity event of the season. Most women would give their right arm to be in your position. Not to mention the fact that Lazzero Di Fiore is the hottest man on the face of the planet. What's not to like?"

Chiara pressed her lips together. Kat didn't know about her history with Antonio. Why Milan was the last place she'd want to be. It wasn't something you casually dropped into conversation with your new roommate, despite how close she and Kat had been getting.

She pursed her lips. "I have my shifts at the café. I need that job."

"Everyone's looking for extra hours right now. Someone will cover for you." Kat stuck a hand on her silk-clad hip. "When's the last time you had a holiday? Had some *fun*? Your life is boring, Chiara. *Booorrring.* You're a senior citizen at age twenty-six."

A hot warmth tinged her cheeks. Her life *was* boring. It revolved around work and more work. When she wasn't on at the café, she was helping out at the bakery on the weekends. There was no *room* for relaxation.

The downstairs buzzer went off. Kat disappeared in a cloud of perfume. Chiara cranked up the air-conditioning against the deadly heat, which wouldn't seem to go below a certain lukewarm temperature no matter how high she turned it up, and made herself dinner.

She ate while she played with a design of a dress she'd seen a girl wearing at the café today, but hadn't quite had the urban chic she favored. Changing the hemline to an angular cut and adding a touch of beading to the bodice, she sketched it out, getting close to what she'd envisioned, but not quite. The heat oppressive, the blaring sound of the television from the apartment below destroying her concentration, she threw the sketchbook and pencil aside.

What was the point? she thought, heart sinking. She was never going to have the time or money to pursue her career in design. Those university classes she'd taken at Parsons had been a waste of time and money. All she was doing was setting herself up for more disappointment in harboring these dreams of hers, because they were never going to happen.

Cradling her tea between her hands, she fought a bitter wave of loneliness that settled over her, a deep, low throb that never seemed to fade. *This* was the time she'd treasured the most—those cups of tea after dinner with her mother when the bakery was closed.

A seamstress by trade, her mother had been brilliant with a needle. They'd talked while they'd sewed—about anything and everything. About Chiara's schoolwork, about that nasty boy in her class who was giving her trouble, about the latest design she'd sketched at the back of her notebook that day. Until life as she'd known it had ended forever on a Friday evening when she was fifteen when her mother had sat her down to talk—not about boys or clothes—but about the breast cancer she'd been diagnosed with. By the next fall, she'd been gone. There had been no more cups of tea, no more confidences, only a big, scary world to navigate as her father had descended into his grief and anger.

The heavy, pulsing weight encompassing all of her now, she rolled to her feet and walked to the window. Hugging her arms tight around herself, she stared out at the colorful graffiti on the apartment buildings across the street. Usually, she managed to keep the hollow emptiness at bay, convince herself that she liked it better this way, because to engage was to *feel*, and to feel hurt too much. But tonight, imagining the fun, glamorous evening Kat was having, she felt scraped raw inside.

For a brief moment in time, she'd had a taste of that life. The fun and frivolity of it. She'd met Antonio at a party full of glamorous types in Chelsea last summer when a fellow barista who traveled in those circles had invited her along. The newly minted vice president of his family's prestigious global investment firm, Antonio Fabrizio had been gorgeous and worldly, intent on having her from the first moment he'd seen her.

She'd been seduced by the effortless glamour of his world, by the beguiling promises he'd made. By the command and authority he seemed to exert over everything around him. By how grounded he'd made her feel for the first time since her mother had died. Little had she known, she'd only been a diversion. That the woman Antonio was slated to marry was waiting for him at home in Milan. That she'd only been his American plaything, a "last fling" before he married.

Antonio had tried to placate her when she'd found out, assuring her his was a marriage of convenience, a fortuitous match for the Fabrizios. That *she* was the one he really wanted. In fact, he'd insisted, nothing would change. He would set her up in her own apartment and she would become his mistress.

Chiara had thrown the offer in his face, along with his penthouse key, shocked he would even think she would be interested in that kind of an arrangement. But Antonio, in his supreme arrogance, had been furious with her for walking out on him. Had pursued her relentlessly in the six months since, sending her flowers, jewelry, tickets to the opera, all of which she'd returned with a message to leave her alone, until finally he had.

Her mouth set as she stared out at the darkening night, a bitter anger sweeping through her. She had changed since him. *He* had made her change. She had become tougher, wiser to the world. *She* was not to blame for what had happened, Antonio was. Why should she be so worried about seeing him again?

If this was, as Lazzero had reasoned, a business proposition, why not turn it around to her own advantage? Use the world that had once used her? Surely she could survive a few days in Milan playing Lazzero's love interest if it meant saving her father's bakery? And if she were to run into Antonio at La Coppa Estiva, which was a real possibility, so what? It was crazy to let him have this power over her still.

She fell asleep on the sofa, the TV still on, roused by Kat at 2 a.m., who sent her stumbling to bed. When she woke for her early morning shift at the café, her decision was made.

Di Fiore's was blissfully free of its contingent of fortune hunters when Lazzero met Santo for a beer on Saturday night to talk La Coppa Estiva and their strategy for Gianni Casale.

He'd been pleasantly surprised when Chiara had called him earlier that afternoon to accept his offer. Was curious to find out why she had. Thinking he could nail those details down along with his game plan for Gianni, he'd arranged to meet her here for a drink after his beer with Santo.

Ensconcing themselves at the bar so they could keep an eye on the door, he and Santo fleshed out a multilayered plan of attack, with contingencies for whatever objections the wily Italian might present. Satisfied they had it nailed, Lazzero leaned back in his stool and took a sip of his beer. Eyed his brother's dark suit.

"Work or pleasure tonight?"

"Damion Howard and his agent are dropping by to pick up their tickets for next week. Thought I'd romance them a bit while I'm at it."

"What?" Lazzero derided. "No beautiful blonde lined up for your pleasure?"

"Too busy." Santo sighed. "This event is a monster. I need to keep my eye on the ball."

Lazzero studied the lines of fatigue etching his brother's face. "You should let Dez handle the athletes. It would free up your time."

His brother cocked a brow. "Says the ultimate control freak?"

Lazzero shrugged. He was a self-professed workaholic. Knew the demons that drove him. It was part of the territory when your father self-destructed, leaving his business and your life in pieces. No amount of success would ever convince him it was *enough*.

Santo gave him an idle look. "Did Nico tell you about his conversation with Carolina?"

Lazzero nodded. Carolina Casale, an interior designer by trade, was coordinating the closing night party for La Coppa Estiva, a job perfectly suited to her extensive project management skills. Nico, who'd negotiated a reprieve from the wedding planning to attend the party with a client, had called her to request an additional couple of tickets for some VIPs, only to find himself consoling a weepy Carolina instead, who had spent the whole conversation telling him how unhappy she was. She'd finished by asking how Lazzero was.

His fingers tightened around his glass. *He could not go through another of those scenes.* It was not his fault Carolina had married a man old enough to be her father.

"I'm working on a solution to that," he said grimly. "Tonight, in fact. Speaking of solutions, you aren't giving me too much field time are you? I can feel my knee creaking as we speak."

Santo's mouth twitched. "I'm afraid the answer is yes. We need a solid midfielder. But it's perfect, actually. Gianni plays midfield."

Lazzero was about to amplify his protest when his brother's gaze narrowed on the door. "Now *she* could persuade me to abandon my plans for the evening."

Lazzero turned around. Found himself equally absorbed by the female standing in the doorway. Her slender body encased in a sheer, flowing blouse that ended at midthigh, her dark jeans tucked into knee-high boots, Chiara had left her hair loose tonight, the silky waves falling to just below her shoulder blades in a dark, shiny cloud.

It wasn't the most provocative outfit he'd ever seen, but with Chiara's curves, she looked amazing. The wave of lust that kicked him hard in the chest irritated the hell out of him. She had labeled him a bloody Lothario, for God's sake. Had told him he was exactly the kind of man she'd never get involved with. He'd do well to remember this was a business arrangement they were embarking on together.

Chiara's scan of the room halted when she found him sitting at the bar. Santo's gaze moved from Chiara to him. "*She's* the one you're meeting?"

"My date for Italy," Lazzero confirmed, sliding off the stool.

"Who *is* she?" His brother frowned. "She looks familiar."

"Her name is Chiara. And she's far too nice a girl for you."

"Which means she's *definitely* too nice for you," Santo tossed after his retreating figure.

Lazzero couldn't disagree. Which was why he was going to keep this strictly business. Pulling to a halt in front of her, he bent to press a kiss to both of her cheeks. An intoxicating scent of orange blossom mixed with a musky, sensual undertone assailed his senses. It suited her perfectly.

"I'm sorry I'm late," she murmured, stepping back. "The barista who was supposed to relieve me was sick. I had to wait until the sub came in."

"It's fine. I was having a beer with my brother." Lazzero whisked her past Santo just as his brother's clients walked in. Chiara cocked her head to the side. "You're not going to introduce us?"

"Not now, no."

"Because I'm a barista?" A spark of fire flared in her green eyes.

"Because my brother likes to ask too many questions," he came back evenly. "Not to mention the fact that we don't have our story straight yet."

"Oh." The heat in her eyes dissipated. "That's true."

"Just for the record," he murmured, pressing a palm to the small of her back to guide her through the crowd, "Santo and I started Supersonic from nothing. We *had* nothing. There is no judgment here about what you do."

Her long dark lashes swept down, dusting her cheeks like miniature black fans. "Is it true what Samara Jones said about you and your brother masterminding your business from here?"

His mouth twisted. "It's become a bit of an urban myth, but yes, we brainstormed the idea for Supersonic at a table near the back when we were students at Columbia. We kept the table for posterity's sake when we bought the place a few years later." He arched a brow at her. "Would you like to sit there? It's nothing special," he warned.

"Yes." She surprised him by answering in the affirmative. "I'll need to know these things about you to make this believable."

"Perhaps," he suggested, his palm nearly spanning her delicate spine as he directed her around a group of people, "you'll discover other things that surprise you. Why did you say yes, by the way?"

"Because my father needs the money. I couldn't afford to say no."

Direct. To the point. Just like the woman who felt so soft and feminine beneath his hand, but undoubtedly had a spine of steel. He was certain she was up to the challenge he was about to hand her.

Seating her at the old, scarred table located in a quiet alcove off the main traffic of the bar, he pushed her chair in and sat opposite her. His long legs brushed hers as he arranged them to get comfortable. Chiara shifted away as if burned. He smothered a smile at her prickly demeanor. *That* they would have to solve if they were going to make this believable.

She traced a finger over the deep indentation carved into the thick mahogany wood, a rough impersonation of the Supersonic logo. "Who did this?"

"I did." A wry smile curved his mouth. "I nearly got us kicked out of here for good that night. But we were so high on the idea we had, we didn't care."

She sat back in her chair, a curious look on her face. "How did you make it happen, then, if you started with nothing?"

"Santo and I put ourselves through university on sports scholarships. We knew a lot of people in the industry, knew what athletes wanted in a product. Supersonic became a 'by athletes, for athletes' line." He lifted a shoulder. "A solid business plan brought our godfather on board for an initial investment, some athletes we went to school with made up the rest."

A smile played at her mouth. "And then you parlayed it into one of the world's most successful athletic-wear companies. Impressive."

"With some detours along the way," he amended. "It's a bitterly competitive industry. But we had a vision. It worked."

"Will Santo be in Milan?"

He nodded. "He's the chairman of the event. He'll have his hands full massaging all of our relationships. When he isn't busy doing that with his posse of women," he qualified drily.

"Clearly runs in the family," Chiara murmured.

Lazzero set a considering gaze on her. "I think you would be surprised by the number of relationships I engage in versus what the tabloids print. I do need some time to run a Fortune 500 company, after all."

"So actually," Chiara suggested, "you are a choir boy."

A smile tugged at his lips. "I wouldn't go that far."

Chiara expelled a breath as a pretty waitress arrived to take their order. In dark jeans and a navy T-shirt, Lazzero was elementally attractive in a way few men could ever hope to emulate. When he smiled, however, he was devastating. It lit up the rugged, aggressive lines of his face, highlighting his beautiful bone structure and the sensual line of his mouth. Made him beautiful in a jaw-dropping kind of way. And that was before you got to his intense black stare that seemed to dissect you into your various assorted parts.

Which was clearly having its effect on their waitress. Dressed in a gray Di Fiore's T-shirt and tight black pants, she flashed Lazzero a high-wattage smile and babbled out the nightly specials. Without asking Chiara's preference, Lazzero rattled off a request for a bottle of Italian red, spring water and an appetizer for them to share.

She eyed him as the waitress disappeared. "Are you always this…*domineering*?"

"Sì," he murmured, eyes on hers. "Most women like it when I take control. It makes them feel feminine and cared for. They don't have to think—they just sit back and… enjoy."

A wave of heat stained her cheeks, her pulse doing a wicked little jump. "I am not most women. And I *like* to think."

"I'm beginning to get that impression," he said drily. "The 'not like most women' part."

"What happens," she countered provocatively, "when you turn this hopelessly addicted contingent of yours back out into the wild? Isn't that exactly the problem you're facing with Carolina Casale?"

He shrugged. "Carolina knew the rules."

"Which are?"

"It lasts as long as she keeps it interesting."

Her jaw dropped. His arrogance was astounding. Carolina, however, had likely believed she was different—her cardinal mistake. As had been hers.

"She married Gianni on the rebound from you," she guessed.

"Perhaps."

She felt a stab of sympathy for Carolina Casale. She knew how raw those dashed hopes felt. Antonio had married within months of their breakup. Because that was what transactionally motivated men like Antonio and Lazzero did. They used people for their own purposes without thought for the consequences. It didn't matter who got hurt in the process.

The waitress returned and poured their wine. Chiara put the conversation firmly back on a business footing after she'd left. "Shall we talk details, then?"

"Yes." Lazzero sat back in his chair, glass in hand. "La Coppa Estiva is a ten-day-long event. It begins next Wednesday with the opening party, continues with the tournament, then wraps up on the following Saturday with the final game and closing party. We will need to leave New York on Tuesday night to fly overnight to Milan."

Her stomach lurched. She was actually doing this.

"That's fine," she said. "There's a girl at work who's looking for extra shifts. I can trade them off."

"Good." He inclined his head. "Have you ever been to Milan?"

She shook her head. "We have family there, but I've never been."

"The game," he elaborated, "is held at the stadium in San Siro, on the outskirts of the city. We'll be staying at my friend Filippo Giordano's luxury hotel in Milan."

Her stomach curled at the thought of sharing a hotel suite with Lazzero. But of course, they were supposedly together and they would be expected to share a room. Which got her wondering. "How do you expect us to act together? I mean—"

"How do I normally act with my girlfriends?"

"Yes."

He shrugged. "I don't expect you to be all over me. But if there is an appropriate moment where some kind of affection is in order, we go with the flow."

Which could involve a kiss. Her gaze landed on his full, sensual mouth, her stomach doing a funny roll as she imagined what it would be like to kiss him. It would be far from forgettable, she concluded with a shiver. That mouth was simply far too...*erotic*.

Which was exactly how she should *not* be thinking.

"You were right," she admitted, firmly redirecting her thoughts. "I don't have the appropriate clothes for this type of an event. I would make them, but I don't have time."

Lazzero waved a hand at her. "That comes with the deal. We have a stylist we use for our commercial shoots. Micaela's offered to outfit you on Monday."

She stiffened. "I don't need a stylist."

He shrugged. "I can send my PA with you with my credit card. But you would lose the benefit of Micaela's experience with an event like this. Which could be invaluable."

She hated the idea of his PA accompanying her even more than she hated the idea of the stylist. And, she grumpily conceded, a stylist's help would be invaluable given her doubts about her ability to pull this off.

"Fine," she capitulated, "the stylist is fine."

"*Bene*. Which brings us to the public story of *us* we will use."

She eyed him. "What were you thinking?"

"I thought we would go with the truth. That we met at the café."

"And you couldn't resist my espressos, nor me?" she filled in sardonically.

His mouth curved. "Now you're getting into the spirit. Except," he drawled, his ebony gaze resting on hers, "I would have gone with the endlessly beautiful green eyes, the razor-sharp brain and the elusive challenge of finding out who the real Chiara Ferrante is underneath all those layers."

Her heart skipped a beat. "There isn't anything to find out."

"No?" His perusal was the lazy study of a big cat. "I could have sworn there was."

"Then you'd be wrong," she came back evenly. "How long has this supposed relationship of ours been going on, then?"

"Let's say a couple of blissful months. So blissful, in fact, that I just put an engagement ring on your finger."

She gaped at him. "You never said anything about being engaged."

He hiked a broad shoulder. "If I put a ring on your finger, it will be clear to Carolina there is no hope for a reconciliation between us."

"Does she think there is?"

"Her marriage is on the rocks. She's unhappy. Gianni is worried he can't hold her."

"Oh, my God," she breathed. "Why don't you just tell Gianni he has nothing to worry about? That you have a heart of stone."

He reached into his jeans pocket and retrieved a box. Flipping it open, he revealed the ring inside. "I think *this* will be more effective. It looked like you. What do you think?"

Her jaw dropped at the enormous asscher-cut diamond with its halo of pave-set stones embedded into the band. It was the most magnificent thing she'd ever seen.

"Lazzero," she said unsteadily. "I did not sign on for this. This is *insane*."

"Think of it as a prop, that's all." He picked up her left hand and slid the glittering diamond on her index finger. Her heart thudded as she drank in how perfectly it suited her hand. How it fit like a glove. How warm and strong his fingers were wrapped around hers, tattooing her skin with the pulse of attraction that beat between them.

How *crazy* this was.

She tugged her hand free. "You can't possibly expect me to wear this. What if I put it down somewhere? What if I lose it?"

"It's insured. There's no need to worry."

"How much is it worth?"

"A couple million."

She yanked the ring off her hand. "No," she said, setting it on the table in front of him. "Absolutely not. Get something cheaper."

"I am not," he said calmly, "giving you a cheaper engagement ring because you are afraid of losing it. Carolina will be all over it. She will notice."

"And what happens when we call this off?" She searched desperately for objections. "What is Gianni going to think about that?"

"I should have him on board by then. We can let it die a slow death when we get back." He took her hand and slid the ring on again.

"I won't sleep," Chiara murmured, staring at the ring, her heart pounding. Not when she would publicly, if only for a few days, be branded the future Mrs. Lazzero Di Fiore. It *was* crazy. *She* would be crazy to agree to do this.

She should shut it down right now. *Would*, if she were wise. But as she and Lazzero sat working out the remaining details, she couldn't seem to find the words to say no. Because saving her father's business was all that mattered. Pulling him out of this depression that was breaking her heart.

CHAPTER THREE

CHIARA, IN FACT, didn't sleep. She spent Sunday morning bleary-eyed, nursing a huge cup of coffee while she filled out the passport application Lazzero was going to fast-track for her in the morning.

The dazzling diamond on her finger flashed in the morning sunlight—a glittering, unmistakable reminder of what she'd signed on to last night. Her heart lurched in her chest, a combination of caffeine and nerves. Playing Lazzero's girlfriend was one thing. Playing his *fiancée* was another matter entirely. She was quickly developing a massive, severe case of cold feet.

She would be to Italy and back—*unengaged*—in ten days' time, she reassured herself. No need to panic or for anyone to know. Except for her father, given she wouldn't be able to help out at the bakery on the weekends. Nor could she check in on him as she always did every night, a fact that left her with an uneasy feeling in the pit of her stomach.

She chewed on her lip as she eyed her cell phone. Telling her father the truth about the trip was not an option. He would never approve of what she was doing, nor would his pride allow him to take the money. Lazzero, for whom logistics were clearly never a problem, had offered to make an angel donation to her father's business through a community organization Supersonic supported which provided assistance to local businesses.

Which solved the problem of the money. It did not, however, help with the little white lie she was going to have to tell her father about why she was going to Italy. Her father had always preached the value of keeping an impeccable truth with yourself and with others. It will, he always said, save you much heartache in life. But in this case, she concluded, the end justified the means.

She called her father and told him she was going to be vacationing with friends in a house they'd rented in Lake Como, feeling like a massive ball of guilt by the time she'd gotten off the phone. Giving in to her need to ensure he would be okay while she was gone, she called Frankie De-Lucca, an old friend of her father's who lived down the street, and asked him to look in on her father while she was away.

She dragged her feet all the way down to meet Gareth, Lazzero's driver, the next morning for her shopping expedition with Micaela Parker. She was intimidated before she'd even stepped out of the car as it halted in front of the posh Madison Avenue boutique where she was to meet the stylist. Everything in the window screamed *one month's salary*.

Micaela was waiting for her in the luxurious lounge area of the boutique. An elegant blonde, all long, lean legs, she was more interesting looking than beautiful. But she was so perfectly put together in jeans, a silk T-shirt and a blazer, funky jewelry at her wrists and neck, Chiara could only conclude she was in excellent hands. Micaela was, after all, the dresser of a quarter of Manhattan's celebrities.

"Tell me a bit about your personal style," Micaela prompted over coffee.

Chiara showed her a few of her own pieces she'd made on her phone. Micaela gave them a critical appraisal. "I like them," she said finally. "Very Coachella boho. Those soft feminine lines look great on you."

"Within reason." A pang moved through her at the praise. "I have too many curves."

"You have perfect curves. You just need to show them off properly." Micaela handed back her phone. "What other staples do you have in your wardrobe we can work with?"

Not much, it turned out.

"Not a problem," Micaela breezed. "We'll get you everything. Luckily," she teased, "Lazzero's PA gave me carte blanche. He must be seriously smitten with you."

Chiara decided no answer was better than attempting one to that statement. Micaela took the hint and reached for her coffee cup to get started. Her eyes nearly popped out of her head when she saw the giant diamond sparkling on Chiara's hand.

"You and Lazzero are *engaged*?"

"It's brand-new," Chiara murmured, as every assistant in the shop turned to stare. "We haven't made a formal announcement yet."

"You won't have to now," Micaela said drily, inclining her head toward the shop girls. "Half the city will know by noon."

Oh, God. Chiara bit her lip. Why had she agreed to do this again?

Micaela led her into the dressing area and started throwing clothes at her with military-like precision. Telling herself it was the armor she needed to face a world in which she'd been declared not good enough, Chiara tried on everything the stylist presented her with and discovered Micaela had impeccable taste that worked well with her own personal style.

It was when they came to the search for the perfect evening dresses that Micaela got intensely critical. Chiara would be in the limelight on these occasions, photographed by paparazzi from around the world. They needed to be flawless. Irreproachable. Eye-catching, but not ostentatious.

Just the thought of walking down a red carpet made her stomach churn.

By the time they'd chosen purses and jewelry to go with her new wardrobe, she was ready to drop. Looking forward to collapsing at the spa appointment Micaela had booked for her, she protested when the stylist dragged her next door to the lingerie boutique.

"I don't need any of that," she said definitively. "I'm good."

"Are you sure what you have isn't going to leave lines?" Micaela asked.

No dammit, she wasn't. And she wasn't about to end up on a red carpet with them. Marching into the fitting room, she tried on the beautiful lingerie Micaela handed over. Felt her throat grow tighter as she stood in front of the mirror in peach silk, the lace on the delicate bra the lingerie's only nod to fuss.

Antonio had loved to buy her lingerie. Had always said it was because he loved having her all to himself—that he didn't want to share her with anyone else. He'd used that excuse when it came to social engagements too—taking her to low-key restaurants rather than his high-profile events because, she'd assumed, he was deciding whether he should make her a Fabrizio or not, and fool that she'd been, she hadn't wanted to mess it up.

Heat lashed her cheeks. Never again would she give a man that power over her. Never again would she be so deluded about the truth.

Sinking her fingers into the clasp of the delicate bra, she stripped it off. She hadn't quite shed the sting of the memory when Micaela whisked her off to the salon for lunch, hair and treatments.

Dimitri, whom Micaela proclaimed the best hair guy in Manhattan, promptly suggested she cut her hair to shoulder length and add bangs for a more sophisticated look.

A rejection rose in her throat, an automatic response, because her hair had always been her thing. Her kryptonite. Antonio had loved it.

That lifted her chin. She wasn't that Chiara anymore. She wanted all signs of her gone. And if there was a chance she was going to run into Antonio in Milan, she would need *all* her armor in place.

"Cut it off," she said to Dimitri. "And yes to the bangs."

Lazzero was on the phone tying up a loose end before he left for Europe on Tuesday evening when Chiara walked into the tiny lounge at Teterboro Airport. Gareth, who'd dropped her off with Lazzero's afternoon meetings on the other side of town, deposited Chiara's suitcase beside her, gave him a wave and melted back outside. But Lazzero was too busy looking at Chiara to notice.

Dressed in black cigarette pants, another pair of those sexy boots she seemed to favor and a silk shirt that skimmed the curve of her amazing backside, she looked cool and sophisticated. It was her hair that had him aghast. Gone were the thick, silky waves that fell down her back, in their place a blunt bob that just skimmed her shoulders. He couldn't deny the sophisticated style and wispy bangs accentuated her lush features and incredible eyes. It just wasn't *her*.

Wrapping up the call, he strode across the lounge toward her. "What the hell did you do to your hair?"

Her eyes widened, a flash of defiance firing their green depths. "It was time for a change. Dimitri, Micaela's hair guy, thinks it looks sophisticated. Wasn't that what you were going for?"

Yes. *No.* Not if it meant cutting her hair. She had gorgeous hair. *Had* gorgeous hair. He wanted to inform *Dimitri* he was an idiot. Except Chiara looked exactly like the type of woman he'd have on his arm. Micaela had done her job well. *So why the hell was he so angry?* Because he'd liked her better the way she'd been before?

"I'm sorry," he said gruffly. "It's been a long day. You look beautiful. And yes, it's chic…very sophisticated."

Her chin lowered a fraction. "Micaela was amazing. She gave me some excellent advice."

"Good." Catching a signal from a waiting official, he inclined his head. "We're good to go. You ready?"

She nodded and went to pick up her bag. He bent to take it from her, his fingers brushing against hers as he did. She flinched and took a step back. He grimaced and hoisted the bag. He was going to have to deal with that reaction before they landed in Italy or this relationship between them wasn't going to be remotely believable.

He carried it and his own bag onto the tarmac, where the sleek corporate jet was waiting. After a quick check of their passports, they were airborne, winging their way across the Atlantic.

He pulled out his laptop as soon as they'd leveled out. Chiara, an herbal tea in hand, fished out a magazine and started reading.

Together they silently coexisted, seated across from each other in the lounge area. Appreciating the time to catch up and finding it heartily refreshing to be with a woman who didn't want to chatter all the way across the ocean about inane things he wasn't the slightest bit interested in, it wasn't until a couple of hours later that he noticed Chiara wasn't really focusing on anything. Staring out the window in between flipping pages, applying multiple coats of lip balm and fidgeting to the point where he finally sighed and set his laptop aside.

"Okay," he murmured. "What's wrong?"

She dug into her bag, pulled out a newspaper and dropped it on the table in front of him. Too busy to have touched the inch-thick pile of press clippings that had been left on his desk that morning, he picked it up and scanned the tabloid page, finding the story Chiara was referring to near the bottom. It was Samara Jones's weekly column, featuring a shot of Chiara leaving a store, shopping bags in hand.

One Down—One to Go!

Sorry, ladies, but this Di Fiore is now taken. According to my sources, Lazzero Di Fiore's new fiancée was seen shopping in fashion hot spot Zazabara on Monday with celebrity stylist Micaela Parker, a four-carat asscher-cut diamond dazzling on her finger. My source wouldn't name names, but revealed an appearance at La Coppa Estiva was the impetus for the shopping excursion.

Lazzero threw the tabloid down. For once he didn't feel like strangling the woman. It was perfect, actually. Word would get around, Carolina would realize the reality of the situation and his problem would be solved.

The pinched expression on Chiara's face, however, made it clear she didn't feel the same way. "It was the point of this, after all," he reasoned. "Don't sweat it. It will be over in a few days."

She shot him a deadly look. "Don't sweat it? Playing your girlfriend is one thing, Lazzero. Having my face plastered across one of New York's dailies as your fiancée is another matter entirely. What if my father sees it? Not to mention the fact that it's going to be the shortest engagement in history. The press will have a field day with it."

He shrugged. "You knew they were going to photograph you in Milan."

"I was hoping it would get buried on page twenty." Her

mouth pursed. "Honestly, I have no idea how we're going to pull this off."

"We won't," he said meaningfully, "if you flinch every time I touch you."

A rosy pink dusted her cheeks. "I don't do that."

"Yes, you do." *Now*, he decided, was the time to get to the bottom of the enigmatic Chiara Ferrante.

"Have a drink with me before dinner."

She frowned. "I'm sure you have far too much work to do."

"It's an eight-hour flight. There's plenty of time. You just said it yourself," he pointed out. "We need to work on making this relationship believable if we're going to pull this off. Part of that is getting to know each other better."

Summoning the attendant, he requested a predinner drink, stood and held out a hand to her.

Chiara took the hand Lazzero offered and rolled to her feet. She could hardly say no. He would only accuse her of being prickly again. And she thought that maybe he was right, maybe if they got to know each other better she wouldn't feel so apprehensive about what she was walking into. About her ability to carry this charade off.

She curled up beside him on the sofa in the lounge area, shoes off, legs tucked beneath her. Tried to relax as she took a sip of her drink, but it was almost impossible to do so with Lazzero looking so ridiculously attractive in dark pants and a white shirt rolled up at the sleeves, dark stubble shadowing his jaw. It was just as disconcerting as she'd imagined it would be. As if the testosterone level had been dialed up to maximum in the tiny airplane cabin with nowhere to go.

God. She took another sip of her drink. Grasped on to the first subject that came to mind. "What sport did you play in university?"

"Basketball." He sat back against the sofa and crossed one long leg over the other. "It was my obsession."

"Santo too?"

His mouth curved. "Santo is too pretty to rough it up. He'd be running straight to his plastic surgeon if he ever got an elbow to the face. Santo played baseball."

She considered him curiously. "How good *were* you? You must have been talented to put yourself through school on a full scholarship."

He shrugged. "I was good. But an injury in my senior year put me on the sidelines. I didn't have enough time to get back to the level I needed to be before the championships and draft." He pursed his lips. "It wasn't meant to be."

She absorbed his matter-of-fact demeanor. She didn't think it could have been so simple. Giving up her design classes had been like leaving a piece of herself behind when money had been prioritized for the bakery. Lazzero had had his fingers on every little boy's dream of becoming a professional athlete, only to have it slip right through them.

"That must have been difficult," she observed, "to have your dream stolen from you."

A cryptic look moved across his face. "Some dreams are too expensive to keep."

"Supersonic was a dream you and your brothers had," she pointed out.

"Which was built on a solid business case backed up by a gap in the market we identified. Opportunity," he qualified, "makes sense to me. Blind idealism does not."

"Too much ambition can also be destructive," she said. "I see plenty of examples of that in New York."

"In the man who broke your heart?" Lazzero inserted smoothly.

Her pulse skipped a beat. "Who says he exists?"

"I do," he drawled. "Your speech at the café…the fact that you've never given any man who comes in there a fighting chance. You have 'smashed to smithereens' written all over you."

She sank her teeth into her lip, finding that an all-too-accurate description of what Antonio had done to her. "There was someone," she acknowledged quietly, "and yes, he broke my heart. But in hindsight, it was for the best. It made me see his true colors."

"Which were?"

"That he was not to be trusted. That men like him are not to be trusted."

He eyed her. "That is a massive generalization. So he hurt you...so he burned you badly. He is only *one* man, Chiara. What are you going to do? Spend the rest of your life avoiding a certain kind of man because he *might* hurt you?"

Her mouth set at a stubborn angle. "I'm not willing to take the risk."

"Did you love him?"

"I thought I did." She gave him a pointed look. "I could ask you the same thing. Where does *your* fear of commitment come from? Because clearly, you have one."

A lift of his broad shoulder. "I simply don't care to."

"Why not?"

"Because relationships are complicated dramas I have no interest in participating in." He took a sip of his drink. Rested his glass on his lean, corded thigh. "What about family?" he asked, tipping his glass at her. "I know nothing about yours other than the fact that your father, Carlo, runs Ferrante's. What about your mother? Brothers? Sisters?"

A shadow whispered across her heart. "My mother died of breast cancer when I was fifteen. I'm an only child."

His gaze darkened. "I'm sorry. You were close to her?"

"Yes," she said quietly. "She ran the bakery with my father. She was amazing—wonderful, *wise*. A pseudo parent to half the kids in the neighborhood. My father always said most of the clientele came in just to talk to her."

"You miss her," he said.

Heat stung the back of her eyes. "Every day." It was a deep, dark hollow in her soul that would never be filled.

Lazzero curled his fingers around hers. Strong and protective, they imparted a warmth that seemed to radiate right through her. "My father died when I was nineteen," he murmured. "I know how it feels."

Oh. She bit her lip. "How?"

"He was an alcoholic. He drank himself to death."

She absorbed his matter-of-fact countenance. "And your mother? Is she still alive?"

He nodded. "She's remarried and lives in California."

"Do you see her much?"

He shook his head. "She isn't a part of our lives."

"Why not?"

"It isn't relevant to this discussion."

She sat back in the sofa as a distinct chill filled the air. *Not a part of their lives?* What did that mean? From the closed-off look on Lazzero's face, it didn't seem as if she was going to find out.

She slid her hand out of his. Took a sip of her drink. "What other things should I know about you?" she asked, deciding the mood needed lightening. "Recreational pursuits? Likes, dislikes?"

His mouth quirked. "Are you looking for the dating show answer?"

"If you like," she agreed.

He took a sip of his wine. Cradled the glass in his palm. "I train in a gym every morning at six with a fighter from the old neighborhood. That's about the extent of my recreational activities other than the odd pickup basketball game with my brothers. I *appreciate*," he continued, eyes glimmering with humor, "honesty and integrity in a person as well as fine Tuscan wines. I *dislike* Samara Jones."

Her mouth curved as she considered her response.

"You've likely gathered from my speech at the café integrity is a big one for me too," she said, picking up on the theme. "*I*, like you, have little downtime. When I'm not working at the café, I'm helping out at the bakery, which makes my life utterly mundane. Although I do," she admitted with a self-deprecating smile, "have a secret obsession with ballroom dancing reality shows. It's the escapism."

Lazzero arched a brow. "Do you? Dance?"

"No." She made a face. "I'm horrible. It's entirely aspirational. You?"

"My mother was a dancer, so yes. She made us take classes. She thought it was an invaluable social skill."

She found the idea of the three powerful Di Fiore brothers taking dance classes highly entertaining. It occurred to her then that she had no idea what a date with Lazzero would look like. Did he take a woman dancing? Perhaps he whisked them off to Paris for lavish dinner dates? Or were the females in his life simply plus-one accompaniments to his endless social calendar?

Was he romantic or entirely transactional? She sank her teeth into her lip. *That* had nothing to do with a business arrangement, but God, was she curious. If she and Lazzero had ever acted on the attraction between them, how would it have played out?

She decided it was a reasonable question to ask, given their situation. "So what would a typical date night look like for you? So I have some sense of what *we* would look like."

He rubbed a palm over the stubble on his jaw, a contemplative look on his face. "We might," he began thoughtfully, "start off with dinner at my favorite little Italian place in the East Village. Nothing fancy, just great food and a good atmosphere. Things would definitely be getting interesting over dinner because I consider stimulating conversation and excellent food the best primer."

For what? she wondered, her stomach coiling.

"So then," he continued, apparently electing to illuminate her, "if my date decided she'd found it as stimulating as I, we'd likely head back to my place on Fifth. You could assume she'd end up well satisfied...*somewhere* in my penthouse."

Heat flared down low, a wave of color staining her cheeks. She wasn't sure if it was the "somewhere" that got her or the "well satisfied" part.

"I see," she said evenly. "Thank you for that very *visual* impression."

"And you?" he prompted smoothly. "What are your dating preferences? Assuming, of course, they involve the working-class, non-power-hungry variety of man?"

"I'm too busy to date."

He gave her a speculative look. "When *was* the last time you had a date?"

She eyed him. "You don't need to know that. It has nothing to do with our deal."

"You're right," he deadpanned. "I just want to know."

"No," she said firmly. "It's *not relevant* to this discussion."

An amused smile tilted his lips. "You could be out of practice, you realize?"

"Out of practice for what?"

"Kissing," he said huskily, his smoky gaze dropping to her mouth. "Maybe we should try one now and get it out of the way. See if we're any good at it."

Something swooped and then dropped in her stomach. She was seriously afraid she *was* out of practice. *Severely* out of practice. But that didn't mean kissing Lazzero was a good idea. In fact, she was sure it was a very *bad* idea.

"I don't think so," she managed, past a sandpaper dry throat.

"Why not?" His ebony eyes gleamed with challenge. "Or are you afraid of the very *real* attraction between us?"

Her pulse racing a mile a minute at the thought of that sensual, erotic mouth taking hers, she could hardly deny it. She *could*, however, shut it down. *Right now.*

She lifted her chin, eyes on his. "This is a business arrangement between us, Lazzero. When we kiss, it will be toward that purpose and that purpose only. Are we clear on that?"

"Crystal," he murmured. "I like a woman who can keep her eye on the ball."

CHAPTER FOUR

CHIARA'S MIND WAS on anything but business after that heated encounter with Lazzero. By putting the attraction between them squarely out in the open, he had created a sexual awareness of each other she couldn't seem to shake. Which absolutely needed to happen because that attraction had no place in this business arrangement of theirs. Particularly when Lazzero had clearly been toying with her with his own ends in mind—making them *believable* for Gianni Casale.

She retreated to a book after dinner, forcing herself to focus on it rather than her ill-advised chemistry with the man sitting across from her. Night fell like a cloak outside the window. With Lazzero still absorbed in his seemingly endless mountain of work, her eyelids began to drift shut. Giving in to the compulsion, she accepted his invitation to use the luxurious bedroom at the back of the plane and caught a few hours of sleep.

When she woke, a golden, early morning light blanketed the white-capped Italian Alps in a magnificent, otherworldly glow. She freshened up in the bathroom, then joined Lazzero in the main cabin. He'd changed and looked crisp and ready to go in a light blue shirt and jeans, his dark stubble traded for a clean-shaven jaw.

Her heart jumped in her chest at how utterly gorgeous he was. Did the man ever look disheveled?

"We're about to land," he said, looking up from the report he was reading. "Do you want coffee and breakfast before we do?"

She wasn't the slightest bit hungry, still groggy from sleep. But she thought the sustenance might do her good. Accepting the offer, she inhaled a cup of strong, black coffee and nibbled on a croissant. Soon, they were landing in Milan and being whisked from the airport to the luxury hotel Lazzero's Milanese friend, hotel magnate Filippo Giordano, owned near the La Scala opera house.

The Orientale occupied four elegant fifteenth-century buildings that had been transformed from a spectacularly beautiful old convent into a luxurious, urban oasis. Chiara was picking her jaw up off the ground when the hotel manager swooped in to greet them.

"We were fully booked when Filippo made the request," he informed them smoothly. "La Coppa Estiva is always *maniaco*. Luckily, the presidential suite became available. Filippo thought it was perfect, given you are newly engaged."

Chiara's stomach dropped. *This is well and truly on. Oh, my God.*

The stately suite they'd been allocated occupied the entire third floor of the hotel, living up to its presidential suite status with its high ceilings and incredible views of the city, including one from the stepped-down infinity pool on the elegantly landscaped terrace.

Sunlight flooded its expansive interiors as the butler gave them a personal tour. The suite's lush, tasteful color scheme in cream and taupe was complemented by its black oak woodwork, the perfect combination of Milanese style with a touch of the Orient.

Chiara's eyes nearly bugged out of her head when the butler showed them the showpiece of a bathroom, its muted lighting, Brazilian marble floors and stand-alone hot tub occupying a space as large as her entire apartment. But it was the gorgeous, palatial bedroom with its French doors and incredible vistas that made her heart drop into her stomach. *One elegant, king-size, four-poster bed.* How was that going to work?

Lazzero eyed her. "I'd asked for a suite, thinking we'd get one with multiple rooms, but clearly this was all that was available. I'll sleep on the sofa in the bedroom."

"No." She shook her head. "You're far too tall for that. I will."

"I'm not a big sleeper." He shut the argument down with a shake of his head.

They got settled into the suite, Chiara waving off the butler who offered to hang up their things because she preferred to do it herself. After a sumptuous lunch on the terrace, Lazzero went off to work in the office, with a directive she should take a nap before the party because it was going to be a late night.

She didn't have the energy to protest yet another of his arrogant commands. Too weary from only a few hours of sleep, she undressed in the serene, beautiful bedroom and put on jersey sweats before she crawled beneath the soft-as-silk sheets of the four-poster bed. The next thing she knew, it was 6 p.m., the alarm she'd set to ensure she'd have enough time to get ready sounding in her ear.

Padding out to the living room, she discovered Lazzero was outside swimming laps in the infinity pool. Deciding she would enjoy the pool with its jaw-dropping view tomorrow, *minus* what she was sure would be an equally spectacular half-naked Lazzero, she had a late tea, then took a long, hot bath in the sunken tub.

Lazzero came in to shower as she sat applying a light coat of makeup in the dressing room. Keeping her brain firmly focused on the mascara wand in her hand rather than on the naked man in the shower, she stroked it over her lashes, transforming them from their ordinary dark abundance to a silky, lush length that swept her cheeks. A light coat of pink gloss finished the subtle look off.

Makeup and hair complete, she slipped on the silver sequined dress she and Micaela had chosen for the party. Long-sleeved and made of a gauzy, figure-hugging material, it clung to every inch of her body, the sexy open back revealing a triangle of bare, creamy flesh.

She stared dubiously at her reflection in the mirror. It was on trend, perfect for the opening party, but it was shorter than anything she normally wore. Micaela, however, had insisted she had an amazing figure and needed to show it off. She just wasn't sure she needed to show so *much* of it off.

Pushing her doubts aside, she slipped on her gold heels, a favorite purchase from her shopping trip because they were just too gorgeous to fault, and a sparkly pair of big hoop earrings, her one concession to her bohemian style. And declared herself done.

She stepped out onto the terrace to wait for Lazzero. The sun was setting on Milan, the magnificent Duomo di Milano, the stunning cathedral that sat in the heart of the city, bathed in a rosy pink light, its Gothic spires crawling high into the sky. But her mind wasn't on the spectacular scenery, it was on the night ahead.

Her stomach knotted with nerves, her fingers closing tight around the metal railing. This wasn't her world. What if she said or did something that would embarrass Lazzero? What if she stumbled on one of the answers they'd prepared to the inevitable questions about them?

Her mouth firmed. She'd been taking care of herself since she was fifteen. She'd learned how to survive in any situation life had thrown at her in tough, gritty Manhattan which would eat you alive if you let it. Every *day* at the Daily Grind was an exercise in diplomacy and small talk.

Surely she could survive a few hours socializing with the world's elite?

And perhaps, she conceded, butterflies circling her stomach, she was winding herself up for nothing over Antonio. Perhaps he wouldn't even be there tonight. Perhaps he was out of town on business. He ran a portfolio of global investments—he very likely could be.

Better to focus on the things she could control. Another of her father's favorite tenets.

Fifty laps of the infinity pool with its incomparable view of Milan should have rid Lazzero of his excess adrenaline. Or so he thought until he walked out onto the balcony and found Chiara sparkling like the brightest jewel in the night.

Dark hair shining in a silken cap that framed her beautiful face, the silver dress highlighting her hourglass figure, her insanely good legs encased in mile-high stilettos—she made his heart stutter in his chest. And that was before he got to her gorgeous eyes, lagoon-green in the fading light, a beauty mark just above one dark-winged brow lending her a distinctly exotic look.

The tension he read there snapped his brain back into working order. "Nervous?" he asked, moving to her side.

"A bit."

"Don't be," he murmured. "You look breathtakingly beautiful. I'm even forgiving Dimitri for the hair."

She tipped her head back to look up at him, her silky hair sliding against her shoulder. A charge vibrated the air between them, sizzling the blood in his veins. "You don't have to feed me lines," she murmured. "We aren't *on* yet."

His mouth curved at her prickly demeanor. "That wasn't a line. You'll soon know me well enough to know I don't deliver them, Chiara. I'm all for the truth in its soul-baring, hard-to-take true colors. Even when it hurts. So how about we make a deal? Nothing but honesty between us this week? It will make this a hell of a lot easier."

An emotion he couldn't read flickered in her eyes. She crossed her arms over her chest and leaned back against the railing. "Tell me why this deal with Gianni is so important for you, then? Why go to such lengths to secure it?"

He lifted a shoulder. "It's crucial to my company's growth plans."

She frowned. "Why so crucial? Fiammata is a fading brand, Supersonic the rising star."

"Fiammata has a shoe technology we're interested in."

"So you want to license it to use in your own designs?"

His mouth curved. "Sharp brain," he drawled. "It's one of the things I appreciate about you." Her legs being the other predominant one at the moment.

She frowned. "What's the holdup, then?"

And wasn't that the multimillion-dollar question? A thorn unearthed itself in his side, burrowing deep. "Fiammata is a family company. Gianni may be having a hard time letting such an important piece of it go."

"As would you," she pointed out, "if it was yours."

"Yes," he agreed, a wry smile twisting his mouth, "I would." He reached across her to point to the Duomo, glittering in the fading light. "There is a myth that Gian Galeazzo Visconti, the aristocrat who ordered the construction of the cathedral, was visited by the devil in his dreams. He ordered Visconti to create a church full of diabolical images or he would steal his soul. Thus the monstrous heads you see on the cathedral's facade."

"Not really much of a choice was it?" Chiara said as she turned her head to look at the magnificent cathedral.

"Not unless you intend to embrace your dark side, no." His gaze slid over the graceful curve of her neck. Noted she'd missed a hook at the back of her dress. *Perhaps more nervous than she admitted.*

He stepped behind her. "You aren't quite done up," he murmured, setting his fingers to the tiny hook. It took a moment to work out the intricate, almost invisible closure, his fingers brushing against the velvet-soft skin that covered her spine.

She went utterly still beneath his hands, the voltage that stretched between them so potent he could almost taste it. Her floral perfume drifting into his nostrils, her soft, sensual body brushing against his, the urge to act on the elemental attraction between them was almost impossible to resist. To set his hands to those delectable hips, to put his mouth to the soft, sensitive skin behind her ear until she melted back into him and offered him her mouth.

But, he admitted, past his accelerating pulse, that would be starting something he couldn't finish because the *only* thing on the agenda tonight was nailing Gianni Casale down, once and for all.

He reluctantly pulled back. Chiara exhaled an audible breath. Turned to look up at him with darkened eyes, her pupils dilated a deep black among a sea of green. "He'll be there tonight? Gianni?" she asked huskily.

"*Sì.* Everyone in Milan will be there." He glanced at his watch. "Speaking of which, we should go or we'll be late."

The sleek Lamborghini Lazzero had borrowed from Filippo made quick work of the drive to the venue. Soon, they were pulling up in front of Il Cattedrale, the historic church where the opening party for La Coppa Estiva was being held.

Turned into a café/nightclub over a decade ago, its stately facade was lit for the festivities, illuminating the cathedral's elegant red brickwork and massive arched front door. Chiara's stomach turned to stone as she took in the scores of paparazzi jostling for position on either side of the stationed-off red carpet, camera flashes snapping like mad as they photographed the arrival of the world's glitterati.

There was the world's most famous Portuguese footballer making his way down the red carpet with his supermodel girlfriend, followed by the eldest princess of a tiny European municipality Chiara recognized from one of the gossip magazines her fellow barista Lucy kept under the counter. The princess's balding, older husband beside her was, Chiara recalled, a huge fan of football.

"Santo will be excited about that," Lazzero murmured as he helped her from the car. "Free publicity right there."

Her damp palm in his, her other clutching the tiny purse that matched her dress, Chiara didn't respond. *What had Micaela said about the etiquette for the red carpet?* Her mind felt as blank as a chalkboard wiped clean.

Lazzero passed the car keys to the valet and bent his head to hers. "Relax," he said softly, his lips brushing her ear. "I will be by your side the entire time."

A current zigzagged through her, one she felt all the way to the pit of her stomach. It didn't get any better as Lazzero straightened and pressed a hand to the small of her back. In a sophisticated black tux that molded his long, muscular frame to perfection, he was undeniably elegant. *Hot.* Utterly in command of his surroundings.

She took a deep breath and nodded. The handler gave them the signal to walk. Lazzero propelled her forward, stopping in front of the logo-emblazoned step-and-repeat banner so the photographers could get a shot of them. The heat from his splayed palm radiated through her bare skin, focusing every available brain cell on those few inches of flesh.

It did the trick in distracting her. Before she could blink, it was over and they were making their way inside the cathedral. Which was *unbelievable.*

Much of the original architecture of the church had been

left intact, stone walls and square pillars made of cream-colored Italian marble rising up to greet the original sweeping balconies of the cathedral. The massive chandelier was incredible, a full story tall, the large canvases on the walls impressive. But the most arresting sight of all had to be the original altar which had been converted into a bar under the dome of the church. Lit tonight in Supersonic red, it was spectacular.

"I've never seen anything like it," Chiara breathed. "It's like we've all come to pray to the gods of entertainment."

Lazzero's mouth twisted. "Exactly what Santo was envisioning. He'll be thrilled."

The crowds were so thick they were difficult to negotiate as they made their way toward the bar, the upbeat music drowned out by the buzz of the hundreds in attendance. Lazzero wrapped a hand around her wrist, guiding her through it as they sought out his brothers who held court at the bar.

Santo, whom she remembered from Di Fiore's, looked supremely sophisticated in a dark suit with a lavender shirt, every bit the blond Adonis the press painted him as. Nico had Lazzero's dark looks, so handsome in a clean-edged, perfect kind of way, he was intimidatingly so.

Both were undeniably charming. "Trust Lazzero to show up with the most beautiful woman in the room when he claims he has been out of circulation," Nico drawled, kissing both of Chiara's cheeks. "Although you picked the wrong brother," Santo interjected, stepping forward and lifting her hand to his mouth. "Why go for the middle brother when you can have the most physically viable of them all? Think of the genetics."

He said it so straight-faced, Chiara burst out laughing. "Yes," she said, "but Lazzero tells me you have a *posse*. I'm afraid that wouldn't do for me."

Santo pouted. "I will give it up when the time comes."

"That will be when you are old and gray." Nico handed her a glass of champagne and Lazzero a tumbler of some dark-colored liquor. Lounging back against the bar, the eldest Di Fiore nodded toward a table beside the dance floor. "Gianni arrived a few minutes ago."

Chiara's gaze moved to Gianni Casale, whose powerful presence stood out amongst the crowd at the table. In his midfifties, he had thick, coarse black hair tinged with gray, expressive dark eyes and a lined face full of character. Impeccably dressed in a charcoal gray suit with a silver-gray tie, he was, she conceded, undeniably handsome still.

Her attention shifted to the woman beside him. She didn't have to wonder if it was Carolina Casale or not because the brunette's eyes were trained on her and the hand Lazzero had rested on her waist. Remarkably beautiful with vivid blue eyes that matched her designer silk dress, dark hair and alabaster skin, the cool elegance she projected was borderline aloof.

She looked, Chiara concluded, as if she'd rather be anywhere than where she was. *Hungry* was the only word she could think of to describe how Carolina looked at Lazzero. She wondered if the other woman had any idea how obvious her feelings were.

Lazzero, on the other hand, looked utterly impassive as he turned around and got the lay of the land from his brothers. When they were suitably caught up, he tightened his fingers at her waist. "We should circulate," he murmured. "You okay with the champagne?"

She pulled in a deep breath. "Yes."

Lazzero spent the next couple of hours attempting to cover off the most important business contacts in the room as he played it cool with Gianni, waiting for the Casales to come to them. He should have been focused solely on business, his game plan with Gianni firmly positioned in his head, but his attention kept straying to the woman at his side.

He was having trouble keeping his eyes off Chiara's legs in that dress, as were half the men in the room. Despite the tension he could sense in her, a tension he couldn't wholly understand given the confidence he was used to from her, she remained poised at his side, charming his business associates with that natural wit and intelligence he had always appreciated about her. It was, he found, a wholly alluring combination.

He was about to acquire another glass of champagne for her from a waiter's tray when Carolina and Gianni approached, Carolina's hand on her husband's arm firmly guiding him toward them.

His ex-lover looked stunning, as beautiful as ever with those icy cool, perfect features, but tonight she left him cold. She had always been too self-contained, too calculating, too bent on getting her own way. Gianni, who'd spent three years putting up with those character flaws, eyed him warily as they approached, his dark eyes betraying none of the undercurrents stretching between them.

"Lazzero." Dropping her hand from her husband's arm, Carolina stood on tiptoe and pressed a kiss to both of Lazzero's cheeks. She lingered a bit too long, and as she did Gianni's eyes flashed with a rare show of emotion.

"Carolina." Lazzero set her firmly away from him so that he could shake Gianni's hand. Releasing it, he drew Chiara forward. "I would like you both to meet my fiancée, Chiara Ferrante."

The color drained from Carolina's face. "I'd heard the gossip," she murmured, her gaze dropping to Chiara's left hand, where the asscher-cut diamond blazed bright. "I thought it must be wrong." She forced a tight smile to her lips as she returned her perusal to Lazzero. "You swore you'd never marry."

"Things change when you meet the right person," Lazzero said blithely.

"Apparently so."

Gianni, ever the gentleman, stepped forward to compensate for his wife's lack of discretion. *"Felicitazoni,"* he said, pressing a kiss to Chiara's cheeks. "Lazzero is a lucky man, clearly."

"Grazie mille," Chiara replied. "It's all very new. We're still…absorbing it."

"When is the big day?" Carolina lifted a brow. "I haven't seen an announcement."

"We're still working that out," said Chiara. "For now, we're just enjoying being engaged."

"I'm sure you are." A wounded look flashed through Carolina's vibrant blue eyes. "You must be very happy."

Lazzero felt a bite of guilt sink into him. He shouldn't have let it go on so long. It was a mistake he would never repeat.

Chiara escaped to the ladies' room after that awkward encounter with the Casales. She felt sorry for Carolina who was so clearly still in love with Lazzero, who hadn't blinked the entire conversation. Because she knew that hurt—that rejection—what it felt like to be discarded for something *better.*

It took her forever to wind her way through the crowd to the powder room. An oasis in the midst of the celebration, it was done in cream and black marble with muted lighting and white lilies covering every available surface. Heading for one of the leather seats in front of the mirror, Chiara ran smack into an older woman on her way out.

An apology rose to her lips. It died in her mouth as she stared at the lined, still handsome face of Esta Fabrizio, Antonio's mother. She froze, unsure of what to do. The older woman swept her gaze over her in a cursory look, not a hint of recognition flaring in her dark eyes. Flashing Chiara an apologetic look, she murmured, *"Scusi,"* then moved around her to the door.

"Is it just you and Maurizio here tonight?" Esta's companion asked.

"Sì," Esta replied. "My son is out of town, so it is us representing the family tonight."

Chiara sank down on the leather seat, relief flooding through her as they left. *Antonio isn't here.* She could put that fear to rest. But quick on its heels came humiliation as she stared at her pale face in the mirror. Esta had looked at her as if she was nothing. But why *would* she remember her?

She'd treated Chiara as if she were a bug to be crushed under her shoe the day she'd shown up unexpectedly at Antonio's penthouse to surprise him for his birthday, only to find Chiara leaving for work. Esta had taken one look at Chiara, absorbed her working-class, Bronx accent and correctly assessed the situation. She'd informed Chiara that Antonio had a fiancée in Milan. That she was simply his American "plaything." The Fabrizio matriarch had added, with a brutal lack of finesse, that a Fabrizio would never marry someone like her. So best if she ended it now.

A bitter taste filled her mouth as she reached for her purse and fumbled inside for her powder and lipstick. Applying a coat of pink gloss and powdering her nose with shaking hands, she willed herself composure. She would *not* let that woman get to her again. The important thing was that Antonio was not here. She could relax.

Now all she had to do was pull herself together.

The party was in full swing when she exited the powder room. The lights had been lowered, the massive chandelier cast a purple hue across the room, the hundreds of smaller disco balls surrounding it glittered like luminescent planets in the sky. High in the ceiling, amidst that stunning celestial display, hung sexily dressed acrobats in beautiful red dresses, hypnotizing to the eye.

Music pulsed through the room, champagne flowed freely as couples packed the dance floor. She headed toward the bar where Lazzero and Santo had ensconced themselves. Almost groaned out loud when Carolina Casale flagged her down, two glasses of champagne in her hand. *That was all she needed right now.*

Carolina handed her a glass of champagne. "I apologize for my behavior earlier. I was caught off guard. I thought I should congratulate you properly. Lazzero and I go a long way back."

"He mentioned." Chiara considered Carolina warily as she took the glass. "*Grazie.* How *do* you know each other?"

"My firm did the interior decorating for Supersonic's offices as well as Lazzero's penthouse when he bought it." A low purr vibrated Carolina's voice. "Lazzero couldn't be bothered with that kind of thing."

Heat seared her skin. She could only imagine how that relationship had started. Carolina walking around Lazzero's penthouse with paint samples in her hand only to find herself in his bed. *Well satisfied*, no doubt.

"How did *you* and Lazzero meet?" Carolina prompted, a speculative glitter in her eyes. "Everyone is very curious about how you did the impossible by catching him."

"We met in a café."

The brunette arched a dark brow. "A café?"

"Where I work." Chiara lifted her chin. "We've known each other for over a year now."

An astonished look crossed the other woman's face. "You're a *waitress*?"

"A barista," Chiara corrected, her encounter with Esta Fabrizio adding a bite to her tone. "Love doesn't discriminate, I guess."

Carolina's face fell at the surgical strike. "Love?" Her

mouth twisted. "I would offer you a piece of advice about Lazzero. He is in *lust* with you, Chiara, not in love with you. He doesn't know *how* to love. So take my advice and make sure that prenup of yours is ironclad."

"Duly noted," Chiara rasped, having had more than enough. "Now, if you'll excuse me, I need to find my *fiancé*."

Santo eyed Chiara as she stood toe-to-toe with Carolina. "Should we intercede?"

"Give it a minute," Lazzero murmured, eyes on the exchange. "Chiara can handle herself."

"That she can." Santo shifted his study back to him. "I remember now where I've seen her before. Chiara. She's the brunette you were chatting up at the *Score* premiere."

"I wasn't chatting her up," Lazzero corrected. "I was saying hello. Her friend won tickets to the launch. I see her every day—it would have been rude not to say hi."

His brother gave him a disbelieving look. "And you're trying to tell me she is all business? That all she does is make your espresso every morning? I don't believe it. Not with that body."

A flash of fire singed his belly. "Watch your words, Santo."

His brother blinked. "You *like* her."

"Of course I like her. I brought her with me."

"No, I mean, you *like* her. You've never once warned me off a woman like that."

"You're overthinking it."

"I think not." Santo gave him a considering look. "She is far from your usual type. I think your taste has improved."

It might have, Lazzero conceded, if Chiara were *his*. Which she was not.

Santo drained his glass as Chiara stalked through the crowd toward them, an infuriated look on her face. "I see a damsel in distress. Off to do my duty. Good luck with *that*."

Santo waltzed off into the crowd. Chiara slid onto the bar stool beside him, her green eyes flashing as she downed a gulp of champagne.

Lazzero eyed her. "What did she say?"

"She is—" Chiara waved a hand at him. "She was *rude*. She told me to make sure my prenup is airtight because it isn't going to last."

"It *isn't* going to last," he said. "This is fake, remember? Why are you so upset?"

She gave him a black look. "She made it clear a barista is *beneath* you."

"That's ridiculous."

"Is it?" Her mouth set in a mutinous line. "Carolina owns her own interior decorating firm. *I* am merely a barista you hired to play your fiancée…someone who couldn't, in a million years, afford to say no to your offer. Someone you would never *consider* marrying." Her eyes darkened. "This is exactly what I was talking about earlier…the games rich people play where people get hurt. Carolina might be a bitch, Lazzero, but she is *wounded*."

A flare of antagonism lanced through him. "I think you have it the wrong way around. I'm doing this so that *no one* gets hurt. If I made a mistake with Carolina, which I might have, it was in letting the relationship drag on for too long. Since I acknowledge I made that mistake, I am rectifying it now by not hurting her further by giving her hope for something that can never be."

She gave him a caustic look. "Exactly what do you think is going to happen if you do commit to a woman? The bogeyman is going to come get you?"

The fuse inside him caught fire. "Speaks the woman who doesn't date?"

"At least I acknowledge my faults."

"I just did," he growled. "And as far as you and Carolina are concerned, you are right, you are *not* in the same class as her. You *outclass* her in every way, Chiara. Carolina is an entitled piece of work who uses everything and everyone in her life to her own advantage. You are hardworking and fiercely independent with an honesty and integrity I admire. So can we please put the subject of your worth to rest?"

Her indignation came to a sliding halt. "So why *did* you date her, then?"

A hint of the devil arrowed through him, fueled by his intense irritation. "She took off her clothes during our consultation appointment at my penthouse. What was I going to do?"

Her eyes widened. "You aren't joking, are you?"

"No."

"I walked right into that one, didn't I?"

"Yes. Now," he murmured, bringing his mouth to her ear, "can we move on? Gianni just sat down at the end of the bar. He's watching us and I'd like to make this somewhat believable."

She blew out a breath. "Yes."

"Bene." He nodded toward her almost empty glass of champagne. "Drink up and let's dance."

She cast a wary eye toward the dance floor, where the couples were moving to the sinuous rhythm of a Latin tune. "Not to this."

"This," he insisted, sliding off the stool and tugging her off hers.

"Lazzero, I don't know how," she protested, setting her glass on the bar and dragging her feet. "It's been years since I took salsa lessons and I was *terrible*. I'm going to look ridiculous out there."

He stopped on the edge of the dance floor and tipped her chin up with his fingers. "All you have to do is let me lead," he said softly. "Give up that formidable control of yours for once, Chiara, because this dance doesn't work without complete and total...submission."

Chiara's heart thumped wildly against her ribs as Lazzero led her onto the dance floor. The feel of his fingers wrapped around her wrist sent a surge of electricity through her, tiny sparks unearthing themselves over every inch of her skin.

This is such a bad, bad idea.

A new song began as they found a free space among the dancers. Sultry and seductive, it brought back memories of the bruised feet and embarrassing silences she'd stumbled through in dance classes. She attempted one last objection as Lazzero pulled her close, clasping one hand around hers, the other resting against her back. "Back on one," he said, cutting off her protest, "forward on five."

She wasn't sure how she was supposed to remember the *first* step with the heat of his tall, muscular body so close to hers, his sexy, spicy aftershave infiltrating her head. But she couldn't just stand there on the dance floor doing nothing with everyone watching, so she took a deep breath and stepped back to mirror Lazzero's basic step.

Her lessons, remarkably, came back immediately, the basic step easy enough to execute. Except she was all out of rhythm and stumbled into him, her cheeks heating.

"Follow my lead," Lazzero growled. "And look at *me*, not at the floor. When I push, you step back, when I pull, you move forward. It's very basic. Follow my signals."

Except that was a dangerous thing to do because his eyes had a sexy, seductive glimmer in them that had nothing to do with a business deal and the champagne had now fully gone to her head, making any attempt at sophisticated steps a concerted effort.

Forcing herself to concentrate, she followed his lead before she fell flat on her face. His grip firm and commanding, he guided her through the steps until she was picking out the basic movement in time to the music.

"Now you've got it," he murmured, as they executed a simple right turn. "See, isn't this fun?"

It was, in fact, with a lead as good as Lazzero. He moved in ways a man shouldn't be able to, his hips fluid and graceful. She started to trust he would place her where she needed to be and gave herself in to the sensual rhythm of the dance. The champagne, fully charging her bloodstream now, had the positive effect of loosening her inhibitions even further as they pulled off some more sophisticated steps and turns.

By the time the song was over, she was having so much fun, she fell laughing into Lazzero's arms on the final turn. Caught up in all that muscle, his powerful body pressed against the length of hers, she swallowed past the racing of her heart as a languorous, slow number began to play. "Maybe we should go get a drink," she suggested, breathlessly. "I am *seriously* thirsty."

"While I have you so soft and compliant and all womanly in my arms?" he mocked lightly, sliding an arm around her waist to pull her closer. "We're actually managing to be convincing at the moment. I'd like to enjoy the novelty before the arrows start flying again."

"I don't do that," she protested.

"Yes, you do." He gave her a considering look. "I think it's a defense mechanism."

"Against what?"

"I'm still trying to figure that out."

She followed him through the slow, lazy steps, excruciatingly aware of the hard press of his powerful thighs against hers, the thump of his heart beneath her hand, *the brush of his mouth against her temple.*

"Lazzero," she breathed.

"The Casales are watching. Relax."

Impossible. Not with the warm touch of those sensual lips on her skin giving her an idea of how they'd feel all over her. The smooth caress of his palm against the small of her back, burning into her bare skin. Definitely not when his mouth traced a path along the length of her jaw.

He was going to kiss her, she registered with a wild jump of her heart. And there was nothing she could do to stop it. Nor could she even pretend she wanted to.

Electric shivers slid up her spine as he tilted her chin up with his thumb, holding her captive to his purposeful ebony gaze. Her breath stopped in her chest as he bent his head and lowered his mouth to hers in a butterfly-light kiss meant to seduce.

This isn't real, she cautioned herself. But it was fruitless, as every nerve ending seemed to catch fire. Lips whispering against hers, his thumb stroking her jaw, he teased and tantalized with so much sensual expertise, she was lost before the battle even began, her lips clinging to his as she tentatively returned the kiss.

Nestling her jaw more securely in his palm, he tugged her up on tiptoe with the hand he held at her waist and took the kiss deeper. Head tilted back, each slide of his mouth over hers sending sparks through her, Chiara forgot everything but what it felt like to be kissed like this. To be *seduced.* As if lightning had struck.

A sound left the back of her throat as her fingers crept around his neck. Clenched tensile, hard muscle. Murmuring his approval, he nudged her mouth apart with the slick glide of his tongue and delved inside with a heated caress that liquefied her insides. Weakened her knees.

She moved closer to him, wanting, *needing* his support. His hand slid to her hip, shifting her closer to all that muscle, until she was molded to every centimeter of him, the languorous drift of his mouth over hers, his deep, drugging kisses, shooting sparks of fire through her.

A low groan tore itself from his throat, the hand he held at her bottom bringing her into direct contact with the shockingly hard ridge of his arousal. She should have been scandalized. Instead, the wave of heat coursing through her crashed deeper, a fission of white-hot sexual awareness arcing through her.

She was so far gone, so lost in him, she almost protested when Lazzero broke the kiss with a nuzzling slowness, his fingers at her waist holding her steady as he dragged his mouth to her ear.

"The song is over," he murmured. "As much as I hate to say it."

The lazy satisfaction in his voice, the beat of a fast new tune, brought the world into focus with shocking swiftness.

What was she doing? Had she lost her mind? Lazzero had kissed her to prove a point to the Casales. This was just a *game* to him, she simply a pawn he was playing. And she had pretty much thrown herself at him.

Head spinning, heart pounding, she pulled herself out of his arms. "Chiara," he murmured, his eyes on hers, "it was just a kiss."

Just a kiss. It felt as if the earth had moved beneath her feet. Like nothing she'd ever experienced before, not even with Antonio who'd been practiced in the art of seduction. But for Lazzero, it had been *just a kiss.*

Had she learned nothing from her experiences?

She took a step back. Lifted her chin. "*Sì,*" she agreed unsteadily, "it was just a kiss. And, now that we've given an award-winning performance, I think I've had enough."

CHAPTER FIVE

JUST A KISS.

Clearly, Lazzero conceded as he drove back to the hotel at the close of the night, that hadn't been the right line to feed Chiara at that particular moment in time. She had given him one of those death glares of hers, stalked off the dance floor and remained distant for the rest of the evening, unless required to turn it on for public consumption.

The chill had continued in the car, with her blowing off his attempts at conversation. But could he blame her, really? A kiss might have been in order, but *that* hadn't been necessary. That had been pure self-gratification on his part.

He should have stopped it before it had gotten hot enough to melt the two of them to the dance floor. Before he'd confirmed what he'd always known about them—that they would be ridiculously, spectacularly hot together. But Chiara's unwarranted, unfair judgments of him had burrowed beneath his skin. And, if he were being honest, so had his need to prove he was not the *last* man on earth she'd ever want, he was *the* one she wanted.

His curiosity about what it would be like to strip away those formidable defenses of hers had been irresistible. To find the passion that lay beneath. And hell, had he found it.

His blood thickened at the memory of her sweet, sensual response. It had knocked him sideways, the feel of those lush, amazing curves beneath his hands as good as he'd imagined they would be. He'd let the kiss get way out of hand, no doubt about it, but he hadn't been the only participant.

Chiara was out of the car and on her way into the lobby as he handed the keys to the Lamborghini to the valet, shocking him with how swiftly she could walk in those insanely high shoes. She had jammed her finger on the call button for the elevator by the time he'd made it into the lobby, her toe tapping impatiently on the marble. It came seconds later and swished them silently up to the third floor.

Kicking off her shoes in the marble foyer of the penthouse, she continued her relentless path through the living room, into the bedroom. He caught up with her before she reached the bathroom door. Curved a hand around her arm. "Chiara," he murmured. "We need to talk."

She swung around, a closed look on her face. "About what? You were right, Lazzero, it was *just a kiss*. And now, if you don't mind, I am going to go to bed. I am exhausted." Her eyes lifted mutinously to his. "*If* I am *off duty*, of course."

Oh, no. Red misted his vision as she pulled out of his grasp and stalked into the bathroom, slamming the door in his face. She wasn't going to go there.

Walk away, he told himself. Shake it off. Deal with this tomorrow when saner heads prevail.

Except nothing about that kiss had been business and they both knew it. It had been a long time coming, *a year* precisely, since he'd walked through the door of the Daily Grind and found Chiara cursing at an espresso machine on a particularly bad day. They *had* something. That was clear. They were consenting adults. What the hell was the problem?

He stalked into the dressing room. Threw his wallet and change on the armoire. The wounded look on Chiara's face in the car filtered through his head. She thought he was playing with her. That this was a *game* to him. Which, admittedly it might have started out as, until he'd gotten as caught up in that kiss as she had been.

Leaving her to stew, he decided as he stripped off his bow tie and cuff links, was not a good idea. Tossing them on the dresser, he rapped on the bedroom door. Walked in. Frowned when he found the room empty, the bed untouched. Then he spotted Chiara on the balcony, her back to him.

Definitely stewing.

He crossed to the French doors. Stopped in his tracks. She was dressed for bed, a factor he hadn't taken into consideration. Which needed to be taken into consideration, because what she was wearing heated his blood.

The simple tank top and shorts were hardly the sexiest nightwear he'd ever seen, covering more of her than most women did on the streets of Manhattan. It was the way the soft jersey material clung to her voluptuous body that made his mouth go dry.

His hands itched to touch, to give in to the craving he'd been fighting all night, but he stayed where he was, framed in the light of the suite.

"It wasn't just a kiss."

His quiet words had Chiara spinning around. An equally spectacular view from the front, he noted, her face bare of makeup, lush mouth pursed in contemplation, her legs a sweep of smooth golden skin that seemed to go on forever.

He set his gaze on hers. "That kiss was spectacular. You and I both know it. I wanted to do it since the first moment I saw you in that dress tonight. Actually," he amended huskily, "since the first day I set eyes on you in the coffee shop. You and I have something, Chiara. It would be ridiculous to deny it."

She swallowed hard, the delicate muscles in her throat

convulsing. A myriad of emotion flickered through her green eyes. "You were toying with me, Lazzero."

He shook his head. "I was satisfying my *curiosity* about the attraction between us. Finding out how it would be. And you were curious too," he added deliberately, eyeing the flare of awareness staining her olive skin. "But you won't admit it, because you're so intent on protecting yourself, on preserving that prickly outer layer of yours, on putting your *labels* on me, you won't admit how you feel."

A fiery light stormed her eyes. "You're damn right I am. I have no interest in becoming your latest conquest, Lazzero. In being bought with a piece of jewelry. In performing ever greater circus tricks to retain your interest, only to be dumped in a cloud of dust when I no longer do. I have *been there* and *done that*."

His jaw dropped. "That's absurd."

"You said it at Di Fiore's. Your relationships only last as long as your interest does." She planted her hands on her hips. "The soul-baring truth and nothing but. Isn't that how you put it?"

He had no response for that, grounded by his own transparency. She tipped her chin up. "Consider my curiosity well and truly satisfied. My *list* ticked off."

His ego took that stunning blow as she turned and stalked inside, effectively ending the conversation. Except which part of it hadn't been true? He was all of that and more.

He followed her inside, stripped off his clothes in the guest bathroom and deposited himself under a chilly shower to cool his body down, still revved up from that almost-sex on the dance floor.

He played by a certain set of rules because that's what he was capable of. He was never going to allow a woman *in*, was never going to commit, because he knew the destructive force a relationship could be. He'd watched his father wind himself in circles over his mother before he'd imploded in spectacular fashion, a roller coaster ride he was never getting on. Ever.

Getting his head tied up in Chiara, no matter how hot he was for her, was insanity with everything riding on this deal with Gianni. He'd best keep that in mind or *he* was going to be the one going down in a cloud of dust.

Pulling on boxer shorts in deference to his company, he braced himself for the far-too-short-looking sofa in the bedroom, the only sleepable surface in the suite other than the extremely comfortable-looking four-poster bed. Which was…*empty*.

What the hell?

He found Chiara curled up on the sofa, a blanket covering her slight form. Her dark hair spread out like silk against the white pillowcase, long, decadent lashes fanned down against her cheeks, she was deep asleep.

Every male instinct growled in irritation. This had clearly been her parting volley. *Clearly*, she didn't know him well enough if she thought he was going to let her sleep there, no matter how amazing that bed looked after the couple of hours of sleep he'd had on the plane.

Moving silently across the room, he slid his arms beneath her, lifted her up and carried her to the bed. Transferring her weight to one arm, he tossed the silk comforter aside and slid her into the bed. She was so deep asleep she didn't blink an eyelash as she shifted onto her stomach and burrowed into the silk sheets. Which gave him a very tantalizing view of her amazing derriere in the feminine shorts.

The reminder of what those curves had felt like beneath his hands, how perfectly she'd fit against him, sizzled the blood in his veins. Revved him up all over again. A low curse leaving his throat, he retreated to the sofa, flicked the blanket aside and settled his hormone-ravaged body onto the ridiculous excuse for a piece of furniture.

His attempts to get comfortable were futile. When he stretched out, his feet hung over the edge, cutting off his circulation. When he attempted to contort himself to fit, his old basketball injury made his knee throb.

The minutes ticked by, his need to sleep growing ever more acute. He had four hours maximum before he had to get up for his practice with a team of world-class athletes who were going to run him into the ground at this rate. He must have been insane to agree to play.

He had shifted positions for what must have been the tenth time when Chiara lifted herself up on her elbow and blinked at him in the darkness. "How did I get into the bed?"

"I carried you there," he said grumpily. "Go back to sleep."

She dropped back to the pillow. A silence followed. Then a drowsy, "Get in the bed, Lazzero. It's as big as Milan. We can share it."

He was off the sofa and in the bed in record time. It *was* the size of Milan and he could restrain himself. Finding a comfortable position on the far side of the bed, he closed his eyes and lost himself to blissful unconsciousness.

Chiara was having the most delicious dream. Plastered against a wall of heat, she was warm and cocooned and thoroughly content after finding the air-conditioning distinctly chilly during the night.

Pressing closer to all that heat, she registered it was hot, hard muscle—hot, hard *male* muscle that was its source. Utterly in tune with the whole picture because she had truly outdone herself with this dream, she pressed even closer.

A big, warm hand slid over the curve of her hip to arrange her more comfortably on top of him. She sighed and went willingly, because he felt deliciously good against her, underneath her, *everywhere*, and it had been so long, so damn long since she'd been touched like this. *Held* like this.

He traced his fingers down her spine, savoring the texture and shape of her. She purred like a cat and arched into him. The sensual slide of his mouth against the delicate skin of her throat stirred her pulse to a drumbeat. Melted her insides. A shiver coursing through her, she turned her head to find the kiss he was offering. *Best dream ever.*

Slow, lazy, decadent, it was perfection. She moved closer still, wanting more. His hand closed possessively over her bottom, a low sound of male pleasure reverberating against her mouth.

Too real.

Oh, my God.

She broke the kiss. Sank her palms into his rock-hard chest, panic arrowing through her as she stared into Lazzero's sleepy, slumberous gaze. Registered the palm he held against her back, the other that cupped her buttock, plastering her against him, exactly as she'd been in her dream.

Except it hadn't been a dream. It had been real. *Good God.*

She pushed frantically against his chest. Scrambled off him. Lazzero eyed her lazily, his ebony eyes blinking awake. "What's the hurry?" he murmured, his husky, sleep-infused voice rumbling down her spine. "That was one hell of a way to wake a man up, *caro*."

She sat back on her heels. Ran a shaky hand through her hair. "You took advantage of the situation."

"I think you have that the wrong way around," he drawled. "I have been on this side of the bed all night, a fact I made damn sure of. Which means it was *you* who found your way over here." He lifted a brow. "Maybe it was your subconscious talking after that kiss last night?"

Her cheeks fired. "I had no idea *who* I was kissing."

He crossed his arms over his chest and lounged back

against the pillows. "Funny that, because you sighed my name. Twice. I'm fairly sure that's what woke me up."

She searched his face for some sign he was joking. "I did *not*."

His smug expression gave her little hope. She dropped her gaze away from his, utterly disconcerted, but that was an even bigger problem because he was jaw dropping—perfectly hewn, bronzed muscle, marred only by the scar that crisscrossed his knee. Better than she could ever have imagined, his low-slung boxers did little to hide his potent masculinity. Which was more than a little stirred up at the moment. *By her.*

"I am," he murmured, pulling her gaze back up to his, "wide-awake now, on the other hand, if you are looking for my full participation."

Her stomach swooped. Searching desperately for sanity, she shimmied across the massive bed and slid off it. Felt the heat of Lazzero's gaze follow her, burning over the exposed length of her legs. "I need to shower," she announced, heading for the bathroom as fast as her legs would carry her.

"Coward," he tossed after her.

She kept going. He could call her what he liked. If she didn't get her head on her shoulders, figure out how to wrangle her attraction to Lazzero under control, she was going to mess this up, because this was *not* her world and she was hopelessly out of her depth. And since messing this up was not an option, she needed to restore her common sense. *Yesterday.*

Joining the other girlfriends, wives and friends of the players in the VIP seating area at San Siro stadium for the practice proved to offer plenty of opportunity for Chiara to recover her composure. It was packed with women in designer outfits and expensive perfume, sophisticated perfection she couldn't hope to emulate.

Dressed in a pair of white capri jeans and a fuchsia-colored blouse she had knotted at the waist, a cute pair of white sneakers on her feet, she looked the part, but how could she possibly participate in the conversations going on around her? What did she know about Cannes for the film festival or an annual Easter weekend on a Russian oligarch's yacht?

She found herself confined to the outer fringe of the group, the cold shoulder Carolina had given her instigating that phenomenon, no doubt. She wasn't sure why she cared. This wasn't her world, she didn't want it to be her world. But that didn't mean it didn't hurt. That it didn't remind her of the mean girls in school who'd ridiculed her for her hopelessly out-of-date, out-of-fashion clothes.

Putting on the aloof face she'd perfected in school, she positioned herself at the end of the bleacher, pretending not to care. The lovely, bubbly wife of the Western European team captain, Valentino Calabria, sat down beside her, dragging one of the other wives with her as she braved the cold front. "Don't pay any attention to them," Pia Calabria murmured. "It takes years to break into their clique."

Pia kept up a continual stream of conversation as the Americas team took to the field for its practice, for which Chiara was inordinately grateful. It was hard, brutal play as the team geared up for its opening match against Western Europe, sweat and curses flying.

Pia sat back as the play halted for a water break, fanning her face with her purse. "The eye candy," she pronounced with a dramatic sigh, "is simply too much for me to handle today."

"Which you are not supposed to be noticing with Valentino, the *magnifico*, right in front of you," Pia's friend reprimanded drily.

Pia slid her a sideways look. "And you are not doing the same? *Looking* is not a crime."

Chiara's gaze moved to Lazzero. It *was* impossible not to ogle. Intense and compelling in black shorts and a sweaty, bright green Americas T-shirt, he looked amazing.

"Him," Pia agreed, following her gaze to Lazzero, who stood in the middle of the field, wiping the sweat off his forehead with the hem of his T-shirt as he yelled at his teammates to get ready for the kick in. "Exactly. Now, there is a *man*. Those abs… You could bounce a football off of them. And those thighs…" She rolled her eyes heavenward. "*Insano*. No wonder Carolina is going ballistic."

Chiara kept her eyes glued to the field. Thought about that ridiculously amazing kiss she'd shared with Lazzero that morning. It had felt undeniably *right*. As if she and Lazzero had something, exactly as he'd said. She would be lying if she said she wasn't desperately curious to know what it would have been like if she'd let it play out to its seductive conclusion, because she knew it would have been incredible.

You're a senior citizen at twenty-six. Kat's jibe flitted tauntingly through her head. Her life *was* pathetic. She *had* no life. But to take a walk on the wild side with Lazzero, who'd surely annihilate her before it was all over? It seemed patently unwise.

She pushed her attention back to the field, rather than allow it to continue down the ridiculous road it was traveling. Watched as Lazzero's squad executed an impressive series of passes to put the ball in the net.

"Hell." Pia covered her eyes. "They look good. Too good. Valentino is going to be unbearable if they lose."

The practice ended shortly thereafter. Chiara dutifully engaged a cool Carolina in a stilted conversation as she'd promised Lazzero she would so that he could catch up with Gianni before the sponsor lunch. When Carolina blew her off a few minutes later, she found herself at loose ends as Pia drifted off to find her husband.

Giving her father a quick call at the bakery before he began work, she assured herself he was okay, then got up to stretch her legs and go look for Lazzero when some of the Americas team players started to drift back onto the field. Heading toward the tunnel where the players were coming out, she stopped dead in her tracks at the sight of Lazzero and Carolina engaged in conversation in the shadowed passage. Carolina, stunning in a bright yellow dress, was leaning against the wall, Lazzero standing in front of her, his head bent close to hers, his hand on the wall beside her.

Intimate, *familiar*, the conversation looked intense. Sharp claws dragged through her. What were they talking about? Was Carolina trying to convince Lazzero she would leave Gianni for him? She had no doubt the other woman would do so in a flash, more than a bit in love with him still.

The jealousy that rocketed through her was illogical, she knew it. She and Lazzero were putting on a charade. It *wasn't* real. But the visceral emotion sweeping through her was.

She swung away, her insides coiling. Walked into a brick wall. She looked up to find Lucca Sousa, the celebrated Brazilian captain of the Americas' squad steadying her, his hands at her waist. Glancing down the tunnel, Lucca absorbed the scene she'd just witnessed, a frown creasing his brow.

"Nothing to see there," he murmured, pressing a hand to her back and guiding her away from the tunnel. "Ancient history, that is."

It hadn't looked so ancient. It had looked very *present*.

"At loose ends?" Lucca queried, giving the group of football wives a glance.

Chiara shot him a distracted look. "I am not part of their clique."

"Nor do you want to be," he said firmly. "Take it from me. Come—kick a ball around with me before lunch."

He was taking pity on her, she registered, a low burn of humiliation moving through her. Helping her save face. It unearthed a wound she'd buried layers deep, because she knew what it was like to be the side amusement for a man who had more than his fair share of willing participants.

But tall, dark and gorgeous Lucca, as smooth as Lazzero was hard around the edges, refused to take no for an answer. Procuring a ball from the sidelines, he ignored his own personal posse lining up to talk to him and shepherded Chiara onto the field. "Do you play?"

She shook her head. "Only a bit in school."

"That will do." Giving her an instruction to move back a few feet, they dribbled the ball back and forth. A couple of the other players and their wives joined in and they played a minigame at one end of the field, a crowd gathering to watch the good-natured fun. Lucca and she proved decent partners, mainly because he was brilliant and as patient as the end of the day.

Chiara, who hadn't been a bad player in school, still found the precision required to get the ball in the net exceedingly frustrating, particularly after all this time. Lucca stopped the play, moved behind her and guided her through the motion of an accurate, straight kick. It took her a few tries, but finally she seemed to master it.

They played the game to five, Chiara's confidence growing as they went. When their team won the game, she jumped in the air in victory. Lucca trotted over and gave her a big hug, lifting her off her feet. "Don't look now," he murmured, glancing at the sidelines, "but your fiancé is watching and he looks, how do I say it in English...*chateado*. Pissed."

Cheeks flushed, exhilarated from the exercise, she stood on tiptoe and gave him a kiss on the cheek, knowing she was stoking the fire, but unable to help herself. "Thank you. That was so much fun."

"You're good at this," Lucca drawled, his eyes sparkling. "Go get him."

Her stomach turned inside out as she walked off the field toward Lazzero, who was standing on the sidelines, dressed in dark jeans and a shirt, arms crossed over his chest.

"Should we go in to lunch?" she suggested coolly when she reached his side. "It looks like it's ready."

"In a minute." He shoved his hands into his jean pockets, his gaze resting on hers. Combustible. *Distinctly combustible.* "Having fun?" he asked.

"Actually, yes, I was. Lucca is lovely."

"He's the biggest playboy on that side of the Atlantic, Chiara."

"I thought that was you," she returned sweetly.

"He had his hands all over you," he murmured. "We are supposed to be newly engaged—madly in love. You might try giving that impression."

Her chin came up, heat coursing through her. "Maybe *you* shouldn't be canoodling with your ex, then. Everyone saw you, Lazzero. You're lucky Gianni didn't."

He raked a hand through his hair. "Carolina was upset. I was doing damage control."

"So was I. If people were watching Lucca and I, then they weren't watching you. And honestly," she purred, "I don't think there is a woman on the planet who would object to having Lucca Sousa's hands on her, so really, it was no hardship. You can thank me later."

His gaze darkened. "Trying to push my buttons, Chiara?"

She lifted a brow. "Now, why would I do that? This isn't real, after all."

Lazzero attempted to douse his incendiary mood with a cold beer at lunch as he sat through the interminably long, posturing event with all its requisite speeches and small

talk. The urge to connect his fist with Lucca Sousa's undeniably handsome jaw was potently appealing. Which was
not a rational response, but then again, Chiara seemed to
inspire that particular frame of mind in him.

His black mood might also, he conceded, be attributed
to Gianni. He'd finally pinned the Italian CEO down before lunch, but their conversation had not been the one he'd
been looking for.

He finessed an escape as dessert ran into ever-lasting
coffee, promising to meet Chiara at the exit once he'd collected his things. Packing his things up, he ran into Santo
on his way out of the locker room.

His brother's eyes gleamed with amusement as he rested
a palm against the frame of the door. "Everything under
control with your fiery little barista? You look a bit hot
under the collar."

"Not now, Santo." Lazzero moved into the hallway for
some privacy. "I talked to Gianni."

Santo lifted a brow. "How did it go?"

"Not great," he admitted. "He seems to have some reservations about how the two brands will work together. If
our design philosophies will match. But he wasn't saying
no. He wants to meet on Tuesday."

"Well that's something." Santo shrugged. "Show him
the design ideas we've developed. They're impressive."

Lazzero shook his head. "Those designs are all wrong.
I'm not happy with them."

A wary look claimed his brother's face. "This is not the
time for your obsessive perfectionism, Laz. The designs
are fine. *Use them.* We might not get another crack at him."

"We definitely won't if we use those drawings," Lazzero
said flatly. "Gianni will hate them. I *know* him. We need
him on board, Santo."

Heat flared in his brother's eyes. "I am clear on that. *I*,
however, wasn't the one who decided to go off half-cocked

on the annual investor call and tell the world we're going to be the number two sportswear brand when number three was a stretch."

A red haze enveloped his brain. "That damn analyst led me on, Santo. You know she did. She loves to push me."

"And *you* shouldn't have bitten. But that's irrelevant now. *Now* we have to deliver. We go back empty-handed and the financial community will crucify us." His brother fixed his gaze on his. "We both know how fast a rising star can crash, Laz. How it's all about perception. What happens if we start to look as if we've overshot our orbit."

Broken, irreparable dreams and all the inherent destruction that comes with it.

His father had been one of the greatest deal-makers on Wall Street—a risk-taking rainmaker who had made a fortune for his clients. Until he'd taken the biggest risk of all, founded a company of his own on a belief those riches could be his, and lost everything.

He *knew* the dangers in making promises you couldn't keep. In trying to grow a company too far, too fast. Had grown up with its repercussions falling down around him, just as Santo and Nico had. But he also knew his instincts weren't wrong on Volare.

"You need to trust me. We have *always* trusted each other. I can do this, Santo. I can make us number two. You just need to give me the room to maneuver."

His brother studied him for a long moment, his dark gaze conflicted. "I do trust you," he said finally. "That's my problem, Laz. I'm not sure if this obsessive drive of yours is going to make us or break us."

"It's going to make us," Lazzero said. *"Trust me."*

CHAPTER SIX

LAZZERO EMERGED FROM the luxurious office space at the Orientale at close to midnight, having spent the evening consulting with his design team in New York, attempting to come up with some sketches for Gianni that worked. An effort which had not yet yielded fruit, but *had* achieved his dual purpose of staying away from Chiara and his inexplicable inability to control himself when it came to her.

Tracing a silent path through the living room to the bedroom, he found the rumpled bed unoccupied and light pooling into the room from the terrace. Crossing to the French doors, he found Chiara curled up on the sofa, staring out at an unparalleled view of Milan. The moon cast an ethereal glow over the beautiful, aristocratic city, but it was Chiara's face that held his attention—the stark vulnerability written across those lush, expressive features, the quiet stillness about her that said she was in another place entirely.

Dressed in the silky, feminine shorts and tank top she seemed to favor, her hair rumpled from sleep, she looked about eighteen. Except there was nothing youthful about the body underneath that wistful packaging. The fine material of her top hugged every last centimeter of her perfect breasts, her hips a voluptuous, irresistible curve beneath the shorts that left her long, golden legs bare.

His blood turned to fire, his good intentions incinerating on a wave of lust that threatened to annihilate his common sense. *So he had a thing for her. Maybe he had a gigantic thing for her. He could control it.*

Maybe if he kept telling himself that, he'd actually believe it.

She turned to look at him, as if sensing his presence. The emotion he read in her brilliant green eyes rocked him back on his heels. It was impossible to decipher—too mixed and too complex, but he could sense a yearning behind it and it turned a key inside of him. Melted that common sense away into so much dust.

"Did you get your designs figured out?" Her voice was husky from lack of use.

He shook his head. "The team's still working on it." He picked up the hardback book she had sitting beside her, a pencil tucked into the binding, and sat down. "You couldn't sleep?"

"My head was too full."

With what? He looked down at the book he held, a sketchbook of some sort, open to a drawing of a dress. "What's this?"

"Nothing. It's just a hobby. I like to make my own clothes." She reached for the book, but he held on to it and flipped through the sketches.

"These are really good. Do you have formal training?"

"I did a few semesters of a fashion design degree at Parsons."

"Only a few semesters?" He directed an inquisitive gaze at her. "It's one of the best design programs in the country. Why did you stop?"

"We needed to prioritize money for the bakery." She shrugged. "It was a long shot anyway."

"Says who? Parsons clearly thought you had talent."

Her expression took on a closed edge. "The program was insanely competitive—the design career I would have had even more so. It just wasn't realistic."

He snapped the book shut and handed it to her. "The best things in life are the hardest to attain. What was the end goal if you'd continued with your degree? To go work for a designer?"

She shook her head. "I wanted to create my own line of affordable urban fashion."

"A big dream," he conceded. "What was your inspiration for it?"

She drew her knees up to her chest and rested her head against the back of the sofa. "My mother," she said, a wistful look in her eyes. "We didn't have much growing up. The bakery did okay, but there was no room for extras. My father considered fashion a luxury, not a necessity, which meant I wore cheap, department store clothes or my cousin's hand-me-downs. Hard," she acknowledged, "for a teenage girl trying to fit in with the cool crowd.

"Thankfully, my mother was an excellent seamstress. After dinner, when the bakery was closed, she'd brew a pot of tea, we'd spread the patterns out on the floor and make the clothes I wanted." A smile curved her lips. "She was incredible. She could make anything. It was magical to me, the way the pieces came together. There was never any doubt as to what I wanted to be."

"And then she passed away," Lazzero murmured.

"Yes. My father, he was—" she hesitated, searching for the right words "—he was never really the same after my mother's death. He was dark, *lost*. He worshipped the ground she walked on. All he seemed to know how to do was to keep the bakery going—to *provide*. But I wouldn't go out with my friends, because of how dark he would get. I was worried about what he would do—what he *might* do. So, I stayed home and took care of him. Made my own clothes. It became a form of self-expression for me."

His heart contracted, the echoes of an ancient wound pulsing his insides. "He was angry. Not at you—at the disease. For taking your mother from him. For shattering his life."

Her dark lashes fanned her cheeks. "You were like that with your father."

He nodded. The difference was, his father's disease had been preventable. Perhaps even more difficult to accept.

Chiara returned her gaze to the glittering city view. "Designing became my obsession. My way of countering the mean girls at school who made fun of my clothes. My lack of designer labels. Sometimes I would make things from scratch, other times I would buy pieces from the thrift store and alter them—not to follow the trends but to reflect what *I* loved about fashion. Eventually," she allowed, "those girls wanted me to make things for them."

"And did you? After what they'd done?"

She nodded.

"Why?"

"Because anger doesn't solve anything," she said quietly. "Only forgiveness does. Allowing my designs to speak for me."

Lazzero felt something stick in his chest. That struck him as phenomenal—*she* struck him as phenomenal—that she would have that sense of maturity, wisdom, at such a young age.

But hadn't he? It was a trait you developed when you were left to fend for yourself. *Sink or swim. Protect yourself at all costs. Arm yourself against the world.* But unlike Chiara, he had had his brothers. She'd had no one.

For the first time he wondered how, in withdrawing when his mother had left, retreating into that aloof, unknowable version of himself he did so well, what effect that had had on his brothers. What it must have been like for Nico, at fifteen, to leave school, to abandon the dreams he'd had for himself to take care of him and Santo. How selflessly he'd done it. How Chiara had had none of that support and turned out to be as strong as she was.

He picked up her hand and tugged it into his lap. Marveled at how small and delicate it was. At the voltage that came from touching her, the connection between them an invisible, electrical thread that lit up his insides in the most dangerous of ways.

"You need to go back to school," he murmured. "Defeating the mean girls was your mission statement in life, Chiara. Some people search a lifetime for one. You *have* one. If you quit—*they* win."

Her gaze clouded over. "That ship has sailed. My classmates are done and building their careers. I'm too old to start again now."

His mouth twisted. "You're only twenty-six. You have plenty of time."

"Speaks the man who put Supersonic on the Nasdaq by the time he was twenty-five."

He shook his head. "You can't compare yourself to others. Santo and I had Martino, our godfather, to back us. To *guide* us. And Nico, who is every bit as brilliant."

She slanted him a curious look. "Was Martino family? What was the relationship between him and your father?"

He shook his head. "Martino and my father were on Wall Street together. Two of the biggest names in their day. Intense competitors and the best of friends."

"Was that where your father's alcoholism began? I've heard stories about the pressure…the crazy lifestyle."

"It started there," he acknowledged. "My father was levelheaded. Smart. Just like Martino. They both swore they'd get out once they'd made their money. Martino, true to his word, did. He founded Evolution with his wife, Juliette, and the rest is history. My father, however, got sucked into the lifestyle. The *temptations* of it.

"My mother," he continued, "didn't make it easier for

him by taking full advantage of that lifestyle and spending his money as if it were water. When Martino finally convinced my father to leave, he was intent on proving he could do it bigger and better than Martino. He bet the bank and his entire life savings on a technology start-up he and a client founded that never made it off the ground."

"And lost everything." Chiara's eyes glittered as they rested on his.

"Yes."

"Did Martino try and help your father? To pull him out of it?"

His mouth flattened. "He tried everything." *Just as they had.* Pouring bottles down the sink. Hiding them. Destroying them. Nico walking their father to AA every night before he'd gone to evening classes. None of it had worked.

Chiara watched him with those expressive eyes. "When did Martino take you under his wing?"

"After my father's funeral. My father was too humiliated to have anything to do with Martino when he was alive. Martino had conquered where he had failed. He refused all help from him. They had," he conceded, staring up at the scattering of stars that dotted the midnight sky, "a complex relationship as you can imagine."

Chiara didn't reply. He looked over at her, found her lost in thought. "What?"

She shrugged a slim shoulder. "I just— I wonder—" She sighed. "Sometimes I wonder if that's why my father withdrew after my mother died. Because I reminded him too much of her. We were mirror images, she and I."

"No." He squashed that imagining dead with a squeeze of his fingers around hers. "You can't take that on. People who are mired in grief get caught up in their own pain. It's as if they're in so deep, they can't dig their way out. They try," he acknowledged, "but it's as if they've made it to the other side, they're clawing their way to the surface, but they can't make it those last few feet to get out."

Her eyes grew dark. "Your father couldn't climb out?"

He nodded. And for the first time in his life, he realized how angry he was. How furious he was that his father who had always been superhuman in his eyes, his *hero*, hadn't had the strength to kick a disease that had destroyed his childhood. How angry he was that, in his supreme selfishness, his father had put his grief above *them*. At those who had created such a culture of reckless greed, his father had been unable to resist, tempted by sirens he didn't have the strength or desire to fight.

"You can't blame yourself," he told her. "This is about your father's inability to put you first, which he *should* have done."

"He did in a financial sense," Chiara pointed out.

"But you needed the emotional support, as well. That's just as important to a fifteen-year-old. And that, he didn't give you."

She sank her teeth into her lip. "Maybe I didn't give him what he needed, either. He was so lost. I didn't know what to do. I keep thinking maybe if I'd gotten him some help, if I'd done *something*, he wouldn't be the way he is. As if he's half-alive. As if he'd rather not be."

Her eyes glittered with tears, unmistakable diamond-edged drops that tugged hard at his insides. The defiant tilt of her chin annihilated his willpower completely. "Chiara," he murmured, pulling her into his arms, his chin coming down on top of her head, her petite body curved against his, "this is not on you. It's about him. You can't find his happiness for him. He has to find it himself."

"And what if he doesn't?"

"Then you were there for him. That's all you can do."

He thought she might pull out of his arms then, a palpable tension in her slight frame. Which would have been the smart move given the chemistry that pulsed between them. Instead, heaving a sigh, she curled closer. Her jasmine-scented hair soft as silk against his skin, the silent, dark night wrapping itself around them, it was a fit so perfect, his brain struggled to articulate it. For once in his life, he didn't even try.

His mouth whispered against the delicate curve of her jaw in an attempt to comfort. The rasp of his stubble against her satiny skin raked a shiver through her. Through *him*.

She went perfectly still. As if she'd forgotten how to move, how to breathe. His palm anchored against her back, her softness pressed against his hardness, his brain slid back to that lazy, sexy kiss this morning. The leisurely, undoubtedly mind-blowing conclusion he would have taken it to if it had been his call.

His blood thickened in his veins, his self-imposed celibacy over the past few months slamming into him hard. His fingers on her jaw, he turned her face to his. Her dark lashes glistening with unshed tears, her lush mouth bare of color, the flare of sensual awareness that darkened her beautiful green eyes was unmistakable. The kind that invited a man to jump in and drown himself in it.

Vulnerable. Too vulnerable.

"Lazzero," she murmured.

This isn't happening.

He lifted her up and carried her inside. In one deft move, he sank his fingers beneath the silky hair at her nape and whisked his arm from beneath her thighs until she slid down his body to her feet, the rasp of her ripe curves against his sensitized flesh almost sending him up into flames.

He doused the vicious heat with a bucketful of cold determination. Because this, *this* could not happen right now. His brain was far too full and she was too damn fragile.

He reached up to tuck a rumpled tendril of her hair behind her ear. "It's late," he rasped. "Go to sleep."

Turning on his heel, he headed for the study and a response from his New York team before he changed his mind and gave in to temptation.

He had a problem. A big one. Now he had to figure out what to do with it.

Chiara woke late, her body still adjusting to the time difference, her mind attempting to wrap itself around the intimate, late-night encounter she'd had with Lazzero the night before. She eyed the unruffled side of the bed opposite her, indicating Lazzero had not joined her. Which actually wasn't the worst thing that could have happened given how he'd walked away last night, shutting things down between them.

Her stomach knotted into a tight, hard ball. She kicked off the silk comforter in deference to the already formidable heat and stared moodily out at another vivid blue, cloudless perfect day through floor-to-ceiling windows bare of the blinds she'd forgotten to close. She might be able to excuse herself for her slip last night because she'd been so vulnerable in the moment, but she couldn't escape the emotional connection she and Lazzero had shared. How *amazing* he'd been.

She buried her teeth in her lip. She had poured her heart and soul out to him last night. Her hopes, her dreams. Instead of brushing them aside as her father had done, pointing to her mother who'd barely been eking out an income as a seamstress before she'd met him, or Antonio, who had advised her she'd be lost in a sea of competition, Lazzero had validated her aspirations.

Defeating the mean girls is your mission statement in life. If you quit—they win.

She'd never thought about it like that. Except now that she had, she couldn't stop. Which was unrealistic, she told herself as a distant, long-ago buried dream clawed itself back to life inside of her. Even with the bakery on a solid financial footing, the rent was astronomical. She'd still need to help her father out on the weekends because he couldn't afford the staff. Which would make studying and working impossible.

She buried the thought and the little twinge her heart gave along with it. It was easy to think fanciful thoughts in Lazzero's world, because he made everything *seem* possible. Everything *was* possible for him. But she was not him and this was not her world.

She conceded, however, that she had misjudged him that day in the café. Had tarred him with the same brush as Antonio, which had been a mistake. Antonio had been born with a silver spoon in his mouth, recklessly wielding his power and privilege, whereas Lazzero had made himself into one of the most powerful men in the world *despite* the significant traumas he'd suffered early on in life. He was a survivor. Just like her.

It made him, she acknowledged with dismay, even more attractive. It also explained so much about who he was, *why* he was the way he was, that insane drive of his. Because he would never be his father. Never see his world shattered beneath his feet again. It also, she surmised, explained why Lazzero was a part of the community angel organization in New York—it was his way of helping when he had been unable to help his father. Another piece of the man she was just beginning to understand.

Then there was last night. He could have used their intense sexual chemistry to persuade her into bed—but he had not. He had walked away instead. Exactly the opposite of what Antonio had done when he had seduced her with his champagne and promises.

Promises Lazzero would never give because he was clear about what he offered a woman. About what he had to give. Which would likely, she concluded, heat blanketing her insides, be the most incredible experience of her life if she allowed it to happen. Which would be *insane*.

She needed coffee. Desperately. She slipped on shorts and a T-shirt and ventured out to the kitchen to procure it. *All* problems could be solved with a good cup of java.

Making an espresso with the machine in the spotless, stainless steel masterpiece of a kitchen, she leaned against the counter and inhaled the dark Italian brew. She had nearly regained her equilibrium when Lazzero came storming into the kitchen dressed in jeans and a T-shirt, a dark cloud on his face. Sliding to an abrupt halt, he scorched his gaze over her fitted T-shirt and bare legs. Back up again.

"Make me one of those, will you?"

Heat snagged her insides. "You might try," she suggested with a lift of her chin, "'please make me one of your amazing espressos, Chiara. I am highly in need.'"

"Yes," he muttered, waving a hand at her. "All of that."

She turned and emptied the tamper into the garbage, relieved to escape all of that mouthwateringly disheveled masculinity. Took her time with the ritualistic packing of the grinds, because she had no idea where she and Lazzero stood after last night. How to navigate this, because it felt as if something fundamental had changed between them. Or maybe it was just *her* that felt that way?

Having artfully packed the tamper with the requisite perfect, round puck, she set the coffee to brew, turned around and leaned a hip against the counter. "You've been up all night?"

Lazzero raked a hand through his rumpled hair. "The designs are not what they need to be."

"When is your meeting with Gianni?"

"Tuesday."

She took a sip of her coffee. Considered his combustible demeanor from over the rim of her cup. "I have a thought."

He gave her a distracted look. "About what?"

Definitely past the moment, he was. "Volare," she elaborated. "I was looking at the Fiammata shoes when I was window-shopping yesterday. The way they are marketed. They're selling a dream with Volare, not a shoe. A *lifestyle*. The ability to fly no matter who you are. Your designs," she said, picking up one of the sheaf of drawings he'd left on the counter, "need to reflect that. They need to be aspirational."

He eyed her contemplatively. "You may have a point there. The designs are *functional*. That's what I don't like about them. Fiammata's approach is very European. Quality of life seems to predominate here. Which, in today's market," he allowed, "might appeal to the American consumer." He slanted her a speculative look. "What would you do with them?"

Chiara found her sketchpad in the bedroom and brought it back to the kitchen. Setting it on the island, she began sketching out a running shoe that was more aspirational than the one Lazzero's designers had done. Something she could see herself wearing.

"Something like this," she said, when she was finished. "Smoother lines. As if the shoe allows you to soar no matter who you are or what you do."

Lazzero rubbed a palm over the thick stubble on his jaw. "I like it, but I think we can go even further with it if that's the direction we were to take. Can you give it the sense that it has wings? My scientists can make sure the aerodynamics work. It's the impression that counts."

She altered the image so it looked even sleeker, with an emphasis on the power of the front of the shoe. Made the back end less clunky. "Like this?"

Lazzero studied it. "Now it's too aspirational. Too ethereal. It needs to be *real* at the same time it's inspirational."

She eyed him. "Are you always this perfectionistic?"

"Sì," he drawled, his gaze glimmering as it rested on

her. "With everything I do. It can be a good quality, I promise you."

Heat pooled beneath her skin, his well-satisfied comment slicing through her head. She wished he'd never said it because she couldn't get it out of her head.

She bent her head and fixed the drawing. Back and forth they went, building off each other's ideas, Lazzero relentlessly pushing her to do better, pulling things out of her she hadn't even known she had. Finally, they finished. She massaged her cramping hand as he examined the drawing from every angle. If he didn't like this version, she decided, he could do it himself.

"I love it," he said slowly, looking up at her. "You're insanely good, Chiara."

A glow warmed her insides. "It's rough."

"It's fantastic." He waved the drawing at her. "Do you mind if I get my New York team to play with the idea? See what they come up with?"

She shook her head. "Go ahead."

He prowled toward her. Dipped his head and grazed her cheek with his lips, the friction of his thick stubble against her skin, the intoxicating whiff of his expensive scent, unearthing a delicious firework of sensation in her. "Thank you."

She sank back against the counter, watching as he strode toward the living room.

"Oh, and, Chiara?"

Her pulse jumped in her throat as he turned around. "Mmm?"

A wicked smile curved his lips. "You make a mean espresso."

CHAPTER SEVEN

"SANTO CIELO."

Pia shaded her eyes from the bright sunlight slanting through the roof of San Siro stadium as the referee added two minutes to the Americas versus Western Europe game, the teams locked two-two in the tense, bitter rivalry being played in front of eighty thousand screaming fans. "I can't bear to watch," her Italian friend groaned. "Valentino is going to be *impossibile* if this ends in a tie."

Chiara, thankful for the one and only ally she had, kept her thoughts to herself. She knew how important this game was to Lazzero. Had witnessed how dedicated he was to the REACH charity he supported in Harlem that kept kids off the street and on the court, the cause he was playing for this week. More layers to the man she had so inaccurately assessed at the beginning of all of this.

Who, along with his penchant to care deeply for the things that mattered to him, had a seemingly inexhaustible appetite for social connection if it contributed to the bottom line. The foreign correspondents' dinner on Saturday, cocktails at the British embassy on Sunday, a dinner meeting with the largest clothing retailer in the world last night at a posh Italian restaurant where they'd consumed wine expensive enough to eat up her entire monthly budget.

Plenty of opportunity for Lazzero to put his hands on her in those supposedly solicitous touches that sent far too much electricity through her body and plenty of opportunity for her to like it far more than she should.

She sank her teeth into her lip as Lazzero took the ball on the sidelines. It had been all business all the time. Which was exactly as it should have been. What she'd signed up for. What she'd *asked* for. Why then, did she feel so barefoot? Because the way she felt when she was with Lazzero made her feel alive in a way she hadn't for a very, very long time? Because feeling *something* felt good?

Her palms damp, her heart pounding, she watched as Lazzero yelled instructions to his teammates, then threw the ball in. Off the Americas team went, roaring down the field. Three neat passes, the final one from Lazzero to Lucca, and the ball was in the net.

The crowd surged to its feet with a mighty roar, Chiara along with it. One last fruitless drive by the Western Europe team and the clock ran out, signaling victory for the Americas. Lazzero, looking utterly nonplussed by his assist in the winning goal, turned and trotted off the field where he and Lucca were enveloped in a melee of congratulations.

Pia groaned. "There goes my chance for romance tonight. You, on the other hand," she said, tugging on Chiara's arm, "must go down to the field. It's La Coppa Estiva tradition to give the winning players a kiss. The television cameras love it."

Oh, no. Chiara dug her heels in. She was *not* doing that. But as the other wives and girlfriends filed onto the field, she realized she had no choice. Getting reluctantly to her feet, she left her purse with Pia and made her way down the stairs.

Lazzero eyed her as she approached, an amused light dancing in his dark eyes. *Thump* went her heart as she took him in. Sweat darkening his T-shirt, his hair slicked back from his brow, his game face still on, he was spectacular.

She pulled to a halt in front of him. Balanced her hands

on his waist as she stood on tiptoe to brush a kiss against his cheek. "Congratulations," she murmured. "You played a fantastic game."

He caught her jaw in his fingers, the wicked glint in his eyes sending a skitter of foreboding through her. "I think," he drawled, "they're going to expect a bit more than that."

Spreading his big palm against her back, he bowed her in a delicate arch, caged her against the unyielding steel frame of his powerful body. Her breath caught in her throat as he bent his head and took her mouth in a pure, unadulterated seduction that weakened her knees.

Her arms wound around his neck out of the pure need to keep herself upright. But then, her fingers got all tangled up in his gorgeous thick hair, *she* got all tangled up in the dark, delicious taste of him and the way he incinerated her insides, and the *plink, plink* of the camera flashes faded to a distant distraction.

Dazed, disoriented, she rocked back on her heels when he ended it, the hand he had wrapped around her hip holding her steady. Light blinding her eyes, a chorus of wolf whistles and applause raining down around them, she struggled to find her equilibrium.

Lazzero swept his sexy, devastating mouth across her cheek to her ear. "It almost felt as if you meant that, *angelo mio.*"

She was afraid she might have.

"Finally got your priorities straight." Lucca issued the jab as he waltzed past, his posse trailing behind him. "You look amazing, *querida.* As always."

Lazzero's face darkened. "I can still put my fist through your face, Sousa."

Lucca only looked amused as he headed to a television interview with Brazilian TV. Chiara looked up at Lazzero, her heartbeat slowing to a more normal rhythm. "How did your meeting with Gianni go?"

His combustible expression turned satisfied. "He loved the sketches. Due in large part, to you. He's invited us to a dinner party on Friday night to discuss the partnership further."

She smiled. "That's amazing. Congratulations."

He retrieved the towel he had slung over his shoulder and wiped the sweat from his brow. "I thought I'd take you out to say thank you. Celebrate."

"With the team, you mean?"

"No," he said casually, slinging the towel over his shoulder. "Just us. I figured you'd had enough socializing. And, I have a surprise for you."

A *surprise*? A break from the relentless socializing? She was most definitely on board.

A slither of excitement skittered up her spine. "What should I wear?"

He shrugged. "Something nice. Wear one of your own dresses if you like. We can just be ourselves tonight."

It was a directive Lazzero might have reconsidered as he and Chiara stood on the tarmac at Milano Linate Airport in the late afternoon sunshine, her light pink dress fluttering in the wind. Empire-waisted and fitted with flowing long sleeves that somehow still left her shoulders bare, it was designed with multiple layers of some gauzy type of silk that looked as if she was wearing a flimsy scarf instead of a dress.

Which only came to midthigh, mind you, exposing a sweep of bare leg that held him transfixed. He was having dreams about those legs and what they would feel like wrapped around him, and that dress wasn't helping. The image of what he would like to do with her wasn't fit for public consumption.

Chiara gave him a sideways look as she proceeded

him up the steps into the jet. "You told me to wear what I wanted."

"I did and you look great." He kept his description to the bare minimum. "The dress is fantastic."

Her mouth curved into a smile that would have lit a small metropolis. "I'm glad you think so. It's one of mine."

The impact of that smile hit him square in the chest. *He was screwed*, he conceded. So royally screwed. But then again, he'd known that the moment she'd told him her story. When she'd quietly revealed her plan to defeat the mean girls of the world. It explained everything about the sharp, spiky skin that encased her. The fierce need for independence. The brave face she put on for the world, because he'd been exactly the same.

The difference between him and Chiara was that he had taught himself not to care. Made himself impervious to the world, and she had not. Which *should* label her as off-limits to him. Instead, he had the reckless desire to peel back more of those layers. To find the Chiara that lay beneath.

They flew down to the boot of Italy to Puglia, known for its sun, sea and amazing views. Sitting in the heel of the boot, it was tranquil and unspoiled, largely untouched by the masses of tourists who flocked to the country.

"It's stunning," Chiara breathed as they landed in Salento, nestled in the clear waters of the Adriatic, its tall cliffs sculpted by the sea.

"A friend of mine has a place here." Lazzero helped her down the steps of the jet, afraid she would topple over in those high heels of hers, which also weren't helping his internal temperature gauge. "It's unbelievably beautiful."

Her dress whipped up in the wind as they walked across the tarmac. He slapped a hand against her thigh as a ground worker stopped to stare. "Can you please *control* this dress?"

Hot color singed her cheeks. "It's the wind. Had I known

we were *flying* to dinner, I would have chosen something else."

And that would have been so, so sad. He ruthlessly pulled his hormones under control as he guided her to the waiting car, allowing her to slide in first, then walked around the car to climb in the other side. The town of Polignano a Mare, perched atop a twenty-meter-high limestone cliff that looked out over the crystal-clear waters of the Adriatic, was only a short drive away.

Known for its cliff diving, jaw-dropping caves carved out of the limestone rock that rose from the sea, as well as its excellent food, it held a wealth of charm as the sunset bathed it in a fiery glow. Suggesting they leave the car behind and walk the rest of the way to their destination to enjoy the view, Lazzero caught Chiara's hand in his.

Her gaze dropped to where their fingers were interlaced. "We're not in public," she murmured. "You don't have to do that."

"Sheer force of habit," he countered blithely. "Don't be so prickly, Chiara. We're holding hands, not necking in the street."

Which brought with it a whole other series of images that involved him backing her into one of the quaint, cobblestoned side streets and taking exactly what he'd wanted from the very beginning. Not helpful when added to *the dress.*

She left her hand in his. Was silent as they walked through the whitewashed streets toward the sea, the lanes bursting with splashes of fluorescent color from the vibrant window boxes full of brightly hued blooms. Then it was him wondering about his presence of mind, because the whole thing felt right in a way he couldn't articulate. Had never experienced before.

The Grotta Nascondiglio Hotel, carved out of the magnificent limestone rocks, rose in front of them as they neared the seafront. Chiara gasped and pointed at something to their right. "Are *those* the cliff divers? Good heavens, look where they're diving from."

They were high—twenty meters above the ground, diving from one of the cliffs that flanked the harbor below. But Lazzero shrugged a shoulder as they moved closer to watch. "It's perfectly safe. The water is more than deep enough."

"I don't care how deep it is," Chiara breathed. "That's *crazy.* I would never do it. Would you?"

"I promised my friend who lives here I would do it next year with him."

Her eyes went wide. "No way."

A smile pulled at his lips. "Sometimes you just have to take the leap. Trust that wherever it takes you, you will come out the other side, better, *stronger* than you were before. Life is about the living, Chiara. Trusting your gut."

Chiara's brain was buzzing as Lazzero escorted her inside the gorgeous Grotta Nascondiglio Hotel. It might have been the challenge he had just laid down in front of her. Or it could simply have been how outrageously attractive he looked in sand-colored trousers and a white shirt that stretched across his muscular torso, emphasizing every rippling muscle to devastating effect.

He didn't need anything else to assert his dominance over the world, she concluded, knees a bit unsteady. Not even the glittering, understated Rolex that contrasted with his deeply tanned skin as he pressed a hand to her back and guided her inside the restaurant. The aura of power, *solidity*, about him was unmistakable, his core strength formed in a life that had been trial by fire.

The warm pressure of his palm against her back as they walked inside the massive, natural cave unearthed an excitement all of its own. It was sensory overload as she looked around her at the warmly lit room that opened onto a spectacular view of the Adriatic.

"Tell me we have a table overlooking the water," she said, "and I will die and go to heaven."

Lazzero's ebony eyes danced with humor. "We have a table overlooking the water. In fact, I think it's that one right there."

She followed his nod toward a candlelit table for two that sat at the mouth of the cave, the only one left unoccupied. The only thing separating it from a sheer, butterfly-inducing drop to the sea was the cast-iron fence that ran along the perimeter of the restaurant. Chiara's stomach tipped over with excitement. It was utterly heart-stopping.

The maître d' appeared and led them toward their table. She slipped into the seat Lazzero held out for her and accepted the menu the host handed her. Pushing her chair in, Lazzero took the seat opposite her.

"Not exactly a little hole in the wall in the East Village," she murmured, in an attempt to distract herself from the thumping of her heart.

A speculative glimmer lit his dark eyes. "Are you calling this a *date*, Chiara Ferrante?"

Her stomach missed its landing and crashed into her heart. "It was a joke."

His sensual mouth curved. "You can't even say it, can you? Are you going to run for the hills now that we've gotten that out of the way?"

"Are you?" she asked pointedly.

"No." He sat back in his chair, the wine list in hand. "I'm going to choose us a wine."

He did not ask her preference because, of course, that wasn't how a date with Lazzero went. His women felt feminine and cared for. And she found herself feeling exactly that as he took control and smoothly ordered a bottle of Barolo.

It was, she discovered, a heady feeling given she'd been the one doing the taking care of for as long as she could remember.

"So," Lazzero said, sitting back in his chair when their glasses were full. "Tell me about this urban line of yours. What kind of a vision do you have for it?"

She snagged her lip between her teeth. "You really want to know?"

"Yes. I do."

She told him about the portfolio of designs she'd been working on ever since she was a teenager. How her vision had been to design a line for both teenagers and young women starting out in the work force, neither of whom had much disposable income.

"Most women in New York can't afford designer fashion. Most are like me—they want to be able to express their individuality without blowing their grocery budget on a handbag."

Lazzero made a face. "I've never understood the whole handbag thing." He pointed his glass at her. "How would you market it, then?"

"Online. My own website, which would include a blog to drive traffic to the retail store. The boutique online fashion retailers… Keep it small and targeted."

"Smart," he agreed. "The trends are definitely headed that way. Very little overhead and no in-store marketing costs."

He swirled the rich red wine in his glass. Set his gaze on hers. "I was speaking with Bianca, my head designer, this morning when I signed off on the sketches. She mentioned to me how talented she thought you were."

Her insides warmed. "That's very nice of her to say."

"She's tough. It's no faint praise. Bianca," he elaborated, "heads up an incubator program in Manhattan, the

MFDA—Manhattan Fashion Designer Association. You've heard of it?"

She nodded. "Of course. They nurture new talent from the community—offer bursaries for school and co-op positions in the industry. It's an amazing mentoring program."

"I told Bianca your story. She wants to meet you." Lazzero's casually delivered statement popped her eyes wide-open. "If you are interested, of course. It would just be for a coffee. To see if you'd be a good fit for the group. There are no guarantees they'd take you on, but Bianca holds a great deal of sway."

Her stomach swooped and then dropped. "It's impossible to crack, Lazzero. Some of the most talented kids at school never made it in."

"They're looking for people with vision. You have one." He shook his head. "You don't second-guess an opportunity like this. You embrace it. See where it goes. It may go somewhere. It may go nowhere. But at least you tried."

She bit the inside of her mouth. She had only been dabbling at the drawing the past few years. What if she'd lost her technique? What if she didn't have *it* anymore? And then there was the part where she'd never get another chance like this.

"It's just a coffee," Lazzero said quietly. "Think about it."

She nodded. Sat back in her chair, her head spinning, and took a sip of her wine. The fact that he believed in her enough to do that for her ignited a glow inside of her. But it wasn't just that. He had invited her opinion about the sketches, had valued her input. He valued her for *who* she was. When was the last time someone had done that?

He might be every bit as much of a playboy as Antonio was, but that, she realized, was where the similarities between the two men began and ended. Lazzero was fascinating and complex, the depth to him undeniably compelling.

He was brutally honest about who he was and what he had to offer a woman, which Antonio had never been.

What he'd said that first night about her had been right. She *was* afraid to get hurt again. Was afraid to admit how she felt about him. But denying this connection between them wasn't getting her anywhere.

A flock of butterflies swooped through her stomach. What if she were to walk into this thing with Lazzero with her eyes wide-open? No wild, dreamy expectations like she'd had with Antonio. Just the cold hard reality that when she and Lazzero went back to New York, it would be over?

It was a heady thought that gained momentum as the conversation drifted from politics to the entertaining stories Lazzero had to tell about the mega-million-dollar athletes he worked with. As she sipped the delicious, full-bodied wine. Absorbed the heart-stoppingly romantic atmosphere as the waves crashed against the cliff below.

And then there was the way Lazzero kept holding her hand as if it was the most natural thing in the world. The brush of his long, muscular legs against the bare skin of her thighs that sent shivers of excitement through her. The way his gaze rested on her mouth with increasing frequency as the night wore on.

She didn't want to feel dead inside anymore. She wanted to walk into the fire with Lazzero. To know every thrilling moment of it. To not look back and wonder *what if.* Because she *wasn't* the same girl she'd once been. She was tougher. Wiser. And she knew what she wanted.

Somewhere along the way, between a discussion of the current state of the EU and the choice of decadent dessert, she lost the plot completely.

Lazzero's gaze darkened. "I have a question," he asked huskily, eyes on hers. "When are we getting to the necking part of the evening?"

Her insides fell apart on a low heated pull. "Lazzero—"

He lifted his hand. Signaled their waiter. Five minutes later, he had the bill paid and something else the waiter had placed in his hand. Extending a purposeful hand to her, he navigated the sea of tables to the exit with an impatience that had her heart slamming into her breastbone. But he didn't lead her toward the entrance, he directed her toward the elevators instead.

"Aren't we getting the car?" she breathed.

"No." Jamming his thumb on the call button Lazzero summoned the elevator. *A key*, she identified past her pounding heart. He had a key in his hand.

She could have cried out with frustration when the elevator doors opened to reveal two couples inside. She smiled politely at them, her knees shaking. Lazzero, noticing her less-than-steady stature, slid an arm around her waist and pulled her back against his hard, solid frame. Which was like touching dry timber to a match. By the time they stopped at their floor, she was trembling so much, she could hardly breathe.

Open slid the elevator doors. Out she and Lazzero stepped. Down the hall he strode, her hand in his. There didn't seem to be any other rooms on this floor, just the one door Lazzero stopped in front of at the end. Expecting him to use the key, she gasped as he backed her up against the wall instead, his mouth dipping to take hers in a hot, hard kiss, one that promised a wildness that echoed the shaking in her knees.

His hand wound around a thick chunk of her hair, he angled her head until he had her exactly where he wanted her, then plunged deeper, until they were consuming each other with a ferocity that was terrifying in its intensity.

When they finally came up for air, they were both breathing hard. Lazzero dragged his mouth up to her ear. "You are so beautiful," he murmured. "Tell me you want this, Chiara."

A moment of complete and utter panic consumed her. She drew back, a handful of his shirt in her fingers. Took a deep breath and grounded herself in his dark, hot gaze. In the man, she was learning, she could trust without reservation. Reaching up, she traced the hard, sensual line of his mouth with her fingers and nodded.

His eyes turned to flame. His brief fumble with the key before he got it into the lock wiped away the last of her reservations. Door unlocked, he picked her up, wrapped her legs around him and walked through the door, kicking it shut.

Wild for her in a way he had never experienced before, Lazzero backed Chiara up against the wall and picked the kiss up where he had left off. Trailing openmouthed caresses down the elegant line of her neck, he sank his teeth into the vein that throbbed for him. Her gasp rang out, hot, needy.

Tempted beyond bearing, he slid his hands beneath the gauzy silk of her dress and cupped her bottom. *Silk.* She was wearing silk panties beneath the dress—light, sheer wisps of nothing. Sliding his hands over her bottom, wanting, *needing* to feel her against him, he lifted her, altered the angle between them so that he was cradled in the heat between her thighs. She gasped as the still-covered length of his erection parted her softness through the silk of her panties.

"God, Lazzero. That feels—"

He smoothed a thumb over the juncture of her thigh and abdomen. She arched against him, his hot, hard length rubbing against her center.

"How?" he whispered, his voice rough. "How does it make you feel?"

"So good," she whimpered. "It feels so good. So *hot*."

He uttered a string of curses. *Slow it down*, his brain warned. Slow it down or he'd be buried in her in about five seconds flat and that was not how this was going to go. Not when the thought of having her was blowing a hole in his brain.

His heart threatening to batter its way through his chest, he sucked in a breath. Unwrapped her legs from around his waist and eased her down his body until her feet touched the floor, the slide of her curves against him hardening him to painful steel. Confused, Chiara stared up at him, her green eyes dazed with desire.

"We need to slow it down," he said huskily, snaring her hand and leading her into the suite, "or this is going to be over way too fast."

The suite, he discovered, was like something straight out of a fantasy. Carved out of the same limestone rock as the rest of the hotel, the circular room was finished with exposed brick and a mosaic-tiled floor illuminated by the soft glow of the lamp that had been left on for them.

Not to be outdone by the view from the restaurant, a luxurious sitting area offered a spectacular view of the sea through the open French doors and the terrace beyond. It was, however, the massive bed dominating the space that held his attention.

He sat down on it. Drew Chiara between his parted legs. His blood fizzled in his veins as he scoured her from head to toe.

"I don't know what to touch first," he admitted huskily. "You are so stunning you make my head want to explode."

Her eyes darkened to twin pools of forest green. She apparently knew exactly what *she* wanted to touch. Hands trembling, she moved her fingers to the buttons of his shirt. Worked her way down the row until she'd reached the last, buried beneath his belt. Dragging his shirt from his pants, she undid it, spread her palms flat against his abs and traced her fingers over each indentation and rise of muscle.

"You are insane," she murmured.

His stomach contracted, a rush of heat flooding through him. Not as insane as he was going to be if he didn't touch her soon. Shrugging off the shirt, he threw it to the floor. Hands at her waist, he turned her around and lowered the zip on her dress, exposing inches of creamy, olive skin as he sent the dress fluttering to the floor in a cloud of dusky-pink silk.

"Step out of it," he instructed, heart jamming in his chest.

She kicked the dress aside and turned around. Absorbed the heat of his gaze as it singed every inch of her skin. The soft, full, oh-so-kissable mouth that had driven him wild from the beginning. The delicate pink bra and panty set she wore that did little to hide the lush femininity beneath.

He sank his hands into her waist and lifted her to straddle him, her knees coming down on either side of his. Cupping her head with the palm of his hand, he brought her mouth down to his. Devoured her until she was soft and malleable beneath his hands and as into this as he was.

Needing to touch, to discover, he dropped his hands to her closure of her bra. Undid it and stripped it off, dropping it to the floor. Her curves, heavy and rose-tipped, filled his hands. Drunk on her, unable to get enough, he traced circles around her flesh with his thumbs, moving ever closer to the swollen tips with every sweep of his fingers, but never where she wanted it, until she groaned and pushed herself into his hands.

"Like this?" he asked softly, rubbing his thumbs over the distended peaks, enflamed by her response. She gasped and muttered her assent. He rolled the hard nubs between his fingers until she was twisting against him, restless and needy.

"You want more?" he murmured. "Show me where."

A wave of color stained her cheeks. "Lazzero—" she whispered.

"Show me."

She sank her teeth into her lip. Spread a palm against her abdomen, low, where those tiny pink panties barely covered her femininity. His blood surged in his veins. Tempted beyond bearing, he covered her palm with his, his eyes on hers. "You want me to touch you?"

Her cheeks turned a deeper, fiery red. Then came a tiny nod. He almost lost it right there, but somehow, he held it together. Easing his fingers beneath the waistband of her panties, he cupped her in his palm. Waited while she got used to his intimate possession, her beautiful green eyes dilating with heat. Then, sliding a finger along her slick cleft, he caressed her with a lazy stroke. Felt his heart slam in his chest at how wet, how aroused she was.

"You feel like honey," he murmured, taking her mouth in a lazy kiss at the same time as he rotated his thumb against her sweet, throbbing center. "Like hot, slick honey."

She moaned into his mouth. He kept teasing her until she was even hotter, slicker, aroused to a fever pitch. Then he slid a finger inside of her—slowly, gently, watching the pleasure flicker across her face as he claimed her with an intimate caress.

"You like that?"

"More," she whispered, arching her back.

Her uninhibited, innocent responses affected him like nothing he could remember, the blood raging in his head now. He slid deeper, each gentle push of his finger taking him further inside her silky body. The feel of her velvet flesh clenching around him was indescribable. She was tight and so damn hot. *Heaven.*

"That's it," he encouraged thickly as she moved into his touch, inviting it now. "Ride me, baby. Take your pleasure."

She closed her eyes. He tangled his tongue with hers, absorbed every broken sound until her harsh pants became desperate. "Lazzero—" she breathed.

He slid two fingers inside of her. Pumped them deep. Once, twice, three times, and she came apart in his arms.

Chiara wasn't sure how long it took her to surface, her bones melted into nothing as his strong arms held her upright. When she finally returned to consciousness, she found herself drowning in the dark glitter of satisfaction in his black gaze.

He had given her extreme pleasure, but had taken none for himself. The tense set of his big body beneath her hands was testament to the control he had exerted over himself. But now it was stretched to the limit.

Emboldened by what they'd just shared, wanting to give him the same pleasure he'd just given her, she dropped her hand to the hard ridge that strained his trousers. Reveled in the harsh intake of air he sucked in. "I think we should abstain from that right now," he murmured, clamping his hand over hers.

"I want to touch you," she said softly, her eyes on his. "Let me."

He considered her for a moment, and then his hands fell away. She curled her fingers around the button of his pants. Released it from its closure. Her fingers moving to his zipper, she lowered it, working it carefully past his straining erection.

The air was so hot and heavy between them as she reached inside his briefs and closed her fingers around him, it was hard to breathe. He was insanely masculine—like smooth, hard steel. Moving her hands over him, she stroked him, petted him, her body going slick all over again at the thought of having him. *Taking* him.

With a low groan, Lazzero rolled off the bed and divested himself of the rest of his clothes. The sound of a foil wrapper sounded inordinately loud in the whisper-quiet room. Prowling back to the bed, he kissed her again, eased her back into the soft sheets with the weight of his body and stripped the panties from her.

An ache building inside of her in a deeper, headier place, she cupped the back of his head and brought his mouth down to hers.

Luxurious, intimate, the meeting of their mouths went on forever. Sliding his hand around the back of her knee, Lazzero curved her leg around his waist. Settled himself into the cradle of her thighs until his heat was positioned against her slick, wet flesh. Her stomach dissolved into dust. He was big. *So big.*

"We go slow," he murmured, reading her expression. "Tell me how it feels, *caro*. What you like."

She arched her hips, desperate for him. He slid a palm beneath her bottom, raised her up and slipped the velvet head of him just inside her, his big body shuddering. "So tight," he said raggedly, "so good. How does that feel?"

"Amazing." She barely got the word out past the pounding of her heart. "More."

He sank inside of her a little bit more. Retreated, then pushed deeper, each stroke giving her time to adjust to the size and girth of him. Gentle, so patient, he tried *her* patience.

She closed her hands around his rock-hard glutes and pulled him deeper. A muttered curse leaving his mouth, he grasped her hips and claimed her with a single, powerful thrust that filled every part of her. Tore the breath from her lungs.

Never had she felt so possessed, so full of *everything*. Mouth glued to his, her air his air, they set a frantic rhythm together until they melted into one. Until she felt herself tighten around him, the pleasure threatening to shatter her all over again.

"That's it." Thick, hoarse, the guttural edge to Lazzero's voice at her ear spurred her on. "Let go."

His big body flexed above her, his muscles bunching as he shifted his position to deepen his thrusts. The connection they shared as his dark gaze burned into hers was so electric, so all-encompassing, it froze her in place. So much more than just the physical, it was the most intimate, soul-baring experience of her life.

Slowly, deliberately, he ground against her where she needed him the most. The delicious friction of his body against hers sent her over the edge with a sharp cry. An animal-like groan leaving his throat, Lazzero unleashed himself and took his pleasure, claiming her so deeply all she saw was white-hot stars as they shattered into one.

CHAPTER EIGHT

CHIARA EMERGED FROM a sex-induced haze to find herself plastered across Lazzero's muscular chest, her legs tangled with his, his heart pounding beneath her ear in almost as wild a rhythm as hers. She had the feeling he was as thrown off balance by what they'd just shared as she was, but he didn't say anything, just stroked a lazy path down her spine with his palm.

Her stomach dipped, settling somewhere around the rocky shore below. She'd just had wild, ridiculously hot sex with Lazzero, the depth of the connection they'd shared frightening in its intensity. She had not only walked *into* the fire, she'd drowned herself in it. She didn't feel dead anymore, she felt unnervingly, terrifyingly alive, like someone had mainlined adrenaline through her veins. As if she'd denied herself this depth of feeling, of *connection*, for so long, it was complete and utter sensory overload.

But there was also fear. Fear she'd spent a lifetime avoiding these feelings. That the one time she'd slipped and allowed herself to be this vulnerable, she'd been destroyed. Fear that it was Lazzero that was making it so scary. Because he was an insane lover. Because she had liked him for a long time and refused to admit it.

Because of how he made her *feel*.

She buried her teeth in her lip. Forced herself to stay in the moment. To absorb it, rather than run from it, because she'd been doing that for far too long and she'd promised herself *this* was not going to be about that. This was about finding a piece of herself again that she'd lost.

"What?" Lazzero's hand stilled on her spine, as if he could read the shift in her emotion.

She buried her teeth deeper into her lip. "Nothing."

He rolled her onto her back and sank his fingers into her hair so that she was forced to look at him. "You are far too easy to read. You have smoke coming out of your ears. Regrets already?"

"No. It was perfect. I—" She shook her head. "Making myself vulnerable isn't the easiest thing for me. You were right about that. It's easier to hide behind my layers—to not engage, rather than let myself feel."

His midnight gaze warmed. "You were engaged just now. You made me a little insane for you, Chiara. Or did you miss the part where we almost didn't make it to the bed?"

A flush crept up her body and warmed her cheeks. She had *not* missed that part. She had been there for every mind-blowing second of it. She'd *liked* that he'd almost lost control. That she could do that to him. That he had been just as crazy for her as she had been for him. It made her feel less self-conscious about the way she felt.

Lazzero ran a finger across the heated surface of her cheek. "Give me five minutes," he murmured, "and I will refresh your memory."

Her gaze slipped away from his, unable to handle the intensity of the moment. Moved over the magnificent length of his muscled body, bathed in the glow of the lamplight. It warmed another part of her entirely, every inch of the honed, sinewy muscle on display, the scar that crisscrossed his knee his only imperfection.

She traced her fingers over the raised ridge of the scar. "What's this?"

"An old basketball injury."

"The one that ended your career?"

"Yes."

When no further information was forthcoming, she sank back on her elbow to look at him. "I sat beside your old basketball coach at lunch yesterday—Hank Peterson. He was wonderful. Full of such great stories. He told me you come to talk to his kids at the REACH program."

A ghost of a smile touched his mouth. "Hank is a legend. I met him when we moved to Greenwich Village. He used to coach a league at The Cage, one of the most famous streetball courts in New York that was right around the corner from our house. It was mythical, where *dreams* are made—where some of the greats were born. I used to ditch my homework and play all night. Until they turned the lights off and Hank sent me home."

Her mouth curved. "I used to do the same thing with my sketching. I was supposed to be doing my homework while my parents finished work at the bakery. Instead, my mother would come home to a whole lot of drawings in the back of my notebook and very little else. It used to drive her crazy."

"At least she cared," he murmured. "That's a good thing."

She frowned. "Yours didn't?"

"There was no one home *to* care. My father was drinking by then and my mother had left. Nico," he allowed, "used to lecture me to study. He was all about school and learning. But I was hopelessly obsessed."

Her eyes widened. *His mother had left?* "I thought she remarried when your father died."

Lazzero shook his head. "She walked out on us when I was fourteen."

Chiara was shocked into silence. *What mother would leave her children like that? When everything was falling*

*apart around them? When her children were at their most
vulnerable and needed her most of all?*

"Was your father's alcoholism an instigator in her leaving?" she asked, trying to understand.

"My mother was a sycophant," he said flatly. "She fell
in love with my father's money and she fell out of love with
him when he lost it."

She bit the inside of her mouth. "I'm sure it wasn't quite
that simple."

"It was just that simple." He tucked his hands behind his
head, an expressionless look on his face. "My mother was
a dancer trying to make it on Broadway when she and my
father met. She wanted a career, the glitz, the glamour. She
didn't want a family. When she got pregnant with Nico, my
father thought he could change her mind. But he never did.
He spent their entire marriage trying to keep her happy,
which in the end failed miserably when he imploded and
she walked out on him."

She absorbed his harshly issued words. "That's only one
side of the story," she said huskily. "I'm sure it couldn't
have been easy on your mother to give up her career. Her
dream. And your father," she pointed out, "sounds as if he
was extremely driven. As if he had his own internal demons to battle. Which couldn't have been easy to live with."

"No," Lazzero agreed evenly, "it wasn't. But he was
a man. He was focused on providing. He was hurt when
he couldn't make her happy. His pride was damaged. He
spent more and more time at work, because he didn't want
to be at home, which eventually devolved into the affairs
he had to compensate. Which were not in any way excusable," he qualified, "but perhaps understandable, given she
drove him to it."

That struck a raw note given what Antonio had done to
her. "Nobody drives anyone to do anything," she refuted.

"Relationships are complicated things, Lazzero. You make a choice to love someone. To see it through."

His eyes glittered. "Exactly why I choose not to do it. Because any way you look at it, someone always messes it up."

She absorbed his intense cynicism. "So basketball," she murmured, seeking to dispel some of the tension in the air, "became your outlet. Like sketching was for me?"

He nodded, sifting his fingers through her hair and watching it in the play of the light. "If I was on the court, I wasn't dealing with the mess my life was. With the shadow of a man my father had become. But I also," he conceded, his gaze darkening, "fell in love. There's a magic about the game when you play it on the streets of New York—an unspoken devotion to the game we all shared. By the time I'd won my first tournament for Hank, I knew I wanted to play basketball for a living."

Her mouth curved. "Hank said you were always the first and last on the court."

"Because I wasn't as physically gifted as some of the other players," he acknowledged. "I didn't have the size some of them did, nor the jumping ability. I had to work harder, *want it more* than all the rest. But I was smart. I could read the court and I built my career around that. I won a division championship for Hank in my junior year at Columbia."

A college career which, according to Hank, had been limitless in its possibilities. Until he'd injured himself.

She curled her fingers around his knee. "Tell me about it? What happened."

He lifted a shoulder. "There isn't much to tell. I was chasing a player down on a breakaway in a key divisional play-off game. I jumped to block the shot, felt something pop in my knee. Shatter. When I tried to stand up, I couldn't. I'd torn the two main ligaments that hold your knee together. It was almost impossible for the surgeons to put it back together."

Her throat felt like gravel. "That must have been devastating."

"It was what it was."

His standard line. But she knew now it hadn't been so simple. "Hank said you were an exceptional player, Lazzero. That you'd been scouted by three professional teams. It had to have hurt to have that taken from you."

A shadow whispered over the clarity of his gaze. "What do you want me to say, Chiara? That I was shattered inside? That watching every dream I'd had since I was eight go up in a puff of smoke tore me apart?"

She flinched at the harsh edge to his voice. Pushed a hand into the mattress to sit up and stare out at the sea, a dark, silent mass beyond the French doors. Maybe she'd been looking for the truth, given she'd poured her heart and soul out to him on the terrace that night. But that was not what this was, she reminded herself, and she'd be a fool to forget it.

Lazzero exhaled an audible breath. Snared an arm around her waist and pulled her back against him, tucking her against his chest.

"I was in denial," he said quietly. "I refused to believe it would end my career. I went for a second opinion and when that doctor told me I would never play at that level again, I set out to prove him wrong. It took me almost a year and hundreds of hours of physio to accept the fact that I was never coming back. That it was *over.*"

A hand fisted her chest. "You didn't give up," she said, absorbing the hard beat of his heart beneath her ear. "Not like I did."

"Giving up wasn't an option. It was everything to me."

Sometimes dreams are too expensive to keep.

Her blood ran jagged in her veins. Suddenly, he made so

much sense to her. Lazzero's world had dissolved beneath his feet, not once, when his father had imploded and his mother had walked out, but twice, when his basketball career had disintegrated beneath his feet on a painful stroke of fate. But instead of allowing himself to become bitter and disillusioned, he'd created Supersonic. Built a company around the sport he loved.

"Hank says you are a great mentor to the kids," she said huskily.

A lift of his shoulder beneath her. "It gives them something to shoot for if a pro basketball career doesn't work out for them. Unfortunately, the statistics are stacked against it."

Her heart did a funny twist. She hadn't needed another reason to like him this much. Because falling for Lazzero wasn't on the agenda in this walk on the wild side of hers. And maybe he decided that too, because before she could take another breath, he had rolled her onto her back, speared a hand into her hair, and there was no escaping the sparks that sizzled and popped between them.

"I think that's enough talking," he murmured, lowering his mouth to hers. "Now that I've gotten you where I want you, I intend to take full advantage of it."

She sucked in a breath, only to lose it as he covered her mouth with his, his kiss dragging her back into the inferno with relentless precision. A gasp left her throat as he slid his tongue inside her mouth, mating with her own in a fiery dance that signaled his carnal ambitions.

It was pure, dominant male at its most blatant and she loved it. Her hands found the thick muscle of his back and shoulders as she surrendered to the hunger that consumed them both.

Her last coherent thought was that it had been worth every second. Exactly as she'd known it would be. And maybe she was in way, way over her head.

* * *

An opera at the stunning Teatro alla Scala in Milan was hardly the thing to put a girl firmly back on her feet after she'd just embarked on a wild, passionate affair with a man who was most definitely out of her league. Chiara, however, attempted to do exactly that the following evening as she and Lazzero attended a private performance of Verdi's *La Traviata* at the beautiful, iconic theater.

An opportunity for the sponsors of La Coppa Estiva to entertain their international guests in a glamorous, glitzy affair that had been enjoyed by the Milanese upper crust since the eighteenth century, she and Lazzero were to host a German retail scion and his wife in their private box.

She thought Micaela had gotten her outfit just right, the ankle-length sleek scarlet dress with its asymmetric cut at the shoulder glamorous, yet understated, a red lip and sparkly heels her only accessories. It was Lazzero in a perfectly tailored black suit, his ebony hair worn fashionably spiky tonight, a five o'clock shadow darkening his jaw, that was making her pulse race.

His touch lingered just a little bit longer than before, the possessive glimmer in his eyes as they worked the crowd doing something funny to her insides. *As if they were lovers.* Which, in fact, they were, a mind-boggling detail she was just beginning to wrap her head around.

Then it was the spectacular theater that was stealing her attention. Six rows of gold stuccoed boxes sat stacked on top of each other in the oval theater, soaring high above the packed crowd below. The massive, Bohemian crystal chandelier was incredible, as was the sumptuous elegance of their box with its red velvet, silk and gilded stucco interior. Since she knew nothing about opera, having never attended one in her life, Chiara nestled her viewing glasses in her lap and scoured the program so she would know the story, but soon the lights were dimming and the curtain came up and she lost herself to the performance instead.

She was hooked from the very first second. Transfixed by the elaborate sets, the hauntingly beautiful music and the poignant story of Violetta Valéry, the heroine of Verdi's opera.

Violetta, a courtesan, knows she will die soon, exhausted by her restless life. Alfredo Germont, played by a handsome, world-famous tenor who strutted across the stage in the opening act, has been fascinated by Violetta for a very long time. When he is introduced to her at a party, he proposes a toast to true love. Enchanted by his candid and forthright manner, Violetta responds with a toast in praise of *free* love.

Enamoured though she may be, Violetta decides there is no room for such emotion in her life and walks away from Alfredo. But she can't quite seem to put him out of her head and eventually, the two embark on a passionate love affair.

Tears filled Chiara's eyes as she watched Alfredo awaken Violetta's desire to be truly loved. They slipped silently down her cheeks amidst the beautiful music. She brushed them from her cheeks, afraid to watch, because she knew what was to come. As in all of the great, tragic love stories it seemed, disaster was about to befall the two lovers.

Alfredo's father, a wealthy aristocrat, pays a visit to Violetta to convince her there can be no future for her and his son. That she is destroying Alfredo's future by encouraging his love, and that of his sister, as well, to marry into the upper echelons of society.

Heartbroken, Chiara watched as Violetta left Alfredo to return to her old life, telling him she didn't love him to set him free. Alfredo, grief stricken and racked with jealousy and hurt at Violetta's supposed betrayal, stalked across the stage as the music reached its crescendo and proposed a duel with her paramour to end the second act.

"Ooh," said the German CEO's wife as the lights came up for the intermission. "It's so good, isn't it?"

Chiara nodded, frantically rifling through her purse for a tissue. Lazzero offered her the handkerchief from his front pocket, a cynical look on his face. She ignored him as they made their way out into the elegant foyer with its fluted columns and crystal chandeliers, her head still caught up in the story. Absorbing its nuances.

Violetta's story had struck so many chords in her, she wasn't sure which one to consider first. How much the character reminded her of herself with her determination to escape her emotions. How she hadn't been good enough for Antonio. How swept up she was becoming in Lazzero. What would happen in the end, because Violetta had to die, didn't she? Would her and Alfredo's love be forever thwarted?

When her opera companion excused herself to the ladies' room, Chiara slipped out onto one of the Juliette balconies to regain her equilibrium while Lazzero introduced the German CEO around. The tiny balcony, set apart from the larger one that was buzzing with activity, boasted a lovely view of the lit Piazza della Scala.

She leaned back against the stone facade of the building and inhaled a deep breath of the sultry, summer night air. It was as far removed from her life as she could possible imagine. And yet, there was something so real about the moment. So revelatory.

She had not been living for far too long, that she knew. But was it worth the consequences that Violetta had feared to fully embrace this new world of emotion? To reap the greatest rewards that life had to offer? She hadn't quite determined the answer to that question when Lazzero stepped out onto the balcony, two glasses of Prosecco in his hands.

She lifted a brow. "You're not networking until you drop?"

"Hans saw someone he knew." He handed her a glass of Prosecco. "I thought you might need this. You looked a little emotionally devastated in there."

A wry smile pulled at her mouth. "It's a beautiful story. I got a little swept up in the emotion. Although you," she conceded, "did not seem quite so captivated. Which part of your jaded view of love did Verdi offend?"

"Not all of it," he drawled, leaning a hip against the wall. "I thought Violetta was spot-on. I'm all for the concept of *free love*. Everybody walks into it with realistic expectations. Nobody gets hurt. Her critical mistake was in buying into Alfredo's vision—into a fantasy that doesn't really exist."

"Who says?" she countered lightly. "My parents had it. They were madly in love with each other."

"So much so that your father is in the dark place that he is?" Lazzero tipped his head to the side. "Some would call that an unhealthy kind of love. A *devastating* kind of love."

She couldn't necessarily disagree with the observation, because loving that deeply had consequences. She had lived with them since she was fifteen. She knew what it was like to be loved and what it felt like to have that love taken away. Had convinced herself she was better off without it after Antonio. But she also believed her parents had shared something special and somewhere, deep down, if she were to be completely honest, she knew she wanted it too.

She met Lazzero's cynical gaze. "You're talking about your parents. That *messy*, kind of love you are so intent on avoiding?"

"They were a disaster from start to finish," he said flatly. "My father fell in love with an illusion rather than the reality of what he got. This," he said, waving a hand toward the doors, "could be their story tonight. And you see how well it turned out for Violetta and Alfredo."

She shook her head. "Violetta *loved* Alfredo. What they had was real. It was his father that messed it up."

"And look how easily she was swayed. One might say she was simply looking for a way out. That she never truly committed."

"She was being selfless. She wanted to set him free. You make a choice to love someone, Lazzero. You *choose* to commit."

"Or you choose to marry for the wrong reasons." He tipped his glass at her. "My mother married my father for the money. Carolina married Gianni on the rebound. Violetta needed to be rescued. Does anyone ever marry for the *right* reason? Because they want to spend their lives together?"

"Violetta's case was different," she disagreed. "For her to set Alfredo free was, in my opinion, the ultimate act of love on her part."

"And what happens when she is gone?" Lazzero lifted a dark brow. "Do you think Alfredo is going to applaud himself for the decision he made when his heart has been smashed to smithereens?"

Exactly as his father's had been? Her insides curled at the parallels. "Maybe," she offered huskily, "he will feel lucky to have experienced that kind of love *once* in his life and he will have that to hang on to when she's gone. Maybe, as much pain as my father is in, he wouldn't trade what he and my mother had for the world."

Lazzero rested an inscrutable gaze on her.

"What?"

"You," he murmured. "I never would have guessed you are a closet romantic with that prickly exterior of yours."

She shrugged. "I'm merely trying to make a point. *You* are the one who said to me that tarring all men of a certain bank balance with the same brush is a mistake. Maybe," she suggested, "lumping all relationships into the same category is an equal error in judgment."

He pushed away from the wall and caged her in with a palm beside her head all in one lazy movement. "So," he drawled, his eyes on hers, "is that what is on offer to Mr. Right? Chiara Ferrante's heart if a man is willing to go *all in*?"

Her breath stalled in her chest. He was so gorgeous, so dark and brooding up close, it was impossible to think. "Stop playing with me," she murmured. "You are inherently skilled in the art of deflection, Lazzero."

"Who says I'm playing? Maybe I'm accepting your challenge. Maybe I just want to know the answer."

"Maybe," she breathed. Because she wasn't sure if she was ready to open herself up again to the full gamut of that emotion she so feared. To the possibility she might be rejected again—that she wouldn't be *good enough*. But maybe that was the risk you had to take. To know, that if you jumped, you were strong enough to handle whatever came on the other side.

"What I *think*," Lazzero murmured, his dark gaze glittering as it rested on hers, "is that you and I have a good thing, Chiara. Honest, up-front, with all of our cards on the table. And *that* is why it works."

Right, she told herself. That was exactly what this was. And she could handle it. Absolutely she could.

"Although," he said softly, lowering his head to hers so their breaths melded in a warm, seductive caress, "I didn't come out here to debate Verdi with you."

Every kiss, every caress, every heart-stopping moment of pleasure from the night before swept through her in a heady rush. "Oh," she breathed, her heart thumping in her chest. "Why did you?"

"Because I wanted to do *this*." He closed his mouth over hers in a lazy, persuasive possession that stormed her senses. She let her eyes flutter shut. Stopped thinking entirely as her fingers curled around the lapel of his jacket, a gasp of warm air leaving her lips as her mouth parted beneath his sensual assault.

The sound of the intermission bell ended the seductive spiral. "We should go back in," Lazzero murmured, nuzzling her mouth.

"Yes," she agreed unsteadily, taking a step back. "Although I'm not so sure I want to see Violetta shatter Alfredo's heart."

CHAPTER NINE

THE THOUGHT OF a dinner party at Villa Alighieri, Gianni Casale's stunning estate in Lake Como, was a much less intimidating prospect for Chiara than many of the events she and Lazzero had attended thus far. She had created the sketches for Volare the Italian CEO had fallen in love with, she had accepted Bianca's offer for coffee which could take her life in a whole new direction and she was knee-deep in a spectacular affair with Lazzero that showed no signs of cooling.

If she was being unwise, foolhardy, in thinking she could handle all of this, telling herself she wasn't in as deep as she was, she brushed those thoughts aside, because being with Lazzero was the most breathtakingly exciting experience of her life, she felt ridiculously alive and it was the headiest of drugs.

Striving for an elegance and composure to match the evening, she chose a midlength, black wrap dress. Simple in design, it was the gorgeous material that made the dress, the light jersey clinging to her body in all the right places, the deeply cut V that revealed the barest hint of the swell of her breasts its only overtly sexy note.

Chiara had loved it because of the huge, red hibiscus that fanned out from her waist, transforming the dress from ordinary to extraordinary. A splash of vibrant color on a perfectly cut canvas.

Adding a dark cherry gloss to her lips and delicate high heels that matched the exotic bloom, she left the golden tan she'd acquired to do the rest of the work, her final touch a series of layered silver bracelets.

Lazzero spent the entire drive up to Lake Como on a conference call, in full mogul mode. It wasn't until they'd parked at the marina and taken possession of the boat that would transport them to Villa Alighieri, that she claimed his attention, his gaze roving over her in a starkly appreciative appraisal that brought a flush to her cheeks.

"You look like an exotic flower come to life," he murmured, brushing a kiss against her cheek. She took in his tapered, light gray pants and lavender shirt as he stepped back. They did everything for his dark good looks and little for her pounding heart that felt as if it might push right through her chest.

On any other man, the pastel color might have come off as less than masculine. On Lazzero, it was a look that would send most women slithering to the ground.

"You don't look so bad yourself," she said breezily, the understatement of the year. But clearly, she needed to do something to diminish the way his eyes on her made her feel. As if this was more than a charade. As if she wanted to fling caution to the wind. Which was so *not* what she should be doing.

His dark gaze trailed lazily over her face. Read the emotions coursing through her as he always seemed to do. "I am," he drawled, "worried about the hair, however."

She produced a scarf from her evening bag. "I was warned." Draping it around her head, she secured the ends beneath her chin in Jackie O fashion before Lazzero handed her into the boat and brought the powerful speedboat rumbling to life. Soon, they were off, headed toward Villa Alighieri, which was perched at the end of a wooded promontory on the far end of the lake, accessible only by boat because the privacy-conscious Gianni liked it that way.

The sun threw up slender fingers of fire into a spectacular vermillion sky, the air was crisp and cool on her skin, the spray of the seawater as they sped across the lake salty, invigorating, life affirming in a way she couldn't describe. Or maybe, she thought, butterflies swooping through her stomach, that was just the way Lazzero made her feel—as if she'd woken up from a life of not really living.

When a particularly strong gust of wind caught her off guard, she swayed in her high heels. Lazzero caught her wrist in his fingers, tugged her to him and tucked her in front of him at the steering wheel. His mouth at her ear, he pointed out the sights, the husky edge to his voice raking across her nerve receptors, backed up by the hard press of his amazing thighs against hers. By the time he cut the throttle and they pulled up to the wide set of stone steps that led up to Villa Alighieri, Chiara was so caught up in him she couldn't see straight.

Lazzero threw the rope to one of the valets who stood waiting, then lifted her out of the boat and onto the steps, his hands remaining on her waist to steady her as her legs adjusted to solid ground. Drawn by the smoky heat in his eyes, she stared up at him, the muscles in her throat convulsing.

"Dammit, Chiara." He raked a gaze over her face. "You pick a hell of a time to go there, you know that?"

You don't pick *these things*, she thought unsteadily, sliding her hand into his as he led her up the path toward the cream stuccoed villa, which rose up out of the spectacular, terraced gardens.

"This is unbelievable," she murmured. *"Heaven."*

"Gianni named it after his favorite poet—Dante Alighieri—who wrote *The Divine Comedy.*"

Her lips curved. "My father loves *The Divine Comedy.*"

He'd been trying to get her to read it for forever. She thought it appealed to the philosopher in him.

He was quiet as they took the winding path through the gardens up to the loggia. But she knew how critical tonight was for him. Read it in the tense set of his face. Which meant she needed to be focused on the task at hand.

"Who's going to be here tonight?"

He threw her an absentminded look. "A few of the Italian players and their wives. A fairly intimate group from what I could gather."

Which it turned out to be. Mingling under the elegant loggia which offered a breathtaking view of the lake and the islands beyond from its perch on the highest point of the promontory, were perhaps a dozen guests.

Carolina and Gianni materialized to greet them. Lazzero slid a proprietary hand around her waist, but Carolina, it seemed, had elected to sheath her claws tonight. Which made it easier for Chiara to let down her guard as she met the Italian players and their wives and girlfriends, as well as Gianni's daughter from his first marriage, Amalia, a beautiful, sophisticated blonde.

The friendly rivalry between Lazzero and the Italian players inspired good-natured jokes and predictions about who would win the tournament, headed for an Americas, Western Europe collision in the final the following day. By the time they'd finished the cocktails, Chiara was relaxed and enjoying herself, finding Amalia, in particular, excellent company.

It was as they were about to sit down to dinner at the elegantly set table for twelve that Amalia's beautiful face lit up. *"Eccoti!"* she exclaimed, walking toward the house. *There you are.* "I thought maybe you were grounded by the bad weather."

Amalia's husband, Chiara assumed, who'd been in London on a business trip. She turned to greet him, a smile on her face. Felt her heart stop in her chest at the sight of the tall, dark-haired male brushing a kiss against Amalia's cheek, the jacket of his sand-colored suit tossed across his shoulder.

It could *not* be. *Not here. Not tonight.*

Amalia came back, her husband's hand caught in hers. "Antonio," she said happily, "please to meet you Lazzero Di Fiore, a member of the Americas team and a business associate of my father's, and his fiancée, Chiara Ferrante."

"Please *meet*." Antonio corrected her English, but his eyes never left Chiara. "*Mi dispiace.* I'm sorry I'm late. We were grounded for an hour."

"You're not late," Amalia said, wilting slightly at the correction. "We were just about to sit down to dinner."

"*Bene.*" Antonio held out a hand to Lazzero. "A pleasure," he drawled in perfectly accented English. "Congratulations on your engagement."

Chiara swayed on her feet. Lazzero tightened his arm around her waist, glancing down at her, but her eyes were glued to the man in front of her. His raven-dark hair, the lantern jaw she'd once loved, the piercing blue eyes that exuded an unmistakable power, an authority that was echoed in every line of his perfectly pressed, handcrafted suit. But it was his eyes that claimed her attention. They were the coldest she'd ever encountered.

How, she wondered, *had she never noticed that?*

Lazzero extended his hand to Antonio. Greeted the man who had once been her lover. Who had smashed her heart into so many pieces she'd wondered if she would ever be able to put herself back together again.

Panic pushed a hundred different flight routes through her head. What was she supposed to do? Admit she knew him? Deny it completely? The latter seemed preferable with his wife standing at his side. Antonio, however, didn't miss a beat. Focusing that cold, blue gaze on her, he bent to press a kiss to both of her cheeks. "Lazzero is clearly a lucky man," he murmured. "When is the big day?"

It was as if he'd asked her the exact date and time a meteor was going to hit the earth and blow them all to smithereens. Lazzero gave her a quizzical look. She swallowed hard and gathered her wits. "Next summer," she murmured. "So many people rush their engagements. We wanted to enjoy it."

"Indeed," agreed Antonio smoothly. "Marriage is a life-long commitment. A serious endeavor. Amalia and I did the same."

Oh, my God. A flare of fury lanced through her. He had not just said that. *A lifelong commitment. A serious endeavor. He* had been willing to break those vows before he'd even embarked on his marriage. He had *planned* on taking a mistress, without deigning to fill her in on the plan. And why? Amalia was beautiful, charming, funny, *with* the impeccable breeding Antonio required.

Gianni joined them, giving Antonio's arm a congenial squeeze. "A good introduction for you," he said to Lazzero. "The Fabrizio family is the largest stakeholder in Fiammata outside of the family. That's how Antonio and Amalia met. You should pick his brain over dinner. He can give you some excellent perspective on the company."

Lazzero nodded and said he would do exactly that. Chiara attempted to absorb the panic seeping through her like smoke infiltrating a burning building. Of course it made complete sense that Antonio owned a stake in Fiammata, she acknowledged numbly. He ran one of Europe's largest investment houses, with a slew of marquee clients across the globe.

Lazzero bent his head to hers as they waited to be seated at the elegant table under the loggia, his lips brushing her cheek in a featherlight caress. "What's wrong?"

"Nothing." She forced a smile past her pounding heart. "I think that cocktail might have gone to my head."

"You should watch the wine, then. It was a hot day."

She absorbed the concern in his ebony gaze. The *warmth*. It was like looking into a mirror of the man. She always knew exactly where she stood with Lazzero—good or bad—just as he'd promised from the beginning.

She did not turn down the excellent Pinot Grigio that was served with the appetizer, desperately needing the steadying edge it gave her nerves. Seated between Amalia and Lazzero, with Antonio directly opposite her and Gianni beside him, she attempted to regain her composure as the men talked business and Amalia chattered on. But it was almost impossible to concentrate.

Antonio kept staring at her, making only a cursory attempt at conversation. Which made her agitated and furious all at the same time. She took a deep sip of her wine. Steeled herself as she pulled her gaze away from his. She was going to do exactly what she'd told herself she would do in this situation. She was going to move past it like the piece of history it was. She was not going to let Antonio get to her and she was not going to let her disarray affect this evening for Lazzero.

Somehow, she made it through the leisurely seven-course meal that seemed to stretch for an eternity on a hot, sultry night in the Lakes, the wine flowing as freely as the delicious food, which Chiara could only manage a few bites of. By the time the *dolce* was served, and Gianni claimed Lazzero for a private conversation over a *digestivo* of grappa, she was ready to crawl out of her skin.

She chatted fashion with Amalia, who was quite the fashionista with the budget she had at her disposal. When Carolina claimed Amalia to speak with someone else, Chiara secured directions to the powder room at the bottom of the loggia stairs and retreated to repair her powder and gloss. A tension headache pounding like the stamp of a sewing machine in her head, she took her time, aware Gianni and Lazzero might be a while and unable to face the thought of yet more social chitchat.

When she could delay no longer, she headed back upstairs. Almost jumped out of her skin when Antonio cut her off at the bottom of the stairs.

"We need to talk," he said grimly.

A thread of unease tightened around her chest, then unraveled so fast her heart began to whirl. "No we don't. We were done the day I walked out of your penthouse. There's nothing to talk about."

He set his piercing blue gaze on her. "I disagree. We can either talk about it here or up there," he said, nodding toward the loggia and the sound of laughter and conversation.

She stared at him, sure he was bluffing. But just unsure enough she couldn't risk it. Nodding her head, she followed him to a viewing spot near the water that sat under the shade of an enormous plane tree, cut in the shape of a chandelier.

He leaned back against the tree. "You look different. You've cut your hair."

Chiara tipped her chin up. "It was time for a change."

He eyed her, as if assessing the temperature in the air. "You don't love him, Chiara. You don't go from being madly in love with me to madly in love with another man in the space of a few months."

"It's been six months," she said quietly. "And I was never in love with you, Antonio." She knew that now when she compared her feelings for him to the ones she had for Lazzero. "I was *infatuated* with you. Bowled over by your good looks and charm. By the attention and care you lavished on me. I thought I meant something to you. When in reality, I never did."

He rubbed a hand over his jaw. Shook his head. "I *was*

in love with you, Chiara. I told you my marriage to Amalia was a political one. Why can't you get that through your head? Why do you keep pushing me away when we could have something?"

She shook her head, everything crystal clear now. "She is beautiful. Lovely, charming, funny. How can she not be enough for you?"

"Because she isn't you." He fixed his gaze on hers. "You are *alive*. You are fire and passion in bed. You do it for me like no other woman ever has, Chiara."

The blood drained from her face at the blunt confirmation of everything she'd known, but hadn't wanted to believe. "So I was good enough to warm your bed, but I wasn't good enough to stand at your side?"

"It wouldn't have worked," he said quietly. "You know that. I needed the match with Amalia. It works. But I hadn't given up on you. I thought you'd be over it by now. I was going to come see you next month in New York when I'm there."

"Save yourself the trouble." Her chin lifted as she slammed the door shut on that piece of her life with devastating finality. "I am in love with Lazzero, Antonio. I am marrying him. We are *over*."

"You don't mean that," he countered, his dark gaze flashing. "You're hurt. A ring on your finger isn't going to increase your value, Chiara. Not to a man like Di Fiore. You'll still be a possession to him. What's the difference if you're his or mine?"

It stung, as if he'd taken a hand to her face. "He is ten times the man you are," she said flatly, refusing to show him how much it hurt. "You can't even make the comparison. And you're wrong, I do care about him."

Which was scarily, undeniably true.

Frustration etched a stormy path across Antonio's handsome face. "What do you want me to do, Chiara? Walk away from Amalia? You know I can't do that."

Her heart tipped over and tumbled to her stomach. He actually *believed* she still wanted him after everything he'd done?

"I want you to leave me alone," she said harshly. "I want you to forget we ever existed."

"Chiara—"

She turned on her heel and walked away.

Lazzero emerged from his after-dinner chat with Gianni infuriated by the Italian's perpetual game of hard to get. Now that he and the Fiammata CEO were aligned when it came to the design sensibility of a potential Supersonic Volare line, Gianni had turned his focus to price and how much he expected to be compensated for Volare. Which was astronomical—far more than Lazzero had offered—and also utterly ridiculous for a single piece of intellectual property.

Firmly immersed in the black mood that had overtaken him, he sought out Chiara. When she wasn't in the group enjoying after-dinner drinks, he looked for her downstairs, concerned she wasn't well. He was about to give up, thinking they'd missed one another, when he found her in one of the viewing areas that overlooked the lake. With Antonio Fabrizio, who hadn't taken his eyes off her all dinner, a liberty he had been content to allow because Chiara was beautiful and he couldn't fault Fabrizio for thinking so.

Tempering his rather insanely possessive streak when it came to Chiara, he started toward the two of them, only to have Chiara turn on her heel and walk toward him, her face set in a look of determination.

"Whoa." He settled his hands on her waist as she nearly walked through him. She blinked and looked up. "Sorry," she muttered, an emotion he couldn't read flaring in her green eyes. "I didn't see you there."

He tipped her chin up with his fingers. "You okay? You look pale."

She nodded. Waved a hand toward Fabrizio, who was making his way up the stairs. "Antonio was just showing me his boat. The *Amalia*. It's quite something."

He studied the play of emotion in her eyes. "You sure?"

"Yes. I am tired though. Do you think we can leave soon?"

Her request mirrored his own desire to end the evening before he self-combusted. Setting a hand to her back, he guided her upstairs where they made a round of goodbyes and said thank you to the Casales.

It was dark on the boat trip back across the lake. This time, he spent the journey focusing on getting them safely back to shore rather than putting his hands on Chiara, doing the same on the stretch of highway back to Milan. She was quiet the whole way, perhaps suffering from the headache Amalia had given her aspirin for. Which worked for him, because he needed to get his antagonism with Gianni out of his system.

Curving a hand around her bare thigh, he focused on the road. Thought about how easy the silences were between them. How easy it was to be with *her*.

She was smart as he'd known, talented as he'd come to find out and compelling in a way he couldn't describe— the most fascinating mix of innocence, toughness and a fierce strength he loved. With more secrets hidden beneath those protective layers, he suspected, glancing over at her shadowed face in the dim light of the car. He shouldn't want to uncover them as much as he did, but the desire was undeniable.

When they arrived back to the Orientale forty-five minutes later, he threw his jacket over a chair and followed Chiara into the dressing room where she stood removing her jewelry. Their sexy moment on the boat infiltrating his head, he came to a halt behind her. Set his hands to her voluptuous hips, his mouth to her throat. "Head better?"

She nodded. Tipped her head back to give him better access, an instinctive response he liked. He pressed a kiss to the sensitive spot between her neck and shoulder. Registered the delicate shiver that went through her.

He should really go work. Crunch some numbers to try and make Gianni's preposterous demands make sense, but he'd been so hot for her from the moment they'd stepped off that boat tonight, he needed to have her. And maybe once he had, he could pry what was wrong out of her in bed. *Fix it.*

He pulled her back against him so she could feel his arousal pressed against her. Her heady gasp made him smile. With a sigh, she melted back into him, the bond between them undeniable. *Incomparable.*

He scraped his teeth across the pulse pounding at the base of her throat. Slid a hand inside the wrap front of her dress and curved it possessively around her breast. Her little moans as he stroked the silky button to an erect peak had him hard as titanium. Setting his hands on her thighs, he slid them up underneath the sleek material of her dress until he found the soft skin of her upper thighs.

"God," he murmured, his mouth against her throat. "You make me so hot for you, Chiara. Like no other woman has... I can't think when I'm around you."

She went stiff as a board. "What did you just say?"

He paused. Racked his brain, numbed with lust. "I said you make me hot for you. Like no other woman does. It's true. You do."

She pulled out of his arms and swung to face him so fast it made his head spin. Set a smoldering green gaze on his. "I am more than just an *object*, Lazzero."

He eyed her warrior pose, arms crossed over her chest, cheeks flushed with arousal. "Of course you are. You know I appreciate everything about you."

Her mouth set in an uncertain line. He swore and shoved his hands in his pockets which only increased his agony. His mother had perfected the hot and cold routine. He'd watched his father spin like a hamster on a wheel trying to keep up. He was *not* doing this tonight. No matter how much he wanted her.

He dug his fingers into the knot of his tie, stripped it off and tossed it on the armoire. "I need to work," he bit out. "Get some sleep. We can talk in the morning."

He saw the hurt flash through those beautiful eyes. Steeled himself against it as he turned on his heel and left. Which was the sane thing to do, because lust was one thing. Getting emotionally involved with her another thing entirely. Particularly when he had already gone way too far down that path.

Chiara paced the terrace, her thoughts funneling through her head fast and hard, like a tornado on rapid approach. Lazzero had requested honesty at the start of all of this. She should tell him. *But why?* her brain countered. Antonio wasn't anyone's business but her own. She'd made it clear it was over a long time ago. It was Antonio's problem if he couldn't accept it. It *was* history. What use would it be to dredge it up?

She kept pacing under the luminous hanging hook of a moon, a tight knot forming in her chest. She and Lazzero *had* something—a fledgling bond they were building she was afraid to break. She'd felt it on that boat tonight. She was falling for him and she thought he might feel something for her too. Unless she was reading him all wrong, she conceded, which she could be because she'd done it before.

Would he understand if she told him the truth about Antonio? Or would he judge her for being as naive as she'd undoubtedly been when it came to him?

There didn't seem to be a right answer. Lost in a circular

storm of confusion, she finally went inside, removed her makeup and stood under a long, hot shower in the steam room, hoping it would ease the tension in her body and provide clarity to the questions racing through her head. But she only felt worse as she dried herself off and put on her pajamas.

She had completely overreacted to what Lazzero had said. Had allowed her history with Antonio to rule her when Lazzero had proven every which way but Sunday how highly he thought of her. And here she was, ruining it all.

She curled up in the big, king-size bed in the shadow of the beautiful silver moon. But her heart hurt too much to sleep.

Lazzero went over his financials in the study. But no matter which way he spun the numbers, they simply didn't make sense. Which left him in an impossible position. Pay more for Volare than it was worth and put Supersonic's growth in jeopardy, or walk away from the deal and admit to the analysts who ruled his future he had been too hasty in his predictions for that rapid growth he'd promised, an admission—as Santo had stated so bluntly—they would crucify him for.

Neither of which he considered options. Which left his only choice to call Gianni's bluff and force him to make a deal. Which wasn't at all a sure bet given the competitors the Italian CEO had hinted he had waiting in the wings—a British sportswear giant the one that worried him the most.

Painted into a corner of his own making, he pushed to his feet, poured himself a glass of whiskey and carried it to the floor-to-ceiling windows that overlooked the city. Gianni he would solve. He was banking on the fact that there wasn't a company in America right now hotter than Supersonic. That the Fiammata CEO was so enamored of his dominant US market share, his offer would outshine the others.

Chiara, on the other hand, was a puzzle he couldn't seem to decipher. The scene they'd just acted out was a perfect demonstration of everything he'd spent his life avoiding. Exactly what happened when you got invested in someone. It got messy. *Complicated.*

Except, he conceded, taking a sip of the whiskey, Chiara was different. She wasn't a practiced manipulator like his mother had been, nor was she a drama queen like Carolina. She was honest and transparent—real in a way he'd never encountered. And something was wrong.

Sure, he might have needed to blow off some steam tonight, but she had never been an object to him. *Ever.* And she knew it. She had been just as into him on that boat tonight as he had been to her, her reaction to him in the dressing room way off.

He polished off the Scotch, battling his inner instincts as he did so. He should stay away. He knew it. But his inability to remain detached from Chiara was a habit he couldn't seem to break.

The bedroom was plunged into darkness when he walked in, the glow of the moon its only light, spilling through the windows and splashing onto the silk-covered bed. Chiara was curled up in it on her side of the mattress, but he could tell she wasn't sleeping from the rhythm of her breathing. Shucking all of his clothes except his boxers, he slid into bed.

Silence.

Sighing at the tension that stretched between them, he reached for her, curving an arm around her waist and pulling her into his warmth. *"Mi dispiace,"* he murmured, pressing a kiss against her shoulder. "I am in a filthy mood because of Gianni. He has me running in circles."

Chiara twisted in his arms to face him. Propped herself

up on her elbow. "No—" she said on a halting note, "—it was me. I let my baggage get the better of me. I'm sorry. It wasn't fair to you."

Dark hair angled across her face, skin bare of makeup, eyes glittering like twin emerald pools, she was impossible to resist. He ran a finger down her flushed cheek. "How about you tell me what happened earlier? Because I don't think that was about *us* and what we have here."

An emotion he couldn't read flickered through those beautiful eyes before she dropped back onto the pillow and fixed her gaze on the ceiling. "It's hard to explain."

"Try," he invited.

She waved a hand at him. "It's always been about the way I look. Ever since high school. While the girls were making fun of my clothes, the boys wanted me for what was underneath them, which only made the girls more vicious to me. I didn't know how to handle it, so I retreated. Which was fine, because mostly, I was at home with my father. But also because I didn't trust. I didn't believe anyone would want me for who I was, so it was easier that way.

"Then," she said, twisting a lock of her hair around her finger, "I finally met someone that I thought did. I opened myself up to him. Trusted him. Only to realize he had no intentions of letting me share his life. He only wanted me in his bed." She pursed her lips. "What you said tonight reminded me of him. Of something he said."

His heart turned over. He'd known that son of a bitch had done a number on her. He'd like to find him and take him apart piece by piece. But hadn't he objectified her too with his offer to come to Italy? With his suggestion he *gloss her up*? To make her fit into his world? Except he'd always seen more in Chiara than just her undeniably beautiful packaging. Had always known there *was* more to her if he could just manage to peel back those layers of hers. And he'd been right.

He caught her hand in his. Uncurled her tight fingers to lace them through his own. "You know I care about you," he said gruffly. Because he did and he wanted her to know that.

She nodded. Eyed him silently.

"What?"

"Gianni," she murmured. "You're letting him make you crazy, Lazzero. Why not develop the technology yourself if he's going to be like this?"

The far too perceptive question stirred the frustration lurking just beneath the surface. "Because I don't have the time," he said evenly, tempering his volatile edge. "Acquiring Volare means we can put the shoe into production immediately. Meet our steep growth trajectory."

"And if Gianni won't sell it to you? What do you do then?"

A muscle jumped in his jaw. "I'll cross that bridge when and if we come to it."

"Maybe," she suggested quietly, "if Gianni *doesn't* work out, it's time to get back to your roots. To make it about the passion again."

He arched a brow. "Who says the passion's missing?"

"I do." She shook her head. "I saw your face at Di Fiore's that night, Lazzero, when you talked about starting Supersonic. How you came alive when we were doing those sketches… You say you don't dream anymore, but you and Santo *had* a dream to make the best products out there for athletes. Because you *are* athletes. Because it's in your blood. *That* is what you should be doing. Not running circles around Gianni Casale."

"It's not that simple," he said curtly. "Dreams grow up. I run a multibillion-dollar business, Chiara. I've made promises to my shareholders I need to keep. This isn't about sitting down in the lab with my engineers playing house. It's about making my numbers."

Her chin lifted. "I'm not talking about playing house. I'm talking about following your passion, just as you've been pushing me to do." She waved a hand at him. "I've been thinking a lot about what you said this week. About what I want out of life. Sometimes dreams *are* too expensive to keep. And sometimes they're all you have."

And now she was threatening to blow up his brain. "I don't need a lecture right now," he said softly, past the shimmering red in his head. "I need some sleep. Tomorrow's a big day."

"Fine." She lay there staring at the ceiling.

He let out a pained sound. "What?"

"I just think if you dish it out, you should be able to take it."

His blood sizzled in his veins. "Oh, I can take it," he purred, eyes on her pajamas, which tonight, had big red kisses plastered across them. "But I'm trying to keep my hands off you at the moment. At *your* request."

Her white incisors bit into her lip, her eyes big as they rested on his. "I thought you wouldn't be in the mood now."

The vulnerable, hesitant look on her face hit him square in the solar plexus. "Baby," he murmured, "if there's a planet in this solar system where I wouldn't want you in that outfit, you're going to have to find it for me."

A river of color spread across her face, a smoky heat darkening her gaze. "Lazzero—" she breathed, her eyes on his.

He pushed a hand into the bed and brought himself down over her. Bracing himself on his palms and knees, he lowered his mouth to her ear. "Say it," he murmured, "and I will."

And so she did, whispering her request for him to make love to her in a husky voice that unearthed a whole new set of foreign emotions inside of him. Ones he had no idea how to verbalize. And then, because actions had always spoken louder than words and he wanted to show her what she did to him, *on every level*, he deified her instead.

Caging her sexy, amazing body with his, he moved his mouth over every centimeter of her satiny skin until her pajamas impeded his progress and he stripped those off too. Exploring every dip and curve, he trailed his mouth over the taut, trembling skin of her abdomen, found the delectable crease between hip and thigh.

Chiara sucked in a breath, fisted her hands in the bedspread. He could tell she loved it when he did this to her. It made her wild for him. But she was also at her most vulnerable—stripped open and exposed to him. And that was exactly the way he wanted her right now. He wanted to obliterate the distance she'd put between them earlier and put them back exactly where they belonged.

He spread her thighs with firm hands. Slid a palm beneath her bottom and lifted her up to him. Her delicate, musky scent made his head spin. He blew a heated breath over her most intimate flesh. Felt her thighs quiver. Heard the rush of air that left her lips. It set his blood on fire.

He explored her first with his mouth and then with his fingers, caressing every pleasure point with a reverent touch. Her tiny whimpers of pleasure, the clutch of her fingers in his hair, threatened to incinerate him.

"Look at me." His throaty voice dragged her out of the vortex, her eyes stormy and hazy as they focused on his. "When you are like this, stripped bare, Chiara, when you allow yourself to be *vulnerable*, you are insanely beautiful."

Her eyes darkened. Drifted shut. He spread her wider with his hands. Feasted on her, devoured her until she was shaking beneath him. He had meant to dismantle her. Instead he dismantled himself as he mercilessly ended it with the hard pull of his mouth on the most sensitive part of her. It tore a cry from her throat, her broken release reverberating through him.

His skin on fire, his heart pounding in his chest, he crawled up her sated, limp body, clasped her arms above her head and, his hands locked with hers, took her in a slow, sweet possession that lasted forever.

Something locked into place as he watched her shatter alongside him. A piece of him he'd never accessed before. A piece of himself he hadn't known existed. He thought it might be the point of no return.

She fell asleep in his arms, her dark lashes fanning her cheeks. He held her, his breath ruffling the silky hair that slid across her cheek. But sleep eluded him, what she'd said about Gianni turning through his head. Maybe because he thought there might be a grain of truth in what she'd said. That he *had* lost his passion somewhere along the way and it had become all about the business. That all he *knew* was how to keep on pushing, because what would he find if he stopped?

CHAPTER TEN

WITH A HEART-STOPPING Americas team win—the first ever for the squad—in the history books at La Coppa Estiva that afternoon, Chiara dressed for the closing party amidst a buoyant air of celebration. To be held at one of the swishest hotels in the city, it was pegged to be the bash of the year.

Smoothing her palms over her hips, she surveyed her appearance in the black oak mirror in the dressing room at the Orientale. She'd spent far too long choosing her dress, vacillating between the two choices Micaela had given her until she'd finally settled on a round-necked, sleeveless cream sheath that showed off the olive tone of her skin and made the most of her figure.

She thought Lazzero would appreciate the sexy slit that came to midthigh. Which was going to be the *last* time she allowed herself to think like that, because tomorrow it was back to reality. Back to their respective lives. And maybe, if everything worked out with Bianca, exciting new possibilities for her. Hoping for more with Lazzero, when she knew his capabilities, would be a fool's errand. Asking for a broken heart.

Except, she conceded, her heart sinking, it might already be too late. That somewhere along the way, the charade had faded and reality had ensued and this relationship had morphed into something exciting and real and she *didn't* want it to end.

If her head told her it was impossible to fall in love with someone so quickly, her heart told her otherwise.

As if she'd summoned him with her thoughts, Lazzero blew into the dressing area, a towel wrapped around his hips, a frown marring his brow. Clearly used to maximizing every minute of the day, he went straight for the wardrobe.

Her eyes moved over his shoulders and biceps bulging with thick muscle, down over abs that looked as if they'd been carved out of rock, to the mouthwatering, V-shaped indentation that disappeared beneath the towel. He was the hottest man she'd ever encountered. Being with him had been the most breathtakingly exciting experience of her life. But he was so much more than that, the glimpses he'd given her into the man that he was making her want *more* of him, not less.

He shot her a distracted glance. "Do you have any idea where Edmondo put the shirt to my tux?"

"In the far closet," she said huskily. "Closest to the door."

He stalked over to the closet. Snared the shirt off the hanger. "*Perfetto*. Now if I can just find my bow tie, we're in business."

She pointed to a drawer. He bent and rustled through it, straightening with the black tie in his hand, a victorious look on his face. "Amazing. How did I ever do this without you?"

She couldn't actually answer that because he'd been serious all day. Too serious, avoiding any kind of personal interaction after that amazing night they'd shared. Except when she'd literally forced him onto the bed to ice his knee after he'd limped away from today's brutally physical match. His eyes had turned to flame then, a suggestion she could ease his pain in another way entirely rolling off his tongue. To which she'd replied they had no time.

And now he was back to serious. As if maybe he'd rethought everything, decided she'd been exactly the kind of high-maintenance female he avoided like the plague last night and it was best to dump her before they got back to New York.

She couldn't read him *at all*. It was making her a little crazy.

Lazzero shifted his distracted survey to her. "You okay?"

She nodded.

"Bene." A smile creased his cheeks. "You look incredible. I'll be ready in five."

The crowds were thick outside the Bvlgari Hotel, located in a renovated, eighteenth-century Milanese palazzo just around the corner from the Orientale. There was that same intimidating red carpet to walk, that same unnerving need to be *on*, but tonight Chiara was too distracted to pay it much heed, relying on the hand Lazzero had resting on the curve of her back to guide her through the throngs of guests and hangers-on.

The party was in full swing in the meticulously land-scaped gardens where trees and hedges created a series of open-air rooms. Lit in La Coppa Estiva blue, the buoyant crowd was buzzing under the influence of one of Italy's most famous DJs, a celebratory atmosphere in the air. Soon, she and Lazzero were caught up in it, acquiring glasses of the champagne that was flowing like water while they made the rounds.

The only minor ripple in the celebration was the appear-ance of Antonio as he worked the party with his interna-tional contacts, minus Amalia who had come down with a cold. Chiara blew off his attempt to talk to her when La-zzero was waylaid by Carolina and one of the other orga-nizers, and determinedly ignored him from that point on.

Pia, accompanied by a surly Valentino, who'd been a part of the losing team, soon came up to whisk her off to the dance floor.

"I need you," Pia said. "He's making me crazy."

Chiara smiled. Looked up at Lazzero. "Okay?"

"Yes," he drawled, subjecting her to one of those looks that could strip the paint from a car. "But don't go far. I need to be able to look at you in that dress."

A flush stained her skin as he bent to brush a kiss against her cheek. *"Go."*

She frowned as he straightened, visibly favoring his left leg. "You should stay off that knee."

"And how," he murmured, dropping his mouth to her ear, "will I get you to play nursemaid if I do?"

"You don't need a nursemaid," she said saucily. "You need to be able to walk tomorrow."

Lazzero watched as Chiara turned on her heel and followed Pia into the crowd. He couldn't take his eyes off her in that dress. The sleek design molded her fabulous figure like a glove and the slit that left an expanse of silky skin bare every time she moved was an invitation to sin.

His head fully immersed in the woman who had just walked away from him, it took him a moment to realize Santo had materialized at his side, sharp in black Armani.

"Sorry?" he said on a distracted note. "What did you say?"

"I said, 'Well if it isn't the man of the hour...'" Santo clapped him on the back. "That was a genius of a final play, *fratello.* Aren't you glad you played?"

Lazzero muttered something in the affirmative. Santo eyed him, a glitter in his eyes. *"Dannazione."*

"What?"

"The dark knight has fallen."

"What the hell are you talking about?"

"Her." Santo nodded at Chiara's retreating figure. "Your barista. You are ten feet under. *Fully brewed.* In case you hadn't noticed."

He had. He just had no idea what the hell to do about it. He'd been thinking about it all night. He should let Chiara walk away. Call it a scorching-hot affair done right. Nobody gets hurt. Everybody wins. *His specialty.* Because Chiara didn't play by the same rules as him. And maybe that was the real reason he'd stayed away from her as long as he had.

And then he'd invited her to come to Italy with him. Had kissed her, made love to her and crossed every line in the book. Which left him exactly where?

"I need a drink," he said flatly.

"A celebratory drink," Santo agreed.

Ensconcing themselves at the bar, they exchanged their fruity glasses of champagne for an excellent measure of off-list smoky bourbon as they recapped the game in glorified detail.

It hit him like a knife edge how much he'd missed the adrenaline that had once been his lifeblood. The *buzz* that came from being on the firing line in a pivotal match.

Competition was in his blood—it was what he thrived on. The *purpose* that had once fueled his days, because if he'd been on the court nothing else had mattered.

Building Supersonic had fulfilled that competitive edge. The need to *conquer.* But somewhere along the way the rush had faded. Carrying the weight of a team, of a school, on his back might rival the necessity to keep ten thousand people in a job, but his soul wasn't in it the way it had once been. Chiara had been right about that.

He watched her on the dance floor with Pia. Wondered what it was about her he couldn't resist. She was beautiful, yes. But he'd dated scores of beautiful women. Chiara was *real* in a way he'd never encountered before. She challenged him, made him think. He was *better* when he was with her. Happy even, a descriptor he would never have used with himself.

If the truth be known, he went into that damn café every

morning because he wanted to see her. Because he didn't feel half-alive when he was around her. And the thought of them going back to the status quo with Chiara serving him an espresso in the morning with one of those cool, controlled expressions on her face made him a little nuts. But what, exactly, did he have to offer her?

She deserved someone who would be there for her. An *Alfredo*. Someone who would offer her that true love she was looking for. Someone who would be that solid force she needed to shine. Who would prove to her she would always be *enough*.

Which was not him. He had never been *that guy*. So why the hell did he want to be so badly?

When he couldn't help himself any longer, he left his brother to the devices of a beautiful redhead and sought Chiara out on the dance floor.

Chiara tipped her head back to look up at Lazzero as they danced, her pulse racing at the banked heat in his gaze. He'd been staring at her the whole time she'd been on the dance floor with Pia, his desire for her undeniable. But maybe, she acknowledged, a hand fisting her chest, that was all it was.

He slid a hand to her hip in a possessive hold. Tugged her closer. "Do you know what I was thinking the opening night when I was holding you like this?"

"What?"

"That I wanted to ditch the party and have you until the sun came up." His gaze darkened. "I am crazy about you, Chiara. You know that I am."

Her heart missed a beat. She'd been so scared she'd been imagining it. Building it up in her head like she'd done before. Getting it all wrong. "You don't want to end this when we get back to New York?"

He shook his head. "I think we should see each other

back in New York. See where this goes. If," he qualified quietly, "you want that too."

She sank her teeth into her lip. "What do you mean, 'see where this goes'?"

"I mean exactly that. We explore what we have. See where it takes us." He shook his head. "I'm not good at this, Chiara. I could mess it up. But I don't want to lose you. *That*, I know."

Her knees went weak. He wasn't making any promises. She could end up with her heart broken all over again. Was likely setting herself up for it. But everything she'd learned about Lazzero made her think he was worth it. That if she was patient, she might be able to breach those tightly held defenses of his. That maybe she could be *the one*.

A whisper of fear fluttered through her belly at the thought of making herself that vulnerable again. Because Lazzero, she knew, could annihilate her far worse than Antonio had ever done. But the chance to have him, to *be* with him, to hold on to that solid force he'd become for her, was far too tempting to resist.

She stood on tiptoe and kissed him by way of response. A long, slow shimmer of a connection, it was perfection. But soon it grew hungrier, *needier*, the flames between them igniting.

Lazzero enclosed the nape of her neck with his hand and took the kiss deeper, delving into her mouth in a hot, languid joining that stole her breath. She settled her palms on his chest. Grabbed a handful of his shirt. Every hot breath, every stroke, every lick, sensual, earthy, built the flames higher.

Tracing a path across her jaw and down to the hollow of her throat, Lazzero pressed an openmouthed kiss to her pulse. It was racing like a jackhammer. He flicked his tongue across the frantic beat, shifted his hands lower to shape her against his hard male contours. A gasp slipped from her lips.

He pulled back. Surveyed her kiss-swollen mouth. "I think this time we *are* leaving," he murmured. "The song's over, *caro*. Go get your things."

Lazzero propped himself up against the bar while Chiara collected her wrap, a supreme feeling of satisfaction settling over him. He was strategizing on all the different ways he would take her apart until she begged for him, when Antonio Fabrizio slid into place beside him at the bar and ordered a Scotch. Turning to face the Italian, he reluctantly switched back into networking mode.

"Enjoying yourself?" he murmured lazily.

"Sì." Fabrizio reclined his lanky frame against the bar, his gaze on Chiara's retreating figure. "Beautiful, isn't she? The most beautiful woman in the room, no doubt."

Lazzero stood up straighter. "I think so," he agreed evenly. "But then again, she's my fiancée, so I would."

"Still," the Italian drawled, "a man would be hard-pressed to resist."

And now he'd had it. Lazzero's blood sizzled, the amount of bourbon warming his blood doing little to leash his temper. He'd been okay with the man admiring Chiara last night, but really, enough was enough. Given, however, Gianni had let it slip that the Fabrizio investment house was one of Fiammata's largest stakeholders, he needed to keep it civil.

"Luckily," he said icily, "I don't have to." He waved a hand at the other man. "I have a suggestion, Fabrizio. You have a beautiful wife. Perhaps you should go home and lavish some attention on her."

The Italian lifted a shoulder. "Amalia is a political match. Unexciting in bed. Chiara, on the other hand, is not."

Lazzero froze. *"Scusi?"*

Fabrizio set a cold, blue gaze on him. "You didn't know? She was mine before she was yours, Di Fiore. Or didn't she tell you that?"

He was lying, was his first thought. But he had no reason to lie. Which meant he was the one in the dark here.

"When?" he grated.

Fabrizio shrugged. "It ended before Christmas. I was engaged to Amalia. Chiara didn't like playing, what do you Americans call it…*second fiddle* to my fiancée, so she broke it off. Gave me an ultimatum—it was Amalia or her." The Italian tipped his glass at Lazzero. "As far as her being in love with you? Highly unlikely given she made a habit of telling me she was in love with me every morning before I left for work."

Lazzero's head snapped back. Fabrizio was telling him he'd had an affair with Chiara months ago? A man she'd calmly pretended she'd never met last night when they'd been introduced. An *engaged man*.

Except she hadn't been calm, he recalled. She'd been off from the moment Antonio Fabrizio had shown up at that party. Had blown off his concern for her as a case of fatigue. His brain putting two and two together, he rocked back on his heels. Fabrizio was the man who'd broken her heart?

A dangerous red settled over his vision. He had just poured out his feelings to her. Had just told her he was crazy about her. And she had lied to his face. Did he even *know* her?

"I get it," Fabrizio murmured. "She's *insano* in bed. Almost worth putting a four-carat ring on her finger."

It was the "almost worth it" that did it. Lazzero had Fabrizio by the collar of his bespoke suit before he knew what he was doing. Blind fury driving him, he balled his hand into a fist and sent it flying toward the Italian's face. Anticipating the supreme satisfaction of watching it connect with that arrogant, square jaw, he found his hand manacled just short of its destination.

"What the hell are you doing?" Santo said, wrapping an arm around him and hauling him backward. "Have you lost your mind?"

Fabrizio straightened the lapel of his suit as a shocked crowd looked on. Picked up his Scotch and shifted away from the bar, his eyes on Lazzero. "By the way," he drawled. "I nudged Gianni in the direction of the British deal. It has a more global scope."

His parting volley hanging in the air, the Italian sauntered off into the crowd. Enraged, Lazzero pulled at Santo's grip to follow him, but his brother held him back. Directed a furious look at Lazzero. "What the hell is wrong with you? He's a key stakeholder in Fiammata, for God's sake."

Lazzero shrugged him off. Raked a hand through his hair. "He's an arrogant bastard."

"So you decided to *hit* him?"

A frisson of fury lanced through him. "No," he bit out. "That was for something else."

"Well, whatever it is, you need to get it together. Everything hinges on this deal, Laz. Or have you forgotten?"

Lazzero's mouth thinned. "He baited me."

"Which appears to be your Achilles' heel," his brother observed. "Perhaps food for thought as you do some damage control here."

Chiara claimed her wrap, practically floating on air. A sharp bite of anticipation nipped at her skin as she made her way back through the crowd to where Lazzero was waiting for her at the bar.

Her progress painfully slow, she looked up to catch his eye. Noted he was deep in conversation. The tall, dark male he was talking to shifted to pick up his drink. *Antonio*, she registered. Which would have been fine. A social chat perhaps. *Business.* Except for the expression on Lazzero's face.

Oh, my God.

Heart pounding, she quickened her pace, desperate to intervene. But the crowd was too tightly packed, her high heels allowing her to move only so fast. By the time she made it to the bar, Santo was hauling Lazzero away from Antonio after some type of an altercation. Antonio, who looked utterly unruffled, straightened his suit, said something to Lazzero, then melted off into the crowd.

She came to a sliding halt in front of the two brothers. Santo said something to Lazzero, a heated look on his face, then stalked off. He looked just as furious as his brother. *Or maybe not.* Lazzero looked *livid.*

"What happened?" she breathed.

Lazzero's face was a wall of concrete. "We are not talking about it here."

She didn't argue because the rage coming off him in waves was making her knees weak. Clutching her purse to her side, she practically ran to keep up with his long strides as they found Carolina and the other organizers of the party, thanked them, then walked the couple of blocks back to their hotel.

When they entered their suite, Lazzero peeled off his jacket and threw it on a chair. Whipping off his bow tie, he tossed it on top of his jacket and walked to the bar to pour himself a drink. Carrying the glass to the windows, he stood looking out at a shimmering view of a night-lit Milan.

Chiara kicked off her heels and threw her wrap on a chair. Her throat too tight to get words past it, her brain rifled through the possible scenarios of what had just happened. Which were too varied and scary to consider, so she stood, arms hugged around herself, and waited for Lazzero to speak. Which he finally did.

"Why didn't you tell me about Fabrizio?"

She blanched. Felt the world fall away from beneath her feet. "I didn't think it was anyone's business but my own," she said, managing to find her voice as he turned to face her. "Antonio and I were over months ago. It was history to me. I didn't see the point in bringing it up."

"You didn't see the point?" His voice was so quiet, so cold, it sent a chill through her. "Because you had an affair with a man who *belonged to someone else*?"

The blood drained from her face. "I didn't have an affair with him. I didn't know he was engaged, Lazzero. He lied to me. I told you what happened last night."

"You didn't tell me it was *Antonio Fabrizio*!" He yelled the words at her with such force she took a stumbling step backward. "Fabrizio is one of Fiammata's largest stakeholders, Chiara. There are three, equally strong deals on the table for Volare. That son of a bitch told Gianni to take the British offer over ours."

Oh, good God, no. The blood froze in her veins. She had known Antonio was angry. That he wasn't one to concede defeat. But she'd been so sure the fact that she was engaged to Lazzero would have driven the point home that she was unavailable. Which, she admitted numbly, had been a gross miscalculation on her part.

"I'm so sorry," she said dazedly, sinking down on the arm of the sofa. "I can't believe he did this."

His gaze glittered like hard, polished ebony. "What were you two talking about by the lake, then? If it's *over*?"

She sank her teeth into her lip. "It's complicated."

"Enlighten me," he growled.

She pressed her palms to her cheeks. Dropped her hands to her sides. "I met Antonio at a party last summer in Chelsea. It was a sophisticated crowd—I was completely out of my league. Worried about my father. You know what it's been like. Antonio—he pursued me relentlessly. He wouldn't give up. He swept me off my feet, made all sorts of promises and within weeks we were living together.

"I thought we had something. That he loved me. Until one morning when I was leaving the penthouse for work, I bumped into his mother. She'd come to surprise Antonio for his birthday—to do some Christmas shopping. She told me Antonio had a fiancée in Milan. That I was just his American plaything."

Her stomach curled at the memory. "I was crushed. *Devastated*. I gave Antonio his key back that night and told him I never wanted to see him again. He was furious. Refused to take no for an answer. He kept sending me flowers, theater tickets, jewelry. Kept calling me. I sent it all back, told him I wanted nothing to do with him. Finally, a couple of months ago, he stopped calling."

Lazzero watched her with a hooded gaze. "And last night?"

"Antonio followed me when I went to the washroom. He said he hadn't given up on me. That he thought I'd be over Amalia by now and he was going to come and see me in New York the next time he was in town."

"Because he wants you back."

A statement, not a question. One she couldn't refute, even with the recrimination written across Lazzero's face. "Yes," she admitted. "He wants me to be his mistress. He asked me what I wanted—if I wanted him to leave Amalia, because he couldn't. I told him I was engaged to you. That I loved you. That I wanted you to forget we ever existed, because I want nothing to do with him."

"He *said* you disliked playing second fiddle to Amalia. That you, in effect, had given him an ultimatum—it was her or you."

Her breath left her in a rush. "That's a lie," she rasped. "He is on a seek and destroy mission. If he can't have me, no one will."

"Why bother?" Lazzero murmured. "I get that all men love you, Chiara, but Fabrizio is a powerful man. He could have any woman he wants."

Her stomach curled at the insinuation she wasn't worth pursuing. That she had somehow *invited* Antonio's attention last night. That she was in some way responsible for what had happened.

"Antonio is entitled," she said quietly, fingers clenching at her sides. "He *does* think he can have anything he wants. I think you forget you're the one who walked into the café and threw that insane amount of money at me to come with you, Lazzero. You're the one who wouldn't take no for an answer. *I* never wanted to be any part of this world."

"Because he is here."

"Yes," she snapped back at the look of condemnation in his eyes, "because he is here. I put him out of my life, Lazzero. I had no idea he was married to Amalia. I was in complete shock last night at the dinner party. But never once did I give him any encouragement that there might still be something between us. You know how I feel about you."

"I don't *know* anything," he lanced back. "I have no idea what the hell to believe, because you lied to my face, Chiara." He pointed the Scotch at her. "I gave you every opportunity to tell me what was wrong last night. Every opportunity you needed. And you told me you were tired. That *nothing* was wrong."

Her stomach dropped, like a book toppling off a high shelf. She should have told him. She had known he had trust issues. Had known he'd let down his walls for her. Had known she'd been playing with fire by not telling him. And still, she had done it.

"I was afraid to lose you," she admitted softly. "Afraid you wouldn't understand."

A choked-off sound of disbelief ripped itself from his throat. "So you did the one thing guaranteed to make that happen? *Maledizione*, Chiara. You know my history on this. I thought we *had* something here. I thought we were building something together. I thought we were different."

"We are," she blurted out, her heart in her mouth. "I'm falling for you, Lazzero. You know that."

"How would you even know *who* you're in love with?" He waved a hand at her. "A few months ago it was him. Now it's me. Do you just turn it on and off at will? Like a tap?"

Her stomach contracted at the low blow. At the closed-off look on his face, getting colder by the minute. "I was never in love with him," she said evenly, her chin lifting. "I *thought* I was. How I feel for you is completely different."

He shrugged that off. "Trust was the one thing that was nonnegotiable in this. You knew that."

"Lazzero," she said huskily, "it was an error in judgment. *One* mistake."

"Which could bury me." He raked a hand through his hair. Eyed her. "Is there anything else I should know? Any other powerful men you have slept with who can annihilate my future?"

Her breath caught in her throat. "You did *not* just say that."

He pushed away from the bar and headed for the study. "I need to go research the competition. See if I can salvage this."

The finality of it, the judgment written across his face said it all. Whatever she said, it wasn't going to be enough.

"Why did you try and hit him?" She tossed the question after him because she had to know.

He turned around, mouth twisting. "He suggested you were *almost* worth a four-carat ring. I was defending your honor, fool that I am."

CHAPTER ELEVEN

CHIARA DIDN'T SLEEP. She lay awake all night in the gorgeous four-poster bed, numb, *frozen*, as she waited for Lazzero to join her. But he never did, pulling one of his all-nighters in an attempt to salvage the deal. And what, she conceded miserably, staring up at the beautiful crystal chandelier, would she have even said to him if he had?

She *should* have told him about Antonio. She could never have predicted what Antonio had done—was still in utter shock that he'd done it. But she had known about Lazzero's trust issues. And instead of believing in what they had, in what they were building together, she'd reverted back to her old ways. Had allowed her insecurities to rule. And in doing so, she'd destroyed everything.

Sleepless and bleary-eyed, she boarded the jet for their flight home to New York the following afternoon. Lazzero devoted the entire journey to his effort to discredit his British competition, which left such a sick feeling in her stomach, she hadn't slept there, either.

If she hadn't known it was over the night before, she knew it was when Lazzero bid her a curt farewell on the tarmac, he and Santo en route to a sports fund-raiser, not one speck of that warmth he usually reserved for her in his gorgeous, dark eyes. She gave him back the ring, unable to bear wearing it a moment longer, only to have Lazzero wave his hand at her and tell her to keep it. *He couldn't take it back and she needed the money.*

It had been all she could do not to throw it at him. She told him instead that she couldn't be bought, that she'd never been for sale and shoved the ring in his hand. Then she'd allowed Gareth, whom Lazzero had handed her off to, to shepherd her into the Bentley for the drive home.

Her carpe diem moment seemed foolish as the car slid smoothly off into the night. She had told herself it was a mistake to accept Lazzero's offer. To allow herself to fall for him. Then she'd gone ahead and done it anyway and fool that she'd been, she'd started to buy into the fairy tale. Of what she and Lazzero could be.

Her chest throbbed in a tight, hot ache as the headlights from the other cars slid across her face. She'd opened herself up exactly as Lazzero had challenged her to—had shown him who she truly was—had taken that leap—only to have him walk away as if what they'd shared had meant nothing. As if *she* wasn't worth the effort. Which might hurt the most of all.

The sun was sinking in a giant, red-orange ball when she arrived at her apartment in Spanish Harlem, bidding the city a sultry, crimson adieu. Gareth, a gentleman to the end, helped her up the three sets of stairs to her door and made sure she was safely inside before he melted back into the sunset like the former special agent he likely was.

The apartment was hot and stuffy, empty with Kat working the closing shift. She dumped her suitcase in the living room, too exhausted to even think about unpacking, because then she would have to look at all those beautiful clothes and the memories that came with them. About the man who'd just walked away from her without a backward glance.

She called her father instead as she made a cup of herbal tea, anxious to talk to him after a week of trading messages. Only to find him bubbling over with the news of a visit by the Five Boroughs Angel Foundation the previous afternoon, in which Ferrante's had been the recipient of an angel investment that would cover the bakery's rent for the remainder of the year.

He'd been so happy and relieved, he'd gone over to Frankie DeLucca's to celebrate. It was almost enough to peel away a layer of her misery as she signed off and promised to see her father the following evening.

She carried the tea into the living room, intent on numbing her brain with one of her dancing shows. But the stiflingly hot room felt like a shoebox after the palatial suite at the Orientale, the sound from her downstairs neighbor's TV was its usual intolerably loud level and the window box air conditioner refused to work.

As if nothing has changed. Except everything had. And maybe that's why her chest felt so tight. Because she'd gone to Italy as one person and come back another. Because of Lazzero.

The tears came then, like hot, silent bandits slipping down her cheeks. And once they started, they wouldn't seem to stop. Which was ridiculous, really, because, in the end, what had Lazzero been offering her? The same no-strings-attached arrangement as Antonio had? A few more weeks of being starry-eyed while she fell harder for a man who had a questionable ability to commit?

She staggered to bed, flattened by jetlag. Rose the next morning with a renewed sense of determination. She was tougher than this. She wasn't going to let Lazzero Di Fiore crush her. She was going to go to this coffee with Bianca and *crush it.* Because if there was one thing Lazzero had taught her, it was that she couldn't depend on anyone else to make her dream happen. That had to come from her.

She met Bianca at the Daily Grind before her shift began. A tall, Katharine Hepburn–like bombshell, Bianca was as tough as Lazzero had described, but also inspiring, brilliant and full of amazing ideas as they looked through her portfolio. When Bianca glanced at her bare left hand for what seemed like the fiftieth time, Chiara waved it in the air. "We broke up," she said shortly. "It was all my fault."

It was the same line she used with the girls at the café when Bianca disappeared out the door with a promise to get back to her with the committee's decision. When a week passed with no sign of Lazzero and his habitual order of a double espresso, her heart jumping every time the bell on the door rang, because maybe he would change his mind. Maybe he would apologize. But it never happened.

Eyes trained on his computer screen, Lazzero pulled the coffee that his PA, Enid, had just delivered within striking distance while he scanned the contents of the email he'd just gotten from Gianni. Only to discover the wily Italian had changed the rules of the game. *Again.*

His mind working a mile a minute at the implications of what the Fiammata CEO was proposing, he lifted the espresso to his lips and took a sip. Almost spit it out.

It was the final straw.

"Enid!" he bellowed, pushing to his feet and heading out to Reception, cup in hand. "What the hell is this?" He arched a brow at her. "Do we not have an espresso machine and do you not know how to use it?"

His exceedingly young, ultraefficient PA, who couldn't be more than twenty-five, gave him a wary look as if considering which angle with which to avoid this new threat. "We do," she agreed evenly, "and I do."

"Then maybe you can try again," he suggested, dumping the cup on her desk. "Because this is filth. *F.I.L.T.H.*"

Enid calmly got to her feet, scooped up the cup and headed toward the kitchen. Santo strolled out of his office, a football palmed between his hands. "Jet lag getting to you?" he asked pointedly.

"Gianni," Lazzero muttered. "He just got back to me."

Santo followed him into his office. "What did he say?"

"'After much consideration,' he's decided to split the global rights for Volare. Supersonic is to receive the North American license, Gladiator, the rest-of-world global rights. Provided we are agreeable with the price tag he has attached to the offer."

"Which is?"

Lazzero named the figure.

Santo blinked. "For the North American rights? That would stretch us."

More than stretch them. It would eliminate other growth opportunities he wanted to pursue. *Close doors.* On a bet that Volare would move heaven and earth for them.

He walked to the window. Looked out at a glittering Manhattan, the sun gilding the skyscrapers the palest shade of gold. If America was the land of opportunity, New York was the epitome of the American Dream. He'd seen it from both sides now—knew what it was like to live one step away from the street with a paralyzing fear as your guiding force and what it was like to have it all. How easily it could flip—in the blink of an eye—with one wrong move.

With one mistake.

He locked his jaw, ignoring the pain riding beneath his chest, because *they* were over and he was better off this way. But that didn't mean she hadn't made him think.

"We're not doing it." He turned around and leaned against the sill, his eyes on Santo. "We take the reputational hit. We tell the analysts it's going to take us a bit longer than we anticipated to make it to number two, and we do it ourselves. The way we do it best."

A wealth of emotion flickered through Santo's dark eyes. "There will be a storm. You know that."

He nodded. The investment community *would* crucify them for missing their targets for the first time in the company's history. There would be that analysis their star had risen too far, too fast. But he hadn't created this company to have it ruled by a bunch of number crunchers in their high-priced offices.

He lifted a shoulder. "We ride it out. We were bound to hit one someday."

Santo palmed the football in his hands. "Okay," he said finally, a rueful smile tilting his lips. "We do it ourselves. We go back to our roots. Tell Gianni to go to hell."

His blood buzzed in his veins. It felt *right* for the first time in forever.

Enid came in with the new espresso. Set it on Lazzero's desk and beat a hasty retreat. Santo eyed the coffee. "You going to do something about that?"

"About what?"

"Your barista."

Lazzero scowled. "What makes you think I need to?"

"Because I've never seen two people try *not* to look at each other as hard as you two did on the plane. Because she lights you up in a way I've never seen before. Because you haven't shaved in a week, you look terrible and you're hurting and you won't admit it." Santo crossed his arms over his chest and cocked a brow. "Have I covered it all?"

Quite possibly. Which didn't mean he wasn't still furious with her.

"You're crazy about her," his brother said quietly. "What's the problem?"

What wasn't? That she had violated the one code of honor he lived his life by, the trust he'd needed to convince himself they could be different. That he'd been *all in for her*, confessed his innermost thoughts and feelings to her when she hadn't shown him the same respect? Because it had felt like the most real thing he'd ever had, when in reality it had been as fake as every other relationship he'd known.

He pushed away from the sill and headed toward his desk. "It was never going to work. She was a temporary thing."

"Good to know," Santo said lazily. "Because I think she's amazing and if you don't go after her, I will." His brother gave a laconic shrug. "I'll give her some time to get over your jaded, broken heart, of course, but then I will."

Lazzero had to smother the urge to go for his brother's throat. He knew he was baiting him and still, the soft taunt twisted a knot in his gut.

He missed her. In the morning giving him sass from the espresso machine…when he walked into the penthouse at night, filling his empty spaces…and definitely, plastered across his bed sketching in those sexy pajamas of hers. But trust and transparency were essential to him.

Santo sauntered out of his office wearing a satisfied look, having stirred him up exactly as he'd known he would. He attempted to anesthetize himself with yet more work alongside the weak, tepid garbage Enid had produced yet again, but he couldn't seem to do it.

The first Monday after the Labor Day weekend was always madness at the Daily Grind. The students were back, relentless in their search of a caffeine injection as they juggled an unfamiliar, highly resented wake-up call, while the flashy-suited urban set struggled to get back to reality after a weekend spent in the Hamptons. And then, there was Sivi, currently having a meltdown over her broken romance with a Wall Street banker who'd ended things over the weekend. Chiara had fixed half a dozen of her messed-up orders already, which wasn't helping her ability to cope with the massive lineup spilling out the door.

"You know what I think?" Sivi announced, handing her

three cups marked with orders of questionable reliability. "*I* think Ted has been reading Samara Jones. I think he decided to dump me because the Athertons' pool party was on the weekend. I was just a *summer shag.* I looked good in a *bathing suit.*"

Kat snorted as she made change for a customer. "Men have been systematically dumping women in Manhattan for little to no reason since the beginning of time. The whole concept of a summer shag is ridiculous."

"Oh, it's a real thing," interjected a twentysomething-blonde regular in the lineup. "The event I held last week? Seventy-five percent of the men came with a plus one. My Fall Extravaganza in a couple of weeks? *Fifty percent.*"

"It's an epidemic," said her friend, a perky, blue-eyed brunette. "My roommate found her kiss-off gift in his underwear drawer over the weekend. She's trying to decide whether to stick around or not."

"At least she got a kiss-off gift," grumbled Sivi. "I loved him, I mean, I really *loved him,* you guys. The BlackBerry in bed? No problem. Football all Sunday? I did my nails. And the snoring? It was like the 6-train coming through the walls. But I excused it all for him because he was *just that good in bed.*"

Oh, my God. Chiara wanted to put her head in her hands, but she had two espressos and an Americano to make, and now a frowning customer was shoving her drink back across the counter. "This is *not* what I ordered. I ordered a *triple venti, half-sweet, nonfat caramel macchiato.*"

Chiara counted to five. Sivi waved a cup in the air. "Are there *any* men left in Manhattan who have serious intentions when it comes to a woman?"

"I do," intoned a husky, lightly accented voice. "Although I might have gone about it the wrong way."

Chiara's heart lurched. She looked up to find the owner of that sexy, familiar voice standing in the lineup, all eyes on him as he answered Sivi's question. Which might also have something to do with the way Lazzero looked. Dressed in a severely cut pinstripe suit, a snowy-white shirt and a dark tie, he was so sinfully good-looking, she could only clutch the cup in her hand and stare, her brain cells fried with the pleasure and pain of seeing him again.

She'd missed him. God, she'd missed him.

Memories of their last meeting bled through. She pulled in air through a chest so tight it hurt to breathe. Lowered her gaze and started remaking the macchiato with hands that shook, because he was not doing this. He was damn well not doing this right here and right now.

But, oh, yes, he was. "I am guilty," Lazzero said evenly, "of being *that guy.* Of callously discarding a woman without a second thought. Of believing a piece of jewelry could buy a weekend in the Hamptons. Of thinking my money could acquire anything I wanted."

The perky brunette drank him in from the tip of his sleek, dark head to his custom-made Italian shoes. "I can't say I would have said no."

"Until," Lazzero continued, his eyes on Chiara, "I met the one woman who was immune to it. Who convinced me that I was *wrong.* That I wanted more. And then I was scrambling," he admitted. "I tried every which way but Sunday to show her how different the man was beneath the suit. And then, when I finally did, I screwed it up."

Chiara's stomach swooped, skimming the shiny surface of the bronze, tiled floor. She set the cup down before she dumped espresso all over herself. Took in Lazzero, intensely private Lazzero, who was loath to talk about his feelings, talking to her as if there was no one else in the room. Except the entire front half of the lineup was watching them now and the café had gone strangely silent.

"We are over," she said quietly. "You made that very clear, Lazzero."

"It was a mistake." A stubborn strength underlaid his tone. "You need to give me another chance."

Like he had her? She dumped the misguided macchiato in the sink, her heart shattering all over again at how completely he'd taken her apart. "I don't *need* to do anything. I no longer make coffee on command for you, Lazzero. I no longer serve as your decorative piece on the side and I definitely don't have to forgive you so that I can once again become as expendable as one of your high-priced suits."

"I'm not interested in having you on a temporary basis," Lazzero said huskily, stepping over to the counter. "I'm interested in having you forever. I walked away from the deal, Chiara. Nothing is right without you."

She stared at him, stunned. *He'd walked away from the deal? Why would he do that?* She noted the dark shadows in his eyes then, the white lines bracketing his mouth, the dark stubble on his jaw. Not cool, collected Lazzero. Another version entirely.

"I'm in love with you, Chiara." He trained his gaze on hers. "Give me another chance."

"I don't know about you," said the brunette, "but he had me at the pinstriped suit."

"Yes, but it was necessary to make him grovel," said the blonde. "Not that we know what he did."

Chiara's heart was too busy melting into the floor at the naked emotion blazing in Lazzero's eyes to pay them much heed.

"And now that we have that decided," said a disgruntled-looking construction worker at the front of the line, "could we please have some coffee here? Some of us have to work for a living."

Chiara stared blankly at the drink orders in front of her. Kat waved a hand at her. "*Go.* You are clearly now useless, as well. Sivi—you're on the bar with Tara. And for heaven sakes, try and get it right."

Chiara had to run to keep up with Lazzero when he took her hand and dragged her out of the café and into the bright morning sunshine. Breathless, she leaned against the brick wall of the coffee shop and stared dazedly up at him. "Did you mean that? That you love me?"

"Yes," he said, setting a palm against the wall beside her. "Although the speech was not intentional. You have a way of provoking a completely irrational response in me."

Happiness bloomed inside of her, a dangerous, insidious warmth that threatened to envelop her completely. She bit her lip, held it in check. "What do you mean you walked away from the deal? Why would you do that?"

"Because you were right. Because somewhere along the way, I *had* lost my passion and I needed to get it back. It's what gets me out of bed in the morning. Or *in it* at night," he murmured, his eyes on her mouth. "Which has also been extremely empty. Too empty because I'd let the best thing that's ever happened to me walk out of my life."

The blaze of warmth in his eyes threatened to throw her completely off balance. She spread her palms against the warm brick wall and steeled herself against the desire to throw herself in his arms. "You hurt me with those things you said, Lazzero. Badly."

"I know." He traced the back of his knuckles across her cheek. "And, I'm sorry. If I had been in my right mind, I would have seen the truth. That Antonio had made a wrong decision in letting you go and was doing everything he could to get you back. Instead, I let him push all my buttons. I was blind with jealousy. I thought you might still love him, because he is clearly still in love with you. And I was angry," he allowed, "because I thought what we had was real."

"It *was* real. I should have trusted you, but you needed to trust me too, Lazzero. It goes both ways."

"Yes," he agreed, "but in the moment, that breach of

trust confirmed everything I thought I knew about relation-ships—that they are messy, complicated things better off avoided. Proved us as false as every other relationship in my life had been. That I was the fool, because there I was, letting a woman play with my head, exactly as my father had done time and time again."

Her stomach curled. "I wish I could take it all back," she whispered. "I hate that I let my insecurities get to me like that."

He shook his head. "I should have realized why you'd done what you'd done. I *did* after I cooled off. No man had ever proven to you he was deserving of your trust. *I* was still hedging my bets by offering you a no-strings-attached relationship when I knew how I felt about you."

"About that," she said, her heart swelling as she lifted her fingertips to trace the hard line of his jaw because she couldn't resist the need to touch him any longer, "how can you be in love with me when you called it a fantasy that doesn't really exist that night at the opera?"

"Because you challenge every belief I've ever had about myself and what I'm capable of," he said huskily. "I've been walking around half-alive for a long time, Chiara. Think-ing I was happy—telling myself I didn't need anyone. Until you walked into my life and showed me what I was miss-ing. In *every* aspect."

She melted into him then, unable to help herself, her fingers tangling in his hair to bring his head down to hers. "I love you," she murmured against his mouth.

Passionate, perfect, the kiss was so all consuming nei-ther of them noticed Claudio ambling past them into the café, a newspaper tucked under his arm. "Took you two long enough," he muttered. "I really don't get modern court-ship at all."

EPILOGUE

NICO DI FIORE MARRIED Chloe Russo in a simple, elegant ceremony at the majestic, storied St. Patrick's Cathedral on Christmas Eve in Manhattan. Dubbed one of the must-attend society events of the season, the nuptials drew guests from around the globe, including many of the famous personalities who represented the face of the Evolution brand.

Chloe, who had chosen the date because Christmas Eve had been her father's favorite night of the year, walked down the aisle in a showstopping, tulip-shaped, ivory Amsale gown which left an inspired Chiara dying for a sketchpad and pencil, dress designs dancing in her head.

The five hundred guests in attendance remarked on Chloe's serene, Grace Kelly–like beauty and timeless elegance. *A dark-haired version*, they qualified. Mireille, who preceded Chloe down the aisle in a bronze gown that matched the glittering metallic theme of the wedding, was her blonde equivalent.

Nico looked devastating in black Armani, as did his two groomsmen, Lazzero and Santo, whom Samara Jones cheekily underscored from her position in the gallery, had been on her summer must-have list. Humor, however, gave way to high emotion when Chloe began to cry the moment she reached Nico's side, overcome by the significance of the evening. Nico held her until she stopped, which hadn't left a dry eye in the house.

Then it was off to the magnificent Great Hall of the Metropolitan Museum of Art in Central Park for the lavish dinner reception and dance. With its immense domes, dramatic arches and marbled mosaic floor, it was suitably glamorous for the sophisticated crowd in attendance.

Chloe had wanted it to be a party, for the guests to dance the night away and celebrate. Which it surely was. As soon as dinner was over, the lights were dimmed to a sparkling gold, and the festivities began with the bride and groom's first dance to Etta James's "At Last," sung by LaShaunta, the famous pop star who fronted Chloe's wildly popular perfume Be.

Chiara found herself caught up in the romantic perfection of it all. With Lazzero consumed by his best man duties, she danced with partner after partner as the live band played. But all night long, she felt his gaze on her in the shimmering, sequined, off-the-shoulder dress she'd chosen especially for him, its glittering latte color somehow apropos.

Mireille, Chloe's sophisticated, irreverent sister she was growing to love, gave Chiara an amused glance after one such scorching look as they stood on the side of the dance floor, recovering with a glass of vintage champagne. "He's so crazy about you, he doesn't know which way is north and which way is south."

Chiara's heartbeat accelerated under the heat of that look. She knew the feeling. And it wasn't getting any more manageable, it was only getting worse, because Lazzero had been there for her every step of the way as she'd taken on the coveted incubator position with Bianca and worked to prove herself amidst so much amazing talent. Through her decision to go back to school. He'd come to mean so much to her, she couldn't actually articulate it in words.

"I never thought I'd see it," Mireille mused. "The Di Fiore brothers fall. Nico, I get. He was always the nurturer and he was always in love with Chloe. But Lazzero? I thought he was *untakeable*. Until I saw him with you."

So had she. Her gaze drifted to Santo, entertaining a bevvy of beauties on the far side of the dance floor. "What about Santo? Do you think he'll ever commit?"

A funny look crossed Mireille's face. "I don't know. There was a girl…a long time ago. Santo was madly in love with her. I think she broke his heart."

Chiara rested her champagne glass against her chin, intrigued. "Is there any chance they'll get back together?"

"I would say that's highly unlikely."

She was about to ask why when Mireille, clearly deciding she'd revealed too much, changed the subject. "Your dress is amazing. Is it one of yours?"

Chiara nodded.

"I need one for Evolution's Valentine's event." Mireille tipped her glass at her. "Would you make me something similar?"

"Of course." Chiara was beyond flattered. Mireille was a PR maven, one of the highest-profile socialite personalities in New York. *Everyone* noticed what she was wearing.

She was still bubbling over at the idea when Lazzero came to claim his dance, his official duties over for the evening. The champagne popped and sparkled in her veins as she tipped her head back to look up at him. "Mireille loves my dress. She asked me to make her one for Evolution's Valentine's event. Can you believe it?"

"Yes." He brushed his lips against her temple in a fleeting caress. "The dress is amazing, as are you. Speaking of which," he prompted, "when are you finishing up work at the bakery?"

"Next week. My aunt Gloria called me today to tell me she's retiring. She's going to take on my shifts at the bakery to give herself something to do, which is so perfect," she bubbled, "because my father adores her. It'll be so good for him. Oh," she added, "and the *jaw-dropping* news? My father is playing *briscola* at Frankie DeLucca's house on Friday nights. Can you believe it?"

Lazzero smiled. "Maybe you going to Italy was exactly what he needed."

"Yes," she agreed contemplatively, "I think it was."

She chattered on until it became clear Lazzero wasn't really listening to her, that absentminded look he'd been wearing all night painted across his face.

"Have you heard a word I've said?" she chastised.

"Yes." He shook his head at her reproving look. "No," he admitted. "I need some air," he said abruptly. "Do you need some air?"

She looked at him as if he was mad. It was December and her flimsy dress was not made for this weather. But she knew Lazzero well enough now to know that when he needed to talk, she needed to listen.

They collected their coats and walked hand in hand out into a winter wonderland, Central Park covered in a dusting of snow that made it look as if it had been dipped in icing sugar. It was magical, as if they had the park all to themselves. She was thinking it had been the *perfect* idea, when Lazzero tugged her to a halt in a pretty clearing flanked by snow-covered trees.

She tilted her head back to look up at him. But now he was holding both her hands in his, and she thought she could detect a slight tremor in them, and her heart started to hammer in her chest. "Lazzero," she breathed, closing her fingers tight around his. "What are you doing?"

He rested his forehead against hers for a moment, took a deep breath, then sank down to one knee. Her legs went so weak at the sight of him there, she thought she might join him.

He delved into the inside pocket of his dark suit. Pulled out his fist. Uncurled his fingers. Her breath caught in her chest as the moonlight revealed the magnificent asscher-cut diamond in his palm.

Her ring. The ring she'd dreamed about. The ring she wanted back. Desperately.

Her eyes brimmed with tears that spilled over and ran down her cheeks. A frown of uncertainty crossed Lazzero's face. "You like the ring, don't you? I've been going back and forth all week on it. I thought maybe I should buy you another, but I bought this one for you. Because it reminded me of you. Full of life, vibrant, *impossibly strong.*"

She stifled a sob. *He* made her feel strong. Impenetrable. Bulletproof. As if she could take on the world.

"I love the ring," she managed to choke as she shoved her hand at him. He slid the ring on, the heavy weight of it sliding a piece of her heart back into place.

His face smoothed out. "I'm no Alfredo," he said huskily. "But I want to have that once-in-a-lifetime love with you, Chiara. I want to be the guy who's always there for you. The one who never lets you down. *If* you will do me the honor of becoming my wife."

Her fingers tugged at the lapels of his coat. Rising to his feet, he collected her against him and kissed her until she was breathless. And then buttons on coats were a problem in their haste to get closer to each other. When that proved too frustrating an exercise, Lazzero swung her up into his arms and carried her out of the park.

"You're giving up your job at the café tomorrow," he commanded, lifting his hand to flag a taxi on Fifth Avenue.

"You just want me to make you coffee every morning," she accused, a massive smile on her face.

"Yes," he agreed, his face an arrogant canvas of satisfaction, "I do. But only if it comes with you."

* * * * *

BOUND TO HER
DESERT CAPTOR

MICHELLE CONDER

This is for Robyn,
who is always warm and welcoming no matter what.

Thanks for taking care of my dad.

CHAPTER ONE

'I'M SORRY, YOUR MAJESTY, but there has been no further information as to your sister's whereabouts.'

Jaeger al-Hadrid, King of Santara, nodded once then turned his back on his silver-haired senior aide. He stared out of the arched windows of his palace office on to the city of Aran below. It was early, the dawn sun bouncing off the Gulf of Ma'an and bathing the sleepy capital of Santara in a golden glow. The pale pink palace perched on the crest of a hill faced the once industrious port that had recently been transformed into a tourist mecca: hotels, restaurants and shopping outlets, tastefully designed to blend the old with the new. It was just one of Jaeger's successful attention-grabbing visions to boost the local economy and showcase the changing face of his kingdom.

He didn't see any of it right now, his mind locked down by the worry brought about by his sister's disappearance.

Where was she? And, more importantly, was she all right?

A week ago he had returned from a business trip to London to find a note on his desk.

Dear Jag,
I know you won't like this but I've taken off for a few weeks. I'm not going to tell you where I'm going be-

*cause this is important to me. That's why I haven't
taken my cell phone.*

*No doubt if I did you'd figure out where I'm going
before I even get there! But don't worry, I'll be fine.
I love you,
Milena xxx*

Don't worry? Don't worry? After what had happened
three years ago, how could he do anything but worry?

He reached for the note on his desk, now enclosed in
an evidence bag, and had to force himself not to crumple
it in his fist. So far the only thing his elite security team
had been able to find out was that she had taken a flight
to Athens and then disappeared with a man. A man who
had been identified as Chad James. An employee, no less,
whom Jaeger had personally allowed his sister to work
alongside for the past six months.

His jaw hardened and he had to force himself to breathe
deeply. Chad James was a brilliant graduate who had been
recruited from the States last year to work for his pet company, GeoTech Industries. The company only employed
high-energy, intelligent men and women who could think
outside the box to create leading-edge technologies that
rivalled anything coming out of Silicon Valley. A week
ago the young graduate had put in for one month's leave
without pay.

Had he coerced Milena into going with him for some
lovers' tryst? Or, worse, kidnapped her and planted the note,
planning to ask for a ransom any day now?

Jag cursed silently. Since becoming King a decade ago
he'd done his best to keep his siblings safe from harm. How
had he failed so extraordinarily in that endeavour? How had
he got it so spectacularly wrong? Again! Because it *was* his

fault. He'd put his sister in harm's way, even if he hadn't known it at the time, and he held himself *fully responsible*.

And it couldn't have come at a worse time.

For the past decade he had worked tirelessly to pull Santara out of the economic and political quagmire his father had inadvertently left it in, and, right when he was on the verge of having Santara recognised as an integral political powerhouse on the world stage, his sister went missing.

The worry was eating him alive.

'How is it possible,' he growled in Tarik's direction, 'that in this day and age no one can find out where she is?'

The elderly man Jag had known since his boyhood shook his head. 'Without her mobile phone or computer there's no way to track her,' Tarik answered, not telling him anything he didn't already know. 'We have accessed security footage in and around the ports of Piraeus, Rafina and Lavrio, as well as the local train stations, but so far we have come up empty-handed.'

A knock at the door cut off Jag's vicious string of curse words. His PA entered, and murmured something to Tarik before casting him a quick, sympathetic glance.

Jaeger's heart thumped into his throat. Please don't let his sister be in trouble.

Noticing his granite-like expression, Tarik shook his head. *No, not the Princess.*

Jag let out a rough breath. Only his tight inner circle knew that Milena was missing. Together they had mobilised a small taskforce of elite soldiers to hunt for her and Chad James, demanding absolute silence in the meantime. Jag hadn't even alerted his brother to Milena's disappearance and he didn't plan to until he had something concrete to give him. Nor had he alerted the Crown Prince of Toran whom Milena was due to marry in a month's time.

The last thing he needed was a scandal of this magnitude, a week out from hosting one of the most important international summits in Santara's history. Leaders from all over the globe would be descending on Santara for four days to discuss world matters including environmental affairs, world health issues, banking and trade deficits. It would be the largest summit of its kind; a pinnacle moment in Santara's rebirth, and his staff had worked tirelessly to see that it came off without a hitch.

'Tell me,' he demanded, noticing the slight hesitation on his aide's pale face.

'I have just been informed that Chad James's older sister landed in Santara an hour ago.'

Jag frowned. 'The sister he emailed the day before he disappeared?'

'I believe so. A report on her has been sent to your inbox.'

Jag sat down at his desk, touching the mouse pad on his computer to awaken the screen. Quickly he found the relevant email, scanned it, and opened the attachment. It was a dossier of sorts.

Name: Regan James
Age: Twenty-five

Height, weight and social security number were all there. Her eyes were brown, her hair brown, and she worked at some posh-sounding school as a teacher. According to the report, she lived alone in Brooklyn, and volunteered at a bereavement centre for kids. No pets and no known convictions or outstanding warrants for her arrest. Parents deceased.

Which Jag already knew from the file that had been compiled on her brother. She also had a photography website. Jaeger flicked to the next page. On it was a photo of

Regan James. It was a half-body shot of her standing on a beach somewhere, her hair tied back in a low ponytail, wisps of it caught by the breeze on the day and flattering her oval-shaped face, her hand raised as if to keep it back. She was smiling, a full-faced smile, showing even white teeth. A camera hung around her slender neck, resting between her breasts. It was a photo of a beautiful woman who didn't look as if she would hurt a fly. And her hair wasn't brown. Not in this photo. It was more auburn. Or russet. And her eyes weren't just brown either, they were…they were… Jag frowned, caught his train of thought and shut it down. They were brown, just as the report said.

'Where is she now?'

'She booked into the Santara International. That's all we know.'

Jag stared at the photo that shimmered on his screen. This woman's brother had taken his sister somewhere and he would move heaven and earth to find them and bring Milena home.

He only hoped Chad James had an army to help him when he finally got his hands around the bastard's scrawny neck, because nothing else would be able to.

'Have her followed,' Jag ordered. 'I want to know where she goes, who she talks to, what she eats and how often she goes to the bathroom. If the woman so much as buys a packet of gum I want to know about it. Is that clear?'

'Crystal, Your Majesty.'

Regan knew as soon as she walked into the shisha bar that she should turn right back around and walk out again. All day she'd trudged around the city of Aran looking for information on Chad, but the only thing she'd learned was that there was hot and then there was *desert* hot.

Despite that, she knew that she would have fallen in

love with the ancient walled city if she were here for any other reason than to find out what had happened to her brother. Unfortunately the more she had searched the city for him the more worried she had become. Which was why she couldn't follow her instinct now and leave the small, dimly lit bar Chad had frequented, no matter how tempting that might be.

The dinky little bar was dressed with various-sized wooden tables and chairs that looked to be filled with mostly local men playing cards or smoking a hookah. Sometimes both. Lilting Arabic music played from some unknown source and the air seemed to be perfumed with a fruity scent she couldn't place. Not wanting to be caught staring, she straightened the scarf she had draped over her head and shoulders in deference to the local custom, and wound her way to the scarred wooden bar lined with faded red leather stools.

The truth was this place was almost her last resort. All day she'd been stymied either by her own sense of inadequacy in trying to navigate the confusing streets of Aran, or by the local people she met who were nowhere near as approachable as the travel-friendly propaganda would suggest. Especially Chad's weasel-like landlord, who had flicked her with a dismissive gaze and informed her that he would not open the apartment without permission from the tenant himself. Having just come from GlobalTech Industries, where she couldn't get anyone at all to answer her questions, Regan hadn't been in the mood to be told no. She'd threatened to sue the shifty little man and when he'd responded by informing her that he would call the police she had said not to bother—she'd go there herself.

Unfortunately the officer on duty had told her that Chad hadn't been missing long enough to warrant an investigation and that she should come back the next day. Everything in Santara functioned at a much slower pace than she was used to. She remembered it was one of the things Chad enjoyed most about the country, but when you were desperate it was hard to appreciate.

Utterly spent and weighed down by both jet lag and worry, she'd nearly cried all over the unhelpful officer. Then she'd remembered Chad mentioning this shisha bar so after a quick shower she had asked for directions from one of the hotel staff. Usually when she went out in New York it was with Penny, and right now she wished she'd persuaded Penny to come with her because she didn't feel completely comfortable arriving at an unknown bar alone. She felt as though everyone was watching her and, truth be told, she'd felt like that all day.

Most likely she was being overly dramatic because she was weighed down by a deep-seated sense of dread that something awful had happened to her brother. She'd felt it as soon as she'd received his off-the-cuff email a week ago warning her not to try and contact him over the next little while because he would be unreachable.

For a man who was so attached to his phone that she often joked it was his 'best friend', that was enough to raise a number of red flags in her head and, try as she might, she hadn't been able to dispel them. A spill-over effect, no doubt, from when she'd had to take over parenting him when he was fourteen. Still, she might have been able to set her worry aside if it hadn't been for her friend and work colleague, Penny, who had regaled her with every morbid story she could remember about how travellers and foreign workers went missing in faraway lands, never to be heard from again.

For two days Regan had ignored her growing fear and tried to contact Chad, but when she'd continued to have no luck Penny had almost bought her the plane ticket to Santara herself. 'Go and make sure everything is okay,' Penny had insisted. 'You won't be any good to the kids here until you do. Plus, you've never been on a decent holiday in the whole time I've known you. At best you'll have a great adventure, at worst...' She'd left the statement unfinished other than to say 'And for God's sake be careful,' which hadn't exactly filled Regan with a lot of confidence.

As she cast a quick glance around the bar as if she knew exactly what she was doing, her gaze was momentarily snagged by a shadowy figure in the far right corner. He was dressed all in black with a *keffiyeh* or *shemagh* of some sort on his head, his wide-shouldered frame relaxed and unmoving in a rickety wooden chair, his long legs extending out from beneath the table. She wasn't sure what it was about him that gave her pause but nor could she shake the feeling that he was dangerous.

A shiver raced down her spine and she told herself not to be paranoid. Still, she felt for the can of mace in her handbag and, satisfied that it was there, pinned a smile on her face and turned towards the bar. A man as big as a fridge stood behind the counter, drying a glass, his expression one of utter boredom.

'What'll it be?' he asked, his voice as rough as chipped cement. As far as greetings went it fell far short of the welcome mark.

'I don't need anything,' Regan began politely. 'I'm looking for a man.'

The bartender's brow rose slowly over black beetled eyes. 'Many men here.'

'Oh, no.' Regan fumbled in her pocket when she realised how that had sounded and pulled out a recent photo of Chad. 'I'm looking for this man.'

The bartender eyed the photo. 'Never seen him before.'

'Are you sure?' She frowned. 'I know he comes here. He said so.'

'I'm sure,' he said, clearly unamused at being questioned. He reached for another glass and started drying it with a dishtowel that looked as if it hadn't seen the inside of a washing machine for days. Maybe weeks. 'You want hookah? I have strawberry, blackberry and peach.' Which would explain the fruity scent she'd noticed when she'd first walked in.

'No, I don't want a hookah,' she said with a note of defeat in her voice. What she needed, she realised, was some sort of guide. Someone who could help her navigate the streets and widen her search for Chad.

She'd thought about hiring a car while she was here but the Santarians drove on the opposite side of the road to what she was used to and, anyway, Regan's sense of direction was not one of her strong points. Some might even call it one of her worst. At least Chad would. Remembering how he had often teased her about how he could turn her in a circle and she wouldn't know which way was north made a lump form in her throat. The thought of never seeing her brother again was too much to bear. He'd been her lifeline after their parents had died. The one thing that had kept her total despair at losing them at bay.

'Suit yourself,' the human fridge grumbled, ambling back down the bar to a waiting customer in local dress. In fact, most of the patrons were dressed in various forms of Arabic clothing. Everyone except the man in the corner. She cast a covetous glance in his direction to find that he was still watching her. And he hadn't moved a muscle. Was he even breathing?

Determined to ignore him, she strengthened her resolve and shoved a dizzying sense of tiredness aside. She was here to find Chad and no oversized bartender, or man in

black, was going to put her off. Feeling better, she clutched
Chad's photo tightly in her hand and started to move from
table to table, asking if anyone knew him or had seen him
recently. Of course, no one knew anything, but then, what
had she expected? It was just a continuation of the theme of
the day. As she grew more and more despondent it wasn't
until she had stopped at a large table of men playing bac-
carat that she realised that the low-level conversation in the
bar had dwindled to almost nothing.

Suddenly nervous, she smiled at the men and asked if
any of them knew Chad. A couple of them smiled back,
their eyes wandering over her. Regan felt the need to cover
herself with her hands but knew that she looked perfectly
respectable in cotton trousers and a white blouse, the scarf
covering her unruly brown hair. One of the men leaned
back in his chair, his tone suggestive as he made a comment in Santarian. The other men at the table laughed and
Regan knew that whatever he'd said, it hadn't been pleas-
ant. She might be on the other side of the world but some
things were universal.

'Okay, thanks for your help,' she said, giving them all
her stern schoolteacher look before turning her back and
quickly moving to the next table.

Which, unfortunately, was *his* table.

Her gaze skimmed across the table with the untouched
hookah on it to his hands folded across his lean abdomen.
From there it travelled up the buttons of his shirtfront to
his tanned neck and square jaw. Moistening her lips with
the tip of her tongue, Regan vaguely registered a sensual
unsmiling mouth, a hawk-like nose and the most piercing sapphire-blue eyes she had ever seen. And that was as
far as she got. As if she was caught in the crosshairs of a
predator's glare she stood frozen to the spot, her gaze held
prisoner by his. His eyes glittered with a lethal energy that

was startling and Regan had the sudden realisation that she'd never come across a more dangerous-looking or un-approachable man in her life. Her heart palpitated wildly inside her chest as if she'd just stepped in quicksand and was about to sink.

Run! echoed throughout her head but, try as she might, she couldn't make her body obey. Because not only was he dangerous-looking, but he was also sinfully good-looking, and, just as that thought hit, so did a wave of unbridled heat that raced through her whole body and warmed her face.

Good lord, what was she doing noticing his looks at a time like this?

She blinked, her sluggish brain struggling to register her options. Before she could come up with something plau-sible he moved, kicking the chair opposite him away from the table and blocking her avenue of escape. The sound of the chair scraping across the stone floor made her jump, and once more her heart took off at a gallop.

'Sit down.' His lips twisted into a mocking smile. 'If you know what's good for you.'

His voice was deep and powerful, commanding her to obey even though she knew it was stupid to do so.

This close she could see that he was far more physi-cally imposing than she'd first thought, and completely, un-ashamedly male. He looked strong enough to be able to pick her up one-handed and take her wherever he pleased. With a start she realised she might not be completely against the idea. A ripple of excitement coursed through her, making her feel even more light-headed than the jet lag.

This was insane.

This *thinking* was insane. She did not react to men like this. Especially not men who looked as if they meandered on the wrong side of the law and won. Every time. Still, what could possibly happen to her in a bar full of patrons? Patrons who were still watching her with curious eyes.

Driven by the need to get out from under those curious glances, she chased off the inner voice of doubt and did as the man suggested, taking a seat and perching her handbag on her lap as some kind of shield between them. He glanced at it as if he'd guessed its purpose and his lips tilted into a knowing smirk.

Feeling exposed under his steady gaze, she somehow defeated the urge to jump back up and leave. It wasn't as if she had many alternatives right now. After this bar she had nowhere to go except back to her hotel room, and then possibly back to Brooklyn. Defeated. She wouldn't do that. Ever.

'Like what you see?'

His deep voice slid over her skin like the richest velvet, making her realise that she'd been caught staring at his mouth. Alarmed, she realised that the tingly sensation swamping her senses was some sort of sexual attraction she couldn't remember ever experiencing before.

A betraying jolt went through her and his lazy, heavy-lidded gaze told her that he was too experienced to have missed it.

Flustered and appalled at her own lack of sense, she dragged her eyes to his. 'You speak English.'

'Evidently.'

His droll tone and imperious gaze made her feel even more stupid than she'd felt already, and she grimaced. 'I meant you speak English *well.*'

His only response was to raise one eyebrow in condescension. Regan got the distinct impression that he didn't like her. But how was that possible when she had never even met him before?

'What are you doing here, American?' His voice was low and rough, his lips curling with disdain.

No, he didn't like her. Not one little bit.

'How do you know I'm American? Are you?'

She hadn't been able to place his accent yet.

He gave her a humourless smile. 'Do I look American to you?'

No, he looked like a man who could tempt a nun to relinquish her vows. And he knew it. 'No. Sorry.'

'So what are you doing here?'

She let out a breath and pulled herself together. She didn't know whether to hold the photo of Chad out to him or not. Despite his relaxed slouch, he looked as if he was ready to pounce on her if she so much as blinked the wrong way. 'I'm…looking for someone.'

'Someone?'

'My brother.' Deciding there couldn't be any harm in showing him the photo, she extended it across the table, making sure their fingers didn't connect when he took it. His eyes held hers for a fraction longer than necessary as if he knew exactly what she was thinking. Which she hoped wasn't true because she was still stuck on the whole sexual attraction thing. 'Have you seen him before?'

'Maybe. Why are you looking for him?'

Regan's eyes widened. Hope welled up inside her at the thought that she might have finally found someone who would be able to help her. 'You have? Where? When?'

'I repeat, why are you looking for him?'

'Because I don't know where he is. Do you?'

'When was the last time you heard from him?'

His tone was blunt. Commanding. And suddenly she felt as though he was the one looking for Chad instead of her.

'Why won't you answer my questions?' she asked, her instincts warning her to tread carefully.

'Why won't you answer mine?'

'I have.' She shifted uncomfortably in her seat. 'How do you know my brother?'

'I didn't say I knew him.'

'But you did…you said…' She shook her head. What exactly had he said? She lifted her hand to her head where it had started to ache. 'Look, if you don't know him just say so. I've had a long day and I'm really tired. Not that you care, I know, but if you know where he is I'd really appreciate you telling me.'

He looked at her for so long she didn't think he was going to say anything. 'I don't know where he is.'

Something in his tone didn't sound right but her brain was so foggy she couldn't pick up on what it was. All she could focus on was a growing despair. After the surge of hope she'd felt moments ago it seemed to weigh more heavily on her than it had all day. 'Okay, well—'

'When was the last time you heard from him?' he asked for a second time.

Regan paused before answering him. She didn't know this man from Adam. He didn't know her either for that matter. So why was he asking her so many questions? 'Why do you want to know that? You already said you don't know where he is.'

He shrugged his broad shoulders. 'I don't. But I didn't say I wouldn't help you.'

Their eyes clashed and Regan had a sudden image of a lethal mountain lion eyeing off a prairie rabbit. 'Help me?'

'Of course. You look like a woman who is almost out of options.'

She *was* a woman who was almost out of options. But how did he know that? Did she look as desperate as she felt?

He smiled at her but it held not a hint of warmth. 'Are you going to deny it?'

Regan's brows drew together. She wanted to deny it but

she couldn't. And really she *could* use some help right now. Especially from someone who was a local and knew the area well. Someone who might even know Chad. But this man had already admitted that he didn't, and frankly he unsettled her. She'd thought he was dangerous when she'd first spotted him from across the room and, while closer inspection might have confirmed that he was incredibly good-looking, it hadn't shifted her initial impression one bit. Which was strange because he hadn't made a single threatening move towards her. Still, she listened to her instincts and there was something about him she didn't trust. 'Thanks anyway, but I'm good.'

'Good?' He gave a humorous laugh. 'You're a foreign woman in a bar, alone at night in a city you don't know. Exactly how are you good, America?'

She pursed her lips at both the nickname he had given her and the element of truth behind his words. When she'd first set out it had been early evening and she hadn't given much thought to the time. All she'd considered was finding information that might lead to Chad. But she wasn't completely vulnerable, was she? She had her mace. 'I just am. I'm from New York. I know what I'm doing.'

'Really? So what's your plan now? You going to go bar-hopping and hold up your little photo to every person you come across?' He made the only idea that had come into her head sound ridiculous. 'That's fine if you're looking for trouble as well as your brother.'

'I'm not looking for trouble,' she retorted hotly.

His gaze narrowed at her haughty tone, his inky black lashes making his blue eyes seem electric. It was totally unfair that she should have brown hair and brown eyes while this man was one of the most beautiful creatures she had ever seen in the flesh.

'Take a look outside. You have been in my country for

less than twenty-four hours and you know nothing about it. You should be glad that I'm offering my assistance.'

Regan narrowed her eyes suspiciously. 'How do you know how long I've been in Santara?'

'Any longer and you would know not to swan into a bar in this part of town without an escort who could take on fifty men.'

Regan felt a trickle of unease roll down her spine. She glanced around the room to find it even busier than before. 'I'd like my photo back, please,' she said, standing to go.

He watched her, unmoving. 'Where are you going?'

As if she was silly enough to tell him that. 'I've taken up enough of your time,' she said briskly, 'and it's getting late.'

'So you're just going to turn around and walk out of here?'

'I am,' she said with more bravado than she felt. 'Do you have a problem with that?'

'I don't know, America; can you take on fifty men?'

Regan shivered at the husky note in his voice, her body responding to him in a way she really couldn't fathom. Their eyes clashed and something raw and elemental passed between them. Again, he hadn't moved but she got the distinct impression that he was a bigger threat to her than fifty other men could ever be.

Not wanting to put that to the test, she gave him a tight smile. 'We'll have to see, won't we?'

Once more conversation slowed as curious eyes surveyed her and Regan stuck her hand in her bag, palming her can of mace, before turning and striding towards the entrance of the bar as if her life depended on it.

Relieved when she made it outside without incident, she sighed and hailed a cab that by some miracle pulled into the kerb in front of her.

'Hello? Are you free?' she asked the pleasant-looking driver wearing some sort of chauffeur's hat.

'Yes, miss.'

'Thank heavens.' She jumped in the back and gave the driver the name of her hotel, only feeling as though she could fully relax when the dark car started moving. Which was when she realised that the stranger in black hadn't given Chad's photo back to her.

She glanced out through the rear window, half expecting to find him standing on the pavement watching her, but of course he wasn't. She was being silly now. And the photo didn't matter. She would print off another one tomorrow.

CHAPTER TWO

Jag stood outside the door to Regan James's hotel room and questioned the validity of his actions. He'd been doing that the whole drive over.

After meeting her in the bar it was clear that she knew nothing about her brother's whereabouts. She also seemed to know nothing about his sister being with him. But then she had grown cagey when he'd probed her about the last time her brother had contacted her, and he didn't know if that was because her sense of self-preservation had kicked in, or whether she had something to hide.

Regardless, she was his only link to Chad James and she would undoubtedly have a wealth of significant information about her brother that could lead him to find his sister.

A predatory stillness entered his body as he raised his hand to knock at the door. Regan James had been a revelation at the bar. He'd been right when he'd first seen her photo. Her eyes were not brown, they were cinnamon, and her hair was a russet gold that reminded him of the desert sands lit by the setting sun. Her voice had also been a revelation; a husky mixture of warmth and pure sex.

She had evidently reminded some of the other men in the bar of the same thing because Jag had noticed the sensual speculation in more than one male gaze as she had moved through the bar. She had a slender grace that drew the eye and her smile was nothing short of stunning. Even his own breathing had quickened at that first sight of her, and when she'd stood in front of his table, her doe eyes wide and uncertain, he'd had the shocking impulse to reach across the table and drag her into his lap.

It had been a long time since he'd responded to a woman with such unchecked desire and the only reason he was even here was because he'd realised that he couldn't interrogate her in the bar. As it was, some of his people had started to recognise him despite the fact that he'd shaved off his customary neat beard and moustache. He rubbed his hand across his clean-shaven jaw, quite liking the sensation of bare skin. Instantly the thought of rubbing his cheek along Regan James's creamy décolletage entered his head and altered his breathing.

He scowled at the unruly thought. It had been a long time since he'd been influenced by his emotions rather than his intellect as well; some might have said never. Milena often accused him of having ice running through his veins, of being inhuman. He wasn't. He was as human as the next man, as his physical reaction to Regan James earlier had proven.

The fact was, Jag had learned to control his emotions at an early age and he didn't see anything wrong with that. As a leader it was essential that he keep a cool head when everyone else was losing theirs. He had certainly never let a pretty face or a sexy body influence his decision-making process and he never would.

Irritated that he was even pondering emotions and sex, he raised his fist to bang on the door.

He heard the sound of water being shut off and a feminine, 'Just a minute.'

He let out a rough breath. Excellent; she was just out of the shower.

The door opened wide and he found himself staring into

Regan James's gorgeous eyes. Seconds seemed to lengthen into minutes as his eyes automatically travelled down her slender form.

'You!'

'Me,' Jaeger growled, his voice roughened by the swift rise of his body at the sight of her in a cotton dressing gown and towel around her head. He pushed past her into the room before she had a chance to collect herself and slam the door in his face.

'Hold on. You can't come barging in here.'

Jag didn't bother to point out the obvious. That he already had. Instead he scanned the small room, looking for any signs that might clue him in as to where her brother might be.

'Did you hear me?' She yanked on his arm to turn him towards her and the move was so unexpected, so shocking that he did indeed turn towards her, a frown on his face. Nobody touched him without first being given permission to do so. Ever.

His eyes narrowed as she clutched the lapels of her robe closed, making him acutely aware that she was naked beneath the thin cloth. He wanted nothing more than to wrench the garment from her body and sink into her feminine softness until he couldn't remember what it felt like to be burdened by duty. Until he couldn't remember what it felt like to be alone. But no one could escape destiny and one night in this woman's arms wouldn't change anything. Duty and loneliness went hand in hand. He'd learned that from watching his father.

Savagely tamping down on needs that had materialised from who knew where, he scowled at her.

'I heard you.'

'Then…' She lifted her chin in response to his brusqueness. 'What are you doing here?'

Jag glanced at the photo of her brother in his hand before flicking it onto the coffee table. 'You left this behind.'

Her gaze landed on the photo. 'Well…thanks for returning it, but you could have left it with the front desk downstairs.'

Ignoring her, Jag raised the flap of her suitcase and peered at the contents. 'Is this all the luggage you have?'

Frowning at him, she crossed the room and slammed it closed. 'That's none of your business.'

Deciding that he'd wasted enough time humouring this woman, Jag gave her a look that usually sent grown men into hiding. 'I asked you a question.'

This close, he dwarfed her in height and form, but her instincts for survival must have been truly lost because she still didn't move back from him.

'And I asked you to leave,' she shot back.

Jag's lip curled. He would have thought her much braver than she looked if not for that pulse point throbbing like a battering ram at the base of her neck.

'I'm not leaving.' His voice held a dark warning. 'Not before you've told me everything you know about your brother.'

'You do know my brother, don't you?' Finally she took a quick step backwards. 'Do you also know where he is? Did you lie about that?'

'I ask the questions. You answer them,' he stated coldly.

She shook her head. 'Who are you?'

'That is not important.'

'Do you have my brother?' Her voice held a fine tremor of panic. 'You do, don't you?'

Jag's lip curled into a snarl. 'If I had your brother, why would I be here?'

'I don't know.' Those cinnamon-brown eyes were riveted to his. 'I don't know what you want or why you're here.'

She swallowed heavily and Jag felt his chest constrict at her obvious fear. The need to soothe it—the need to soothe her—took him completely by surprise.

Knowing this would go a lot easier if she were relaxed he tried for a conciliatory tone. 'There's no need to be afraid, Miss James. I merely want to ask you some questions.'

His saying her name seemed to jolt something loose inside of her. He saw the rise of panic in the way her eyes darted to the side, clearly searching out an avenue of escape. Before he could think of how to placate her, to put her at ease, she darted, quick as a whippet, towards the hotel room phone.

If he'd wanted to alert hotel security to his presence he'd have called them himself and he had no choice but to stop her, wrapping his arms around her from behind and lifting her bodily off the ground.

She fought him like a little cat with its tail caught in a door, her nails digging into his forearms, the towel around her head whipping him in the face before falling to the ground.

'Keep still,' Jag growled, wincing as her heel connected with his shin. For a little thing she had a lot of spunk in her and if he wasn't so irritated he'd be impressed. 'Dammit, I'm not—' Jag grunted out an expletive as her elbow came perilously close to connecting with his groin.

Deciding to put an end to her thrashing, he spun her around to face him and gripped her hands behind her back, bringing her body into full contact with his. Her flimsy robe had become dislodged during the struggle and this new position put her barely constrained breasts flat up against the wall of his chest. His traitorous body registered the impact and responded as if it belonged to a fifteen-year-old youth rather than a thirty-year-old man who was also a king.

She panted as she glared up at him, her wet hair wild around her flushed face. Jag's breath stalled. Like this, with her cheeks flushed, her lips parted, her breathing ragged, she looked absolutely magnificent. And that was *absolutely* irrelevant.

'I'm going to put you down,' he said carefully. 'If you run again, or go for the weapon in your handbag, I'll restrain you. If you stay put this will be a lot easier.'

For him at least.

Her fulminating glare told him she didn't believe him, but at least she'd stopped struggling.

He shook his head when she remained stubbornly silent and released her anyway. He was twice her size; if she ran again he'd stop her again. Only he'd prefer not to. It was most likely due to the stress of his sister's disappearance, but being this close to Regan James was playing havoc with his senses.

'Where is your phone?'

He'd check to see if she'd received any calls during the day and move on from there. He glanced into her angry face when she didn't immediately answer. By the set of her jaw she had no intention of doing so.

'Miss James, do not infuriate me again by making this more difficult than it has to be.'

'Infuriate you! That's rich! You follow me to my hotel, barge into my room and then attack me. And you're the one who's infuriated?'

'I did not attack you,' Jag said with all the patience of a saint. 'I restrained you and I will do so again if you run again. Be warned.'

She folded her arms across her chest, a shiver racing down her body. 'What do you want?' She lifted her chin at a haughty angle.

'Not you,' he grated, 'so you can rest easy about that.'

She looked at him as if she didn't believe him and he could hardly blame her after the way he'd handled her. Still, it was true. He preferred his lovers sophisticated, compliant and willing. She was none of those three. So why was he so affected by her?

'Take a seat,' he growled, 'so we can get down to what it is that I do want. Which is information about your brother.'

When she remained stubbornly standing Jag sighed and sat himself.

'A week ago your brother wrote to you. Have you spoken to him since?'

'How do you know he wrote to me?'

'I ask the questions, Miss James,' he reminded her with forced patience. 'You answer them.'

'I'm not telling you anything.'

'I would seriously advise you to reconsider that approach.' His voice was steely soft. She might not know it but there wasn't anything he wouldn't do to find his sister, and the reminder that this woman's brother had her reignited his anger. She looked at him as if she wanted to bite him and he felt another unbidden surge of lust hit him hard.

'No, I haven't heard from him,' she finally bit out.

'What made you come to Santara?'

Her lips compressed and for a moment he thought she might defy him again. 'Because he lives here. And I was worried when he didn't answer his cell phone.'

'He did live here.' He wasn't going to for much longer.

She shook her head. 'He wouldn't move without telling me.'

'I take it you're close.'

'Very.'

The soft conviction in her voice jolted something loose inside his chest. He had once been that close to his own siblings. Then his father had died in a light-aircraft crash that had made him King. There hadn't been time for close-ness after that. There hadn't been *room* for it.

'What do you know about what your brother has been up to lately?'

'Nothing.'

'Really?' He watched the flush of guilt rise along her neck with satisfaction.

'I don't,' she said, shifting from one foot to the other, her eyes flashing fire and brimstone at him as she fought her desire to defy him. He would have been amused if he didn't find her audacity so invigorating. So arousing.

'I mean, I know that he was enjoying work, that he liked to explore the countryside on weekends, that he had just bought a new toaster oven he was particularly proud of, and that he had a new assistant.'

'A new assistant?'

'Yes. Look, I'm not answering any more of your ques-tions until you answer mine.' She planted her hands on her hips, inadvertently widening the neck of her robe. 'Why are you so interested in my brother?'

Dragging his gaze up from her shadowy cleavage, he savagely tamped down on his persistent libido. 'He has something of mine.' His jaw clenched as he wondered how Milena was. Whether she was okay, or if she was in trou-ble. If she needed him.

'He stole from you?'

The shock in her voice pulled his mouth into a grim slash. 'You could say that.'

Regan noted the subtle shift in his muscles when he an-swered her, the coiled tension that clenched his jaw and his fists at the same time. Again she thought of a mountain lion ready to spring. Whatever her brother had taken it was important to this man. And that, at least, explained his interest in Chad. But, while her brother had gone through a couple of rough years after their parents died, he wasn't a bad person. He was smart, much smarter than her, which was why she had worked so hard to make sure he finished high school, finally fulfilling his potential with a university degree in AI at the top of his class. An achievement that had brought him to this country that was, from the little she had seen, both untamed and beautiful.

Much like the stranger in front of her who left her breathless whenever he trained his blue gaze on her as if he was trying to see inside her. Possibly she hated that most of all; the way her body responded to his with just a look.

He was watching her now and it took all her concentration to ignore the sensations spiralling through her. If he hadn't touched her before, grabbed her and held her hard against him it might have been easier.

Regan's nipples tightened at the memory of his arm brushing over her. He was built like a rock, all hard dips and plains that had been a perfect foil for her own curves. And she was in a hotel room alone with him. A man who outweighed her by about a hundred pounds.

'It wasn't Chad,' she said fiercely, forcing her mind back on track.

'It was.'

'My brother isn't a thief,' she said with conviction. 'You've made a mistake.'

'I don't have the luxury of making mistakes in my line of work. Which I have to get back to. Where's your phone?'

'Why do you want my phone?'

Thick black lashes narrowed so that the blue of his eyes was almost completely concealed. 'I've humoured you enough, Miss James. Where is it?'

He uncoiled from the sofa, all latent, angry male energy, and she instinctively stepped back. He noticed, causing her temper to override her anxiety. 'First tell me who you are. You owe me at least that for scaring the life out of me before.'

'Actually I don't owe you anything, America.' His gaze travelled over her with blatant male appraisal. 'I am the King of Santara, Sheikh Jaeger Salim al-Hadrid.'

'The King?' Regan clapped a hand over her mouth to stifle a laugh. The man might have an expensive-looking haircut, now that she could see it without the headdress he'd worn earlier, but with his dark clothing and scuffed boots he looked more like a mercenary than a king. And then another thought struck. Had he been hired to kill Chad? Did he think she would inadvertently lead him to her brother? 'I doubt that. Who are you really?'

She saw instantly that laughing at this man was the wrong thing to do. His blue gaze pinned her to the spot, his body going hunting-still. 'I am the King,' he said coldly, taking a step towards her.

'Okay, okay.' Regan held her hand out to ward him off. 'I believe you.' She didn't but he didn't need to know that. As long as he left—and soon—that was all she needed him to do.

She forced her brain to forget about the perfect symmetry of his face and start thinking more about surviving. He was clearly a madman—or a potential killer—and she was alone with him in her room.

Fresh fear spiked along her spine. She tried to remember that everyone said she had a gift for communicating but this was no recalcitrant seven-year-old with a smartphone hidden beneath his desk.

'You think I'm lying?' he said softly.

'No, no.' Regan rushed to assure him, only to have him bark out a harsh sound that was possibly laughter.

'Unbelievable.'

He shook his head and Regan briefly measured the distance from her to the door.

'Too far,' he murmured, as if reading her mind. Probably not difficult, since she was staring at the door as if she was willing it to open by itself. Which she was.

'Look—'

He moved so quickly she barely got one word out before he was in front of her. 'No more questions. No more games. Give me your phone or I'll tear everything apart until I find it.'

'Bathroom.'

His eyes narrowed.

'I was taking a shower when you turned up,' she said. 'I like to play music while I'm in there.'

'Get it.'

Nearly demanding that he say 'please', Regan decided that the best thing she could do was to stay quiet. The sooner he got what he was looking for, the sooner he would leave.

Moving on wooden legs, she walked towards the bathroom, coming up short when he followed her. Staring back at him in the bathroom mirror, she saw just how big he was, his wide shoulders filling the doorway and completely blocking out the view of the room behind him.

Their eyes connected and for a brief moment awareness charged the air between them, turning her hot. Flustered, she dropped her eyes and picked up her phone. She handed it to him, crossing her arms over her chest in a purely protective gesture.

'Password?'

Heat radiated from his body, surrounding her, and she wished he'd move back. 'Trudyjack,' she said grudgingly.

'Your parents' names?' He gave her a bemused look. 'You might as well have used ABC.'

Regan's eyes flashed to his. How did he know they were her parents' names? *How did he know so much about her?*

'Who are you?' she whispered, frightened all over again.

'I told you. I am the King of Santara. I knew everything about you less than an hour after your plane landed in my country.'

Regan swallowed hard and pressed herself against the basin behind her. Could he really be who he said he was? It didn't seem possible, and yet he did have an unmistakable aura of power and authority about him. But then so did killers, she imagined.

She watched him scroll through her contact list and emails, his scowl darkening in the lengthening silence.

'Chad's phone is switched off,' she said, unable to keep her vow of silence from moments ago. She couldn't help it. She'd never been good with silences and when she was nervous that only became worse. 'I know because I've tried to call him daily.'

'He doesn't have his phone with him.'

'Then what are you searching for on my phone?'

'A burner number. An email from an unknown source.'

'How do you know he doesn't have it with him?'

Ignoring her question, he asked another one of his own. 'Does he have a second phone?'

Regan frowned. Why would Chad not take his phone with him? His phone was his lifeline. 'No. But I wouldn't tell you even if he did.'

His blue eyes melded with hers, a zing of heat landing low in her belly.

'You like to provoke me, don't you, Miss James?'

Regan's heart skipped a beat at his warning tone. No, she didn't like to provoke him. She really didn't.

With a look of disgust he pocketed her phone. She wanted to tell him that he couldn't keep it because her phone was her lifeline too, but at this point she'd do almost anything to placate him and make him go away.

'Satisfied?' she asked, the word husky on her lips.

'Hardly.' His gaze raked down over her again and she became acutely aware of her nudity beneath her robe. The small room seemed to shrink even more and the air grew heavy between them, making it nearly impossible for her to breathe. The man had a dire effect on her system, there was no question about that.

'Why were you so keen to jump on a plane and fly here after that one email?'

'I…' Regan swallowed. 'I was worried. It's not like Chad to be out of contact.'

'So you rushed over here because you thought he might be in trouble? Do you always put your brother first, or is it that you like to feel indispensable?'

Regan's pride jolted at his words because there was some truth to them. Becoming Chad's guardian and throwing herself into the role had helped to fill a void in her life and move on from her grief.

Hot colour flamed in her face. 'You don't know me.'

'Nor do I want to. Get dressed,' he ordered before turning and walking back into the main room.

Regan exhaled, willing herself to be calm. She moved to the doorway to find him going through the photos on her camera. Instantly she went into panic mode. 'Hey, don't touch that. It's old and I can't afford to replace it.'

She lunged to retrieve her precious camera and he held it aloft. 'I'm not going to break it,' he snapped. 'Not unless you keep trying to grab it.'

Snatching her hand back from where it had landed on the hard ball of his shoulder, she slapped her hands on her hips. 'I don't care who you are, you have no right to go through my things.'

He gave her a dismissive glance to say that he had every right and even if he didn't there wasn't a damned thing she could do about it. 'There isn't anything I won't do to get my sister back, Miss James. You'd better get used to that idea.'

His sister?

Regan frowned. 'What has your sister got to do with anything?'

Slowly his gaze returned to hers, the blue so clear and so cold she could have been staring into a glacier. 'Your brother has my sister. And now I have his.'

'That's insane.'

'For once we agree on something.'

'No, I mean you're insane. My brother isn't with your sister. He would have told me.'

'Really?'

Maybe. Maybe not. 'Are they in a relationship or something?' If they were she was a bit hurt that he hadn't told her. They had always shared everything in the past.

'You'd better hope not. Now move. My patience is at an end. I need to return to the palace.'

Wait? Was he really the King of Santara?

'I'm… I'm not going anywhere with you.'

'If you insist on going as you are I won't stop you. But you'll get far more looks than you did earlier, parading around in tight jeans and a flimsy shirt.'

'My clothes were perfectly respectable, thank you very much.'

'You have five minutes.'

'I'm not going with you.'

'That's your choice, of course, but the alternative is that you remain in this room until your brother returns.'

Regan frowned. 'You mean as in *locked* in here?'

'I can't afford to have my sister's disappearance become public knowledge. With you asking questions and wandering around on your own you'll only draw attention to yourself. And, no doubt, get yourself into trouble in the process.'

'I won't say anything. I promise!'

Regan knew she sounded desperate and she was. The thought of being locked in a hotel room for who knew how long was not acceptable. If what this man said was true she wanted freedom to find Chad and figure out what was going on. Preferably before this man found him.

He shook his head. 'Make your decision. I don't have all night.'

'I'm not staying here!'

'Then get dressed.'

Regan's mind was spinning out of control. Her head, already fuzzy from lack of sleep, was struggling to keep pace with the rate at which things were moving. 'I need more time to think about this.'

'I gave you five minutes. You now have four.'

'I don't think I've ever met a more arrogant person than you. Actually, strike that: I know I haven't.'

He folded his hands across his chest, his muscular legs braced wide, his expression hard. Like this he looked as if he could take on fifty men blindfolded and win.

'Your telephone service will be disconnected and I will have guards posted outside your door. I do not advise you to try to leave.'

'But how do I know you are who you say you are?' she said on a rush. 'You could be an imposter for all I know. A murderer. I'd be crazy to go with you.'

'I am not a murderer.'

'I don't know that!'

'Get dressed and I'll prove it to you.'

'How?'

He heaved an impatient sigh. 'You can ask any member of the hotel staff downstairs. They will know who I am.'

For the first time since he had barged into her room Regan saw a way out. If he was really going to take her downstairs then she had a chance of alerting someone as to what was going on.

'Okay, just…' She grabbed a clean pair of jeans and a long-sleeved shirt from her case. 'Just give me a minute.'

Locking herself in the bathroom, she very nearly didn't come back out but decided that he'd most likely break the door down if she aggravated him too much. He had the arms for it.

Concentrating more on his abundant negative qualities, she opened the door to find him propping up the opposite wall, looking at his watch. 'One minute early. I'm impressed.'

Arrogant jerk.

Regan grabbed her handbag and walked ahead of him out the door. She waited as he stabbed the elevator button. 'If you're really a king, where are all your guards?'

'I rarely take guards with me on unofficial business. I can take care of myself.'

Convenient, she thought.

'And why was it that no one in the shisha bar knew your identity? If you're really the King I would have expected some bowing and scraping.'

The slow smile he gave her told her he wouldn't mind making her bow and scrape for him. 'I've found that people rarely see what they're least expecting.'

Regan raised a brow. She couldn't argue with that. She might have thought he looked dangerous when she had first seen him, but she hadn't expected him to turn up at her door making outrageous accusations about her brother. Nor had she expected him to tell her he was the King. Though whether or not that was true still remained to be seen.

'How's the headache?' he asked, watching her in the mirrored wall. Regan slid her gaze to his. 'Don't bother denying it,' he continued. 'You're so pale you look like you're about to pass out.'

'My head is fine.' She wasn't about to admit that he was right. She wasn't sure what he would do with the information. She wouldn't put it past him to try to make it worse.

When they arrived at the lobby Regan felt a surge of adrenaline race through her. Glancing around, she was disappointed to find that the large lobby was mostly empty. Before she could make a move in either direction her arm was gripped, vice-like, and she was towed along towards the reception desk.

The smile on the young man's face faltered as he took them in. They probably looked quite a sight, she thought grimly. Her with her fast-drying hair no doubt resembling a wavy cloud around her head, and her unwanted companion with a scowl as dark as his clothing.

'Ah, Your Majesty, it is an honour.' The man bowed towards the desk, his expression one of eternal deference. Then he said something in Santarian that her companion answered. The younger man's eyes went as big and as round as a harvest moon.

'But…' He gave her a panicked look. 'Miss James, this is His Majesty the King of Santara.' The words almost came out in a stutter, as if he couldn't quite believe he was saying them.

Frankly, nor could Regan. 'How do I know you haven't just set this up?' she said with disdain. 'One man's opinion is hardly folk law.' Turning back to the concierge, Regan said, 'Actually, I'd like to report—'

She didn't get any further as the stranger beside her growled something low under his breath and then towed her further into the lobby, veering off towards the sound of a pianist playing a soulful song. Through French windows Regan saw a room full of people.

Stopping just inside the entrance, they stood waiting until finally most of the room grew silent, staring at the two of them. Then half of the occupants stood and bowed low towards the man still holding her arm.

Regan shook her head, her brain refusing to compute the evidence that he really was the King of Santara. Which meant that if he was right then maybe her brother was with his sister, *Princess* Milena, his new research assistant. She swallowed, swaying on her feet.

Clearly worried she was about to do something girly, like swoon in his presence, the King snaked a hand around her waist, pulling her up against him. Regan set her hand flat against his chest to stop their bodies colliding. Her head fell back on the stem of her neck as the heat from his body sapped the last of her strength. She could feel his heart pounding a steady rhythm to match her own but all she could focus on was the blue of his eyes, indigo in the soft light. Time seemed to disappear as he looked back at her with such heat Regan's thoughts ceased to exist. It didn't matter who she was or what he was. All that mattered was that he kiss her. Kiss her so that the ache building inside her subsided.

A soft growl left his throat, his eyes devouring her lips, and for a brief moment she thought he *would* kiss her.

But then his eyes turned as sharp as chipped jewels and his hand tightened on her hip. 'Satisfied?' he murmured, throwing her earlier question back at her.

Regan shook her head, her balance precarious despite his firm hold. She heard the word 'no' coming from a long, dark tunnel right before she did something she'd never done before. She fainted.

CHAPTER THREE

TWO NIGHTS LATER Jag sat behind his large desk brooding over the voice message he had received from Milena.

'Hi Jag. I know you're worried—you're you—and I'm sorry I can't tell you where I am, or what I'm doing, but I want you to know that I'm with a friend and I'm fine. I'll explain everything when I return. I love you.'

'Any idea where the call originated from?' he asked Tarik.

'Unfortunately not. It was likely made from a burner phone and it was sent through several different carriers. Whoever scrambled the transmission is good.'

Chad had scrambled the transmission, of that Jag was one hundred percent certain; he'd hired the kid in the first place because he was a borderline genius with technology. Anger coursed through him, a hot and welcome replacement for the impotence he'd felt since she'd gone.

He turned to stare outside the window, brooding. On the one hand he was happy that his sister was safe and well, but the reality was that she could have been forced into making that phone call. Not that she'd sounded forced. She'd sounded full of vigour. Almost buoyant. A state he hadn't seen her in for quite a while. A state he would welcome if the memory of what had transpired three years ago wasn't like a smoking gun in his mind.

Then there was the obvious assumption that if she hadn't

been forced to leave Santara then she'd gone somewhere with Chad James of her own free will, and that raised a whole host of ugly questions Jag didn't want to consider. Questions like, what were they doing together that Milena wasn't able to tell him about? Like maybe she was considering not going through with the marriage to the Crown Prince of Toran? Questions like, was she unhappy, and, if so, why hadn't she come to him the way she used to when she was a child?

He rubbed his fingers hard across his forehead. Well, of course she'd been coerced. There was no other way to look at this. Just as he had coerced Regan James into coming to the palace. He recalled the moment she had fainted when she had discovered that he was actually the King, the dead weight of her body as she'd slumped in his arms. He'd had a lot of reactions from women in the past when they'd found out he was royalty—everything from obsequious preening to outright manipulation—but he'd never had a woman faint on him before. Which had been a good thing because right before that he'd nearly given in to an urge he'd been fighting all night and leant down and kissed her. In public! He didn't know what bothered him about that the most: the fact that his inimitable self-control had taken a long hike, or that he would have shocked the hell out of those watching.

Shocked himself, he'd quickly scooped her into his arms and taken her out to his waiting SUV. She'd come to fairly quickly in the car, demanding that he return her to her hotel, but he had calmly reminded her that it had been her choice to come with him and that she was now out of options.

Well aware that his behaviour had been less than stellar with regard to the American woman, he pushed thoughts of her, and his sister, from his head and picked up the raft of reports he needed to sign off. 'These can go to Helen to have the corrections worked up, these can go back to Finance, and this one I still have to read. Tell Ryan I'll get to it later tonight.'

'Very good.'

He rubbed the back of his neck. 'For once I hope that's it for the night.' He gave Tarik a faint smile and saw the old man hesitate. It was only the slightest of movements but Jag knew him too well to miss it. His body immediately shifted into combat mode. 'What is it? And please tell me it has nothing to do with the American.'

As much as he had been trying to keep her presence in the palace under wraps, she had been trying to stop him. Banging on the door of her suite, demanding that she be given her phone and her computer, demanding that she be released, demanding that he come to her. But Jag didn't want to go to her. Already her voice and the memory of her scent had imprinted themselves on his brain. He couldn't imagine that seeing her was going to make that any better.

'Unfortunately it does. She is refusing to eat,' Tarik said.

'Refusing to eat?' Jaeger felt his stomach knot. 'Since when?'

'Since last night, sir. She did not eat her evening meal and today she has rejected all food.'

Jag's jaw hardened. If Regan thought she was going to make herself ill by not eating she had another thing coming.

Trying not to overreact, he pushed himself to his feet. 'What time is her evening meal due to be delivered?'

'It has been delivered. She sent it away.'

Jaeger scowled. 'Have my dinner taken to her suite in half an hour.'

He made to leave but again Tarik hesitated.

'Please tell me you've left the best to last,' Jag drawled.

Tarik grimaced. 'Not exactly, Your Majesty, but I have it in hand.' He passed Jaeger a printout from a local news website. On it were two photos of himself and Regan standing close together. They must have been snapped by one of the patrons in the hotel, the camera perfectly capturing the moment she had discovered he was the King: her eyes wide, lips softly parted, wild mane cascading down her back like a silken waterfall. The next was right before she'd fainted. Jag had tangled his fingers through her hair to cup the nape of her neck, his other hand tight around her waist. Her face had been upturned, her mouth inches from his own. Would those pink lips have tasted as pure and sweet as they looked? Would the skin of her abdomen feel as soft beneath his fingertips as the nape of her neck? Would—?

Tarik cleared his throat. Jag inhaled deeply, uncomfortably aware that his trousers were fitting a little snugger than they were before. What the hell was wrong with him?

'Fortunately they were taken down before any damage was done,' Tarik informed him. 'And the woman's name was not discovered. But I thought you should be informed.'

'Of course I should be informed.' He glanced at the images again, an idea forming in his mind at rapid speed. If he was going to detain Regan James until her brother returned then by damned he would make her useful to him. 'Republish the photos.'

'Your Majesty?'

'Make sure her name is attached and that the images are picked up by the international Press. If the sight of her in my arms doesn't bring her brother out of the woodwork, I don't know what will.'

Tarik looked at him as if he wanted to protest but Jag wasn't in the mood to listen. He wanted a hot meal, a cool shower and a peaceful night's sleep. Since meeting her the American woman had interfered with the latter; now it seemed she would be interfering with the first two as well.

* * *

Regan's stomach grumbled loudly in the silent room and she pressed her palm against her belly. 'It's been one day,' she told her objectionable organ. 'People can survive a lot longer than that without food, so stop complaining.'

She didn't know exactly how long a human being could survive without food, but she recalled various movies about survival and knew it was more than a day.

Mind you she was starving and her errant brain advised her that food would help to keep her strength up. And that the arrogant ruler of Santara wouldn't care about her eating habits anyway.

But it wasn't just the lack of food bothering her. It was the boredom and worry. She'd come to Santara to make sure Chad was okay. Not only was she not doing that but she wasn't doing anything at all. She'd never had so much time on her hands and she was going crazy. The first day she had kept herself busy taking photos of the amazing garden suite she was imprisoned in; the arched Moorish windows, the Byzantine blues and greens that were used to colour the room and the amazing studded teak doors, the one keeping her locked in being the most beautiful of all, which she refused to see as ironic in any way.

Then there was the garden with the swaying palm trees, and deep blue tiled pool. The whole place was stunning and she itched to download her images onto her laptop and play around with the lighting and composition. If she'd been in this magical place under any other circumstances she doubted she'd want to leave.

But more than that she wanted to see the King again. Not because she wanted to see him per se, but because she wanted to know if he had an update on Chad. She hadn't realised when she'd made the choice to leave her hotel room that she'd be swapping one prison for another. Perhaps if she hadn't been so tired and strung-out, if he'd given her more time to consider her options, she would have made a different choice. She certainly wouldn't have thought about what it would feel like to kiss him!

She groaned softly in mortification as she recalled the moment he'd held her against him in the hotel lobby, the moment he'd held her inside her hotel room, his hot eyes on her cleavage, their bodies melded together so tightly she was convinced she'd felt... *Don't go there*, she warned herself. Bad enough that she'd recounted those times second by second in her dreams. The man might be stunningly attractive, but he was holding her against her will and accusing her brother of a terrible crime.

A crime she was even more convinced, now that she'd had some sleep, that he would never commit. If only that blasted King would give her the time of day so she could explain that to him. Explain what a gentle soul her brother was. Explain that Chad was the type to save baby birds in their back garden, not stomp on them.

When her brother had finished university and taken the prestigious opening at GeoTech Industries she'd thought her days of worrying about him had come to an end.

She'd been eighteen when their parents died and she'd been thrust into the role of parent. And she'd thought she'd done okay. But if Chad really had run off with the King's sister... She rubbed at her bare forearms, chilled despite the humid warmth of the night air. She couldn't take the King's claim seriously. Chad just wouldn't do something like that, she knew it. She knew him!

Sensing more than hearing a presence behind her, Regan slowly turned to find the man who had taken her captive standing in her living area. Her heart skipped a beat before taking off at a gallop. He looked magnificent in a white robe that enhanced his olive skin and blue eyes to perfection. He wasn't wearing a headdress tonight, his black hair thick and a little mussed from where it looked as though he had dragged his fingers through it countless times during the day. The glow from the elaborate overhead chandeliers threw interesting light and shadows over his face, making him even more handsome than she remembered.

'Miss James.'

Her name was like thick, rich treacle on his lips and she shivered, hiding her unwanted reaction by stepping forward. 'So you've finally decided to show up,' she grouched, instinct advising her that attack was the best form of defence with a man like this. 'How kind of you.'

He gave her a faint smile. 'I understand you're not eating.'

A small thrill of satisfaction shot through her. So her self-imposed starvation had worked. 'Yes. And I won't until you release me.'

He shrugged one broad shoulder as if to say that his care factor couldn't be lower. 'That's your choice. You won't die.'

'How do you know?' she shot back.

'It takes three weeks for a person to starve to death. You're in no danger yet.'

Resenting his sense of superiority, Regan frowned as he clapped his hands together and two servants wheeled a dining cart into the room. One by one they set an array of platters on the dining table near the window.

'Will that be all, Your Majesty?'

'For now.'

Regan gave him a look as they bowed and exited the room. 'Don't expect that clapping trick to work with me,' she warned. 'I'm not one of your minions.'

His silky gaze drifted over her and she wished she were wearing more than a pair of shorts and a T-shirt. If she'd thought he might actually show up she'd have pulled a curtain from the wall and draped herself in it. Anything so that she didn't feel so exposed.

'No, that would take far more optimism than even I have for that to occur.'

He moved to the dining table and took a seat, inspecting the array of stainless-steel dishes the servers had laid out.

'No matter what you say,' she advised him, 'I won't eat.'

He gave her a long-suffering look. 'Believe it or not, Miss James, I do not wish for you to have a bad experience during your stay in the palace. I even hoped that we might be…friends.'

'Friends?'

He shrugged. 'Acquaintances, then.'

Regan couldn't have been more incredulous if he'd suggested they take a spaceship to Mars. 'And you say you're not optimistic.' She scoffed. 'The only thing I want from you is for you to release me.'

'I can't do that. I already told you that I will do whatever it takes to have my sister returned home safely.'

'Just as I would do whatever it takes to have my brother returned home safely as well.'

He inclined his head, a reluctant smile tugging at the corners of his mouth. 'On this we understand each other.'

Not wanting to have anything in common with the man, Regan set him straight. 'What I understand is that you're an autocratic, stubborn, overbearing tyrant.'

He didn't respond to her litany of his faults and she narrowed her eyes as he uncovered the small platters of delicious-smelling food. His imperviousness to her only made her temper flare hotter.

Then her stomach growled, making her feel even more irritable. She watched him scoop up a dip with a piece of flatbread, his eyes on her the whole time. His tongue came

out to lick at the corner of his mouth and a tremor went
through her. 'You look ridiculous when you eat,' she lied.
'Can't you do that somewhere else?'

Expecting him to become angry with her, she was
shocked when he laughed. 'You know, your disposition
might be improved if you stopped denying yourself your
basic needs. Hunger strikes are very childish.'

Stung to be called childish, Regan stared down at him.
'My disposition will only improve when you release me
and stop saying awful things about my brother.'

His eyes narrowed when she mentioned Chad, but other
than that he didn't show an ounce of emotion; instead he
scooped up more food with his fingers and tempted her
with it.

Irritated, she thought about moving outside but then decided against it. If he was going to antagonise her she would
do the same back.

'You cannot think to stick with this plan,' she said, wandering closer to him.

Curious blue eyes met hers. 'What plan?'

'The one to keep me here until my brother returns with
your sister.'

He leaned back in his chair, wiping his mouth with his
napkin. As he regarded her Regan's eyes drifted over the
hard planes of his face, those slashing eyebrows and his
surly, oh, so sinful mouth. He would photograph beautifully, she thought. All that dominant masculine virility
just waiting to be harnessed... It gave a girl the shivers.
She could picture him astride a horse, outlined against the
desert dunes with the sun at his muscled back. Or asleep
on soft rumpled sheets, his muscular arms supporting his
head, his powerful thighs—

Regan frowned. Sometimes her creative side was a
real pain.

'Is that my plan?' His deep voice held a smooth superiority that set her teeth on edge.

'Well, obviously. But I already told you that I wouldn't say anything about your sister being missing. I'm even willing to sign something to say that I won't.'

'But how do I know I can trust you?'

'Because I'm a very trustworthy person. Call my boss. She'll tell you. I never say anything I don't mean or do anything I say I won't.'

'Admirable.'

'Don't patronise me.' She gripped the back of the carved teak dining chair opposite him. The smell of something delicious wafted into her sinuses and she nearly groaned. 'You're really horrible, you know that?'

'I've been called worse.'

'I don't doubt it. Oh…' She clenched her aching stomach as it moaned again, and glared at him. 'You did this on purpose, didn't you?'

'Did what?' he asked innocently.

'Brought food in here. You're trying to make me so hungry that I'll eat despite myself. Well, it won't work.' She glared into his sapphire-blue eyes. 'You can't break me.'

She wheeled away from the table, intending to spend the rest of the night in the garden until he left, but she didn't make it two steps before he stopped her, wrapping his arm around her waist and hauling her against him.

Regan let out a cry of annoyance and banged her fists down on his forearms.

'Stop doing that,' she demanded. Already her skin felt hot, her unreliable senses urging her to turn in his arms and press up against him. 'I hate it when you touch me.'

'Then stop defying me,' he grated in her ear, yanking the chair she'd just been gripping out from the table and dumping her in it.

'You like doing that, don't you?' she accused, rubbing her bottom to erase the impression left behind from being welded to his hard stomach. 'Using your brute strength to get what you want.'

He picked up his fork and pointed it at her. 'Eat. Before I really lose my temper and ask the palace doctor to get a tube and feed you that way.'

'You wouldn't dare.'

The smile on his face said he would, and that he'd enjoy it.

'I'm only doing this because now that I know you won't let me go I'm going to need my strength to escape,' she said, snatching up a delicate pastry from a silver platter and shoving it into her mouth. It dissolved with flaky deliciousness on her tongue, making her reach for another. She murmured appreciatively and blushed when she found him staring at her. 'What?' she grouched. 'Isn't this what you wanted all along?'

'Yes.' His voice was deep and low, and turned her insides to liquid.

Not wanting him to know just how much he affected her, she decided to take another tack. 'This is preposterous, you know?'

He glanced at her. 'The food? My chef will not be pleased to hear that.'

'Keeping me here.' She picked up her fork and stabbed at something delicious looking. 'It's the twenty-first century and you appear to be an educated man.' Though that was popular opinion, not hers. 'A ruler, for heaven's sake. You can't just impose your will on others whenever you feel like it.'

He gave a short bark of laughter. 'Actually I can.' He piled more food onto his plate. 'And I am aware of the century. But in my country the King creates the laws, which pretty much gives me carte blanche to do what I want, whenever I want.'

'That can't be true.' She frowned. 'You must have checks and balances. A government of some sort.'

'I have a cabinet that helps me govern, if that's what you mean.'

'And what's their job? To rubber-stamp whatever you say?'

'Not quite.'

'They must be able to order you to let me go.'

'Not quite.'

Completely exasperated, Regan put down her fork. 'Look, you're making a big mistake here. I know my brother is innocent.'

His eyes narrowed on hers. 'We've had this conversation. Eat.'

'I can't. The conversation is killing my appetite.'

'Then stop talking.'

'God, you're impossible. Tell me, what makes you think that my brother has taken your sister? Because it's not something my brother would do. He's not a criminal.'

'He stole a car when he was sixteen and copies of his finals exams when he was seventeen.'

'Both times the charges were dropped,' she defended. 'And how do you even know this? Those files are closed because he was a minor.'

He gave her a look and she rolled her eyes. 'Right, you know everything.' She took a deep breath and let it out slowly. 'Chad got into the wrong crowd with the car thing and he stole the exam papers to sell them to help me out financially. We had a hot-water system to replace in our house and no money. He didn't need to steal the exams for himself. He's a straight-A student. Anyway, that's a lot different from *kidnapping* someone,' she shot at him.

'To say that you've been kidnapped is a trifle dramatic. You came to my country of your own free will. Now you are being detained because you're a threat to my sister's security.'

'I had nothing to do with your sister's disappearance!'

'No, but your brother did,' he pointed out silkily, 'and as you've already confirmed he has the capability for criminal activity.'

'He was young and he was going through a hard time,' she cried. 'That doesn't mean he's a career criminal.'

'Why was he having a hard time?'

'I'm surprised you don't know,' she mumbled; 'you seem to know everything else.'

He handed her a warm triangle of pastry. 'I know that your parents both died of cancer seven weeks apart. Is that what you're referring to?'

'Yes.' Emotion tightened her chest. 'Chad was only fourteen at the time. It hit him hard and he didn't really grieve properly… I think it caught up with him.'

'That must have been hard to have both parents struck down by such a terrible disease. I'm sorry.'

'Thank you.' She shook her head and bit into the food he'd handed her, closing her eyes at the exquisite burst of flavours on her tongue. 'This is delicious. What is it?'

'It is called a *bureek*, a common delicacy in our region.' He frowned as he dragged his eyes up from her mouth. 'Who looked after the two of you when your parents died?'

'I was eighteen,' she said, unconsciously lifting her chin. 'I deferred my photography studies, got a job and took care of us both.'

He frowned. 'You had no other family who could take you in?'

'We had grandparents who lived across the country, and

an aunt and uncle we saw on occasion, but they only had room for Chad and neither one of us wanted to be parted.'

His blue eyes studied her for a long time, then he handed her another morsel of food. She took it, completely unprepared for his next words. 'I lost my father when I was nineteen.'

'Oh, I'm sorry,' she said instinctively. She missed her parents every day and her heart went out to him. 'How did he die?'

'He was killed in a helicopter crash.'

'Oh that's awful. What happened to you?'

'I became King.'

'At nineteen? But that's so young.'

He handed her another type of pastry. 'I was born to lead. For me it wasn't an issue.'

Wasn't an issue?

Regan stared at him. He might say it wasn't an issue but she knew how hard it was to take on the responsibility of one brother, let alone an entire country. 'It couldn't have been easy. Did you have time to mourn him at least?'

She noticed a flicker of surprise behind his steady gaze. 'I was studying in America when his light aircraft went down. By the time I arrived home the country was in turmoil. There were things to be done. Try the *manakeesh*.' He indicted the food she forgot she was holding. 'I think you'll like it.'

That would be a no, then, she thought, biting into a delicious mixture of bread, spice and mince. His slight grin told her he knew that she'd enjoyed it. She shook her head, trying to make sense of their conversation.

He might sound as if he were talking about little more than a walk in the park, but Regan could tell by the slight tightening of the skin around his eyes that his father's death

had affected him very deeply. 'How old was your sister at
the time?'

'My sister was eight.' He tore off a piece of flatbread and
dipped it in a dark purple dip. 'My brother was sixteen.'
He handed her the bread.

'You have a brother?'

'Rafa. He lives in England. The *baba ganoush* is good,
yes?'

'Yes, it's delicious.' She licked a remnant of the dip from
the corner of her mouth, frowning when she realised what
he was doing. 'Why are you feeding me?'

His piercing gaze met hers. 'I like feeding you.'

Something happened to the air between them because
suddenly Regan found it hard to draw breath. She reached
for her water glass. Their conversation had taken on a
deeply personal nature and it was extremely disconcerting.

'I can't stay here,' she husked. For one thing, she needed
to find Chad, and for another…for another, this man affected her on levels she didn't even know she had and she
had no idea what to do about it.

'You have no proof that my brother did anything wrong.'

His gaze became shuttered. 'That topic of conversation
is now closed.'

Agitated, Regan stared at him. 'Not until you tell me
what makes you so certain Chad has taken your sister.'

Leaning back in his chair, he took so long to answer her
she didn't think that he would. 'We have CCTV footage of
them together and after she'd gone my sister left a message
on my voicemail informing me that she was with a friend.'

Regan frowned. 'That hardly sounds like someone who
has been taken against her will.'

'Milena is due to marry a very important man next
month. She would not have put all of that at stake if she
wasn't forced to do so.'

'Maybe she doesn't want to marry him any more.'

A muscle jumped in the King's jaw. 'She agreed to the marriage and she would never shirk her duties. Ever.'

His sister might have agreed, Regan mused silently, but having to marry out of duty would make most women think twice. 'Does she love the important man she's going to marry?'

'Love is of no importance in a royal marriage agreement.'

'Okay.' Regan thought love was important in *any* marriage agreement. 'I'll take that as a no.'

'You can take it any way you want,' he ground out. 'Love is an emotional concept and does not belong in the merger of two great houses.'

'Merger? You make it sound like a business proposition.'

'That is as good a way of looking at it as any.'

'It's also harsh. What about affection? Mutual respect? What about *passion*?'

She had no idea where that last had come from—she'd meant to say *love*.

His gaze narrowed in on her mouth and a hot tide of colour stung her cheeks. 'Those things can come later. After the marriage is consummated.'

'That's provided you marry someone nice,' Regan pointed out. 'What if this important man is horrible to her?'

'The Crown Prince of Toran will not be horrible to my sister or he will have me to answer to.'

'That's all well and good in principle, but it doesn't mean your sister *wants* it. I mean, don't get me wrong, there isn't anything I wouldn't do for my family, but when it comes to marriage I'd like to choose my own husband. Most women would.'

'And what would you choose?' His voice was deep and mocking. 'Money? Power? Status?'

His questions made Regan feel sorry for him. Clearly he'd met some shallow women in his time, which went some way to explaining his attitude. 'That is such a cynical point of view,' she replied. 'But no, those things wouldn't make my top three.'

'Let me guess,' he said, a sneer in his voice. 'You want kindness, a sense of humour, and someone to want you just for you.'

Surprised that he'd hit the nail on the head, Regan was flummoxed when he started laughing.

'I don't see what's so funny,' she griped. 'That's what most women want.'

'That's what most women *say* they want,' he retorted with masculine derision. 'I've found that those things fall far short of the mark unless money and power are involved.'

'Then I'd say you've been dating women far short of the mark. Maybe you need to raise your expectations.'

'When I marry, Miss James, it will not be for kindness, love or humour.'

'No,' Regan agreed, 'I'm sure there'll be nothing funny about it. Or loving.'

His lips tightened at her comment. 'I don't need love.'

'Everyone needs love. Believe me, I see the kids in my classroom who aren't properly loved and it's heartbreaking.'

'I agree that a parent should love a child,' he rasped, 'but it's irrelevant in a marriage.'

'I disagree. My parents were deeply in love until the day they died. My father was someone who showed genuine love and affection to all of us.'

'No wonder you have a fairy-tale view of relationships.'

Regan tilted her head, wondering where his *un-fairy-tale-like* view had come from. 'What about your parents? Were they happily married?'

'My parents' marriage was a merger.'

'Not a surprise, I suppose, given your attitude, but I didn't ask why they married, I asked if they were happy.'

One minute he was sitting opposite her and the next he was standing at the windows, staring out at the darkening sky. He took so long to respond to her question, and was so still, Regan would have assumed he'd gone to sleep if not for the fact that he was standing up. Just as she was wondering what she could say to break the tension in the room he turned back to her, a scowl darkening his face. 'Whether my parents were happy or not is unimportant. But actually they weren't. They rarely saw each other. My mother found that she didn't have the stamina to be a queen and spent most of her time in Paris or Geneva. My father was King. A job that leaves little time for anything else. He did what needed to be done. As my sister will. As my brother will, and as I will.'

His words painted a somewhat bleak picture of his early years.

'That sounds a bit cold. Maybe your sister wants something different. Maybe she and my brother are in love. Have you considered that?'

If the muscle jerking in his jaw was any indication, then yes, he had considered it. And not happily.

'You'd better hope not,' he growled.

'Why not? What if they're in love and want to get married?' God, what if they were *already* married? This man would probably skewer Chad like a pig on a spit-roast. 'Would that be such a big deal at the end of the day?'

The look he gave her was dangerous. Dangerous and uncompromising. 'Milena is already betrothed,' he bit out softly. 'And that betrothal cannot be broken. It *will not* be broken.'

'Tell me,' she said, narrowing her eyes, 'are you concerned about your sister's welfare because she's your sister or because she might ruin your precious plans with this so-called Crown Prince?'

'Are you questioning my affection for my sister?' he asked with deadly softness.

'No. I'm saying that if it's true and she and Chad are in love, what can you do about it? I mean, it's not like you can punish my brother for falling in love with your sister. You might not think it's important but falling in love is surely not a crime. Even here.'

The smile he gave her didn't reach his eyes. 'You don't know my country very well at all, Miss James, do you?' He stalked towards her and leaned over her chair, caging her in with his hands on either armrest.

Regan's heart knocked against her chest so loudly she thought he'd be able to hear it. She wasn't afraid of him, although perhaps if she had any sense she would be, because the look in his eyes could chill lava. 'I can have your brother executed for just looking at my sister.'

Regan drew in a shocked breath. 'You cannot.'

His mouth twisted into a grim smile. 'You have no idea what I'm capable of.' His eyes drifted over her face and down to her body. Regan's breath hitched inside her chest. He was so close, his scent filled her senses and started acting like solvent on her brain. She wanted to tell him that she didn't care what he was capable of but neither her brain nor her body seemed to be functioning on normal speed.

'But all that is irrelevant. If you and your brother are as close as you claim to be then he will come running soon.'

With that arrogant prediction he straightened away from her, giving her body enough respite that she could finally drag air into her lungs.

'Goodnight, Miss James. I hope you enjoyed your dinner.'

Discombobulated by his nearness and the vacuum left by

his sudden departure, Regan jumped to her feet and went after him, grabbing hold of the sleeve of his robe. 'Hold on a minute.' She blinked a few times to clear her head. 'What do you mean by that? Why will my brother come running?'

'Because hopefully he's seen the photos I've had released of the two of us.'

'Photos?'

'Yes.' His blue eyes glittered down into hers. 'It seems you and I were photographed together in the hotel lobby. By now they should be splashed all over the European news networks with your name attached.'

'You're using me as bait,' she whispered on a rushed breath.

'I like to think of it as insurance.' His superior smile did little to ease her rising temper. 'When your brother finds out you're here I'm hoping those familial connections you spoke so movingly about will have him scurrying out of the woodwork.'

'Oh, you are t-truly awful,' she stammered furiously. 'Your sister has run away because you're mean and trying to marry her off to someone who is probably just as horrible as you, and you're going to scare my brother in the process.'

'Your brother will pay for his sins, Miss James, and if you two are as close as you say you are he'll come running.'

Regan shook her head. 'I've never met a man as cold and heartless as you. Something you're no doubt very proud of.' She shoved her hands on her hips and stared him down. 'You can't keep me here like this. When I tell the American consulate what you've done you'll be an international pariah.'

The look he gave her was cold and deadly, not a shred of compassion on the stark planes of his beautiful face. 'Are you threatening me, Miss James? You do know it's a crime to threaten the King?'

Regan tossed her hair back from her face. 'It's no doubt a crime to hit him as well but if I had a baseball bat handy, Sheikh Hadrid, or King Jaeger, or whatever your title is, I'd use it.'

She saw his nostrils flare and she suddenly realised how close together they were standing. If she took another step forward they'd be plastered up against each other. She told herself to do the opposite and step back but once again her body and her brain were on divergent paths.

'The correct title is *Your Majesty*,' he said softly. 'Unless we're in bed. Then you can call me Jaeger, or Jag.'

Oh, God, why had he said that?

And why was he looking at her as if he wanted to devour her? As if he wanted to kiss her as much as she wanted to kiss him?

This is stupid, Regan, she warned herself. *Step back. Step back before it's too late.*

But she didn't step back; instead she poked the bear. Quite literally, with her pointer finger. 'Like that will ever happen,' she threw at him. 'I hate you. The only time I would *ever* sleep with you is in your dreams.'

'Is that so?'

He grabbed hold of the finger she was using to jab him and brought it to his mouth. Regan's breath backed up in her lungs as he ran the tip of her finger back and forth across his lower lip. Heat raced through her, consuming every ounce of good sense she'd ever owned. 'Don't do that,' she begged, her voice husky.

He looked down at her, his blue eyes blazing. 'Don't fool yourself. You don't hate me, little America. Far from it.'

CHAPTER FOUR

THE FOLLOWING MORNING Regan was still incensed by the King's high-handedness. Clearly nothing was beyond him: imprisonment, trickery, *sexual domination*.

'Don't fool yourself. You don't hate me, little America. Far from it.'

She did hate him. Of course she did. He was autocratic… arrogant… He was… The memory of the way his warm breath had moistened the tip of her finger, hinting at the dark heat of his mouth, made her shiver. He was unbelievably sexy!

Not that she was thinking about that. Or her response. She liked men who saw themselves as equal with women. King Jaeger obviously saw himself as equal with no one. Not even the gods!

'I make the rules here,' she muttered under her breath, completely oblivious to the beautiful, sultry day outside. 'You'll do as I say.'

How could she find a man like that sexy? Stress. Lingering jet lag. Inconvenient chemistry.

If only he were a rational man you could reason with. But he wasn't. He had decided her brother was guilty, and appealing to reason wasn't going to work.

Which left her with no option but to get away, or at the very least get word to Chad that she was fine and that he needn't worry about her. As much as she wanted to find out what was going on with him, she couldn't bear it if he panicked and did something crazy. Such as put himself in King Jaeger's path.

She glanced around the high walls that surrounded the gardens. She had thought about scaling them but had almost immediately dismissed the idea. They were about twenty feet high and smoothly rendered. There wasn't a foothold anywhere. She had also tried brazening it out and simply walking out of the door on the first day but it was always locked. The only time it wasn't was when the maid was cleaning, as she was now, but on those occasions a security guard was stationed outside the door.

Regan knew because she had tried to sneak out the day before and been met with his implacable, blank stare. Maybe the King trained them personally.

Frustrated at how utterly helpless she felt, she strode back inside. Had the photo of her in the King's arms been released to the media yet? Probably. She hated the thought that Chad had seen it and was worried about her, but more, she hated the thought of what would happen once King Jaeger got hold of her brother.

Good God, what had her brother been thinking, running off with a princess? Was he personally involved with her? And could the King really have him executed? More importantly, would he? He definitely seemed ruthless enough to do it but something told her that he wasn't as bad as he made out. Closed, yes. Bad…no.

Regan fought back a wave of helpless frustration, absently watching the maid enter something into her tablet before picking up the feather duster again. Regan didn't know what she could possibly be dusting—the room was immaculate. The maid was young, no more than twenty, at a guess, and seemed sweet enough. Unfortunately she spoke limited English, totally clamming up that first day when Regan had informed her that she wasn't a guest of the King and needed to leave the palace as quickly as possible.

The girl had given her a confused, shy smile and told her in broken English how wonderful the King was, at which point Regan knew she wouldn't be getting any help from her direction.

But if King Jaeger thought she would sit back while he planned her brother's demise he was very much mistaken. As soon as she was free she would contact the American Embassy and demand that they…that they…what? Put in place economic sanctions against Santara? Ban tourism to the smaller nation? Most likely Jaeger would laugh and shrug those impossibly broad shoulders with a care factor of zero.

Irritated, she watched as the maid returned to her trolley and retrieved a cloth and cleaning agent before heading into the bathroom, leaving the trolley behind. Wandering around the room like a caged tiger in need of exercise, Regan passed the trolley and abruptly stopped when she realised that the maid had not only left her trolley unattended, but she'd left the tablet on it as well.

Heart thumping, she glanced towards the bathroom, where she could hear the maid singing softly to herself, and grabbed the electronic device. Praying that it wasn't password-protected, she nearly gave a cry of relief when the screen lit up at her touch.

Ignoring her sweaty palms, she quickly connected to the internet and chewed on her lip as she thought about what to do next. Not having expected to get access to the web, she had no idea who to contact. The American Embassy? Did they have an emergency email on their website? But even if she contacted them they would have no way of telling Chad that she was fine. That she wasn't at the mercy of King Jaeger. Worse, they might not even believe her.

Thinking on her feet, she pulled up her social-media account and had a brainwave. Rushing over to a sun lounger, she quickly unbuttoned her shirt so that her bra looked like a bikini. With trembling fingers she angled the tablet, plastered a bright smile on her face and took a photo of herself with the pool in the background. Then she quickly captioned a message underneath.

Having fun chez King Jag. Hope you are too. The King is a wonderful host! 💙💙💙

She grinned as she added the three heart emojis. They were a fun joke between her and Chad that she had started when he had been an easily embarrassed teenager. It was something her mother would have taken great joy in doing to both of them.

Before she could reconsider her actions she hit 'post' and watched it come up on her home page. It wasn't much, and she had no guarantee that Chad would check the site, but it was a way they had kept up with each other's lives after he'd gone to university. With any luck he would check it before panicking about what the heck she was doing in the King's arms.

Spiked with adrenaline at having outsmarted His high-and-mighty Majesty, she was about to write Chad a private message when she heard a noise in the room. Not wanting to alert the maid to what she had done, Regan quickly closed down the page she was on and strolled back inside, the tablet behind her back.

The maid didn't even look her way and Regan only realised that her whole body was shaking after she quickly put the device back on the trolley. She exhaled a rushed breath and tried to calm her heartbeat. The tablet wasn't in the same place as where she'd found it, but with any luck the maid would think that she had moved it herself.

Glancing at Regan quizzically, the young girl returned to the trolley and gave her a small smile as she wheeled it out of the room.

A shiver snaked its way down Regan's spine. She had managed to thwart the King. She only hoped he never found out. A small smile touched her lips. But, even if he did, it wasn't as if he could do anything about it. The man didn't control the world.

Jag pounded his opponent so hard the man's knees nearly buckled beneath him.

He should never have gone to her suite. Never have argued with her and certainly never have brought her fingers to his lips.

He swung hard again, grunting as his gloved fists connected with solid muscle.

From now on she would stay on one side of the palace and he would stay on the other.

His opponent groaned loudly. 'Either I'm in really poor form, or you're in extremely good form today, boss-man.' Zumar winced as he prodded the side of his jaw. 'If I'm lucky I might get out of this bout still standing.'

Jag rolled his aching shoulders and waited for Zumar to resume his fighting stance. Zumar was six feet six, built like an iron tank, and the head chef in the palace. He'd once been a black belt in karate and a kick-boxing champion before injury had forced him into another career as a street fighter. Many years ago Jag had assisted him in a five-against-one street brawl and given him a second chance. Zumar had studied as a chef, and could now run a Michelin-star establishment if he so chose. He didn't. Instead he'd made a life for himself in Santara and remained loyal to Jag. Loyal until they faced off in the ring during their regular training sessions.

'Stop complaining,' Jag growled. 'I can't help it if you're going soft on all those pastries you bake.'

'Soft, is it?' Zumar laughed. 'Bring it on, boss-man.'

Jag did…taking out his pent-up energy and frustration in the ring rather than on the woman currently occupying his garden suite.

He still couldn't believe how close he'd come to kissing her again last night. The woman did things to his equilibrium he didn't want to contemplate. Because, for a man who was used to being in the utmost control at all times, it was a sad indictment to admit that when he'd taken one look at her in those cut-off shorts he'd nearly forgotten his own name.

Then there was all her talk of love and happiness…as if they were goals that motivated his life!

What did motivate him was success, position, power. Providing for his country and his family. Making sure everything ran smoothly and that Santara would never be in an inferior political position with its neighbours—Berenia and Toran—again. And if that made him a—what had she called him?—a stubborn, autocratic, overbearing tyrant, then so be it.

Usually steady on his feet, he felt Zumar's fist connect with his right cheekbone. He staggered sideways and scowled at his chef's ecstatic expression.

'Lucky shot,' he growled.

'I'll take it, boss-man,' Zumar chortled, raising his fists again.

Jag feinted a right hook to his jaw and then did a kickboxing manoeuvre that brought the other man down.

'You learn too fast,' Zumar complained. 'I'm calling time.'

'You can't,' Jag stated. 'I'm not finished.'

'You want to cook your own meal tonight, boss-man?'

Jag grunted, wrapping his gloved hand around Zumar's and hauling him to his feet. He glanced around the basement gymnasium many of his senior officers also used, to see if there was anyone else who would help him work off some steam.

Regan James might, his recalcitrant libido whispered, *though that would be a very different type of workout from this.*

Ignoring that unhelpful thought, he tried to catch the eye of a few of his army officers. Unfortunately Jag had never been known to employ idiots and every man in the room kept his gaze averted. It wasn't hard to sense that their leader wasn't quite himself right now.

'What's up with you anyways, boss-man?' Zumar asked, wiping the sweat from his brow with a sports towel. 'This big-deal summit tying you up in knots?'

'It's not the summit.'

'A woman, then.'

'A woman?' Jag gave him a baleful look, yanking his gloves off. 'Why would you say that?'

The Nigerian shrugged. 'When a man is as worked up as you are it usually means trouble of the female variety.' He gave Jag a knowing grin. 'But there is no escape, huh? The heart knows what the heart wants.'

The heart?

'What about your parents? Were they happily married?'

From out of nowhere, Regan's unexpected question from the night before dredged up unwelcome memories of his childhood. He still couldn't fathom how he had become embroiled in a conversation about his family with her. He never talked about his parents, not his father's death, nor his mother leaving them when they were young. It had happened, he'd dealt with both events and moved on, as was befitting for the as then future King of Santara.

And no, he hadn't mourned his father's death. He hadn't thought to. He had respected his father and always done his duty by him, but he hadn't really known the man, other than as his King. And as for his mother…she had never asked for Jag's love and never wanted him to give it.

His throat thickened. Regan James didn't know what she was talking about with her fairy-tale ideas about life. She'd never known duty or hardship. She had never… He frowned. Actually, she had known duty and hardship. And still she remained soft and open. Trusting that people behaved the way that they should. *Little fool.*

Yes, he would be on one side of the palace, she on the other. Because whenever he was around her she managed to twist logic and common sense into something unrecognisable. And really, why would he see her again? She was a means to an end. When that end came about they'd part company and never see each other again. And wasn't that a cause for celebration?

He gave Zumar a hearty slap on the back. 'Thanks, Chef.'

Zumar blinked. 'What for?'

'For helping me realise what was wrong.'

Zumar cracked his jaw. 'Next time I'd appreciate you working that out *before* we get into the ring, boss-man.'

Jag laughed. It felt good to be on solid ground again. Back in charge.

Last night…the chemistry between them, the way she made him question himself… Gone. Completely gone.

At least it was right up until Tarik burst into his dressing room thirty minutes later, his forehead pleated like an accordion.

Jag immediately stopped whistling. 'Milena?'

'No, no, I have no updates on Milena, Your Majesty.'

Jag let out a relieved breath, pulling on his trousers. 'Then it's something to do with the American. I can see the signs of frustration on your face. Don't let it bother you. I imagine she has that effect on everyone she meets.'

'Yes, sir, it is the American woman.'

'What has she done now? Tied her bed sheets together and scaled the palace wall? Planned out my demise in three easy steps? Whatever it is,' Jag assured him as he pulled a white shirt from its hanger, 'I'm not going to let it ruin my good mood.'

'She connected to the internet and uploaded a picture of herself at the palace.'

'Say what?' Jag nearly tore a new armhole in his shirt as he thrust his arm through it. 'Let me see.'

Tarik turned the tablet around so that the screen faced him. He scanned the photo that showed way too much of Regan's sexy cleavage in an ice-blue bra.

Jag knew five Santarian dialects and he swore in all five of them. 'Isn't that the pool in the garden suite?' he bit out.

'Yes, sir. This is a social-media post from the palace.'

He went still. 'The palace is not on social media.'

'No, sir, but Miss James is.'

'Miss James does not have a phone or any other device with her.'

'No. But she somehow got access to one and two hours ago she uploaded this post.'

'She got access to one?' Jag repeated softly. 'How?'

'The IT department is working on obtaining that information. They should know very soon.' There was a touch of desperation in Tarik's voice and Jag knew that his aide was trying to handle him.

'Take it down before anyone sees it,' he ground out. Like

her brother, whom he had no doubt had been the trouble-some woman's intended audience.

'I already ordered it to be taken down, Your Majesty.' Tarik swallowed heavily. 'Unfortunately it has already been seen.'

Jag paused in the process of buttoning his shirt, a sense of foreboding turning his powerful frame tense. 'By whom?'

'The post has been shared across various multimedia outlets six million times, sir.'

'Six mill...' Jag scowled. 'How is that possible in so short a time frame?'

'You are a very popular monarch, Your Majesty, espe-cially since the world is expecting you to announce your betrothal to Princess Alexa this weekend. And, with all eyes on Santara at present because of the impending sum-mit, I'm surprised it's not more.'

Jaeger cursed viciously. He had completely forgotten about Princess Alexa.

'Quite,' Tarik agreed. 'But, speaking of your prospec-tive engagement, I have King Ronan on the phone. He is furious that it seems you are entertaining a *concubine*— his words, sir—after agreeing to marry his daughter. He is threatening to call off the engagement and boycott the summit.'

Jag stared at Tarik. For the first time in his life his brain was struggling to keep up with the turn of events. As beau-tiful as Princess Alexa was, Jag had no real desire to marry her other than the convenience of it. She understood his world and, from what he knew of her, she was as logical and pragmatic as he was. She was also polished and poised. Any leader would be fortunate to have her on his arm. Not only that, but marrying her would strengthen ties with Ber-enia, Santara's third neighbour.

'Miss James is *not* my live-in mistress,' he bit out. 'And I have *not* formally agreed to marry Princess Alexa.'

'I know, Your Majesty, but King Ronan is clearly of the impression that you have.'

'That's because King Ronan is a pushy bastard who tries to manipulate people.'

'Of course, sir. But it is important that you have a plus-one this weekend. If King Ronan is not pacified he will not allow Princess Alexa to attend as your escort. And you know it is never a good idea to attend these events alone.'

Yes, he did, but he had more pressing matters to consider right now than a plus-one. He dragged a hand through his still damp hair. By rights he should be furious with Regan for this stunt—and he was—but part of him couldn't fault her ingenuity. Hell, he might even admire it if she wasn't causing him so much grief in the process.

'King Ronan is holding for you, Your Majesty. He wants to speak with you personally.'

'Of course he does.' Jag snatched up his cell phone from his dresser. 'Transfer the call to my personal number,' he ordered, his brain having gone from sluggish to full-on alert as he went into automatic problem-solving mode.

'Yes, sir.' Tarik flicked his finger quickly across the screen on his tablet. 'And Miss James?'

Jag scowled. 'Leave Miss James to me.' He'd strangle her as soon as he placated the volatile King of Berenia and made a decision about whether or not to marry the Princess.

Striding down the marble staircase en route to the garden suite, he brought his phone to his ear. 'King Ronan,' he said smoothly. 'I believe we have a small problem.'

CHAPTER FIVE

'COME ON, JUST sit still,' Regan crooned. 'Please, just for another few seconds.'

Her camera shutter clicked as she photographed a pair of olive and yellow birds with elegantly turned-down beaks. It was clear by the way they danced around each other and rubbed their beaks together that they were a couple, and their antics made her smile. They reminded her of hummingbirds back home, and she'd always had a soft spot for photographing couples—both animal and human. Everyone loved the notion of finding their soulmate, and she found that 'couples' sold well as stock photos.

She checked her viewfinder, satisfied that the pretty pair would be very popular when they were uploaded onto her website. The light was magnificent in Santara, making the exotic colours of this timeless land pop. Just looking at the sweeping sands of the desert beyond the palace made her itch to explore it.

As concentrated as she was on capturing a shimmering mauve dragonfly hovering above the azure-blue of the pool with her lens, there was no mistaking the moment the King stormed into her suite. She heard the heavy door to her room bang forcefully against the wall, and turned to see a small cloud of white powder float to the floor from where the ornate handle had gouged the plaster.

Regan moved to the arched doorway and then blinked.

King Jaeger stood inside her room, dressed in a pair of tailored trousers that hugged his powerful legs, an unbuttoned pristine white shirt, and that was it. His legs were braced wide, his hands held loosely at his sides, and he wore an expression on his face that could level a mountain. Regan couldn't prevent her eyes from running down the darkly tanned strip of flesh from his neck to the trousers that sat low on his hips. Dark hair covered his leanly muscled chest, arrowing down to bisect abdominal muscles you could probably bounce a coin off.

Her mouth ran dry as her gaze continued on down to his feet.

'I think you forgot your shoes,' she said, appalled to find that she even found the sight of his bare feet sexy.

The door closed behind him with a thud.

'And possibly your sense of humour,' she added, trying to lighten the mood and stop herself from obsessing about his body.

'If I were you I'd be very worried right about now,' he drawled menacingly.

She was. Worried that she couldn't stop thinking about sex whenever he was around. It was becoming insidious.

'About?' she asked, deciding to brave out his obviously bad mood. It wasn't possible that he'd found out about her post so quickly. Not unless he had ESP, or security cameras in her room. She cast a quick glance at the corners of the ceilings. Nothing there. Thank heavens.

'How did you do it?' he asked softly.

Damn. He did know. 'Do what?'

'Don't play cute with me—it won't work. How did you access the internet?'

'Oh, that…' She strolled further into the room until she'd put the protection of the sofa between them. He didn't have the look of a man who was about to do her physical harm, and indeed, every time he had restrained her she'd felt him leash his physical strength so as not to hurt her, but she suspected that if his temper ever did blow it would make Mount Vesuvius look as innocuous as a child throwing sand.

'Yes. *That*.' He came towards her, with animal grace, the muscles in his abdomen rippling with every silent footfall. Regan swallowed, her own stomach muscles pulling tight at the sight. A rush of excitement shot through her. *Excitement?* Was she completely daft? The man looked as if he was coming up with new ways she was going to die!

He stopped in front of the sofa, his eyes briefly scanning it before returning to her. It wouldn't be enough, she thought wildly; the Great Wall of China wouldn't be enough to keep her from him if he wanted to get to her.

'So I accessed the internet,' she murmured vaguely. 'I didn't write anything negative. I actually implied that I liked you. Which I don't, in case you get any ideas.'

Or, at least, any more ideas...

'You implied a lot more than that,' he muttered furiously.

'You're just unhappy because I countered your move and foiled your horrible plan to worry Chad. How did you find out so quickly, by the way? Do you have cameras in this room, watching my every move? That would be truly creepy if you did.'

'I do not have cameras in here, though I might after this,' he bit out. 'But, in answer to your question, your post has been shared a number of times.'

'Good,' she said. 'I hope Chad has managed to see it.'

'I know Chad was your intended audience.' His thick dark lashes narrowed, making his blue eyes seem impossibly vibrant. 'Unfortunately you picked up a few more *interested* parties.'

Regan frowned at his deceptively light tone. 'How many more?'

'Six million more.'

'Six mill—! That can't be true. I only have forty-eight followers and most of those are work-related.'

'You might not be popular, Miss James, but I am.'

'Lucky you,' she retorted, wishing he'd worn more clothing. 'Don't you want to button your shirt?' she said, inwardly cringing at the husky note in her voice when she'd been aiming for cool. 'It's quite chilly today.'

'It's forty degrees in the shade. And I'll button my shirt when I'm good and ready.' His voice became a lethal purr. 'Unless it's bothering you…'

'No. Not at all.' She waved off his suggestion as if it were ludicrous. 'I was just thinking that it didn't look very… *kingly*.'

His smile said that he knew she was lying. 'Good, because I'm not feeling very *kingly* right now.' His eyes drifted to her lips and Regan barely resisted the urge to moisten them. Sexual tension arced between them like a tightrope, and she had no idea what to do with all the jittery energy that coursed through her. She felt like a small child in a room full of sweets who had been told to stand in the corner and not touch anything.

Heat suffused her cheeks and she tried not to think about how warm and resilient his skin would feel if she were to slide her hands inside his open shirt. 'Of course, how you walk around the palace is entirely up to you. Don't mind me.'

She bit into her lip to stop the nervous chatter. She hoped the sharp little pain would also stop all the inappropriate thoughts running through her head.

'Thanks for the memo,' he bit out tautly. 'Now stop prevaricating and tell me how you did it.'

'I can't.' One thing she wouldn't do was get the lovely girl who cleaned her room into trouble.

A muscle ticked in his jaw. 'Miss James, I am two seconds away from strangling you with my bare hands and feeding your body to a lake full of alligators. I suggest you don't push me any further.'

'There are alligators in the desert?'

'Regan!'

She jumped as he bellowed her name. He'd never used her first name before and it scattered her thoughts. 'Calm down.' She didn't know if she was referring to him or herself, but it didn't matter. 'I was only asking. But...' She couldn't think of any more stalling tactics, so she just went with honesty. 'I have no intention of telling you how I accessed the internet, so stop asking me.'

'If someone in my employ helped you they will be punished.'

Regan planted her hands on her hips. 'It wasn't her fault.'

Jaeger's blue eyes narrowed, assessing. 'The maid helped you.'

'She didn't help me. She had a tablet and I...borrowed it.'

The muscle in his jaw flexed rigidly.

'If you punish her I'll never forgive you,' she said earnestly, 'because it wasn't her fault.'

'I have no doubt it wasn't her fault but it is obvious she was negligent.'

'I took advantage.'

'Believe me, I'm in no doubt about that.'

'So you won't do anything to her?' she implored. 'Because I can't allow it.'

'*You* can't allow it?'

He coughed out a laugh and Regan folded her arms across her chest. 'No. It wouldn't be fair. And you strike me as a very fair man.'

'Stop playing to my vanity.' He shook his head. 'It

hasn't worked with women before you; it won't work for you either.'

'I was only—'

'Quiet,' he growled. 'I need to think.'

He might need to but she could really use some air.

'Where are you going?'

Regan looked over her shoulder to find him watching her. 'There's no need to shout,' she grouched. 'I'm right here. And you clearly don't need me to think.'

'I never shout,' he corrected her. 'At least, I didn't before I met you.'

Seriously unnerved by the effect his near naked body was having on her Regan's heart hammered inside her chest. 'You know how to fix that,' she said faintly. 'You can let me go.'

He laughed. 'I wish I could. Believe me, you're a nuisance I could well do without.'

For some reason his words hurt. For all the unconventional nature of their meeting, and their missing siblings, Regan couldn't deny that he was the most exciting man she had ever met. Since her parents had died she'd become cautious and responsible. She always played it safe. One look at this man, one touch, made her feel electrified and more alive than she'd felt in so long. The feeling was at once thrilling and completely appalling. The man didn't *do* love and that was all she knew how to do.

He let out a rough breath that brought her eyes back to his. 'You have no idea what you've done, do you?' he muttered.

Something in his tone stayed her. 'Should I?'

'No. I suppose not.' He dragged a hand through his hair, mussing it further. 'In your world, posting a provocative image on social media would barely raise a ripple. Here it is very different. Here we have morals and ethics.'

'We have morals and ethics in America,' Regan said a little defensively. Well, they used to, at least, and most still did.

'Be that as it may, what you have done, Miss James,' he said with palpable restraint, 'is create a diplomatic crisis I am now in a position to have to fix.'

'A diplomatic crisis? I don't see how.'

'I have probably the most important summit my country has ever hosted starting tomorrow and a raft of people wondering who the American woman is I'm entertaining in my palace.'

'You're hardly entertaining me.'

'Further, I am now without an escort for the next four days.'

'I fail to see what this has to do with me.'

'Then let me explain it to you.' His blue eyes glittered down into hers. 'Since you have created this issue, you will become the escort you made me lose.'

'I didn't make you lose anyone,' she denied hotly. 'And there's no way I'm going to be your escort.' She gave a shaky laugh. Just the thought of it made her hot. 'Do you know what people would think if they saw us together?'

His eyes turned smoky and he leant against the back of the sofa, one bare foot crossed over the other, his eyes on her denim shorts. 'I think that horse has already bolted, *habiba*.'

Regan swallowed heavily. 'Well, I don't intend to make it worse by being seen on your arm. And anyway, this is all really your fault for bringing me here in the first place.'

'I agree. But that horse has also bolted, and now we deal with the consequences.' His eyes turned hard. 'Usually Milena would step in during these situations, but we both know why she can't do that, don't we?'

Regan grimaced. 'My brother had nothing to do with

your sister going AWOL! But okay,' she added quickly when she noticed the betraying muscle clench in his jaw. 'I think the best thing we can do now is leave things as they are. I won't cause any more problems,' she promised. 'And soon enough everyone will forget all about my little photo.'

'No one will forget you're here after that *little* photo. But even if they did, that doesn't solve all of my problems.'

'Surely you have women on speed dial all over the world who could play hostess—escort—for you. Probably any one of them would jump at the chance to do it.'

'I'm sure you're right.' His gaze travelled over her in blatant male appraisal. 'But the women I have on speed dial fulfil a very different function from hostessing, *habiba*.' His lazy drawl left her in no doubt as to what that function was. 'And I don't want to spend the weekend with a woman who might think that I'm more interested in her than I am. With you I know that won't happen.'

'Oh, you can count on that.'

A smile played around the edges of his mouth, amusement lighting his eyes. 'Why is it you're the only person who ever has the gumption to argue with me?'

'Probably if someone else had we wouldn't be in this dilemma because you'd have developed a sense of reason.'

'Oh, we'd be in it.'

'You might be,' she said irritably. 'But I wouldn't. I work at a prestigious private school. I have my reputation to think about, and once this is all over I'll be returning to my normal life and I'm not doing that as some hot desert king's mistress!'

'Hot?'

'As in temperature,' she said, her face flushing. 'You're like a furnace.' He laughed, which only irritated her more.

'Probably my friend, Penny, has already left me a tonne of messages on my phone asking me what's going on. Not that I'd know about those.'

'She has. My staff have replied on your behalf.'

'Oh…!' Her lips pressed into a flat line. 'I promised myself I wasn't going to let you make me angry again, but I'm struggling.'

'Good to know. And I understand your dilemma.'

'You do?'

'Yes. Which is why I won't present you as my partner, or escort. I'll present you as my fiancée.'

'Your *what*?'

Ignoring her shocked outburst, he paced back and forth. 'Yes, this is a much better solution. It will not only satisfy the curiosity of those wondering why you're in my palace, but, since the photo of you in my arms didn't bring your brother running to your rescue, news of our betrothal might do that job too.'

'You're as ruthless as a snake,' she spluttered. 'But it won't work. Chad would never believe it.'

'He doesn't have to believe it.' His bright blue eyes connected with hers. 'He just has to bring my sister back unharmed.'

Regan frowned. If Chad knew she was engaged to the King there was no doubt he'd come running. And maybe that was for the best. Then this whole situation would be resolved and she could go home. 'And if it doesn't work?'

'It has to work.'

'Why? Because your mightiness has decreed that it will?'

He stopped pacing to stare at her. 'You like challenging me, don't you, Regan?' His gaze lingered on her lips and her pulse jumped erratically in her throat.

'Yes, you should look wary,' he murmured. 'Right now

I want to put my hands on you and I'm not sure if I want to make it pleasurable or painful.'

Regan jumped away from him, her insides jittery. 'We were talking about my brother,' she reminded him huskily.

'The whole reason you're here.'

He slowly prowled towards her, crowding her to the point where all she could think about was him. How tall he was. How big. How the stubble on his jaw would feel beneath her fingertips.

'Stop thinking of our betrothal in the romantic sense,' he advised. 'It's a business arrangement and it's temporary.'

'Two things you're obviously exceptionally good at.'

His jaw hardened and his gaze dropped to her mouth. 'I'm good at a lot of things, Regan, and if you're not careful you'll find out which of those things I'm *particularly* good at.'

Regan's mouth went dry at the sensual threat and once more she was acutely aware that he *still hadn't buttoned his shirt*.

He shook his head. 'Your desperation not to marry me serves you well, but it only reinforces that this is the right thing to do. My personal aide has been insisting for years that I need a partner at these major events, and having you by my side will mitigate any potential fallout from your ill-timed photo—'

'*My* ill-timed photo?'

'—And stop any untoward gossip from developing about the Western woman residing in my palace.'

'Residing?' She huffed out an astonished breath. 'You mean imprisoned.'

'If you were imprisoned you'd be in jail.'

'But this is all one-way. This is all about you and what you want. But what about what I want?'

'You're not in any position to make demands.'

'Actually, I am.' She threw back her head and stared at him. 'If you want my co-operation this weekend then I want something too.'

His body went preternaturally still and Regan got the distinct impression he thought she was going to ask him for money or jewels or something. 'You must have really dated some shallow women if the look of dread that just crossed your face is anything to go by.'

His eyes flashed blue sparks at her. 'Don't keep me waiting, Miss James; what is it you want?'

'A deal.'

'Excuse me?'

'Since deals are the only thing you seem to understand, I'll make one with you. I'll agree to be your escort, or rather, your partner this weekend if you let Chad go when he returns.'

'Absolutely not.' He swung away from her and then back. 'Your brother has my sister. That will not go unpunished.'

'But you don't really know what's happened or why they're together.'

'I will. And when I do your brother will be in serious trouble.'

'Fine; then you'll have to pull out your little black book and explain why you've locked me up some other way.'

He stalked over to the window and dug his hands into his pockets. Regan did her best not to notice the way the fabric of his trousers pulled tight across his well-defined glutes.

They're just muscles, she told herself, *just like the ones in his arms, his chest, his thighs...*

'Deal.'

What?

Her head came up, a betraying blush burning her face when she realised he had caught her staring.

'I'm agreeing with you. You become my fiancée for

three nights and four days and when your brother returns, as long as my sister is unharmed, I'll let him leave the country. Unharmed.' He prowled towards her and she unconsciously backed up a step at the light of battle in his eyes. 'Rest assured, though.' He stopped just short of touching her. 'If my sister is hurt in any way I'll kill him, are we clear?'

'Rest assured,' Regan fired back at him. 'If my brother has caused your sister harm in any way you won't have to kill him—I will. But he won't have,' she added softly. 'Chad isn't like that. He's not a macho kind of guy who takes what he wants. He's kind and considerate.'

'Unlike me?' he suggested silkily.

'I didn't say that.'

'You didn't have to, *habiba*; your face is very expressive.'

God, she hoped not.

'Like for the last half hour,' he murmured, taking another step towards her, 'you've been wondering what it would be like to kiss me.'

Regan sputtered out some unintelligible noise that might have had the words 'massive' and 'ego' in it, her hands coming up between them to press firmly against his hard, *naked* chest. She bit her lip against the urge to slide them up that warm wall of muscle and twine them together at the nape of his neck. 'You're wrong,' she husked.

A light came into his eyes that turned her lips as dry as his dusty desert land. 'I'm not wrong. Your pupils are dilated and your pulse is hammering, begging for me to put my mouth on it.'

His words caused hot colour to surge into her face. 'That's fear.'

His eyes lifted to hers. 'Fear of what?' he asked softly. 'That I will kiss you, or that I won't?'

Regan started to shake her head, a soft cry escaping her lips when his hands threaded into her hair and framed her face. His gaze held hers for an interminable second and then something coalesced behind his blue eyes and his head lowered to hers.

Regan's body jerked against his, her hands gripping his wrists with the intention of dragging them away from her, but it didn't happen. His mouth moved on hers with such heat and skill she went still beneath the onslaught. He gave a husky groan as his tongue traced the line between her lips, urging them to part. Sensation rocked through her and without any conscious thought her lips were shaping themselves to his, her mouth matching his hungry intensity.

With consummate skill, he completely controlled the kiss, one of his hands tunnelling further into her hair, angling her head so he could deepen the contact, the other pressed to the small of her back, urging her lower body to fit against his.

At the feel of his rock-hard desire, Regan moaned, wrapping her arms around his shoulders, her senses spinning out of control as she moved against him, her neck arching for the glide of his lips and tongue scraping against her skin.

He made a growling noise in the back of his throat that she felt deep in her pelvis, making her ache.

'Regan, I...' His lips returned to hers, his tongue exploring her mouth with a carnal intimacy that shocked her, the kiss going from hot to incendiary within seconds.

Regan heard herself moan, felt awash with sensations she couldn't contain. Her breasts were heavy and aching, desperate for relief, and her pelvis felt hollow. Beyond thought or reason her hands kneaded his shoulders, her fingers pushing aside his shirt to stroke his heated flesh.

He vibrated against the contact and his own hands must

have moved, because suddenly he was cupping her breast, his thumb strumming the hard nub of her nipple, drawing a keening sound from deep inside her. She felt the need in him ramp up, his movements hungrier, more urgent as his hands skimmed over her body, his fingers tugging on her blouse to release the row of buttons, revealing the upper swell of her breasts to his lips and teeth.

Regan's hands gripped fistfuls of his hair, urging him closer. 'Jaeger... Jag. Please...' His name on her lips seemed to shift something in both of them. He lifted his mouth from her body, his breathing hard, his eyes almost black.

She sucked in a breath, tried to clear her head. She saw shock register on his face and knew instantly that he regretted what had just happened.

'Why did you do that?' She touched her fingers to her tender lips, swollen from the force of his kisses.

His eyes narrowed on her, somehow a lot clearer than hers. 'I've wanted to taste you since the first moment I met you. Now I have.' He stepped further away from her, his eyes mirroring the mental distance he was placing between them as well as the physical. 'Tomorrow you will be provided with a wardrobe that should cover everything you need for the next four days. As long as you stick to your side of the agreement, I'll stick to mine.'

With that he pivoted on his feet and walked out of the door.

As soon as it clicked closed Regan let out a pent-up breath and pressed her hand to her abdomen.

'I've wanted to taste you since the first moment I met you. Now I have.'

Her hand trembled as she pushed her hair back from her face.

Was he serious?

How could he kiss her like that and then walk away?

How was that possible when she felt as if her world had been tipped upside down and shaken loose?

Well, because he must have kissed a thousand women to the half a dozen men she had kissed, most of which had occurred in high school before her parents had died. She'd never been great with boys and as she'd matured she hadn't been great with men either. The ones who liked her she had zero interest in, and the ones she thought had potential were not interested in a woman raising a teenage boy. Even if that boy was her brother. No way had anyone ever kissed her with the sensual expertise she'd just experienced with King Jaeger. But maybe kings were good at everything. Jag certainly claimed to know everything.

She shook her head, pride fortifying her spine. If he could walk away from that kiss without a backward glance then so could she.

Unconsciously her fingers went to her mouth and stroked down the side of her neck along the same path his lips had taken. When she realised what she was doing she dropped her hand and picked up her camera.

Reliving whatever it was that had just happened between them was not conducive to forgetting it. And forgetting it was exactly what she needed to do. She wasn't here for him. She was here for Chad. And now a deal she'd made on the fly.

A deal with the devil.

A deal she knew she could *never* go through with.

CHAPTER SIX

JAG KNEW AS soon as he spotted her in the small anteroom beside the grand ballroom that she was going to renege on their deal. And really he should let her. He didn't really give a damn about having a plus-one for the weekend. He'd done hundreds of these events before on his own. What would one more matter? And as to her unexplained presence in the palace…that was tougher to handle, but not impossible.

He paused for a moment, just watching her. She was pacing back and forth, her teeth delicately worrying her lower lip. A lower lip he had taken gently between his teeth not twenty-four hours earlier.

She looked astonishingly beautiful dressed in a slender column of burnished copper silk overlaid with a sheer organza bodice that accentuated the long line of her neck and hinted at the delicate swell of her breasts. The colour perfectly matched her hair, as he'd known it would, and turned her skin to polished ivory. Skin that was as soft as it looked.

Regan paused in front of the ornate mirror above the fireplace, tucking a strand of hair back behind her ear. Their gazes met in the mirror, her wide cinnamon eyes bright and lovely, her luscious lips painted a subtle pink. With her hair piled on top of her head in an elaborate style, she looked like an ethereal queen from a bygone era, and in that moment he knew he couldn't release her from their deal. Not yet.

Unwilling to analyse his motivations for that decision too closely, he leaned against the doorjamb. 'It's too late to change your mind, *jamila*,' he said gruffly.

She turned towards him with a suddenness that made the skirt of her gown swirl around her body, outlining her long legs before resettling. 'How do you know I want to change my mind?' she asked, her eyes gliding down over his body as if she couldn't help herself. He knew the feeling.

'Body language.'

He only hoped she wasn't as good at reading it as he was. If she was she'd know his was shouting, *I want you. Now.*

Uneasy at the depth of his primal response to her, he reminded himself that he'd already had this discussion with himself in the shower and it wasn't going to happen. He was not going to touch her again, or kiss her, and if that was all he could think about, well, that was just too bad. He wouldn't allow himself to complicate an already complicated situation. It wasn't logical. Just as kissing her hadn't been. One minute he'd been staring into her beautiful, expressive eyes and the next his hands were in her hair and his lips were soldered to hers.

She was like a magnet, and in that moment he'd had all the willpower of a metal shaving. It wasn't something he liked to acknowledge, even to himself.

Pushing away from the door, he strolled into the room. 'We have a few housekeeping issues to sort out before we—'

'Your Majesty, wait. Please.' She drifted closer and his nostrils flared as he picked up her delicate jasmine scent. He'd made sure that she'd been kept busy all day with spa treatments and massages, and just the thought of how supple her scented body would be was a sweet torture he could well do without.

'It's Jaeger,' he reminded her. 'Or Jag. Remember?'

She blushed a becoming shade of pink and pursed her lips. 'I'm trying not to.'

'Look, if this is about that kiss yesterday—'

'It's not about the kiss,' she cut him off quickly. 'I know what that was. You've already said. You wanted to know what it would be like to kiss me, you found out, and now you don't want to repeat the experience. We can move on from that.'

Move on? He wasn't sure that he could.

'The fact is, there's no way I can pose as your fiancée. I'm not royal, or a supermodel. I'm an ordinary school-teacher. Everyone will know instantly that I'm a fraud.'

'You're not ordinary and I don't want you to pretend to be anyone but yourself. As a teacher you must be used to standing in front of large groups of people. I'm sure this won't be any different.'

He paced away from her, his mind still spinning at what she'd just said to him. Should he correct her misconception that he didn't want to repeat their kiss, or would it be easier to let it stand?

Unable to form a decision about that on the spot, he shelved it for later.

'I'm used to standing up in front of primary-school children,' she explained, 'which is not the same as what will be expected of me this weekend. And honestly, I'm a better behind-the-scenes person. I don't do well when the focus is directly on me. I get nervous.'

'Why?' Jag had dealt with crowds and attention his whole life. He was so used to being scrutinised from afar he didn't even give it a second thought. It was being scrutinised from up close that made him uncomfortable.

'I think it stems from all the impromptu interviews from the child-protection services I had to undergo in the early years. Whenever I was under the spotlight there was always the chance that Chad would be taken away from me. I never wanted to let him down by not being good enough and as a result I really dislike surprises and I especially dislike being the centre of attention.'

Shocked that she would tell him something so deeply personal, Jag felt something grip tight in his chest. 'I promise you that you won't be the centre of attention.' He reached out to stroke the side of her face and thought better of it. 'Don't forget, this is a political summit, not a day at Royal Ascot. That means I'll be the one in demand.' He kept his voice deliberately light, wanting to put her at ease and erase the vulnerability he saw in her expression. Vulnerability led to pain and the last thing he wanted was for her to suffer because of him. 'Now, the first part of housekeeping...' he reached into his pocket and pulled out a matte red box '...is for you to wear this.' He opened the box and turned it towards her.

'Oh, my God. It's as big as an iceberg,' she said, snatching her hands behind her back. 'I can't wear that.'

Jag smiled at her response. 'It was the biggest one I could find. Give me your hand.'

'No.'

Ignoring her small act of rebellion, he gently took hold of her left forearm and dragged her hand out from behind her back. 'I hope it fits. I had to guess the size of your fingers. They're so slender the jeweller thought I'd made a mistake.'

They both stared down at the intricately cut diamond glowing on her finger as if it had its own light source. 'But of course you didn't,' she said huskily. 'Are you sure it's not loaded with some beacon so you always know where I am?'

'Don't give me any ideas, *jamila*.'

She blinked up at him. 'You called me that before. What does it mean?'

'Beautiful.'

'I'm not—'

'Yes, you are.'

Awareness throbbed between them and Jag fought with the need to drag her into his arms and ruin her pink lipstick.

'Your Maj—'

'Jag,' he growled.

'This is too much,' she said thickly, keeping her eyes averted from his. 'I hope it's not real. I'll be afraid someone will rob me.'

'Nobody is going to rob you. Not in this crowd, but if it makes you feel any better my security detail will not let you out of their sights.'

'Are you sure that's not so I won't run off with it myself?'

'You won't run off with it. If you did I'd catch you. And yes, it is real.'

She pressed her lips together, staring at the ring, and he had to curb another powerful need to soften the strain around her mouth with a kiss.

'There are three other items of housekeeping to go through,' he said briskly. 'Protocol demands that you always walk two paces behind me, and you also cannot touch me.' He noticed her tapered brows rise with astonishment, and he nodded. 'Santarians do not go in for PDAs.'

'Not ever?'

'Sometimes with children. If the family is a tactile one.'

'Wow, my parents would have been locked up, then. They were always hanging all over each other. And us. Chad and I definitely inherited their affectionate nature. Oh…' She gave him a disconcerted look. 'You probably didn't want to hear that.'

No, he hadn't. But more because he couldn't stop thinking about how wild she'd been in his arms the night before. And of course he didn't want to entertain the idea that

Milena was having a relationship with Chad. *She wouldn't be strong enough to cope if it turned bad.* 'The third item is that I do not intend to spend the evening talking about your brother or my sister. It is a topic that is off the table from this moment on. Understood?'

'Perfectly. And I agree. It wouldn't look good if we started arguing in front of your guests.'

'My lords, ladies and gentlemen, *mesdames et messieurs*, I give you Sheikh Jaeger al-Hadrid, our lord and King of Santara, and his intended, the future Queen of Santara, Miss Regan James.'

Regan gave a small gasp at the formal introduction. She stood two steps behind Jag, waiting for him to descend the grand staircase, craning her neck to see over his wide shoulders to the room below. What she could see took her breath away. The room looked like a golden cloud, the walls gilt-edged and inlaid with dark turquoise wallpaper. Ancient frescoes and golden bell-shaped chandeliers adorned the high ceilings, while circular tables, elegantly laid with silverware and crystal, filled the floor space. Beautifully dressed men and women, some in military garb and traditional robes, milled in small groups and stared up at them with eager, over-bright eyes. Some, mostly the women, were craning their own necks to get a look at her, and it made Regan shrink back just a little more in the shadows.

When Jag had first informed her that she would have to walk two steps behind him at all times she'd been offended. Now she wondered if that wasn't a blessing. It might mean that she went unnoticed the whole night!

She twisted the egg-sized diamond on her finger, eyeing the endless row of steps they needed to descend with mounting dread. She just hoped she didn't trip over the beautiful gown she'd been squeezed into. It was the most delicate, the most exquisite piece of clothing she had ever worn and it made her feel like a fairy princess.

Queen, she amended with a grimace. Had Tarik really needed to introduce her as the future Queen? Couldn't he have just said her name? Or, better yet, nothing at all?

She noticed Jag shift in front of her and her heartbeat quickened. *Here we go*, she thought, preparing to follow him down the staircase. Only that didn't happen. As if sensing her unease, he turned towards her, his hand out-stretched.

Regan glanced up to find sapphire-blue eyes trained on her with an intensity that made her burn. And just like that she was back in his arms with his mouth open over hers. She moistened her lips and saw his eyes darken in response. His chest rose and fell as he took a couple of deep breaths and she wondered if he wasn't thinking about the same thing. Then he gestured for her to approach him.

She took a small step, then another. 'What?' she whispered self-consciously. 'Why have we stopped?'

'The thing is…' A wry grin curled one side of his mouth and he looked so impossibly handsome in that moment she could have stared at him forever. 'The thing is, I've always hated protocol.' He drew her to his side and clasped her hand.

A low murmur rippled through the crowd as he raised her hand to his lips, a sexy smile lighting his eyes. It was a chivalrous gesture. A gesture meant to impress, and it did, melting Regan's heart right along with every other woman's in the ballroom.

Do not get caught up in all this, she warned herself, instantly suppressing the shiver of emotion that welled up inside her. This was not a fairy-tale situation. She was not Cinderella, and Jag was not going to be the Prince—or

King—who promised to adore her for ever. Real life didn't work out that way. Real life was often a painful slog.

She gave him a faltering smile, wondering why he was still stalling. 'It's too late to change your mind now,' she whispered, throwing his earlier words back at him.

His smile widened. 'I have no intention of changing my mind, my little America.'

Regan told herself not to get lost in that smile. Or the nickname that sounded too much like an endearment. He had walked away from their kiss last night without a backward glance. The only interest he had in her was with regard to thwarting diplomatic crises and getting his sister back. That settled in her mind, she took a deep breath and concentrated on not tripping.

Unbelievably the night went much faster than Regan had expected. The people she met were mostly lovely and interesting, and Jag never let her very far out of his sight, instinctively sensing when she was feeling out of her depth and coming to her side.

'He's divine,' more than one woman had said with unabashed envy throughout the night, giggling like schoolgirls when Jag paid them personal attention. She watched with fascination at how he skilfully worked the room and put the people around him at ease. It was such a contrast to the way they had met, and yet she saw both elements of him in the superbly tailored tuxedo that did wicked things to his body. He was at once incredibly sophisticated and also inherently dangerous. Not physically. At least not to her. No, King Jaeger's danger was in the masculine charisma he exuded with unassailable ease. It made everyone in the room want to be near him. Especially her.

Realising that the wife of a Spanish diplomat had just spoken to her, Regan smiled apologetically. She cast a sideways glance at Jaeger, watching the way he easily commanded the conversation in the small group of delegates clustered around him. A stunning woman at his side leaned close to him and whispered something in his ear, her hand placing something into his trouser pocket so effortlessly Regan nearly missed it.

'You are very lucky,' the woman, Esmeralda, said again, forcing Regan to refocus.

'Lucky?' Regan murmured, wondering what they were talking about now.

'Yes. He is a king amongst kings.' She gave Regan a knowing smile. 'Although I'm not sure I could handle all that latent sexuality, and I'm Latin.'

Regan's face flamed as she recalled the sexual skill with which he'd kissed her, the way his hands had moulded her to him and stroked her breasts.

'Ooh-la-la…' Esmeralda chortled. 'I can see that you can.'

'Can what?' Jag asked smoothly, placing his arm around Regan's waist.

'Just girl talk, Your Majesty,' the older woman said, raking her eyes over his torso as if she wished it were her blood-red fingernails instead.

But Regan was embarrassed, knowing for a fact that the woman's assumptions were completely wrong. She didn't have the experience, or the expertise, to handle someone of Jaeger's sexual nature and she never would.

Excusing them both, Jag led her towards their table.

'What's in your pocket?' Regan asked, leaning close to him so no one could overhear.

He stopped and looked at her, stepping to the side to avoid anyone else following in their path. His eyes glinted with amusement at her. 'I suspect it's a phone number. I haven't looked.'

Regan's mouth fell open. She wasn't sure what astonished her the most. That he hadn't looked or that a woman would slip a man her phone number in plain sight of anyone who happened to be paying attention.

'But you're engaged,' she said on a rush. 'At least, that woman thinks you are.'

'She's also married.' His eyes twinkled as they gazed into hers.

'That's terrible. I don't know who to feel sorry for more—her or her husband. She's clearly not happy in her marriage.'

'Some people just want the excitement of being with someone new.'

'Well, I wouldn't. If I committed to someone I'd always be faithful to them.'

'As would I, *habiba*.' His voice was rough, as if he were speaking directly to her and not in generalities.

Her heart bumped inside her chest. 'So you do have scruples,' she said huskily.

'Just because I don't let anyone mess with my family, that doesn't make me the bad guy you think I am, Regan.'

He settled his hands on her waist and Regan's pulse leapt in her throat. 'I didn't think Santarians were into public displays of affection,' she murmured breathlessly.

'We're not,' he confirmed, leading her back towards their table. 'But I figured I'd already broken protocol once tonight and the sky didn't fall in.'

She shook her head. 'You're a real rebel, aren't you?'

He laughed softly. 'Actually I'm not. I was always the child who did the right thing and toed the line growing up.'

'The dutiful son. Was that because it was expected of you as the first born?'

'That and because it was the only thing that made sense.'

'Love makes sense,' she said softly.

'For you, not for me.'

'Why do you think that?'

'Because I know how the world works. Both my parents were emotional. Their relationship unbearably volatile. Whenever emotion took over my mother left and my father worked harder. If there's one thing I've learned from watching my parents it's never to let emotion get in the way of making decisions.'

'But how do you control that so well?'

Right now all she could think about was wrapping her arms around his neck and dragging his mouth down to hers. It was actually frightening, the amount of times she thought about touching him. It felt as if she'd been in a deep sleep for a long time, only to waken and imprint on him like a baby bird.

'Practice.' He smiled at her, his teeth impossibly white against the dark stubble that had already started shading his jaw, taking him from merely handsome to outrageously gorgeous.

'Okay, well, I'm going to start practising emotionlessness right now. If you'll excuse me, I'm going to freshen up.'

'Don't be long.'

Regan let out a ragged breath as his gaze held hers. For a split second his eyes had been on her mouth and she could have sworn they had turned hungry. Most likely wishful thinking on her part.

She really didn't want to like him after the way he had threatened her brother and detained her as bait, but she knew that she did. Maybe if he hadn't kissed her she'd feel differently. But that wasn't entirely true. She'd found herself drawn to him even before she knew he kissed like a god. But he wasn't the only one who tried not to let their emotions dominate their decisions. She'd had to put her own aside after her parents died. And worse, she knew no one was indispensable, so why put yourself out there in the first place?

'Excuse me.'

'Oh, I'm sorry.' Regan smiled at a beautiful dark-haired woman as she exited the ladies' room. She stepped to the side so the woman could enter but she shook her head.

'I'm not going in.'

'Okay.' Regan smiled again and was about to return to the ballroom when the woman took a hesitant step forward. A prickle of unease raised the hairs on the back of Regan's neck. 'Is something wrong?'

'No, I—'

'Have you been crying?' Regan stepped closer to her. 'Your eyes are damp.'

'I'm fine.' The woman sniffed, clearly not fine. 'I just wanted to get a closer look at you.'

During the night many guests had wanted to get a closer look at her, and, while it hadn't been as daunting as she'd first thought, she still didn't like it.

'Why are you crying?'

'I'm Princess Alexa of Berenia.'

'I'm Regan James.'

The woman gave a brief laugh. 'I know.'

'Well, at least I made you smile.' She frowned with concern. 'Has someone hurt you? Are you feeling ill? Why don't I take you back to your table so you can—?'

'No. I don't want to go back to my table.' She gave her a hard look. 'You don't even know who I am, do you?'

Getting an uneasy feeling in the pit of her stomach, Regan shook her head. 'Should I?'

'Considering I was the King's fiancée up until yesterday, I would have thought so. I can't believe he would keep you in his palace and then *marry* you.'

Regan felt as if someone had poked her in the stomach with a sharp stick. 'Do you mean King Jaeger?'

'Who else?' Tears welled up in her eyes again. 'My father thinks you have bewitched him. He blames me, of course.'

'I haven't bewitched anyone,' Regan said vehemently, feeling sick. 'It's just... I mean... I can't explain it to you but I'm really sorry this has happened to you.'

'He loves you. It's obvious by the way he looks at you.' More tears leaked out of her eyes and she valiantly tried to hold them back. 'The way he touches you.'

Regan agreed that he had touched her a little too much. It had kept her in a heightened state of awareness all night. But she knew for a fact that he didn't love her. 'I don't know what to say to you.' Her own emotions felt as if they were being buffeted in a fierce wind. She was at once upset for this woman, who clearly cared for the King a great deal, and incredibly angry at Jag's obvious insensitivity. Why hadn't he told her about his engagement? Why hadn't he warned her that his ex might show up and approach her? Because surely he had known Alexa was invited? He'd signed off the guest list.

'There's nothing you can say.' The Princess raised her regal chin in a show of bravado that only made Regan feel worse for her. 'I tried to tell my father that those photos didn't matter, that you were nothing to the King, but I was wrong.'

'You're not wrong.' Regan bit her lip, anger making her muscles rigid. 'Look, I can't be sure but...maybe things will still work out for you. Maybe you should keep your fingers crossed. You never know what can happen in a couple of days. But if I were you, and I wanted him as much as you seem to then I *wouldn't* give up hope.'

The Princess looked at her as if she was crazy. She wasn't. She was just really angry.

'Are you going to talk to me at all about what's bothering you or are you going to continue to give me frostbite?'

Regan had been giving him the cold shoulder for the last hour until Jag had finally had enough and called it a night.

'Why have we stopped here?' she asked curtly, brushing aside his question and glancing along the unfamiliar corridor.

'You've been moved from the garden suite to the one adjoining mine.'

She glared up at him, her mouth tight. 'I don't want the room adjoining yours.'

Growing more and more irritated because he'd actually enjoyed what was usually a tedious formal evening, he pushed the door to his room wide open. 'Too bad. The garden suite is now occupied by the King and Queen of Norway. Feel free to join them if you like.'

She looked at him with such venom he thought she'd decide to do it. But then she lifted her dainty nose in the air and swept past him into the room. Sighing heavily, he followed her into his private living room, wondering what had gone wrong in the last hour.

'You don't need to accompany me,' she said; 'I know how to undress myself.'

Jag's eyes dragged down over her lush body and all the way back up. A flush of colour tinged her cheeks and heat surged through his veins. Graphic images of her spread out on his elegant sofa wearing nothing but her delicate gold stilettos drove his frustration levels higher. 'You sure about that?' He shrugged out of his jacket and tossed it across the back of said sofa. 'I'd be happy to lend a hand if you need it.'

'Oh, I'm sure you would.' She folded her arms over her chest. 'I'm sure you've helped many women out of their clothing in your time. Women like Princess Alexa perhaps. Your *ex-fiancée*.'

Ah…suddenly the reason for her cool hauteur made sense. 'Princess Alexa was not my fiancée. Whoever told you that is mistaken.'

'She did,' she said, challenge lighting her golden-brown eyes. 'In between bouts of crying.'

Jag stared at her. He'd spoken to King Ronan personally ahead of the opening dinner, reminding the elderly King that he had never actually committed to marrying his daughter and now he wouldn't be.

'Princess Alexa and I—'

'Please.' Regan held up her hand dismissively, cutting him off. 'Don't feel as if you have to explain anything to me. It's none of my business. I'm only the stand-in. Lucky that you find women so interchangeable, no doubt it's water off a duck's back for you.'

'I *do not* find women interchangeable.'

'No, you just see them as part of a package deal to be moved about according to your needs and political machinations. Is this her ring?' She tugged at the diamond he had given her earlier. 'She stared at it long and hard when she saw it. Did you choose it together?'

'Would you stand still and listen to me?' Her pacing was starting to give him whiplash.

'It doesn't matter. I find I can't abide wearing another woman's ring, even if it is just a prop.'

She held it out to him and Jag gritted his teeth, locking his hands around her wrists and jamming the ring back on her finger. 'That is not Alexa's ring. It is yours. I never chose a ring for Alexa.' Unused to explaining himself to anyone, Jag found himself in unfamiliar territory. 'A few months ago King Ronan approached me about marrying his daughter. I believed the idea had merit and said I would consider it. In the meantime someone from the Berenian Palace has been feeding information to the Press to create speculation and, I suspect, a way to encourage me to seal the deal.'

'As far as I could tell, it was definitely sealed for her. She sounds as if she's in love with you.'

'I met the woman twice. Do you really believe that's enough time to fall in love with someone?'

She hesitated a fraction of a second before staring down her nose at him. 'Clearly it was for her.'

'I doubt that. The woman is more in love with the idea of being Queen than being my wife, and her father wants easy access to Santara's wealth.'

'I find that hard to believe. She was incredibly upset.' She tugged at her wrists and he released her to put some much-needed space between them. 'But just say your version is the correct one and she's only marrying you for political gain, I would have thought that was right up your alley. No messy emotions involved to muddy the waters.'

His jaw ached from clenching it so hard. Tarik had pointed the same things out to him the day before. So why, with all the political advantages it also offered, had he killed the idea completely? 'I have explained as much as I am willing to explain to you.'

'Oh, right, because I'm just one of your minions. I suppose you're about to clap your hands next to make me disappear.'

'Don't tempt me,' he grated.

'I think it was really insensitive of you not to tell me about her. You knew that I was nervous about meeting all those people and you just threw me to the wolves.'

'I did not throw you to the wolves. I made sure you were

by my side the whole night. And I am not happy that Alexa approached you, but in the end no harm was done.'

'To you maybe,' she said, clearly not placated by his response. 'But that's because you don't care about people. You're so caught up in your duty and your wheeling and dealing you've forgotten the human element. You should make sure you donate your body to science after you die— you'll be the only person in the world who has been able to exist minus a heart.'

'I am not heartless and at the end of the day this is not about you and me as a couple. We're not a couple. We are a means to an end.'

'Yes, my brother's end.'

Feeling an overload of emotion, Jag walked away from her. 'I refuse to get into this with you.'

'Why?' she volleyed at him. 'Because you're selling Milena off the way King Ronan is his daughter?'

'I am not selling my sister off.'

She gave him a look as if to say 'dream on' and Jag's hands balled into fists. This woman was driving him crazy. 'I'm getting very tired of you questioning my decisions regarding my sister.' He watched as her eyes widened when he paced towards her. 'When Milena was sixteen she became infatuated with an international farrier that had come to work at the royal stables. I assumed it was harmless. I *assumed* he would be a gentleman, given her station and her age. I was a fool. He tried to seduce her even though he was married and he ended up breaking her heart.' He took a slow even breath, anger returning along with his memories. 'Not long after he left she stopped eating and lost an enormous amount of weight. Then I found her with a bottle of sleeping pills clasped in her hand.' He still remembered that feeling of having his heart in his mouth when he'd realised how gravely ill his sister had become, and he'd do anything to ensure that she was never hurt like that again.

'Oh, poor Milena. And poor you.' Regan's sympathy was a tangible force that threatened to wrap around him and never let him go. 'No wonder you're so protective of her. I assumed it was just for political reasons.'

Jag moved away from her so that he couldn't absorb any more of her warmth. 'The political aspect *is* vital. But more than that Milena has always struggled with the need to feel wanted, to feel of value to anyone. She has always blamed herself for our mother's defection. What she fails to realise is that our mother was never maternal. When this marriage arrangement was first presented to me I believed it would give Milena the stability and sense of purpose her life has always lacked. The last thing I need is you coming along and making me second-guess myself.' Shocked to realise how much he kept revealing to a woman who was virtually a stranger, he strode to the windows and stared out at the black, starless night.

'I'm sorry I probably brought back bad memories for you when I refused to eat the other day.' Hearing the deep emotion in her voice, Jag couldn't stop himself from turning to look at her. He'd never met a woman so open with her emotions and so willing to take ownership of her actions. 'And I'm sorry for saying you were heartless. I can see that you really do care very deeply for your sister and it was wrong of me to suggest otherwise.'

'I don't need your sympathy.' Put on the spot by the raw emotion in her voice that paradoxically tugged at his own, Jag put the brakes on the conversation. What he needed was her to get naked so he could work off some of the excess energy coursing through him, not to feel even more than he already did.

He heard her murmur a soft goodnight before she disappeared through one of the closed doors. As he was about to tell her that she'd entered his bedroom instead of her own she returned, red-faced. 'I think I just went into your room. It smells like you.'

Jag's jaw clenched. 'You did.' He pointed to the door on the far side of the room. 'You can access your bedroom through there.'

She ran her hands down the sides of her dress and threw him a nervous smile. 'Okay. Take two.'

Needing to lower his tension levels with something other than her, Jag headed for the bar. He'd just picked up the crystal decanter when she screamed.

Striding through the connecting door, he pulled up short when he found Regan standing on the bed, holding a stiletto sandal in her hand and wearing nothing but a nude-coloured slip. A very short nude-coloured slip.

'Sp-p-pider,' she stammered, her lovely eyes as wide as dinner plates. 'I swear it's as big as a wildebeest.'

'Where?'

'In the…in the wardrobe.'

Finding the offending arachnid, he had to concede that the spider was indeed huge. Maybe not a wildebeest, but if you'd never seen a camel spider before it probably looked as bad as one. Retrieving an empty glass from her bathroom, he captured the spider and tossed it outside the window, closing it after him.

'Technically it's not a spider,' he informed her, returning to find her still on the bed, her long, lithe legs braced apart. 'It's known as a *Solifugae*.'

'As long as it's technically gone I don't care what it's known as. Are there any more?'

Jag checked around the bed, welcoming the diversion from her legs. 'All clear. I'll make sure the staff do a regular sweep of the rooms tomorrow. But rest assured, we don't tend to see very many of them inside the palace. They prefer the open desert.'

'This one got lost,' she said, still warily eyeing the carpet as if she expected to see an army of them come out of the woodwork.

'Come.' He held his hand out to her, even though he told himself not to touch her. 'I'll help you down.'

Still in a state of shock, she took his hand without argument, becoming unbalanced as she stepped off the bed.

Jag caught her in his arms, her body fitting against his like a silken glove, her arms winding around his neck, her legs wrapping around his hips.

Somehow her bottom, round and firm, was cupped in the palms of his hands.

The kiss from the night before spiralled through his head, taking over.

'You wanted to know what I tasted like and now you don't want to repeat it.'

At one point during the night he'd wanted to repeat it so badly he'd nearly cleared the grand ballroom. Part of the problem was that her taste was damned addictive.

The air-conditioning whirred overhead.

Was she breathing?

He wasn't.

Her body was open to his, clinging, her scent winding him up. He was so aroused, he shook with it. All it would take was for him to bunch her silk slip a fraction higher, test her readiness with the tips of his fingers, release himself from his trousers and bury himself deep inside her.

His hands moved to her thighs, tightening on the soft resilience of her skin, then he inhaled raggedly, letting her slide down his torso until her feet touched the floor, biting back a groan.

She stared up at him, as dazed as he was, her eyes dark

with unslaked lust. Her nipples were hard, her breathing as uneven as his, and he knew if he put his hand between her legs he'd find she was equally turned on.

A muscle ticked in his jaw. She wasn't here for this. He hadn't asked her to pose as his fiancée so that he could satisfy a hunger for her he was barely able to comprehend. He'd done it to avert an international crisis; he'd done it to get his sister back. How would it look if he threw sex into the mix for the hell of it?

If Chad James was out there having sex with his sister he'd kill him. He'd expect no less in return. He took a step back from her, called himself ten types of a fool and headed for the door before he could change his mind.

CHAPTER SEVEN

REGAN WAS ALREADY up when breakfast arrived on the King's private terrace. She'd showered and changed into her own clothes—jeans and a T-shirt—ignoring the beautiful items the King had provided for her, since she had no idea what would be expected of her today. She thought about the woman who had slipped him her phone number the night before and wondered if he had gone to find her after he'd walked away from her. And then reminded herself yet again that she didn't care.

She stared at the selection of local pastries and fruits and thought about his revelation concerning his sister the night before. She honestly hadn't thought he had the potential to feel anything on a personal level, but after the disclosure about Milena was torn from his chest she could see that he did. He felt things incredibly deeply and she was coming to understand that the way he had coped with taking control of a family and a country so young was to close down his emotions and just get on with it.

She recalled the way he had fed her in the garden suite when she'd gone on a hunger strike. At the time she'd assumed that he'd fed her for purely selfish reasons, but had he done it because deep down he was a nice person? Somehow she preferred the first option. It made it much easier to dislike him if she thought he was a hard-hearted tyrant.

She spied the food now and tried to stop thinking about

him so that she could figure out if she was hungry or not when he walked through the glass doors and joined her.

Smoothing the napkin on her lap, she told her heartbeat to settle down.

'You were right last night,' he said quietly, his eyes on her face. 'It was insensitive of me not to have informed you about the situation with Princess Alexa. I hadn't looked at it from your point of view, and I also genuinely believed that Alexa would not be overly disappointed if the betrothal didn't go ahead. I'm sorry I put you in that position.'

Not expecting him to apologise, Regan felt taken aback. 'I probably overreacted a little,' she admitted, knowing that really, she had overreacted a lot because she'd been unexpectedly jealous of the other woman. Something that didn't make sense at all given their circumstances. 'But it's okay.' She forced a lightness into her voice. 'I told Princess Alexa not to give up hope.'

His brows drew together. 'Why would you tell her that?'

'Because I felt sorry for her. She was really upset and she's perfect for you.' That thought had kept her up a lot during the night. 'She's beautiful and poised *and* royal. In terms of matches you'd make beautiful babies together. You should definitely go ahead with it.'

He moved towards the table and picked up a peach, testing it for ripeness. She hadn't realised how much she wanted him to deny her advice until he didn't. 'You're always looking for the silver lining, aren't you?'

'I prefer silver linings to thunderclouds. Life's tough enough without always waiting to be rained on.'

'That's a romantic way of looking at the world. If you're not careful you'll be blindsided when you least expect it. And you hate surprises.'

'I hate bad surprises.'

'Is there any other kind?'

Well, there was her reaction to his kisses. That was definitely a thundercloud because, as intoxicating as they were,
as much as they made her burn for more, she would never
be what he was looking for in a woman.

'Good point,' she agreed, frowning as a thought came
to her. 'You're not going to say anything to Princess Alexa,
are you? I wouldn't want her to get into trouble for approaching me.'

'First you protect my staff, and now the Princess? Who
are you going to protect next? Because I don't ever see you
protecting yourself and you make yourself vulnerable in
the process.'

'That's not true.'

'It is true.' He leant against the table beside her. 'You
didn't even realise how much danger you were in that night
at the shisha bar, or walking around a strange city alone.
Anything could have happened to you.'

'It didn't,' she said, feeling the need to defend herself.

'All evidence to the contrary,' he said, bringing a slice
of peach to his mouth. His eyes held hers and the air in the
room grew unbearably hot.

'How is it you can eat that and not spill a drop?' she
began on a rushed breath. 'Did you go to a special etiquette
school for royals or is it something you're born knowing
how to do?'

'I'm careful.'

'Well, if I was eating that I'd have juice all over me by
now. When I was younger my mother used to secure a tea
towel around my neck whenever I sat down to a meal.'
Aware that she was babbling because he made her so nervous, and he was so close, she stopped when he deftly
sliced a sliver of peach and held it out to her. 'Open,' he
ordered softly.

Open?

Without thinking she parted her lips and the sweet, fragrant fruit slipped inside. Regan's tongue came out to capture it and her heart beat a primal warning through every cell in her body as his eyes lingered on her sticky lips.

Kiss me, she thought. *Please, please, just kiss me before I die.*

'Your Majesty?' A male voice interrupted the awareness sparking between them as brightly as the Christmas lights at Macy's.

Tarik walked into the room, bowing formally. 'Excuse me,' he murmured, seeming to sense that he had interrupted something he shouldn't have. 'You asked me to brief you here and... I did knock.'

'That's fine.' The King recovered from the moment a lot quicker than she did and yet again Regan got the impression that he affected her a lot more than she affected him. 'You didn't interrupt anything important.' He moved away from the table and sat in the seat opposite her. 'What have you got for me?'

'The agenda for the day.' Tarik handed them each a one-page document. 'There have been a few amendments made to yours, sir, that I need to run through with you.'

Jag poured himself a short black coffee and held the pot aloft in question to Regan. She shook her head, hoping that she wasn't blushing in the process. She really had to stop letting him feed her.

'Okay, Tarik, tell me what I need to know.'

The older man ran through a list of morning meetings Jag was required to attend that made Regan feel exhausted just listening to it. 'After the round-table meeting on international banking reform, you're supposed to open the new sports complex at the local primary school followed by a tour of the facilities to drive more economic investment in the area. Unfortunately we've had to reschedule the meeting on foreign policy and counter-terrorism, which you shouldn't miss either, and there's no chance you can do both.'

Jag paused and poured himself another coffee. By the sound of his schedule he'd need to have a jug of the stuff on standby. Regan glanced at her own schedule, which consisted of another day of pampering in preparation for another dinner that evening. She frowned. 'Excuse me, I don't like to interrupt but is there any way I can help out?'

Both men looked at her as if she'd grown an extra head.

Regan rolled her eyes. 'Surely, as your supposed fiancée, I can be of more use to you than window dressing and keeping other men's wives at bay.'

His lips quirked at her attempted joke. 'What did you have in mind?'

'Well, I am a teacher. Is there any way I can do the school tour so that you're free to attend the other meeting? I mean, I would offer to attend the counter-terrorism meeting but other than just tell everyone to love each other I'm not sure what I can offer.'

He shook his head at the incongruity of her comment, his eyes sparkling with amusement.

'What do you think, Tarik?' he surprised her by asking the older man. 'I broke with protocol last night. Would this be stretching it?'

'Not really,' Tarik said slowly. 'I mean, if Miss James were really your fiancée it would be highly acceptable, even delightful, for her to take on a task such as this. It's not as if she needs to contribute anything specific. And her presence would add credence to your pet project, given that you're unable to attend.'

The morning sun glinted off the King's tanned face and made his blue eyes seem impossibly bright. 'Are you sure you want to do this, *habiba*? You know if I'm not there all the attention will be on you and you alone.'

Regan shook her head. 'Pretty much all the attention was on me last night anyway—as you knew it would be. But, as you can't be in two places at once, I'm happy to do it. Seriously, there are only so many times you can get your nails and hair done, and I'm not used to having so much time on my hands. It doesn't sit well with me.'

'If you're sure, then…thank you.' Something sparked behind his eyes, some emotion that Regan couldn't identify but then he blinked and it was gone. 'Tarik will accompany you. If at any time you think it's too much for you, tell him and he will return you immediately to the palace.'

Jag paced around his room and checked his watch for the hundredth time in half an hour. Regan should have been back an hour ago. Tarik had sent him a text saying they were on their way. So what was keeping them?

About to contact the security detail he had sent along with them, he heard quick footsteps racing down the marble hallway and knew immediately who it was.

Regan burst into the room, her cheeks rosy with exertion, Tarik hot on her heels. They were both laughing at some shared joke and his eyes narrowed. 'Is either one of you aware of the time? We are expected downstairs at the dinner in thirty minutes.'

Immediately Regan stopped smiling. 'It's my fault,' she assured him. 'Tarik told me that I had to finish up earlier but it was really hard to leave.'

'Miss James was magnificent, Your Majesty.'

Jag watched her roll her eyes at his aide in mocking rebuke. 'That's not true. If anyone's magnificent this man is. I can't believe he's seventy years old. He was kicking a soccer ball around with ten-year-olds.'

'As were you, my lady.'

'I'm just glad I wore flat shoes for the occasion,' she said, pulling the band from her ponytail and letting her glorious mane of hair swirl around her shoulders. 'I'm dead on my feet after today.'

'You're hardly going to be any use to me dead on your feet, Miss James.'

Stark silence greeted his blunt statement and, as Jag became aware that he was experiencing an unexpected jolt of…jealousy…at the obvious camaraderie between his aide and his temporary fiancée, his agitation levels rose. 'I don't remember seeing soccer on the itinerary.'

'It wasn't,' she said demurely. 'Again, that was my fault. We were touring the new gymnasium and sports grounds, which are incredible by the way—hats off to you because I know it was your vision to provide such an amazing space for the kids—and one of the boys rolled the ball my way. I returned it and noticed that the girls were sitting on the sidelines and I encouraged them to join in. Before we knew it we were all playing.'

Tarik was looking at him oddly and Jag drew in a deep breath. 'It's fine. Regan, you need to go and get ready for the dinner. We have…' he consulted his watch '…twenty-five minutes before it's due to commence.'

'Oh, right, of course.' She ran a hand through her hair, tousling it more. 'Oh, Tarik, if it's not too much of a bother, do you mind providing me with the postal address of the school? I have a lot on my mind but I don't want to forget.'

'Of course, my lady.'

'Hold on,' Jag said, feeling his irritation levels rise even higher at their unexpected mutual-appreciation society. 'Why would you need the postal address of the school?'

Regan gave him a faint smile. 'It's nothing. I promised one of the teachers I'd send them some art supplies because it's the one area in the school that isn't flourishing and it's really important.'

'I'm sorry?' Jag was finding it hard to keep up with her.

'The curriculum is really strong on maths, science and English, which can be a bit limiting, particularly for really young kids. They need music and art and lots of time to play so that their love of learning doesn't wither and die in the later years.'

'The reason the curriculum is set up that way is because when I took over as King the school system was in an appalling state.'

'I heard. All the teachers, and local dignitaries, were singing your praises. Apparently ten years ago Santara was in the bottom three percent for literacy and now it's only in the bottom twenty-five percent.'

Jag winced. That was mainly due to the remote country schools that were slow to keep pace with changes made in the cities, but he'd have liked things to be further along than they currently were. The problem was that he couldn't be on top of everything, as Tarik was wont to tell him.

As if reading his mind, his loyal aide raised a brow, seeming to remind him that he wasn't an island, and he scowled.

'Anyway, I said I would send some specialist supplies I know my kids back home love to use.'

Jag shook his head. He should be used to women taking advantage of his position and thinking they could spend his money out of hand. Just because she was spending it on kids didn't make him feel any more generous towards her. In fact, the disappointment that she was like so many other women, who couldn't wait to get their hands on a man's money, made his tone harsh.

'Next time you think to abuse my generosity and allocate palace funds you might care to run it by me.' His eyes were cool as they held hers. 'I will, of course, honour your promise this time, but next time I won't.'

A heavy silence filled the air and just when he was feeling that he had everything in hand Tarik moved to correct him.

'Your Maj—'

'Tarik, please don't.'

Surprisingly Tarik did as Regan requested and Jag stared from one to the other. 'What were you going to tell me, Tarik?'

Before his aide could speak Regan lifted her eyes to his. 'He was going to tell you that I was planning to pay for the art supplies myself.'

Another silence followed her statement. This time a fulminating one. Jag dragged a hand through his hair. 'How is it that you always seem to wrong-foot me, Miss James?'

'I don't know. Maybe it's because you're always looking for the worst in people.'

'That would be because I've seen the worst in people.' He sighed. 'And you will not be spending your money on supplies for the school.'

'But—'

'The palace will provide whatever is needed. Education is of vital importance to our nation. Write up a list of what you want and give it to Tarik.'

'Really?' Her face lit up and she gave him a smile that stopped his heart. 'You don't know how happy that makes me to hear a world leader speaking that way about education. Too often governments just pay lip service to education issues and it's completely debilitating for those who work in the industry. Do you have enough funds set aside for musical instruments too? From what I could tell, they're woefully under-represented as well.'

At the term 'lip service' Jag's gaze dropped to her sexy

mouth and he reminded himself that he was not an un-tried fifteen-year-old boy but a grown man in full control of his faculties. 'Don't push your luck, *habiba*.' If she did he wouldn't be responsible for his actions. 'And now you only have fifteen minutes to get ready. Should I tell them to hold dinner?'

'No, no.' Regan pivoted on her light feet and raced to-wards the connecting door to her room. 'Give me ten min-utes. And thank you. You've made me really happy.'

Swamped by emotions he couldn't pin down, Jag im-mediately poured himself a stiff drink.

'Everyone loved her today, Your Majesty; she's—'

'Here temporarily,' Jag reminded Tarik, cutting off what was sure to be an enthusiastic diatribe as to Regan's vir-tues. 'Or have you forgotten that?'

'No, Your Majesty, it's just—'

'I think you're needed elsewhere, Tarik,' Jag informed him, not at all in the mood to hear any more. 'I'm quite sure I can await my fiancée's reappearance on my own.'

'Of course, Your Majesty.'

As soon as the older man departed the room Jag felt like a heel. It wasn't Tarik's fault that the woman was tying him up in knots.

And where the hell was his sister? If she was putting him through this for nothing he'd be furious.

'Okay.' A breathless Regan appeared in the doorway in record time. 'I hope I look all right. Since you're only wearing a suit and tie, I opted for something less formal than last night.' Her hands brushed over the waist of her sleeveless all-in-one trouser suit that faithfully followed the feminine curves of her body, accentuating her toned arms. Her face looked as if it was almost bare of make-up, and her hair fell around her shoulders in a silky russet cloud. 'I didn't have time to put my hair up,' she said, raising a hand to self-consciously pat it into place. 'If you think I should then I can—'

'It's fine.' He cut off her chatter, aware that this was something she did when she was really nervous. 'You look…' incredible. Stunning. *Beddable* '…very elegant.'

Sexual chemistry arced in the space between them, pulling him towards her as if by an invisible pulley system.

She fiddled with her engagement ring and Jag had to forcibly stop himself from reaching for her and wrapping those slender fingers around another part of his anatomy. A stranger to fighting desires as strong as this, Jag found himself growing increasingly frustrated. 'Let's go,' he growled, appalled at how she could arouse him without even trying.

'Okay. Oh, wait.' She stopped beside him at the door and smiled up at him. 'In all the rush before, I forgot to ask—how was your day?'

How was his day?

Shock made him go so still he could have been nailed to the spot. He couldn't remember the last time he'd been asked that question. Usually people were too busy reeling off a litany of complaints, or asking him to solve problems, to even consider asking him how his day had been.

A lengthy silence filled the room. How was it that this woman managed to uncover weaknesses in him he thought he'd long got over. 'My day was fine.'

'Sorry.' She gave him a faint smile. 'I've upset you again. I always seem to say the wrong thing around you.'

'I'm not upset,' he denied, 'I was just…' He took a deep breath. Let it out. 'Actually my day went very well.'

'Great, then we both had a good day, only…' Her brow scrunched and she paused to look up at him. 'Are you sure everything's okay? You've gone a little pale.'

No, everything was not okay. He was fighting with a very strong instinct to lock her up and throw away the key.

And not in the palace this time but some distant location he couldn't get to.

He thought about last night. The roundness of her bottom against his palms, her arms locked around his neck. The chemistry between them had been explosive but he'd possessed enough sanity at the time to know that doing anything about it would produce a list of regrets that would rival his inbox.

He felt his insides coil tight as the need to have her tried to edge out logic and reason.

As if she sensed the direction of his thoughts her throat bobbed as she swallowed, her eyes wary. As they should be. Because nothing good could come of constantly thinking about how much he wanted her and so he ruthlessly clamped down on emotions that he didn't want to feel, and needs he didn't want to have, and focused on his duties for the night. 'Everything's fine,' he finally said, directing her towards the door. 'Let's not keep my chef waiting any longer. His retribution isn't worth it.'

CHAPTER EIGHT

STANDING ON THE back steps of the palace balcony as the last of the summit delegates boarded a helicopter, Regan let out a long sigh. Presumably her duties as the king's escort would be over now that the four days were up, and she wondered why she didn't feel better about that.

For the past two days she had barely seen Jaeger. They had crossed paths only at social functions when he required her company, but always he seemed distantly polite and at the end of the evening he had done little more than bid her goodnight before heading to his office to do even more work.

She couldn't escape the feeling that he had been avoiding her a little, which had suited her fine. Spending time with him only gave her a false sense of connection with him that she didn't want to feel. Already all he had to do was look at her to make her burn, and she hated the fact that her senses had been awakened by a man who couldn't make it any plainer that he didn't want her. And why would he want her when she was merely a means to an end for him?

Wondering what would happen next given that their missing siblings had not yet returned she steeled her spine when he detached himself from the small party he was speaking with to approach her, his expression serious.

'I know the summit is officially over,' he began, 'and

that our deal only extended to today, however there is one more obligation that is required of you.'

'Obligation?' She forced herself to sound as composed as he did. 'Is this to do with Milena and Chad? Have you located them?'

Yesterday the security detail searching for Milena had reported that there might have been a sighting of her and Chad in a hiking store in Bhutan five days ago. It had eased Regan's mind because Chad was an avid hiker, but it still begged the question that if the two of them were merely hiking why hadn't they been more open about the whole thing?

'No I have no new information on our missing siblings,' Jag said grimly. 'This is a business obligation. The President of Spain is thinking about investing in our agricultural infrastructure. He wishes to see how he might utilise it in his own country and I have organised a short trip to the interior of Santara. As his wife is accompanying us, it would seem strange if you stayed behind. Particularly since she tells me that you have bonded over the past few days.'

'Yes, she's lovely.'

His head cocked to the side, his eyes curious. 'She also tells me that you speak fluent Spanish. Why didn't you tell me that you speak another language?'

'You didn't ask.'

Annoyance briefly pulled his brow together. 'I'm asking you now. How is it that you live on the East coast of America but have come to speak Spanish? It's not as if the language is prevalent there.'

'My mother was a Russian immigrant. She could speak five languages and spoke them often at home. I picked up my love of languages from her.'

'Does that mean you speak Russian too?'

Regan nodded. 'And French and German. Though my German is really basic. I wouldn't want to put it to the test.'

His eyes gleamed as he looked at her. 'A woman of hidden talents.'

Regan glanced at a pair of butterflies as they flitted over a row of flowers hedging the expansive lawn area, the admiration in Jaeger's eyes making her chest tight. The strain of hiding her physical reaction to him over the last few days was wearing her down.

'We will be gone most of the day. I suggest you wear something light and loose. The interior of my country gets very hot.'

Regan watched him stride away from her, immediately feeling a sense of deflation. She supposed it was to be expected since she felt as if she'd been on a roller-coaster ride since she'd arrived in Santara. It was as if she was living someone else's life. It didn't help that her feelings for the King were all over the place. One minute she didn't want to see him ever again, and the next she wanted to plaster herself all over him.

Back in her room she scanned the elaborate wardrobe Jag had provided for her, choosing camel-coloured trousers and a long-sleeved white linen shirt. Remembering the spider from the other night, and knowing they would be outdoors, she ignored the more delicate open-toed sandals and shook out a pair of her own white running shoes. Tying her hair into a low ponytail, she waited for Jag to return. When he did he looked ruggedly masculine in low-riding jeans, boots and a lightweight shirt similar to hers.

'Do you mind if I bring my camera?'

'Of course not. As long as you don't post any photos of me on social media.'

'No fear of that.' Regan grimaced self-consciously. 'I've learned the consequences of that particular lesson.'

His gaze turned thoughtful as he stopped beside her. 'Has it been so bad, *habiba*? Being here with me?'

Regan blinked. He could ask that after ignoring her for the last two days?

Fortunately she was saved from having to find an answer to his question when one of his bodyguards informed him that their helicopter was ready for boarding.

Never having taken a helicopter ride before, Regan was thrilled. Once they had left Aran her eyes were riveted to the vast expanse of sand dunes that stretched in peaks and valleys in an endless sea of gold and brown. In the distance she could see rocky mountain ranges with hints of green, and tiny villages dotted here and there. Jag sat opposite her and she felt his curious eyes on her. She listened as the two other occupants chatted about the sights but didn't join in, enjoying the sound of Jag's voice coming through the headset now and then as he pointed out some of the more interesting aspects of the countryside. At one point she nearly jumped out of her skin when he tapped her on the knee and said her name at the same time. Her eyes flew to his, her heart pounding even at that small contact, to find him pointing out of the window on her other side. 'Camel train,' he said and Regan couldn't contain a smile as she spotted the line of over twenty camels meandering across the top of a distant dune. He grinned back at her and for a moment the connection between them was so strong it was as if they were the only two people in the world. Then Isadora, the First Lady, fired off some questions in rapid-fire Spanish and Jag answered.

As they neared their destination Regan was amazed to see miles and miles of brilliant green fields. Jag explained how the ground was watered by both underground springs and the water that ran off the mountains. An engineering team had devised a revolutionary method for storing the water so that it didn't evaporate in the harsh sun that was a year-round issue for the desert nation.

Landing, they had lunch and took a tour of the various garden centres before the President asked if they could also stop at Jag's nearby thoroughbred stables. Climbing into a cavalcade of SUVs, they were once more whisked through an ever-changing landscape towards the stables.

Not being a horsewoman, Isadora was taken into the main house to rest from the harsh rays of the sun, while Regan headed to the stables, declining an invitation to join the men in the fertility clinic. She wandered from box to box, petting the muzzles of the horses she met and taking photos.

'Oh, you're a beauty,' she crooned as she came upon a giant white stallion, snapping off another photo. She grinned as the horse angled his head. 'And a real poser.' She laughed. The stallion snorted at her from the rear of the box, his black eyes studying her intently.

'You must be at least sixteen hands high,' she praised him. 'Come on. Come say hello.' The stallion stamped his foot a couple of times and then dropped his head, moving towards her and nuzzling her palm, inhaling her smell. 'I wish I had a carrot to give you,' she murmured, leaning in and breathing his horsey scent deep into her lungs.

'Actually he prefers sugar.'

At the sound of Jag's voice the horse whinnied and lifted his head. Man and horse eyed each other like long-time friends.

'I see you've become mesmerised by Miss James's soft touch,' he said, putting his hand in his pocket and pulling out a sugar cube. Instantly the horse nuzzled his palm, devouring the treat.

'He likes that,' Regan said, laughing when the stallion bumped her shoulder, urging her hand back up to his nose. 'You're a demanding thing,' she murmured, happily acqui escing and caressing beneath his mane where the hair grew as silky as duck down.

'Like his owner,' Jag said, his eyes following the movement of her fingers as she combed them through the horse's mane.

She wanted to ask him why he was suddenly paying her attention again, but the gleam in his bright blue eyes made the words die in her throat. Instead she asked, 'What's his name?'

'Bariq. It means lightning.'

The horse whinnied and Regan laughed. 'And I'm sure it suits you,' she assured him.

'He doesn't usually take to strangers so readily. You must know horses.'

'Yes.' Her throat thickened. Horse riding had been one of those things they had all done as a family when her parents had been alive. An activity that had stopped when her parents had become sick. She leaned into the stallion's neck and breathed him in. 'I love horses.'

'Why does that make you sad?' Jag asked softly.

Embarrassed at having given herself away, Regan shifted uncomfortably. 'It was my parents' favourite pastime. They used to take Chad and me riding as often as possible.'

He frowned, his finger lightly tapping the bridge of her nose. 'You have one or two new freckles.'

Regan rubbed at the place he had touched. 'Deft subject change, Your Majesty,' she said with a small smile. 'Unfortunately the freckles come with the hair colour.'

'Not unfortunately. Your colouring is as warm as your personality.' His voice had roughened and sent sparks careening through Regan's body. 'And I don't like to see you sad.'

Not knowing what to say to that, Regan focused on the

stallion. Why didn't he like to see her sad? She was only a means to an end for him, wasn't she?

'Good afternoon, Your Majesty.' A man in a groom's uniform strode down the blue stone aisle towards them. 'Would you like me to saddle Bariq for you to ride?'

Jag hesitated, his eyes on her. 'Care to take a ride with me, Regan?'

Regan immediately shook her head. 'I don't think so… I haven't ridden in a long time,' she admitted huskily.

'I guessed that, *habiba*,' he said, his eyes soft. 'But there is nothing to worry about. I'll be with you the whole time.'

'What about the President and his wife?'

'He is joining his wife for iced tea, after which they will be returning to the airport, where their plane is waiting to return them to Spain. I said goodbye on your behalf.'

Unable to think of another reason to not take this moment to enjoy herself, Regan smiled shyly. 'If you're sure?'

'I am.'

Twenty minutes later, having changed into jodhpurs and a fitted tunic, Regan waited with barely leashed excitement to mount her horse, a lovely palomino mare called Alsukar. Or sugar.

It had been more than a decade since she had ridden but she remembered it as if it were yesterday, bittersweet memories of shared family time filling her head.

'Okay?' Jaeger pulled up alongside her, his magnificent white stallion snorting and champing at the bit in his eagerness to gallop.

Jaeger barely tightened his hands on the reins, his deep voice alone enough to bring his prancing horse under his control.

'Yes, I feel like Bariq. I can't wait to get going.' A groom gave Regan a leg-up into the saddle. Regan took the reins and felt the energy of the horse beneath her.

She couldn't contain her smile. She was looking forward to testing her riding legs, and creating some new memories that were not entirely based on the loss of her parents. And then she wondered if Jaeger had suggested they ride for precisely that reason and told herself not to be fanciful. He had done this for no other reason than that his stallion needed a run, and she'd be a fool to entertain any other notion.

Before moving out Jag brought his horse close to hers. Leaning over, he shook out a piece of cloth and proceeded to fashion it on top of her head into what he told her was a *shemagh*. 'When we get outside you take this piece and tuck it into here so that it covers your mouth and nose.'

His fingers grazed along her jaw as he fixed the headdress into place, sending a cascade of shivers across her skin. Sensing her reaction, Sugar shifted sideways and Jag grabbed hold of her bridle to steady her.

'Thanks,' Regan said, not quite meeting his eyes.

He nodded and then proceeded to expertly fold his own royal blue *shemagh* that perfectly matched his eyes. He was a visual feast and she wondered what it would be like to be able to truly claim this man as her own.

They rode across oceans of sand dunes, taking the horses through their paces, and giving them their head from time to time. Jag tempered his horse to stay by her side and she felt sorry for the big stallion, who just wanted to gallop.

Finally they stopped to rest at a small watering hole on the outskirts of a village. Regan dismounted on jelly legs and immediately went to one of the guards who had trailed them to retrieve her camera from his pack. Completely enthralled by the humble beauty of the place, she snapped off a few photos of the contrasting colours and textures surrounding her.

A few locals came out of the low-lying buildings, bowing low when they saw who had arrived to greet them.

Jaeger was clearly a revered leader, greeting his people with kindness and respect.

Born to lead, he had said, or words to that effect, and, seeing him in action, as she had done over the past four days, she knew it was true.

A group of local men approached Jaeger and the two guards that had followed them dismounted and joined their King.

Regan snapped a photo of the impressive trio, raising her brow when he looked at her.

Is this okay? her look enquired.

Fine, his slight nod replied.

Feeling happy, she turned to find two young girls approaching her, carefully carrying a tray full of clay mugs. They curtseyed and offered one to her.

Taking the cup of cool water gratefully, Regan smiled. '*Shukran.*'

'*Shukran, shukran,*' the young girls tittered, dancing away as if they couldn't believe she had taken their offering.

She watched as they approached Jaeger, bemused at how beautifully he handled their shy attention, taking a mug and bowing to them in return.

Regan couldn't prevent the smile on her face, hot colour stinging her cheekbones as he looked across at her. Could he read her thoughts? Did he know how much she was enjoying herself with him? Did he know how hard it was for her to remember that she was only here with him like this because Chad and Milena were missing? That he believed Chad had committed a crime in running off with his sister?

Not wanting to dwell on any of that now, she turned back to the vast open space of the desert, the light breeze moving gently across the sand like a whisper. Enthralled by the deep quiet of the land, she raised her viewfinder again. When Jaeger came into view across the way she paused. He had unwound his blue *shemagh* and it framed his handsome face, giving his skin tone a golden-brown hue. Curious, she watched an old man approach, handing Jag an enormous bird of prey.

The bird made a noise in greeting and clung to Jag's gloved hand. As wild and untamed as its master, its proud profile perfectly mirroring Jag's.

Regan felt her breath catch. He really was the most magnificent creature, and before she could stop herself she depressed the shutter and snapped a round of photos.

A small crowd had gathered around him and he released the bird into full flight, watching as it soared into the air on ginormous wings. Jaeger gave a short, sharp whistle and the magnificent bird swooped and dived above them, putting on a magical display. Regan couldn't take her eyes off either man or bird as they worked together in perfect harmony, the bird circling high and waiting for Jaeger's commands before plummeting to earth like a bullet from a gun, completely trusting that the King would provide a safe landing for it. Which he did, without even flinching as those huge talons wrapped around his thick leather glove.

As if sensing the lens on him, Jaeger turned in her direction and stared at her, his features proud, his blue eyes piercing as if he were gazing directly into her soul. Regan depressed her finger on the shutter again, her lens capturing the moment before she lowered the camera. She swallowed as he continued to look at her, completely captivated by the heat and masculine energy that emanated from his riveting gaze. It was as if she had become the prey and he were the falcon, with her firmly trapped in his sights.

The memory of his fingers threading through her hair, cupping her face as he kissed her, thrusting his tongue into the moist heat of her mouth, made her breath catch in her throat. It was so easy to imagine him coming to her now, bending to her and kissing the breath from her body, tasting her with his tongue, and gripping her waist in his powerful hands, telling her everything he wanted to do to her. Then doing those things...

One of his men spoke in his ear, breaking the spell between them, and Regan realised it was time for them to ride back. The sun had already started to sink towards the horizon, the heat of the day also starting to ebb away.

Handing the falcon back to the old man, Jag made his way over to her. 'You look flushed, *habiba*,' he said softly. 'I should have given you a wide-brimmed hat as well.'

Regan felt flushed but she knew it had more to do with the scorching hot images of the two of them together than the sun. Safer, though, to have him believe that her heightened state was to do with mother nature than for him to realise that she couldn't look at him lately without wanting him.

'How did you find the ride?' he asked, adjusting the front of her *shemagh*.

'Wonderful.' She shaded her eyes from the sun as she looked up at him. 'It was truly wonderful.'

'No sad memories?'

'At the start but... I didn't realise how much I miss being around horses until now so...thank you.'

'It was my pleasure.'

'That bird—'

'Arrow?'

'Fitting name,' she said. 'He's magnificent.'

'*She's* magnificent. I found her as a chick at the base of a cliff when I was out riding years ago. She had fallen from her nest and wasn't ready to fly. The mother could do nothing for her and there was no way I could scale the side of the cliff to return her to her nest so I took her home with me. We've been firm friends ever since but I hardly get time to take her out any more. She wanted to hunt today but I didn't think you would want to see that.'

'What does she hunt?'

'Mice, hares, smaller birds.'

'Spiders?'

Jag laughed. 'Don't sound so hopeful, *habiba*.'

At the memory of the giant eight-legged monster in her wardrobe, Regan scoured the ground around them. 'You're safe. From creepy crawlies.'

His amused eyes grinned into hers and Regan felt the intimacy of the moment even though they hadn't even touched. For a split second she wondered if he was about to bend down and kiss her. And she wanted him to.

'We need to leave. It is getting late.'

'Of course. I can see the sun already dipping down towards the horizon and it gets cold in the desert at night. Or so I've heard.'

She was babbling, she knew it, and, by the way his lips tilted up at one side, he knew it too. 'It does. The desert is very unforgiving. It is not a place you want to get caught in during the day or the night.'

'Okay, well…'

'Sire, your horse.'

Thankful for the interruption, Regan turned blindly to the man who had brought their horses. Or, rather, Jag's stallion.

'What happened to my mare?'

'She grew tired from the ride out. She will be stabled here for the night and one of the men will return for her tomorrow.' Jaeger collected the reins from the man.

Placing a sure foot in the stirrup, he swung himself up onto the enormous horse, reaching his hand down to her, palm facing up. 'You will ride with me.'

Ride with him? No way. She was trying to lower her awareness of him, not elevate it into the stratosphere. 'That's okay.' She gave him a wan smile. 'I can...' She looked around, hoping to see some other mode of transport at her disposal.

'I'm afraid the A train uptown has left for the day.'

Regan laughed. 'Was that a New York joke, Your Majesty?'

'A pretty lame one,' he admitted unselfconsciously. 'Come. Give me your hand.'

Regan stared up at him. Everything inside of her said that she should not do this. That she should insist that he find another way for her to make it back to the stables. Maybe with one of his trusted guards, but she knew she'd be wasting her breath and really...just the thought of riding with him atop that massive horse gave her goosebumps.

She moistened her lips and placed her hand in his. Right now, out here in the desert, where it was wild and free, she felt very unlike her usually cautious self.

Jaeger's hand closed around hers and seconds later he had her seated on the horse behind him. He twisted around to face her, adjusting her *shemagh* once more so that it covered most of her face. Regan's heart beat fast as she stared back at him, so close she could smell the combined scent of horse and man. It was quite the aphrodisiac. She couldn't see his expression because his sunglasses were back in place, his own *shemagh* drawn across his face. He looked like the dangerous outlaw she had imagined him to be when they met and a thrill went through her. Back then her instincts had screamed at her to run. Now they were begging her to draw closer.

'You'll have to hang on tight, *habiba*. Bariq likes to have his head.'

Before she could respond Jag whirled the stallion on

his hind legs and raced them out of the small village and across the sand, giving Regan no choice but to comply with his suggestion or fly off the back of the horse and land on her rear end.

Determined to remain steadfastly immune to his proximity, she lasted about five seconds before she became aware of the lean, hard layer of muscle at his abdomen as her fingers flattened across his middle. Remembering what those muscles looked like without his shirt led to thoughts of sex, and the harder she tried to banish the word from her mind the more it stuck until it was all she could think about.

Between that and the smooth, powerful motion of the horse, she was decidedly rubber-legged when they arrived back at the stables.

Jag dismounted, his blue eyes hot and stormy as he looked up at her with his arms outstretched. Regan automatically swung her leg over the saddle, holding herself still in the circle of his arms as she waited for her legs to be firm enough to hold her upright.

Not wanting to meet his eyes in case he read every single hot thought she had ever had about him, she focused on the front of his shirt, glad when one of his bodyguards strode over and handed him a phone.

Thankful for the reprieve, she stroked the sweaty sides of the stallion's neck, telling him how big and strong he was.

'Careful, *habiba*, you don't want it to go to his head,' Jag mused as he turned back to her. 'This is supposed to be one of the fiercest horses in the land but he looks as if one word from you would send him to his knees.'

Regan smiled. 'He looks fierce because I suspect people have always been scared of him, but all he needs is to hear how amazing he is.'

Jaeger quirked a brow. 'Don't we all?'

Regan paused. Was that what Jaeger needed? To hear how amazing he was?

'That was Tarik. He has just informed me that the tribe of my ancestors has invited us to attend a congratulatory dinner tonight.'

Regan blinked at him. 'Because the summit is over?'

'No, because I have decided to take a bride.'

She stared at him blankly and he let out a rough laugh. 'You, *habiba.*'

'But we're not really going to be married!' she said, shock sending her voice high.

'To them we are.'

Regan shook her head, frowning. 'I'm not sure it's wise for me to meet even more of your people.' She shook her head, compelled to state the obvious. 'I mean, I'm not your fiancée. I'm a pawn. We both are because I'm using you to ensure Chad doesn't spend the rest of his life in some dungeon, and you're using me to get Milena back.'

A muscle flickered in his jaw, the one that worked every time he got angry. 'I don't have a dungeon,' he growled.

Before she had time to react he caught her face in his strong hands and raised her lips to his. Momentarily stunned, Regan stood there, her body flush against his. It wasn't a gentle kiss, or an exploratory kiss. It wasn't even a nice kiss. It was hot and demanding, skilfully divesting her of any willpower to resist. Not that she was trying to.

Instead her arms hooked around his neck and she rose up onto her toes, meeting the sensual onslaught of his attack with a hunger as deep as his own.

At her total acquiescence he groaned, shifting her so that she was pressed between him and the stable wall, her head tilted back so that she was his to command. And he did, softening the kiss, taking her lips one at a time before plundering her mouth with his tongue.

Her lips clung to his, a sob of pure need rising up inside of her. This was what she wanted, what she needed, what she had craved ever since he had kissed her and touched her that night in the garden suite. This thrilling throb of desire that she had only ever experienced in his arms. It was like a fever in her blood, a rush of sensation that couldn't be denied.

And then it was over just as quickly as it had begun. Once more he pulled back and she was left panting and unsteady, her body aching and empty.

She heard him curse as he turned his back on her. Then he spun towards her, breathing hard.

A groom exited a nearby stall carrying a tack box and Regan wondered if that was why he'd stopped.

She glanced up to see Jag watching her and for once he didn't seem completely immune to what had just happened between them.

'I think that should clear up any misconceptions you have that I didn't want a repeat of our kiss the other night.'

She blinked up at him, shocked at what he had just disclosed.

He looked shocked himself and shook his head. 'Wise or not, we have to attend the dinner tonight. It would be an insult not to, since we are already in the region. We will spend the night at my oasis and return to the palace first thing tomorrow morning.'

'Your oasis?'

'The place I come to when I want to unwind.'

CHAPTER NINE

WHEN WAS HE going to learn that kissing her was not the way to expunge her from his system?

He shook his head and strode inside his Bedouin tent. Set on the edge of a private rock pool and surrounded by palm trees, it was an upscale version of those his ancestors had used to live in. Usually he felt a sense of peace wash over him as he shed the suits and royal robes to reconnect with the man beneath, but not tonight.

He yanked his shirt over his head and made his way to the purpose-built shower at the back. He should not have let her words anger him, he thought savagely; that had been the problem.

He wasn't used to someone questioning the wisdom of his decisions and he didn't like the reminder of how they were using each other even though it was true. Riding Bariq back to the stables with her tucked against his back hadn't done his nerves any good either. If at any time she had shifted her hand an inch lower she would have realised that the only thing on his mind was sex.

Wondering how she was finding her own accommodation and whether she was wishing it was a five-star hotel, he donned a white *thawb* and royal headdress and went outside.

The sun was low on the horizon, his favourite time of day in the desert, the ambient light turning the sky a dusky mauve. Hearing a sound behind him, he turned to see Regan dressed in a brightly coloured *thawb* and flowing floor-length headdress. As soon as they had arrived at the village a group of local women had descended upon their future Queen to give her a traditional makeover. The results were stunning. She was completely covered from head to toe, and yet she managed to look like an exotic treat waiting to be unwrapped. Her chin tilted upwards in a tiny gesture he had first assumed was haughtiness, but now realised was one of self-consciousness. Despite her fair skin, she looked as if she was born to be here. Born to be his.

Perturbed by that last thought, Jag didn't realise he was frowning until Regan raised a brow. 'I did try to tell them to stop with the black kohl and henna. I look like I'm dressed for a Halloween party, don't I?'

Jag felt instantly chagrined at her pained expression. 'You look stunning. I just had something else on my mind.' Such as the fact that he might be slowly losing it.

'Well, whatever it was it obviously wasn't nice. Which is hard to believe when you're in a place like this.' Her gaze swept across the small cluster of tents and the deep blue lagoon. 'This is like something out of a fairy tale.'

'You don't wish for more modern accommodation?'

'Are you kidding?' Regan gaped at him. 'People pay a fortune to have experiences like this. I had no idea tents had carpets and real beds.'

'You're getting the upscale version. Come. It is a short drive to the village.'

'We're not going by camel?'

Jag couldn't prevent a grin at her teasing comment. 'I draw the line at some traditions.'

He held the door wide and her sheer veil caught on his arm as she made to step into the car. As he lifted his hand to disengage it his fingers caught around her silky hair and he nearly threw caution to the wind and buried his hands in the sexy mass and brought her mouth up to his again.

Moments later their car pulled up alongside a large pur-pose-built marquee. Inside low tables were set in a wide cir-cle with cushions scattered throughout the tent for seating, soft music playing from the edge of the entertainment area.

He watched Regan as she greeted his local tribespeople, speaking softly and attempting a few words in his native tongue, her adept mind already picking up a few phrases. He remembered the way her face had lit up when they had ridden first in the helicopter, and then on horseback through the desert. He had half expected her to hate his homeland but to his surprise she had seemed enamoured by it.

As his people were fast becoming enamoured by her.

'Your Majesty, your table.'

The tribal chieftain guided them to the central spot in the marquee, where everyone would be able to watch him and Regan interact.

Seeing the smiles on his people's faces was like a punch in the stomach. He hadn't given much thought to how much they wanted this to be real and he conceded that Regan had been right to be hesitant in accepting the invitation. Prob-ably he could have got out of it but once again he found himself making a decision to keep this woman close when it wasn't necessary.

He frowned. What was necessary was getting back to the palace and to what was important—work and find-ing Milena. But before that could happen he had tonight to get through.

'How are you feeling?' he asked Regan softly. 'Over-whelmed? Nervous? I should apologise because you're the centre of attention again.'

'I'm fine.' She gazed around the wide, brightly decorated space. 'Maybe you dragging me to your palace has been good for me. I think I've become a bit reclusive at home, keeping to my usual routine and never stepping outside of my comfort zone. My world is so small compared to yours. I don't know how you do it; having to be switched on all the time.'

'Sometimes it's tough,' he admitted, something he'd never said out loud before. 'Sometimes I'm presented with problems and challenges with no clear answers, and I find that the hardest of all.'

Especially now that Regan had started making him question his relationship with his siblings. Did Rafa stay away from Santara because Jag had not created a clear role for him at the palace? Had Milena run off with Chad James because she didn't want to go through with her royal marriage and couldn't tell him?

'We don't always get it right,' she said softly, as if reading his mind.

But he did. He had people depending on him. People who needed him to get it right. Especially when his father had been too caught up in his domestic dramas to lead the country as it deserved to be led.

Fortunately the tempo of the music increased, cutting off any further chance of conversation. A good thing, since he had a habit of revealing too much of himself around this woman.

Dancers poured into the tent, smiling and clapping, and, despite her misgivings about being here, Regan decided she was going to enjoy the evening. It wasn't as if she was likely to get a chance to experience something like this again any time soon. And yes, it would be better if she wasn't so aware of the man beside her, but there wasn't much she could do about that. Try as she had…

They might not have met in the most conventional of

circumstances, but the way her body responded to him was one hundred percent *conventionally* female.

And knowing that he was just as attracted to her was driving her crazy. It made her wonder what might have been if he had been an ordinary guy she had met at her local park. But he wasn't. He was a king, a man of supreme importance—and her brother had run off with his sister.

She gave an inward groan, wishing that Chad would return, wishing that this crazy situation was over so that she could go back to normal. If that was even possible after the way Jaeger had touched her, kissed her...

A kaleidoscope of butterflies took flight in her stomach as she absently watched his strong hands as he gestured with the person next to him. His wrists were thick, his forearms sinewy and dusted with dark hair. Everything about him was so potently male it made her feel breathless with need.

I'm falling for him, she realised with a jolt of dismay. *I'm really falling for him.*

She must have made a small sound of distress because he immediately turned towards her, his eyes scanning her face.

'*Habiba*, what is it?'

Regan shrugged helplessly. 'Nothing.'

His frown told her that he didn't believe her but he was prevented from asking more when she joined in the energetic clapping as a troop of new dancers took to the floor. This time the group was made up entirely of women in brightly coloured outfits and carrying sheer scarves.

You're not falling for him, she assured herself sternly. You're suffering from a serious case of lust for a man who knows how to kiss a woman into a stupor. You're not the first, and you certainly won't be the last, to imagine themselves in love with the sheikh. Princess Alexa was a good case in point. She'd met the King twice and fallen for him

And maybe Jag was right in that the Princess only wanted to marry him for political reasons, but Regan had her doubts. She'd seen the woman's heartfelt misery in thinking she had lost him.

Blindly she turned back to concentrate on the dancers. The women were undulating their hips with practised ease, gracefully weaving silken scarves around their bodies in a coordinated display of confidence and femininity. Combined with the lyrical music, it was both provocative and sensual. But all Regan could really concentrate on was the man seated so closely beside her.

Glancing at him through her lashes, she noticed a fine line of tension bracketing his mouth. She wondered why he was having such a reaction to the beautiful display when the story behind the dance hit her on the head. This was no ordinary dance. The scarves, the hip bumps, the sensual spell that held the crowd captivated…this was a type of love dance.

One of the performers broke from the circle and Regan held her breath, only to release it again when she approached a young woman, encouraging her to join her on the floor.

The woman did, smiling shyly at the young man she had been seated next to.

The crowd cheered and clapped encouragingly.

'Please tell me they're not going to expect me to go up here?' she whispered raggedly.

Jag's blue eyes snagged with hers and she knew the answer before he even opened his mouth.

She shook her head. 'I'm a hopeless dancer. I have no coordination at all.'

'You forget I've seen you on horseback, so I know that's blatantly untrue.'

'Riding a horse is nothing like dancing. At least with

horseback riding if something goes wrong I can blame the horse.'

Jag laughed. '*Habiba*, I—'

Before he could finish one of the dancers undulated in front of her, beckoning to her. By this time three other women had joined the dance, mimicking the sensual movements in a joyful display of passion and love.

Oh, God, she was seriously going to die of embarrassment.

Jag's eyes were a deep blue as she slowly rose to her feet. His hand caught hers. 'Regan, you don't have to do this.'

It was kind of him to say so, but Regan knew she'd be disappointed in herself if she didn't do it. Not only because she would be disappointing the people watching, but also because it was another chance to step outside her comfort zone and own it.

'I'll be fine,' she murmured with more bravado than she felt, throwing him one last beseeching look, and she followed the dancer out onto the floor, accepting the rose-coloured scarf that was offered to her.

At first she felt rigid and clumsy, conscious of everyone watching her, but slowly, and by some miracle, the sensual music started to flow through her, luring her to lower her inhibitions.

Telling herself to stop being a coward, she raised her arms and twined her hands together above her head, undulating her hips slowly. The crowd clapped and the music throbbed in time with her heartbeat. Laughingly, she tried to emulate the movements of the other dancers. And then she just let go, closing her eyes and giving herself up to the moment.

Unbidden, Jag's tender kiss against the stable wall invaded her head. Her breasts rose and fell at the memory of his hard body pressed to hers, his mouth devouring her tasting her, arousing her. A sweet lethargy spread through her limbs and she made the mistake of opening her eyes and staring directly into his.

It was like being torched by an open flame. The heat and hunger in his gaze was so intimate it took her breath away. His whole body transmitted unmistakable masculine desire and it seared her to her core.

The scarf floated teasingly in the air between them as she mimicked the earlier movements of the women, the delicate fabric wafting in front of him. With lightning-quick reflexes he grabbed hold of the end, bringing her to a standstill.

She couldn't do anything but stare at him, and then, as if in slow motion, he started to reel her in.

Regan was completely undone to see the delicate skein of silk wrapping around his big, tanned hand, the sight somehow enhancing his potent masculinity when it might have diminished it in a lesser man. But there was nothing lesser about Jaeger al-Hadrid and Regan knew that once she reached him there would be no turning back.

'Regan.'

His eyes were as hot as the sun, his rough tone pure sex.

Regan's breath hitched in her throat. There was only one thing she could say to that look.

'Yes.'

Understanding completely that the word hadn't been a question, he unfolded lithely to his feet. His height dwarfed her, the *thawb* making him seem even more powerful than usual. As soon as he stood the music stopped, but really Regan only vaguely registered the change.

He took her hand and not a single sound was uttered as he led her from the tent.

Once they were outside, the cool night air was a welcome relief against her heated cheeks but it did nothing to relieve the hot, pulsing desire that thrummed through her and turned her insides liquid with need.

When they reached his black SUV he dismissed his driver with a single nod.

Regan hesitated beside the open passenger door, forcing her eyes to meet his. 'I need to know one thing,' she said, her voice breathless with longing. 'Are you going to stop again and pull back from me?' Because if he did she didn't think she could bear it.

His large hand rose to cup her face, his thumb brushing along her cheekbone, his eyes as dark as the night sky above them. 'I've tried that. It doesn't work.'

A quiver went through her at his rough, gravelly tone. She gave him a tremulous smile and his fingers tightened against her scalp. 'Jump in.'

The big car flew across the desert road, eating up the distance between the marquee and his private tent in no time. Neither of them spoke, the air in the car so thick it made talking impossible. It made thinking impossible too and then he was beside her door, opening it, his warm hand pressing to the small of her back as he guided her towards the large tent she knew to be his. He raised the flap and she moved inside, suddenly nervous, the sound of it dropping back into place behind them like the crack of a whip in the stillness.

His hands framed her face and for a heartbeat he just looked at her. Then he lowered his head and took her mouth in a kiss of devastating expertise.

Regan could feel her heart racing, her body turning to liquid.

The kiss, slow and gentle at first, quickly turned urgent. He tasted of wine and coffee, and a deep male hunger that fed her own.

The only thing she managed to whisper was his name

but that must have been enough because suddenly she was being lifted and he was carrying her towards the rear of the tent. He placed her on the edge of the enormous mattress, taking a moment to reef his robe off over his head, leaving him in low riding cotton pants that left little to her imagination.

Her lips went dry as he stood before her, gloriously male, from the thick muscular arms and shoulders down to his lean hips and long legs.

'I won't stop this time, *habiba*, not unless you want me to.'

Regan's heart hammered inside her chest. Maybe she should stop, maybe she should say no, but she couldn't. Spending time with him these past few days, watching him command a room, seeing his quick mind in action, and then today, the way he handled Bariq and Arrow, seeing his gentleness with those less physically capable than himself, was… He was everything a woman could ever hope to find in a man and she loved him. Completely and utterly; as scary as that felt. 'I don't want to stop. I want this. I want you.'

She knew her words held a deeper meaning than he would attribute to them, and suddenly she was aware that this might not be the smartest decision she had ever made.

He lifted his hand to her, beckoning, and she no longer cared about being smart.

'Then come to me, Regan. Let me show you what you do to me.'

CHAPTER TEN

JAG COULDN'T CONTROL the shudder that went through him as Regan gracefully rose from the bed and came towards him. He wasn't sure how he had restrained himself thus far but he forced the aching need riding him hard to subside. He didn't want to impose himself on her or scare her with the strength of his desire. He wanted her to come to him as his equal. As a woman who wanted him regardless of how they had met, or why they were together. He needed her stripped bare because it was exactly how she made him feel.

She stopped a pace away from him, her eyes luminous in the soft light, the silky floor-length veil she still wore framing her beautiful face.

He lifted his hands and searched out the pins that held the veil in place until the fabric pooled at her feet, leaving her glorious hair unadorned.

'Turn around,' he instructed, his voice hoarse.

Silently she complied and he lowered the zipper in the back of her *thawb*. She wasn't wearing a bra and his blood surged at the sight of her pale, slender back. His fingers traced a line down her delicate vertebrae and back up, rejoicing in the tremor that went through her.

'Cold?' he asked, his hands sweeping her hair aside and lowering his head to the tender skin where her neck and shoulder joined.

'No.' She shook her head, resting it back against his

chest. He smoothed the gown over her narrow shoulders and held his breath as it too slithered to the floor.

'Then turn around, *ya amar*. Let me see you.'

Slowly she did as he instructed, her little chin lifted ever so slightly as she stood before him in only a tiny pair of black panties and delicate sandals.

He had been with many women in his life. Women he had admired and even liked, but he had never been with a woman who created in him this deep, gnawing hunger to possess, to brand, to claim as his own for ever and beyond.

Shaking off the sensation that he was in much deeper than he'd ever been before, Jag drew her closer. 'You're beautiful,' he said, his eyes memorising every sensual detail of her supple body; her straight shoulders and slender torso, the rise of her round breasts, high and firm, the narrowness of her waist, and the subtle flare of her hips and long legs. Hips designed to cradle a man's body, legs designed to wrap around him and hold him tight. 'Perfect.'

Unable to hold himself back, he gathered her close, groaning as the tips of her breasts nestled in the hair on his chest. She arched into him, her hands grasping his shoulders to pull him even closer. 'Kiss me, please.'

He did more than that, he devoured her, taking her mouth in a long, searing kiss that was a promise to how he intended to possess her with his body.

She made a soft keening sound, her hands kneading and caressing his naked shoulders. Jag dragged his hands down her ribcage, sweeping along her spine, before bringing his hands to her breasts. He cupped them gently, plucking at her tight nipples between his fingers.

She moaned deeply, arching against him, her body rising to his, climbing his until she was fully in his arms with her legs wrapped around his waist, her breasts inches from his mouth.

He gave a husky laugh. '*Habiba*, how very nice to meet you.' He leaned forward and cut off her answering chuckle by taking her nipple into his mouth. She clung to him, crying out in an agony of pleasure. He wanted to give her that pleasure. He wanted to give her everything.

He suckled her gently, flicking her nipple. Her thighs tightened around him as her arousal heightened and he rewarded her responsiveness with firmer and firmer pulls of his mouth. First on one breast then the other.

'Jaeger! Jag!' She writhed against him and he sensed she was close to climaxing. The knowledge sent his own arousal into the stratosphere.

'Regan, I—' He cursed as he laid her on his bed, his movements clumsy with his own imminent loss of control.

Shaking, he tried to steady himself, but she reached up to frame his face as he came down over the top of her, pulling his mouth back to hers.

'Wait,' he growled as her fingers trailed down over his muscled back and slipped beneath the waistband of his trousers. She was driving him to the edge of control and he needed to pull back for a moment, centre himself. But she didn't listen, her mouth opening wider under his, her tongue gliding into his mouth to mate with his, her clever fingers shattering his ability to keep a part of himself back.

'I don't want to wait,' she murmured against his neck. 'I need you. I need you inside me.'

'If you don't wait,' he growled, 'this is going to be over before it's begun.'

'I don't care. I need—'

He grabbed her hands and shackled them above her head with one hand. With the other he ruthlessly divested himself of his clothing. 'I know what you need.'

He came down over the top of her, pressing her into

the mattress. She parted her thighs and her hips rose to meet his.

'Dammit, Regan, I need to see if you're...' He'd been going to say *ready for me*, but he had already discovered the answer. 'Regan.' He positioned himself over her, his legs nudging her thighs wider.

'Yes. Please, Jag, do it.'

Her fingers dug into his hips and he surged into her, completely sheathing himself inside her.

She gasped and he instantly stilled. He smoothed her hair back from her forehead, putting his weight on his elbows. 'Okay?'

Breathing heavily through her mouth, she nodded. 'You're just so... Oh, that feels fantastic.'

He flexed again and felt her body go liquid around him. Then he stilled.

'Protection.' How in the world had he forgotten that?

She shook her head. 'We don't need it. I'm on the Pill and I've only been with one other man. Years ago.'

One other man?

'And I trust you.'

It was those last words that made his heart leap inside his chest and tipped him over the edge. Or perhaps it was the way her inner muscles rippled around him, drawing him further inside. Either way he no longer cared. All he cared about, all he could think about was taking them both higher, driving them deeper until time and space became irrelevant.

'Jag!' Her body gripped him tighter, growing taut as she moved more frantically beneath him.

'That's it, *habiba, ya amar*, like that... Yes, just...'

He felt the instant her body reached its peak, revelling in the way she screamed his name as she came apart in his arms. And then he couldn't think at all because her muscles were clenching around him like a silken fist. His body surged forward, driving into her with none of his usual finesse, until, with his own cry of release, he lost himself inside her.

Jag woke some time later to find Regan wrapped around him like ivy. One arm slung over his chest, her thigh positioned high over his. He couldn't remember the last time he'd slept all night with a woman. Sleep was a luxury he usually caught in snatches. Was that what had woken him so suddenly? The fact that he wasn't up? Or was it the warm, naked woman at his side who had given him more pleasure than he could ever remember having in bed?

His flesh stirred, definitely liking that second idea better than the first.

She must have registered the change in him because she made a small, sleepy noise, her body snuggling deeper against his.

Jag smiled, shifting a strand of her hair back from her forehead. He loved her hair. The colour, the texture… It felt like silk and fairly vibrated under the sunlight.

He told himself that he wouldn't wake her. She deserved to sleep and she would no doubt be a little tender from not having made love in such a long time.

She had only had one lover before him. He'd had no idea she was that inexperienced but he wasn't unhappy about it. Had he ever had a woman who had given herself to him so openly? So *wholeheartedly*? It was as if she'd held nothing back from him and he wasn't sure he entirely liked how that made him feel. Vulnerable. Open. A little raw, perhaps.

Slowly he became aware of his heart beating and knew it wasn't a sensation he registered very often.

Regan shifted again, her arm moving as if she was searching for something in her sleep.

Him?

Heat coiled through him.

On some elemental level Jag recognised that Regan had unlocked a deep-seated hunger inside him he wasn't altogether comfortable with. She made him think of things like loss and longing, like desire and need, and...

'The heart knows what the heart wants.'

Zumar's statement came to him from out of nowhere. *The heart?*

This wasn't about his heart. It was about sex. Very good, very hot sex.

His hand tightened in her hair as she made another little sleepy sound. It was meant to reassure her that everything was okay but deep inside he wasn't all that sure that it was true. 'It's okay, *habiba*, you're only dreaming.'

'Jag?' Her brown eyes fluttered open, dark and confused in the pre-dawn light. She leaned up on one elbow, her lovely autumn hair sliding across one shoulder, the hint of jasmine and sunshine drifting between them.

'Is it morning?'

'No.'

They stared at each other. Common sense asserted itself, warning him to back away, to put some distance between them.

Obviously picking up on his thoughts she frowned. 'I should go back to my tent. You must want to sleep.' She swallowed, her eyes darting from his, presumably searching for the gown he had dumped on the floor.

Jag wanted to tell her that was a really good idea. The best idea. But he couldn't because it was neither of those things.

'That's a terrible idea, *habiba*,' he said, his voice husky.

Rolling her beneath him, he clasped her hands above her head. 'Especially when I have many more delicious plans for you.'

She gasped as their lower bodies connected, the uncertainty in her eyes replaced with a burning hunger that matched his own. She softened beneath him, her lips raised to his. He didn't hold back, sealing his lips over hers and swallowing her groan of pleasure with a deeper one of his own.

Nudging her thighs apart with his knees, he entered her in one smooth, deep thrust.

'Oh!'

Her eyes went wide, her lips parting.

'*Oh* is right.' He kissed her temple, her eyes and along the side of her jaw. She whimpered beneath him, her lips seeking his 'You're so beautiful, Regan. The sexiest woman I have ever met.'

'Jag.' His name was a sigh against his neck, her arms enfolding him, holding him to her as her hips moved under him.

Without warning he deftly rolled them both until he was on his back and she was held over him.

Her glorious hair fell around them. He moved it back, finding and cupping her breasts. She moaned, her head falling back on her neck. Using only his stomach muscles, he levered upwards and drew one of her nipples into his mouth. Her arms clasped around his back.

'Oh, I like this position.'

Revelling in her enjoyment of their bodies, he surged upwards, taking her hips in his hands and moving them both closer and closer to a place he knew he'd never been with any other woman.

Regan depressed the shutter button on her camera and hoped that she'd captured the moment the two hawks flew side by side in a perfect mirror of each other.

Hearing footsteps behind her, she glanced over her shoulder as Jag crested the small rise above the oasis.

A week ago if someone had told her that she could be so uninhibited with a man in bed, so relaxed, she would have laughed in their face. But there was something about this man that made her feel free and able to be herself. Maybe it was his inherent honesty and desire to do the right thing. It spoke to her and made her want to reciprocate in kind.

All morning she had refused to let herself overthink things as she was wont to do. What was the point? They had shared an incredible night of amazing sex and that was that. Yes, he had asked her to spend the day with him at his oasis, but again she wouldn't overthink it. The fact was, the man worked like a Trojan, he was entitled to a day off and this was his place to come and unwind. And if he wanted to spend time with her…well, that was nice, but he'd made his position about relationships and love clear from the start and, even though she could guess that those beliefs were driven by parents who hadn't loved each other or their kids enough, it didn't change anything.

It would be beyond arrogant for her to imagine that she could be the one to change him.

And what would that even mean anyway? That she would upend her life and move to Santara and really become his queen? She nearly snorted at the thought. Yes, those things happened to some people, but it was a one-in-a-billion chance, and it took both parties to want it. At the end of the day Jag didn't think love was important and she thought it was vital. And of course, there was still the issue of their siblings to sort out…

'Can I see?'

He gestured to her camera and she handed it to him. 'Go ahead.'

A lock of hair fell forward over his brow and she let out a sigh at the sudden urge she felt to push it back.

He paused on the photo she had taken of him with Arrow on his arm, his eyes staring at her.

'I wanted to know what you were thinking when I took that,' she said, her voice husky.

He looked up, his eyes intense, and for once she hoped he couldn't read what was on her mind. It would be beyond embarrassing if he realised she had fallen hopelessly in love with him.

'I don't remember.' He adjusted her *shemagh* and handed her camera back. 'You're very good.'

'You don't need to say that. You've already got me into bed.'

He gave a short burst of laughter at her deadpan comment, hauling her against him for a quick kiss. 'I never have any idea what you're going to say next. But I meant it.'

Regan shook her head. She knew her limitations as a photographer and it didn't bother her. 'Which goes to show that the almighty King of Santara doesn't know everything after all,' she said with a smile. 'I'm no Robert Doisneau.'

His eyebrows rose. 'Robert Dois—who? Is this someone I should be worried about?'

Regan laughed. 'No. He's a famous photographer from last century. When I was a teenager I became enthralled by a photograph of two lovers kissing on a Parisian sidewalk. It was one he had taken. There's a magic to it, a sincerity. The couple look so in love…it's as if they can't wait to get back home and had to kiss in the street or die.'

And suddenly Regan realised why she spent so much time photographing couples. They satisfied a deep longing to find the kind of love her parents had shared and which she feared she'd never experience. Unfortunately making love with the King of Santara had created the same longing inside of her.

She gave a little laugh at the improbability of it all. 'I've always wanted to take photos like that and go to Paris. Neither one has happened yet.'

'Both still could.'

'Paris, maybe. Some day. But photography, no. I'm a teacher now and I love my job. I love inspiring kids to learn, and one of my joys is taking a special photo of them during the year and presenting it to them on their birthday. They love it. And I'm not convinced that being a professional photographer would give me the same level of satisfaction. Oh, look, the hawks are back.' She shaded her eyes as she watched their majestic antics. 'Or are they falcons? I can't tell.'

'Hawks.' He watched them with her. 'Falcons are smaller but have a longer wingspan. And falcons grab their prey with their beaks, whereas the hawk uses its talons.'

'*Ouch.* Fortunately they don't seem hungry right now. Look, they're circling each other.'

She raised her camera and started clicking away right when their talons joined together.

'Oh, wow, did you see that? They're dancing.' She couldn't suppress the smile on her face.

'They're not dancing, *habiba*,' he said roughly, his eyes on her mouth. 'He wants to mate with her.'

Regan's breath caught at the raw, elemental hunger in his gaze as he looked at her.

'Falcons mate for life,' he continued. 'And once they've established a home they never stray from it.'

Regan's throat went thick. 'That's so lovely.'

They both watched the birds skim across the top of the blue lagoon. 'Now, that looks lovely.' His hands found her waist and he lowered his head to hers. 'Come swimming with me.'

* * *

Much later Regan lay with her head in his lap, shaded by the huge palm trees bordering the pool, the breeze gently rustling the fronds overhead.

Jag held a small piece of something or other to her lips. 'Try this—you'll like it.'

Regan opened her eyes to look up at him. 'You have to stop feeding me. I think my stomach is going to burst.'

'Just one more,' he said lazily, tempting her. 'You know I like feeding you.'

Regan felt herself flush with pleasure. Being with him that morning and afternoon had been wonderful and, despite her better judgment, she had let herself soak it up. Let herself soak him up.

They'd made love twice more, once in the lagoon and then again on the blanket. He'd done things to her that made her body instantly tighten with anticipation but she knew reality would set in again soon.

'What are you thinking about, *habiba*?'

'You,' she said honestly.

He gave a purr of appreciation, his thigh muscle tensing beneath her cheek as he shifted. He prowled over the top of her, his powerful arms and shoulders flexing as he moved. 'Anything specific about me?'

She ran her fingers through his hair, loving the way his eyes darkened to almost black as he looked at her.

'That you're not as scary as I first thought you were.'

'Not as scary, huh?'

'No.' Happiness surged inside her as he gazed at her with wicked playfulness. 'You're like a big domestic pussycat when it comes down to it.'

'Is that so?' She gave a squeal of delight as he flicked her sarong aside and lightly tickled her ribcage. 'Want me to show you how much of a pussycat I am?'

The sensual intent in his eyes was unmistakable.

'Are you sure no one can see us?' she asked, breathless with longing.

He nuzzled her breast, tugging her nipple into his mouth. 'I'm sure.' He licked her and tortured her until she was a mass of pure sensation. 'I told you this place is totally off-limits to anyone else.'

'Your own private paradise,' she husked, reaching to touch him anywhere she could.

His smile turned sexy as he kissed his way down her body. 'I think that's what I might start calling you,' he murmured, parting her legs so that he could press his tongue high along the inside of her thigh.

Regan cried out, gripping his shoulders, her insides pulsing with sensual anticipation of his wicked touch.

'My own private paradise,' he agreed, dipping his head to take her to her own private paradise, and leaving her wondering how she was ever going to get over him.

What must have been at least an hour later, given the placement of the sun, she woke to find Jag sitting on a nearby rock and staring out at the water. She took a moment to study him, drinking him in so that later, when he was no longer around, she could recall exactly how he looked. The feeling was at once bittersweet and utterly frightening.

As always, he sensed her eyes on him and turned to her. Their eyes met and for a moment they just stared at each other. Shockingly, the connection between them was almost more intimate than the sex. She blushed, wondering what thoughts were going through his mind, but she was too cowardly to ask. He wanted her; she knew that without a doubt, so she was determined just to enjoy it for what it was.

He held out his hand to her and a small smile tilted her lips. She loved the way he did that, offered her his hand as if it was the most natural thing in the world. As if she was the most important person in the world to him.

A rush of emotion made her fingers uncoordinated as she fixed the sarong over her breasts and tried to untangle the knots in her hair formed by his nimble fingers. When she reached him he slowly drew her to him and wedged her between his legs, her back to his front. She felt him bury his face against her hair and breathe deeply. Warmth suffused her and she turned, lifting her face for his kiss, when his phone rang.

Grimacing with annoyance, he reached around her and pressed the button. Regan heard an outpouring of Santarian and felt the immediate tensing of his body.

Slowly he disengaged them and strode across the sand. Watching him, Regan knew instantly what had happened even before he turned to her, a coolness in his eyes when before there had only been heat and need.

'They're back, aren't they?'

He nodded. 'Time to get dressed.'

CHAPTER ELEVEN

A HEAVY SILENCE permeated the helicopter ride on the trip back to the palace, making it seem interminable. Jag appeared to be as caught up in his thoughts as she was in hers, neither one of them making any overtures to the other. It was as if the lover she had spent the day with had vanished, to be replaced by the cold man she had met at the bar. Gone was the domesticated pussycat indulging her in endless pleasure by the side of the lagoon.

A sense of rising dread churned her stomach the further they flew, her feelings divided between wanting Chad to be okay, and concern over what had happened and how that would impact on the man beside her. She wondered if Jag remembered the deal they had struck. She knew that he would honour it. But then what?

With expert precision the pilot landed on the helipad and Jag jumped to the ground, only absently reaching back to assist her to duck beneath the whirring overhead blades.

He strode ahead of her up the path towards the rear of the palace, and Regan finally got to experience what it felt like to walk two paces behind him. Or maybe four. Quickening her pace, she barely noticed the decadent scent of the magnolia trees that lined the path, or the velvet dark sky above.

Jag pushed open a heavy set of doors at the end of a long corridor, his stride not faltering as he strode up to his sister and enfolded her in his arms.

He held her to him for a long moment. A lump rose in Regan's throat and then her eyes sought out the other occupant of the room.

'Chad.' His lanky frame looked as hale and hearty as always and she rushed over and hugged him tightly. 'I've been so worried.'

Chad hugged her back. 'Me too.'

The hairs on the nape of her neck prickled and she turned to see Jag staring at her brother.

Tension rocketed into the room like an incoming sandstorm. 'You have a lot to answer for.'

'No.' Milena placed her hand on Jag's arm. 'Don't blame Chad. It was all my idea.'

Jag's thunderous expression returned to Milena. 'What exactly was all your idea?'

'It's a long story.' Milena sighed. 'And I'm sorry I worried you. I know I did the wrong thing but I felt as if I had no choice. But first…you're engaged…' Her lovely eyes fastened on Regan. 'Is that right? Chad said it wasn't possible, but you're wearing the most important family heirloom in the collection, so it must be.'

Shocked, Regan stared down at the beautiful ring before lifting her eyes to Jag's, only to find his eyes completely devoid of emotion.

'Regan?' Chad stared at her hand. 'How is this possible?'

Regan shook her head, her brain struggling to keep up with the fact that Jag had trusted her not to lose something so precious.

'There are more important things to discuss,' Jag cut in coldly. 'Like, *where have you been*?'

Milena's face went pale as he bellowed at her, clearly unable to handle her brother's wrath.

'I think we need to calm down first,' Regan suggested

quietly. 'They're both safe and home. That's the most important thing.'

As well as her getting this ring off her finger and back in a vault.

'Stay out of this, Regan,' Jag rasped with icy precision. 'You will not influence how I deal with this.'

She felt Chad bristle beside her. 'I don't think you should speak to my sister that way.'

'I'm not interested in what you think.' Jag turned his lethally sharp gaze on Chad. 'And you're lucky she's here. If she wasn't you'd already be in jail.'

'Jag!' Milena cried.

'One of you had better start talking,' he grated. 'And if you have compromised my sister in any way, James, you'll be sorry you ever set foot on Santarian soil.'

'As you have compromised mine!' Chad burst out.

'Chad!' Regan stared at him. As he had grown up he had become as protective of her as she was of him, but she'd never experienced him coming to her defence so avidly before.... 'You have no idea what you're talking about.'

'Don't I?' Her brother puffed out his chest. 'There's obviously something going on between the two of you. I can tell by the way he looks at you.'

By the way he looked at her?

Right now he was looking at her as if she were chewing gum stuck to the bottom of his shoe.

'What has happened between myself and Regan is not your concern,' Jag advised with a killing softness. 'What has happened between you and Milena is.'

'That's your opinion, Your Majesty, but I can't believe my sister would be with you of her own free will.'

'Chad, stop,' Regan implored him. 'Don't make this about me. You've been gone for two weeks. Of course the King wants answers. So do I.'

'I feel terrible,' Milena mumbled. 'This is all my fault. Please, Jag; Chad isn't to blame.'

Regan watched him run a hand through his hair, clearly trying to rein himself in for his sister's sake. Her heart went out to him because she knew why he'd been so worried about her. 'Why don't you both sit down and tell us what happened?'

Chad threw Milena a quick glance but was wise enough not to approach her.

Milena cleared her throat. 'I'm sorry if I've caused a big mess, Jag, but I couldn't go into my marriage next month without having some time to myself.'

'You did this for time to yourself?' Jag thundered.

'No. Not just that.' Milena looked to Chad for reassurance. 'I just wanted to feel normal for once. No bodyguards, no photographers, no having to be polite all the time. I know you won't understand this because it all comes so easily to you, but sometimes I don't think I know who I am.'

'Milena—'

'No, let me finish,' she said, taking a deep breath. 'Chad and I have grown close over the last few months and…when I told him my plan to take a secret holiday he insisted that he come with me to make sure nothing happened to me.' She threw Chad a quick smile. 'I knew it would be a mistake, but I also thought that if you knew I was with a friend you would worry less. I was only hoping you'd find out it was a male friend after we returned.'

Jag's expression told her that it hadn't made an ounce of difference, but Regan heard the note in Milena's voice that said that she'd been hoping to return in triumph, presumably so that she could prove to her over-protective big brother that she had grown up. Unfortunately such a tactic was likely to have the opposite effect. Milena winced at Jag's continued silence. 'I guess not. But please, don't blame

Chad. If anything, you should be thanking him for being there for me. I didn't even know how to buy a train ticket!'

'I would be thanking Mr James if he had come to me with your hare-brained scheme instead of sneaking off and foiling my attempts to find you. Do you have any idea what would have happened if anyone had got wind of your disappearance? If the Prince of Toran had?' He paced away from her. 'It's only fortunate for us that he expects Santara to take care of all the wedding arrangements. If he'd once tried to call you—'

'I knew he wouldn't.'

'That's beside the point.' Jag turned to stare at Regan's brother. 'Tell me, just how close have you become?'

'Not as close as you and my sister,' Chad ground out.

'Chad, please,' Regan admonished. 'Don't make this worse.'

'How can my stating the obvious make things worse? I've been without internet access this past week, and when I reconnected I nearly died seeing photos of you and him together. You're everywhere in the news, do you realise that?'

She hadn't because she hadn't been given any access to the internet herself. 'I'm sure it's nothing.'

'Nothing? It's not nothing. Ask the King.'

Regan's eyes flew to Jag's. He stared back at her and she saw that he knew how big this had become and that he hadn't cared. The only thing he'd wanted was for Milena to come back and now she had. 'Chad, it's not important. I agreed to do it because we both wanted you to return to Santara.'

'You both agreed to what?' He looked from her to the King and back. 'To becoming engaged to him? My God. I can see it's true. Please tell me you didn't sleep with him for that as well.'

'Chad!'

Ignoring her, he glared at the King. 'How could you involve my sister? She had nothing to do with any of this.'

'I don't think you're in a position to question me,' Jag growled softly.

Before her brother could get any more aggravated and say something really stupid, Regan stepped in. 'I came to Santara to look for you, Chad. No one forced me to do that.'

'Why? I sent you an email explaining that I would be out of reach.'

Regan narrowed her eyes. 'The last time you told me not to worry I got a call from the police precinct to come and bail you out.'

'I was sixteen!' he exclaimed. 'And this is a completely different thing.'

'Yes,' Jag interjected coldly. 'It's far worse. And you should be thanking your sister, not haranguing her. If she wasn't here you'd be in a far worse position than you currently are.'

'I don't think—'

Jag turned on him then, using his formidable height and years of authority to silence her brother. 'No, for a smart man you didn't think.'

'Chad, please,' Milena pleaded. 'It will only make things worse and it's all my fault.'

'It's not your fault,' Chad corrected. 'It's that you live under the reign of your autocratic brother, who never takes anyone's needs into consideration except his own.'

'Okay, enough.' Regan stood up. 'Jag is not like that and you clearly have no real understanding of the worry you've both caused by sneaking off together.'

'Just tell me.' Jag pinned her brother with his icy gaze. 'Did you compromise my sister?'

Milena gave a shocked gasp. 'Jag—'

'Silence,' Jaeger snapped at his sister. 'You are betrothed

o be married to a very important man. If you've slept with Chad James I need to know.'

'She hasn't,' Chad bit out, facing the King with his shoulders back. 'Your sister is a beautiful person and I would never take advantage of her like that.'

Regan heard the protective way Chad spoke about the younger woman and stared at him. *Was he in love with Milena?*

'We didn't do anything like that, Jag,' Milena said crossly. 'Chad was a perfect gentleman. If you're going to be angry then be angry with me.'

'Don't worry,' Jaeger bit out. 'I'm furious with you.'

'I'm sorry,' Milena said, tears forming at the edges of her eyes. 'I was really desperate and I thought you'd say no if I asked.'

The stark truth of that flashed across the king's taut features. 'Who else knows about this?' he asked stiffly.

'Only Chad.'

Jag nodded curtly. 'You look exhausted. We will talk more about this in the morning. Mr James, you will not leave the palace until this situation has been officially resolved.'

'What are you going to do to him?' Milena asked.

'That is not your concern.'

Milena leapt to her feet, her small fists clenched. 'Damnit, Jag, sometimes I wonder if you're even human any more.'

'Milena!'

His harsh call stayed her exit, her slight body vibrating with tension. She didn't turn to look at him. 'Permission to leave your presence, Your Majesty.'

The muscle in Jag's jaw clenched tight. Regan's heart jumped into her throat because she could tell by the flash of emotion across his face that he had taken Milena's words to heart. No doubt he felt responsible for everything that had happened, and she knew he wouldn't welcome her attempts to make him feel better about that.

'Go. We'll talk more in the morning.'

'Don't expect me to go anywhere without my sister,' Chad said.

Jag gave him a faint smile. 'I would expect nothing less.'

Finally he turned to face Regan. 'I believe this is where you say "I told you so".'

A lump formed in her throat, her hands trembling. 'I don't want to say that.'

What she wanted to say was that she loved him, that she wanted to be with him, that she understood his anger, and wanted to be the one to soothe it, but knowing that he had never wanted anything like that from her held her silent.

'Gracious of you. But this is definitely the time I apologise for inconveniencing you. I was wrong.'

'I don't want your apology,' she whispered fiercely. What she wanted was for this formal stranger to disappear and bring back the lover she had known at the oasis.

His gaze seemed to take her all in at once, and then there was nothing. It was as if he had closed down every emotion he'd ever had. 'Mr James, please follow me.'

Regan felt shell-shocked by Jag's departure. Was he coming back after he'd talked to Chad? Or was that it?

But of course that was it. The reason she was even here had been resolved. His sister was safe and the summit was over. Did life just return to normal for him now?

A breath shuddered out of her body and she clamped her arms around her waist. Was it that easy for him? That simple? But then, what had she expected? It had always been going to end when Chad returned. She'd known that. All day she'd reminded herself of the same thing and had convinced herself that she was just taking it for what was. Well, now was the time to prove that. He'd told her that practice helped him contain his emotions and, well... now would be the time for her to try that too.

Only she wasn't so sure she could move on from him that easily. She'd fallen in love with him. It was exactly the scenario she had feared. Falling for someone who didn't want her back. It was almost as if she'd willed into being the very experience she'd spent years avoiding. But then, fate had a way of making you face your worst fears. She should have known that. And what was the mantra after you faced your fears and survived? You'd be stronger for it?

A sob rose up in her throat and she stifled it. That might take a while.

An hour later someone knocked at the door of the garden suite and she immediately assumed it was Chad.

It wasn't, it was Tarik. He smiled at her soberly and handed her a document.

Regan scanned it. It was a press release stating that her engagement to the King was over. It completely exonerated her of any responsibility, merely stating that after careful consideration she had decided to return home.

'If you're happy with the wording, my lady, the King asks that you sign it.'

Regan nodded, her heart in her throat. 'That was fast.'

Tarik handed her a pen. 'His Majesty likes to work that way.'

'Yes, I know,' she said, moving to a table and scrawling her signature at the bottom. She took a deep breath and wondered if the buzzing noise she could hear was inside her head, or outside.

'His Majesty has also given you a settlement for inconveniencing you but said that if it wasn't enough to name your price.'

'His Majesty is very keen to see me go,' she said softly,

wondering if he would renew his engagement to the Princess Alexa now that he was free. It seemed unlikely but then this world wasn't her usual one. Royals made deals and arrangements in the blink of an eye. 'And Chad?' she asked.

'Chad is here,' a voice said from the doorway.

Regan glanced up at him blankly and then felt her resolve start to crumble. 'Oh, Chad!'

He stepped into the room and she raced into his arms.

'I'll leave you alone now, my lady,' Tarik said courteously. 'If there is anything you need, please let me know.'

'Wait, Tarik, there is.' She pulled away from Chad and tugged at the diamond on her finger. It resisted her initial attempt to remove it, but with enough force she worked it free. 'Please return this to His Majesty.'

'The King said that you were to keep it.'

The lump in her throat got bigger. 'No.' She shook her head to hold back tears that suddenly sprang up behind her eyes. 'It's not mine to keep.'

'As you wish, my lady.'

Regan nodded. 'And thank you.' She gave him a watery smile. 'It was nice to get to know you.'

Tarik nodded, bowing as he slowly turned to leave.

'Wow,' Chad said, releasing a long breath. 'This is really full-on.'

'What did you expect?' Regan asked. 'Did you really think you could go off with Milena and there would be no consequences?'

Chad sighed. 'I suppose I didn't really think about the consequences. Milena is a princess. If anything, I thought that once she returned everything would be fine and go back to normal.'

'Wrong.'

'Oh, Reggie, I can see you're upset. I'm sorry you got dragged into all of this.'

'It's okay.' She sniffed knowing that it was very far from okay. 'I'm fine.' It was the way it had always been in the past: her taking care of Chad, not the other way around.

'No, you're not. You look like you're about to cry.' He gave her a wan smile. 'I'm truly sorry. I had no idea that you would rush over to Santara to try and find me.'

'I probably should have stayed home in hindsight but… How did your meeting with the King go?'

Chad made a face. 'He pretty much bawled me out over what I'd done.'

'I don't doubt it. He was worried sick about his sister. It was pretty irresponsible.'

'It didn't seem like it at the time. But he didn't ball me out so much over Milena as over you.'

'Me?'

'Yeah, he dragged me over the coals for scaring you the way that I did. Told me I had to take better care of you.'

'Oh…that was…' She took a breath. It was typical of a man who took his familial responsibilities seriously is what it was. 'He's a decent person when you get to know him.' Funny. Sexy. Strong. Smart. 'And you? What happens for you next?'

'King Jaeger has ordained that I am allowed to continue to work for GeoTech if I want to, but I'm to have no contact with the Princess ever again.'

Regan heard the slight strain in his voice and groaned. 'You're in love with her, aren't you?'

'In love with her?' Chad looked at her, astonishment widening his eyes. 'Of course I'm not in love with her, we're just friends. I mean, she's incredibly beautiful inside and out but…honestly, she reminded me a bit of myself at the same age. When I felt unsure about my place in the world.' He grimaced at the memory. 'I felt bad that she didn't have anyone supportive in her life the way I had you and I wanted to be there for her. But right now I'm more worried about you.' He took her hands in his. 'Did the King hurt you in any way? Did he force himself on you? Because if he did I'll… I'll—'

'He didn't force me, Chad.' She gave his hands a reassuring squeeze before moving towards the windows overlooking the garden. 'Not in the way you mean. He was just incredibly worried about his sister. I might have done the same thing he did if our situations had been reversed.'

A sort of pained silence followed her statement and she glanced over to see Chad watching her. 'You're in love with him aren't you?'

Regan gave a shuddering smile. 'Is it that obvious?'

'Oh, Reggie. What are you going to do?'

'Nothing,' she said. 'There's nothing I can do. He's made it more than clear that he wants me gone, so I guess I'll go home.'

'Have you told him how you feel?'

'God, no.' Regan gave a resigned shake of her head. 'Believe me, Chad, if King Jaeger had wanted me to stay with him he would have said so. But the fact is he has everything he needs already.' And all she had to do was find a way to get over him.

'There's a car waiting to take me back to my apartment. Do you want to come with me?'

'Of course. It's not like I have anywhere else to go.'

'But the King… Are you going to at least say goodbye to him?'

Regan thought about it but she knew she couldn't do it. 'He knows where I am, Chad, and he knows I'll be going with you. Prolonging the inevitable isn't going to change anything.' In fact, it would only make her feel worse.

CHAPTER TWELVE

JAEGER LOOKED DOWN at the report in his hand that detailed just how phenomenally successful the summit had been. It was everything he could have hoped for and yet he had to force himself to feel enthusiastic about it. He'd had to force himself to feel enthusiastic about anything since Regan had walked out of his life a week ago.

It was as if every day was a test of his endurance. A test of his stamina.

He recalled the day the phone call had come through about his father's accident. At first the words coming out of Tarik's mouth had been surreal and then his brain had kicked into high gear. He'd made sure Milena was taken care of. Then he'd flown home to Santara and been met by a legion of cabinet ministers and officials, all awaiting direction on how to handle the death of the King and what to do next. It had been an immense learning curve, and Regan had been right when she'd said that he hadn't grieved properly. He'd been almost numb through those first difficult months and by the time he might have had some time to take a breath it had seemed indulgent to do so. He had a job to do and he'd done it to the best of his ability.

He'd thought *that* had been the greatest test of his stamina. Turned out it was nothing compared to watching Regan get into that car with her brother without a backward glance.

But what else had he expected? He'd scared her in the shisha bar and then again in her hotel room, he'd forced her to come to the palace, where he'd detained her, then he'd forced her to play hostess for him at an international summit, after which he'd forced her to go to his oasis and…

His mind blanked out the events that had taken place in his bed after the celebratory dinner his tribesmen had put on. It had been the only way he hadn't jumped on a plane and immediately followed her to New York. But he hadn't forced himself on her that night. He knew she had come to his bed willingly, her ability to deny the chemistry between them about as strong as his had been.

Zero.

But what was the point in reliving it all? She was back in New York, back to her normal life, and so was he. Back to…back to…

A knock at the door prevented his brooding thoughts from continuing. Thank the heavens.

Tarik entered, looking harassed. The last time he'd looked this way a russet haired, cinnamon-eyed American had been the cause.

'I thought you'd finished for the day,' he told his aide.

'Almost, Your Majesty.'

'Did you see Milena?'

'I did. She is fine. The dress-fitting went very well.'

That surprised him. He still didn't know if his sister really want to marry the Prince of Toran. She hadn't said. In fact she hadn't said anything much to him these past few days, still angry with him for banning her from seeing Chad James. But what had she expected? That he would welcome their friendship with open arms? The man was lucky enough to still have a job. A concession he'd only made because of Regan.

'Good. So what's put that look on your face?'

'The PR department are querying the statement about the end of your engagement to Miss James…'

'What of it?'

'Well, sir, they'd like to know when you plan to release it to the media?'

Jag swivelled his chair to stare out at the dusky night sky. It was orange and mauve, almost a replica of the night he'd lain with Regan by the side of the lagoon. 'When I'm ready. I'm still not happy with the wording.'

'The wording, sir?'

'I don't want there to be any fallout for Miss James. I want the responsibility for what has happened to fall on my shoulders, not hers.'

'Admirable, Your Majesty, but it's a bit late for that.'

Jag's eyes narrowed as he studied his trusted aide. 'What are you talking about?' he asked, as fingers of unease whispered across the nape of his neck.

'The Press have been hounding Miss James ever since she returned to America, sir. I thought that, with the release of the statement ending your engagement, that might ease up for her.'

'What do you mean, the Press have been hounding her? I organised a full security detail to accompany Regan on the jet home. They were to keep the Press at bay for as long as necessary once she got there.'

'Miss James took a commercial flight home, sir.'

Jag surged to his feet, every muscle in his body tight. 'Why wasn't I told about this?' he asked with a deadly sense of calm.

'Because the staff are too afraid to mention her name around you, Your Majesty.'

'You're not.'

'Actually I…' His aide flushed. 'After I returned the ring to you I dared not saying anything again. But if you don't mind me asking, sir, why did you let her go? I thought she was wonderful for you. All the staff did.'

Why had he let her go?

Because he hadn't had any choice. He'd wronged her. A woman whose company he enjoyed. A woman he had come to respect above all others. A woman he had… A rush of emotion threatened to overtake him and he ruthlessly drove it back. This time, though, his formidable mind failed him. This time the emotions kept surging.

'The heart knows what the heart wants.'

Was it possible? Had he fallen in love with Regan? Logic told him that he hadn't spent enough time with her for that to happen but his heart wasn't listening.

He stared at his aide as all the pieces finally fell into place. 'Fear,' he enunciated succinctly, reefing his jacket from the hanger near his door and striding out of his office. 'Nothing but fear.'

'Are they still outside?'

'Still outside?' Penny turned from glancing out of the sitting-room window of Regan's apartment. 'They're outside, up the street, and in the trees. In fact I think there are more of them today than yesterday.'

Regan sighed. 'I was hoping they'd have started to lose interest by now.'

'This is ridiculous, Regan,' Penny snapped. 'You have to do something about it. They've been chasing after you like you're an animal. It's terrible.'

'I know. But what can I do? I told them I wasn't with the King any more but they don't believe me.'

Penny pulled a face. 'Once you become mistress to the King—voila, instant celebrity as far as the Press is concerned.'

'Who would want it?' Regan groaned into her hands. 'And I wasn't his mistress.'

'You did say you slept with him.'

'One night. That hardly makes me his mistress.'

'You know you blush every time you mention him, don't you? Was the sex that good?'

Regan blushed harder.

'Don't answer that.' Penny sighed. 'One day I want great sex like that. Even if it is just for one night.'

'You don't,' Regan returned. 'Believe me, I've been pracising getting over him and...' Her voice choked up. 'I'm getting there.'

Regan knew from losing her parents that time healed all wounds. And when it didn't it at least dulled the pain to a manageable level. Unfortunately that didn't seem to be happening yet.

'I suppose in hindsight agreeing to pose as his fiancée was really naive,' Regan admitted. 'I thought there would be less fallout from that but there's been more.'

'That's because it's a romance story for the ages. Everyone wants it to be true.' She took a long sip of coffee. 'Whatever happened to the press release you said you signed?'

'I don't know.' Regan frowned; the lack of a press release had continued to perturb her. 'He must have only put it out locally.'

'It wouldn't matter if he'd put it out in the palace toilets... the world would still know about it by now.'

Regan gave Penny a faint smile. Having her by her side the past week had been a godsend. Penny had taken one look at her face the first day back at work and shuffled her into the staffroom and closed the door behind them, giving her a hug. Having been through heartache herself, she understood the signs.

The other teachers at the school hadn't been so under-standing, some asking her intimate questions about what the King was like, obviously looking for some insider's scoop, and others upset because she had brought a caval-cade of media to the school gates and it just wasn't done.

'Have you had another look online?' Penny asked.

Regan didn't want to look online. When she did she was bombarded with photo after photo of herself and the King. It was too painful to look at.

'At least if you called the palace you could ask about it,' Penny persisted. 'Regan, you have a right to live your life without being harassed.' She slapped her mug on the coun-ter. 'Give me the number. If you're not going to call, I will. It's not as if they'll put me through to the King or anything.'

'Penny, I love you for wanting to help but I don't think it will. I—'

A hard rap at the door brought both their heads around. 'How did they get up here? You have a security door down-stairs.'

'Maybe one of the neighbours accidentally let them through,' Regan whispered.

Penny went to the window again and peered outside. 'Well, don't answer the door whatever you do—I can't see a single photographer outside, which means that they're all piled up against your front door.'

Regan groaned. 'What am I going to do?'

'Regan! I know you're in there. Open the door.'

Regan froze, her eyes flying to Penny's.

'Damn, but whoever that is they have a yummy voice,' Penny said. 'Pity they're probably scum as well.'

'It's him.'

Penny frowned. 'Who?'

Regan had to swallow before she could get the word out. 'The King,' she whispered.

'Are you sure?'

'Regan!'

Regan nodded. 'I'd know his voice anywhere.'

'Good lord…what do you think he wants?'

'I have no idea.'

'Regan, please open the door.'

Penny raised a brow. 'He said please that time. Do you want me to get it?'

Regan shook her head. 'I will.'

On legs that felt like overcooked spaghetti, Regan walked to the door and opened it. As soon as she did her heart stopped beating. When it started again it jumped into her mouth.

Jag stood on her doorstep with what looked like two paratroopers behind him, a dark scowl on his face. 'You're lucky you answered it when you did. I was just about to break it down.'

'Why?'

'I thought something had happened to you. You haven't answered a single call I've made in the last ten hours.'

'Oh.' Still trying to take in the fact that he was here, in New York, on her doorstep, she stared at him blankly. 'I've stopped carrying my phone around with me because it never stops ringing.'

'Do you know how dangerous that is?'

'At the minute I go from work to home and back again. Anything else is impossible.'

'That's because you didn't take the security detail I organised for you. That was not a good call.'

'You're not responsible for me.'

'The hell I'm not.' His blue eyes turned fierce. 'Didn't you think something like this would happen? That the paparazzi would want your story?'

'No. I told you my world is usually a lot smaller than

yours. I didn't know what to expect until I got here and then…'

'You should have called me to tell me!'

'I wasn't sure you'd take my call.' And she couldn't have lived with that. 'Listen, I'm fine. I appreciate your concern but… I can cope.'

He ran his eyes over her and she felt terribly exposed in her cut-off shorts and worn T-shirt.

'I know you can cope. You're the strongest woman I've ever met.' He dragged a hand through his hair and her pulse rocketed at the memory of how it had felt on her fingers.

The air between them seemed to throb as it usually did when he was this close, and she saw him swallow heavily.

'We're not having this conversation out here, Regan.' He strode past her into her flat and Regan felt helpless to stop him.

She nearly ran smack into the back of him when he stopped in the doorway to her living room.

'Who are you?'

'I'm ah… I'm ah… Penny, Regan's friend.'

'Well, Penny, Regan's friend, I'm King Jaeger of Santara, Regan's fiancée, and I'd really like to talk to her alone.'

'Oh, sure. Of course.' Penny seemed to visibly pull herself together at being confronted by royalty. 'Well, that is, if it's okay with Regan.'

Regan was still trying to process what he had just announced. 'You're not still my fiancée.'

He turned his piercing blue eyes on her. 'Actually I am. I haven't officially ended things between us yet.'

'You haven't…' She frowned. 'I gave you back the ring and Milena is home. The deal ended then.'

'I'm changing the terms of it.'

'You can't do that.'

He looked at her with patient exasperation. 'Will you

please give your friend permission to leave? Unless you want an audience for the rest of this conversation.'

'Oh, sorry. Yes, Penny, I'm fine. He won't hurt me.'

At least he wouldn't intentionally hurt her, but looking at him, being this close to him… Her chest felt tight with the strain of holding her emotions inside.

'I'll call you,' Penny promised before slipping out of the door. When it clicked closed behind her Regan had to place her hand over her chest to keep her emotions back. It was only then that she noticed how dishevelled and tired he looked.

'Look, I know you feel responsible about the paparazzi,' she began, 'but I don't know how you can fix it. I don't want to walk around town swamped by security guards. It will only make things worse. Did you release the press statement yet? Penny thinks that will make it easier.' She pulled a face. 'Even without the ring, they refuse to believe we're not still together. They think I'm trying to play coy.'

She plonked herself down on her favourite armchair and remembered the shelling of questions she'd received ever since landing back in New York.

'Where's the King? When is he planning to visit you?'
'Have you set a wedding date yet?'
'Give us a smile, Regan. Tell us how you met.'

She'd even been invited on a talk show.

'I didn't release the statement,' he said, pacing around her small flat and dwarfing it with his superior size.

'Why not? And what do you mean, you're changing the terms of our deal? Why would you want to do that?'

'Because I was wrong, and that's not easy for me to admit.' He came to stand in front of her. 'You were right when you said that Milena didn't want to marry the Prince of Toran. She doesn't. At least, she doesn't yet. You'll be happy to know that I spoke to her on my way over here and the wedding has been postponed for a year. I've also agreed that she can resume her job at GeoTech and keep working with your brother.'

'That's really nice of you. But you know you're not responsible for Milena's actions, don't you?'

'Not completely no, but after her health scare a few years back I stopped listening to what she wanted and thought I knew best. A mistake I don't want to make with you.'

'How could you make that mistake with me?'

'By presuming you want the same thing that I do.' He squatted down in front of her so they were at eye level.

Regan's heart leapt into her throat. 'What is it you want?'

'You.'

'Me?'

He gave her a small smile. 'When you left, *habiba*, you took a part of me with you. A part of me I wasn't even aware existed.'

The bleak look in his eyes made her feel suddenly hot and cold all over. 'What did I take?'

'My heart, *habiba*; you took my heart.'

A bubble of something that felt faintly like hope swelled inside her chest. 'What are you saying?'

He released a heavy sigh, his eyes full of emotion when they met hers. 'I'm saying that I love you.'

'But that's impossible.'

'You doubt it?' He gave a self-deprecating laugh. 'I detained you. I bound you to my side by making you my fiancée.'

'For your sister.'

'I told myself that too, but the truth is you got under my skin from the first moment I saw you in that shisha bar and every decision I made from then on defied logic and reason. That should have been my first clue.'

Regan felt dazed. Dizzy. 'But you don't believe in love

'That's not strictly true, *ya amar.*' He gave her a small smile. 'I do believe in it. I just didn't think I needed it.' He took her trembling hands and drew her to her feet. 'The thing is, Regan, I'm hopeless when it comes to emotions. All my life it's been easier to shut down than to expose myself to pain. If you don't feel anything you don't hurt.' He gave a sharp laugh as if the concept was ludicrous to him now. 'It was that simple. I thought it made me stronger. I convinced myself a long time ago that I didn't need love in my life—I even thought I wasn't able to feel it—but I was wrong. I just didn't realise *how* wrong until I lost you.'

'You didn't lose me,' Regan said softly, stepping closer to him. 'I only left because I thought you didn't want me.'

He shook his head. 'Not want you? I can't stop wanting you.'

'Then why did you always find it so easy to turn away from me?'

'Practice. But I'm sick of practising walking away. It's what both my parents did my whole life and I didn't even know I'd taken on that part of them until you left. Now I want to practise staying put. I want to practise being open. I want to practise being in love. With you.'

Regan smiled so wide her cheeks hurt. 'You do?'

'I do.' A slow smile started on his face. 'Will you have me, *habiba*, flaws and all?'

'Only if you'll have me, flaws and all.'

'You have none.'

Regan laughed. 'Now I know you really do love me because I have loads.'

He swung her into his arms, his head coming down to hers for a desperate, heated kiss. 'I've missed you, *habiba*. Tell me you've missed me too.'

'Oh, Jag, I have.' Happiness swelled inside her chest. 'I really have.'

'Regan, *ya amar…*' He kissed her again. Harder. Deeper. 'I love you, so much.'

Regan stared at him dreamily. 'I can't really believe it.'

'Believe it, *habiba*. Do you remember that photo you took of me with Arrow? The one in the desert?'

'Yes.'

'You asked me what I was thinking when you took it and I told you that I didn't remember.' He smoothed her hair back from her face. 'Ask me again.'

'What were you thinking?' she asked dreamily.

'I was thinking how happy I was being in the desert with you. I was thinking that I couldn't remember ever being that happy before.'

Regan couldn't contain her joy and didn't try. 'I was thinking the exact same thing. You looked so magnificent I couldn't take my eyes off you.'

Jag dragged her mouth back to his, his hands skating over her back, holding her tightly. Finally he lifted his head, groaning with the effort. 'I want forever with you, *habiba*. Can you give me that, even though it means you'll be the centre of everyone's attention for ever and a day?'

'Jag, I could give you anything at all as long as I'm the centre of *your* attention.'

'*Habiba*, you already are. You're the centre of my world.'

EPILOGUE

MILENA STOOD BEHIND Regan and adjusted the train on her
ivory wedding dress.

'You look so beautiful,' she murmured, misty-eyed.

Regan smiled, unable to believe that today was her wedding day. 'Thank you. I feel so nervous and I don't know
why.'

'Bridal nerves,' Milena said, smoothing down her own
rose-gold gown. 'But you don't have to worry about my
brother. You've transformed him. I've never seen him so
happy and it fills my heart with joy.'

'He makes me happy too. These past three months of
being with him have given me more happiness than I could
have ever hoped to feel.'

More than she had ever expected to feel. For so many
years she had put her own needs aside and, although she
would never regret any of those years, being with Jag had
made her truly blossom. She gazed at the solid-gold bracelet
on her wrist that he had given her as a pre-wedding present. The jeweller had inlaid a photo of her parents on their
wedding day and she stroked a finger across their smiling
faces. 'Thank you,' she murmured. 'For loving me and in
the process showing me how to love in turn.'

Tears formed behind her eyes and she blinked them
back. Jag had given it as a token of his love, asking that
she be patient with him if he ever forgot how to express

his feelings towards her, but she hadn't needed to be. He told her he loved her every time he looked at her, his eyes alight with emotion.

Milena stopped fussing with her veil. 'You already feel like the sister I never had, and I want you to know that I'm well aware that you're the reason my brother is allowing me to go and study in London later in the year.'

'You'll always be his little sister, and he'll always worry about you. But I think you're doing the right thing.'

'I do too. And I can't believe the Crown Prince is still willing to marry me even though I'm postponing things. But I want what you and my brother have and I'm determined not to settle for anything less.'

Regan smiled. 'Good for you. I can promise you that it's worth the wait.'

Brimming with happiness, Regan turned when Penny poked her head around the corner. 'You'd better get out here,' she said, stern-faced. 'Your King isn't going to wait for ever, Reggie. He looks like he's about to come tearing down the aisle and drag you to the altar himself.'

Regan grinned. She wouldn't put it past him and she wouldn't mind a bit. All her life she'd dreamed of finding a love that could rival her parents' and she had. Feeling her nerves finally settle, she took a deep breath. 'Where's Chad?'

'Waiting.'

Regan nodded and stepped onto the red carpet. The assembled crowd gave a collective gasp as they saw her. Chad stepped forward. 'You look beautiful, sis.' His eyes, the same shade of brown as her own, sparkled into hers.

'I love you, you know that, right?' she said softly.

He gave her a tiny smile. 'I love you too. Now, let's move before your possessive fiancé accuses me of holding up the wedding proceedings.'

Regan laughed, and placed her hand in the crook of his arm. 'Then let's go,' she said, turning to lock eyes with the man of her dreams waiting with barely leashed patience for her to join him at the end of the aisle.

* * * * *

COMING SOON!

We really hope you enjoyed reading this book. If you're looking for more romance, be sure to head to the shops when new books are available on

Thursday
26th July